The Peasant Prince

Stephen Cody

TRAJAN
BOOKS

Copyright © 2012 Trajan Books, Inc.

ISBN: 0615695078

ISBN-13: 978-0615695075

DEDICATION

To my darling daughter, Aimée Anastasia Cody,
who long ago proved that
little girls are made of magic.

CONTENTS

ACKNOWLEDGMENTS

To my Round Table of Readers:

Christopher Cody, Ann-Britt Bennett, and Aimée Cody.
Thank you for your thoughtful comments. You helped me
improve this story and catch mistakes in plotting,
grammar, and spelling.

Any errors that remain are my own.

And to my wife, Rita Herrera-Cody:

She hated one of the characters in this book
so much, she wanted to send her death threats.

A writer could ask for no greater compliment.

ONE
THE BANSHEES

Zefrom Arthur Williams IV turned sixteen, but there was no celebration. It was not for lack of money. Art's parents were rich. Art blamed it on the President of the United States.

The new President took his oath of office on January 20th, which was Art's birthday. Since the inaugural date was set in the Constitution, his birthday had to wait. Art had been at the inaugural, seated in the VIP section with his parents. His father, Zefrom Arthur Williams III was on the verge of confirmation as the new Ambassador to England. After the President took his oath and the pomp and circumstance and ceremony finished, the Senate met briefly to confirm a number of new appointments, including his father's. Before the first inaugural parade float made its way down Pennsylvania Avenue, he and his mother and father were rushed over to the State Department, where his father took his oath of office from the new Secretary of State.

There was little for Art to do. He was left to wait in a large suite at the Willard Hotel while his parents went to several of the inaugural balls. His mother insisted on it.

Her name was Mildred Harrison Williams. America did not have a royal family, but hers was as close as it came. Her great-great-great-grandfather was President Benjamin Harrison and his grandfather was President William Henry Harrison. Benjamin Harrison V, one of the signers of the Declaration of Independence, was an even more distant ancestor. There were governors, senators, generals, admirals, Cabinet secretaries, and even a Vice President seeded throughout the newer branches of her family tree.

"You have a heritage of greatness to live up to," she frequently told Art as he was growing up.

His father had come from a less regal background. He was the kind of man who made his money on his own, rather than being lucky enough to inherit it from a dying relative. The Ambassador was tall and tanned from weekends spent on the tennis court and hours under a bronzing lamp. He was a whiz at numbers, able to scan a troubled company's balance sheet and know in an instant how to save the corporation – for a price.

Art was as tall as his father, having finally crossed the six-foot threshold. He had a thick mane of brown hair and green eyes like his mother's. What he had not inherited was his mother's understanding of power or his father's innate financial ability. His father had tried to get him into his old boarding school, Fillmore Academy. Even the hint of a large donation to the building fund did not earn him an acceptance letter. He attended a public high school in Boston, which suited Art, where maintaining a "C" average required little study and even less thought.

"It's because of you," he had overheard his mother say to his father, "that the President got elected. You raised all that money for the President. You should bask in some of the glory. And don't forget that the first George Bush got to be President after he was Ambassador to China. With the right guidance, you could be standing up there in eight years taking your own oath of office."

So the two of them went to the inaugural balls without him, as much to be seen as to join in the festivities. This was also their night to shine. Art's parents were back at the hotel just before midnight in the last few minutes of his birthday.

"Hey, sport," his father said, as he awakened him. "Change of plans. There's a crisis in Europe. The President wants me in London right away. They're holding a plane for us."

"There's always a crisis in Europe," Art told his father and tried to roll over and go back to sleep.

It did not work. In less than half an hour, they were at Andrews Air Force Base, boarded onto a military Gulfstream jet, and were wheels up and in the air.

All his friends were falling behind him. By the time the plane touched down, they would be 3,300 miles away across an ocean. He would be cut off and alone in London.

"Oh," his mother said, as she settled back on takeoff. "Happy Birthday, Art."

Art looked at his watch. "That was yesterday."

His father looked up from a briefing book he was given as they got on the plane. "Really? Are you sure?"

"Yeah, Dad. I think I know when my birthday was."

"Son of a gun," his father said. "I'm sorry. I promise we'll make it up to you when we get to London. Okay?"

Art shrugged and put the earbuds from his iPod Touch in his ears and wrapped himself in a sonic cocoon. He slept most of the flight. The Embassy limousine was waiting for them on the tarmac and took them to Winfield House, the American Ambassador's residence in London.

Winfield House reminded Art of a castle in a way, but without the moat or high stone walls. It was located on twelve acres of land in the center of London, not far from Buckingham Palace, the official residence of the Queen. The front yard was as big as a football field. The main house had forty-eight rooms. Except for Buckingham

Palace, it was the largest private estate in London.

Once inside Winfield House, Art was free of his professional shadow. One of the drawbacks of being the American ambassador's son was that his very own security agent went everywhere with him.

The only time his agent showed even a hint of emotion was when he told Art's parents that his security nickname was "Hedgehog." The agent actually chuckled.

Art's internal clock was still running on Boston time. After his first day in London, he had finally fallen to sleep in the hour just before dawn. As his body fully relaxed, he was startled awake by mournful screams. It was more than a single voice.

It was two voices.

No, three.

It sounded like it was very close, maybe coming from inside the mansion in a room just below his.

He listened for a moment, but he heard nothing more than the cries and the screaming. Somebody should have heard the noise by now. He had been told that the security staff was always in the house.

Where were they now? Why hadn't they tackled this threat to the ground? Or at least gotten it to shut up so he could get some sleep? When one pillow and then another pulled tightly over his head did not muffle the sound, Art decided to get up to see what was the matter.

He was dressed as he always did on a winter night, in long flannel sleep pants and a t-shirt. He padded silently out of his room barefoot and over to the back stairs.

When he reached the bottom of the stairs, the door to the restaurant-sized kitchen was on his right. One of the black suited agents was face down on the floor in front of the swinging kitchen door. The man's suit jacket was shifted off to one side, exposing the pistol he kept holstered on his hip. Alarmed, Art dropped to one knee and tried to rouse the man. He moaned, which Art took as a good sign. At least he was not dead. Art bent forward and grabbed the man's arm to activate his wrist mic like he had seen the agent do. Maybe someone would hear him and get help.

"Mayday, mayday!," Art called out. "This is Hedgehog. If you can hear me, we have an agent down in the back hallway on the first floor. He's next to the kitchen. Send some help."

Art plucked the earphone from the man's head and listened to see if anyone was responding to his distress call. All he could hear was the loud pop of static.

Help was not on the way.

He heard a crash from the doorway to his left. That one, Art knew, led down to the basement. There was a huge laundry down there. Perhaps some of the staff was already here and one of them would be able to summon help. Not wanting to rely totally on luck, Art popped the leather strap on the unconscious agent's holster and took his weapon. As he opened the door down to the basement, Art could tell that the source of the caterwauling was beneath him.

Art braced the gun with both hands in front of him and came down the stairs into the laundry room. There were several industrial sized washing machines and dryers against the far wall. The long sorting tables had been knocked back and were lying flipped over.

There was a large cauldron resting on a pile of flaming logs in the center of the room. Art could see the flames, but he could not feel the heat. There were three translucent figures around the giant black pot and they cried out, wailing and beating their closed fists against their chests.

"Who are you?," Art yelled, trying to speak above their weeping. "What do you want?"

From the corner of his eye, Art saw something move. It was a small black kitten with a blaze of white fur on its forehead. Its eyes glowed red, like coals in a fire, and the pupils were pin-dots of black. It began to purr softly and walk towards Art. He released the safety on the side of the pistol with his thumb, and then pulled back the hammer until it clicked loudly.

The kitten stopped and eyed Art. A soft rumble from the kitten began to deepen as the cat swelled in size. In a few seconds it was a black saber tooth tiger. It gestured with its head towards the three women still screeching their lamentations.

"Do you know what they are, boy?," the massive feline asked him in a deep throated growl.

Art shook his head warily and raised the pistol to eye level.

The animal seemed to take offense that Art was aiming for the blaze of white fur on its forehead, but continued.

"They are Banshees," it said. "If a single banshee shows up and starts to wail, someone nearby is going to die. If three Banshees arrive at the same time, then someone as great as a king will soon draw his last breath. Feel flattered, boy? They've come to sing you to your rest. Either you," the cat said and then sniffed the air, "or your parents."

The black tiger took a half step forward. "Lay down your weapon, child. I promise I will make your death swift. Otherwise," it said, extending its claws, "I like to play with my food before taking the first bite."

As the big cat coiled back, ready to pounce, Art began firing the weapon. The slide atop the gun jumped back, ejecting a brass casing, then raced into position as one new bullet after another was chambered and fired. The cat turned its head away from the spray of lead, but it did not drop. It turned back to Art as the fifteenth and final bullet was fired.

"You should have accepted my offer, child. Agony and regret will form your final thoughts."

There was a rumble from beneath and the creature was knocked off its feet. Art staggered back towards the stairs. Suddenly, the basement floor split, opening a crack ten feet wide across the laundry. Art was sure that the deadly feline would be able to leap that with ease. Just as he was set to run up the basement stairs to warn his parents, a dozen short men emerged leaping from the gash in the earth. All but one wore helmets that looked like they had been chipped from stone. There was a small box on the front of each helm that held a tiny blue glowing orb. None of them was taller than four feet, but their arms were massively muscled and they had big, broad barreled chests. All had shoulder length hair and beards of various colors and they each held a shovel, a pickaxe, or a pry bar.

The twelfth man was dressed in a suit of shining metal armor and drew a long sword from a sheath on his back. His long white hair and flowing beard were tied in braids.

"Be gone, Sidhe," the dwarf knight bellowed. "Tell your mistress that you failed. You'll nay taste this boy's blood tonight."

"You and your feeble band cannot stop me," the Sidhe answered in a hiss. "There is no hope for the child. Listen, the Banshees sing for him. They are never wrong."

The knight stepped forward, holding the pommel of his long sword in both hands. He jabbed at the cat, probing it. Six of the dwarf miners formed a semi-circle around the two combatants, brandishing their tools like weapons. The other five leapt across the tear in the earth with ease and took up positions around Art. The one nearest him tried to push him up the basement stairs.

"Wait," Art said, and the miners obeyed, standing their ground with him.

The knight and the cat parried again and again, a single blade against two paws filled with razor claws. The knight swung his sword, counting on a killing blow, but missed. The cat swept one of its giant paws forward and up. It caught the knight under his ribs and knocked him into the air and up and over the break in the floor. The old warrior landed with his leg crumpled up under his back, unconscious. The polished long sword dropped from his grip and slid across the floor to rest at Arthur's feet.

The miners on the other side of the divide tried to assault the beast, but they were no match.

Arthur picked up the sword, which was thick and heavy in his hands. He looked at the beast and pointed the tip of the blade at it. "This ends, right here, right now," he said.

The demon seemed to smile. "I dine on your heart first and then on your parents'," it said, sweeping the miners away with the back of its paw.

Arthur waited on the ready as the cat launched itself into the air, leaping towards his face with its claws and fangs bared. He slid forward, dropping to his back with his legs folded beneath him, as the beast reached the height of its jump. He thrust the old knight's sword upward. The tip found the unguarded stomach of the monster. Art drove it even higher with a grunt of determination. The tip of the blade exited the creature's back and, before its feet could reach the ground, it transformed into an old woman in a long black dress.

The woman tried to land steadily on her feet, but could only stagger to her right. With the handle of the sword in her stomach and the long blade sticking out her back, she dropped before the cauldron and the three Banshees. The trio had gone silent as soon as Art struck the witch's cat form.

The old hag looked up at the three apparitions with her mouth agape. "How? You sang for the boy!"

The first banshee shook her head and whispered before dissolving into mist, "No, dearie. We sang for you."

The house began to shake.

The miner who had stood at Art's side looked at the dwarves standing around him. "Clear the house." He looked to those who had fought alongside the knight. "Get the King to safety."

Six of the small men moved as one, hoisting the old knight onto their shoulders. They rushed forward and leapt down into the earth's open wound.

Art started towards the stairs, but the miner at his side stopped him.

"My parents!," Art protested.

"They and the others are being looked after as we speak. They'll awaken soon. The banshees' cries will wear off in a few minutes. The Sidhe put a curse on the house in case she failed. It isn't safe."

Just as the little man finished speaking, there was a rumble from within the house above. Chunks of the ceiling began to fall in on them.

"No time," the man yelled.

He pulled Art forward to the edge of the open hole and threw him down into it. Art yelled as the inky black void swallowed him. He was falling head first, down towards the center of the earth.

TWO
THE RAVENS

Edward Flummox-Jones almost spilled his bucket of blood and beef and biscuits as he made his way in the dark down the back stone staircase. The biscuits were a predawn snack, but they were not for him.

He was the Yeoman Warder Ravenmaster of Her Majesty's Royal Palace and Fortress Tower of London, Member of the Sovereign's Body Guard of the Yeoman Guard Extraordinary. The Tower of London would not open for hours, but he was out before dawn as he had done every morning for the past 60 years, bringing the ravens of the Tower of London their first feeding of the day.

There was an ancient legend that the crows, which had always lived on the hill where the Tower was built, would protect England, but if they left the Tower, England would fall and the Tower of London would crumble into the River Thames. From the day in the year 501 that King Bran Hen of Bryneich had made that prophecy, there had always been a Ravenmaster to look after the birds and the Ravenmaster had always been a Flummox-Jones. Edward would be the last Flummox-Jones to hold the office. He had no son. No child for that matter, either. The ravens were as close to children as he would ever have.

He fumbled for his keys and opened the door to the massive cage out on the Tower Green. He was surprised. By now his ravens would have been cawing in anticipation of their first meal of the day. Instead, they were silent.

"Loki, Apollo, Ajax," he called out, but was met by silence. "Aphrodite, you naughty girl, where are you? Margaret? Matilde?"

Although the moon was full, the thick clouds over London obscured the light. Edward's eyesight had begun to deteriorate with age and he could no longer see into the shadows. The clouds parted briefly and a shaft of silver light illuminated the back of the cage. The iron fencing had been ripped opened. It looked like something had forced its way through the bars to get inside.

Edward pulled a small flashlight from his tunic pocket and depressed the button, sending out a tight beam of white LED light that he focused on the first perch in front of him.

He took a step back, dropping his bucket of biscuits and blood. There was something seated on the perch. It made a low, guttural sound, like a lion growling. It was jet black, covered in fine wisps of feathers, and where Edward's torchlight touched them, they glowed an iridescent blue. It unfolded dark, leathery wings that it flapped to steady itself. Its head was pointed, but free of the pinfeathers that covered its body. Instead, it wore row upon row of scales like tiny beads. It moved slight forearms that seemed useless, like the arms on the Tyrannosaurus Rex he had seen once in a museum. Its feet were like hawk's talons with three toes in front.

The creature narrowed its dark red eyes at Edward and bobbed its head. Although it was just a little larger than his ravens, he feared that the creature was about to strike.

The animal raised itself up on its perch and flapped its

wings forward once and began to cough. In a moment, there was an explosion of black feathers coming from its toothy mouth. Edward heard something clang in the darkness and hit his boot. He shined his flashlight downward.

It was a small metal leg band bearing the Queen's seal and the embossed name, "Loki."

As Edward leaned down to pick it up, he heard more coughing. He straightened up and shined his light from perch to perch. There were eight more of them. Each expelled a fine cloud of black feathers that hung in the air for a moment, followed by the sounds of falling metal rings.

Edward focused his lamp on the first creature again, which was looking at him with its head turned sideways. It looked down at the bucket, then back up to Edward, and back to the bucket.

"Are you still hungry?," Edward asked, hoping that it was not viewing him as its next meal.

He slowly reached into the bucket and tossed a blood soaked biscuit to the creature, which caught it and swallowed it down with a single gulp. The creature's eyes widened as it looked at Edward, who swore it was starting to act like an obedient pup.

"Want more?," he asked, holding up a small piece of biscuit.

The creature's tail began to move rhythmically from side to side. Then he saw the other eight were doing exactly the same. He started tossing biscuits and bloody beef to them all. When he was done, he turned it over and then showed them the empty bucket.

"See," he said, "nom-noms are all gone. I want you all to be good ... whatever you are ... and leave. I'll have no more truck with you."

He pointed at the first creature he encountered. "Oy, you. I bet you punched right through that, didn't you. I wish you hadn't done that. It's going to make an awful lot of work for me this morning."

Edward shook his head. "I don't know what I'm going to do. People are expecting to see ravens, not ... lizards with feathers. I wish there was some way I could hold onto my job, but you lot have seen to that, haven't you?"

He picked up his bucket. "Well, turn out the lights when you leave, boys. I'll be sacked, for sure. The Tower has no use for a Ravenmaster when there aren't any ravens."

THREE
THE PRINCESS

Guinevere walked into her mother's breakfast room before dawn and stood in front of the Queen, waiting to be recognized. Even on holiday, her mother was an early riser. Guinevere stood perfectly straight. Her posture was perfect. It had to be. She was The Royal Princess.

Her full name was The Royal Princess Guinevere Melisande Victoria Anne. At fifteen, she was already a member of the Order of the Garter, the Order of the Thistle, the Royal Victorian Order, the Queens' Service Order, the Royal Society of London for Improving Natural Knowledge, and was the patron head of the Royal College of Veterinary Surgeons.

She was a head shorter than her mother and only weighed seven and a half stone. Her long auburn hair had been pulled up high upon her head and was held in place with a headband studded with small rhinestones, reminiscent of a tiara.

Guinevere had a governess who looked after her when she was home, but when she was attending Benendon School in Kent, about an hour southeast of London, she was on her own. Guinevere's governess coughed, causing the Queen to lower the newspaper she was reading. The Princess shot an angry glare at her keeper.

"Darling, I'm sorry," Queen Caroline said, "I didn't see you standing there. Why didn't you say something?"

"I've been reading an account of old customs and manners in our Court. One of the unpardonable sins was to interrupt the sovereign."

The Queen stood. She was wearing a brown and tan jacketed suit made of raw silk and a smooth yellow cream silk blouse. There was not a hair out of place. There was also nothing to indicate that she was the Queen of England, no crown or scepter, no long trailing ermine cape. Unlike the royal women before her, she detested hats and had done away with the custom of always appearing with her head covered in public. She had large blue eyes that flashed and a smile that dazzled.

The people of England, with her, had mourned the sudden passing of her father, the King, the year before. The people of the kingdom had embraced their new Queen and held her husband, Prince Francis, in warm regard. Their feelings toward Princess Guinevere were more reserved.

"You're not interrupting me, Gwennie. I was just reading the newspaper. Your father's friends, the Williamses and their son, Art, will be joining us for tea this afternoon."

Guinevere dropped her gaze for a moment. "That's what I wanted to talk you about. Do a really have to spend time with these —" She struggled to find the right word, then finally spat out, "— Americans?"

"Ambassador Williams is one of your father's oldest friends." The Queen laughed. "Goodness, dear, what do you have against Americans?"

"You've seen them, haven't you? They invade London every summer. Shorts and vests and stupid hats. They're loud and boorish and so ..." She held her hands up and shuddered, as if the very thought of them made her feel unclean. "... common. They're as common as they can be. These Americans," Guinevere continued, "I've read all about them. Traitors to the Crown. They revolted. We should have hung every one of them. Washington. Jefferson. Franklin. Forced them back into the Empire. And I suspect these Williamses are just as common as their countrymen."

"They're lovely people. I haven't seen their son since you were both babies. They attended the coronation, but that was before he was appointed Ambassador. There was so much to do. We couldn't meet up, not even for a moment. If you won't do this for me, do it for your father."

"He's the most common of them all," Guinevere said.

"Guinevere Melisande Victoria Anne!," the Queen scolded her. "I won't have you talking about your father that way."

"Its true, Mother. What was he before you married him? A commoner. He was just a businessman when he met you. No title. No lands. The nearest his family ever got to the House of Lords was taking a walking tour with a bunch of sweaty Americans."

"Guinevere! Stop it this instant. He is your father and he loves you."

Suddenly the door to the breakfast room burst open. Prince Francis, Duke of Dorchester, galloped in and whinnied like a horse. He stopped beside his wife and daughter and clopped his foot.

"Presenting," he said, "Saint George, just back from hunting dragons." The Prince rolled his shoulders forward to reveal Gregory, the eleven-month-old Prince and heir to the throne, sitting astride his father's shoulders.

Behind the two princes, father and son, was a retinue of followers: Gregory's nanny, Francis' staff, and their combined security details. All looked on with panic as the baby tossed back his head in laughter. Gregory pulled back on the salt and pepper hair he held in both hands and kicked his father's collarbones with his heels. Francis leaned forward and gave his wife a peck on the lips.

He nodded to his daughter. "Hello, darling. Love to stay and chat, but St. George here thinks he saw dragons in the drawing room. Tally ho!," he called out as he left with the crowd following behind them.

Guinevere folded her arms across her chest and pursed her lips as she watched her mother smiling at her father's antics.

"Do you see?", Guinevere asked with impatience when her mother turned back to her.

"I think he's adorable," the Queen said with a smile.

"I think he's a loon."

FOUR
THE PRODIGAL SON

A hand reached out in the darkness and slowed Art's descent, but then let go. Another reached for him in the blackness and slowed his fall further. Time after time, a friendly hand slowed him. Finally, an arm caught his and this time, Art stopped. He was lowered a few inches to what felt like solid ground. As his eyes adjusted to the gloom, he could see a large crowd of miners, many more than had been on the surface, with their lighted stone helmets shining down on the old knight, who was now sitting up against the wall of a tunnel that looked like it had been hewn by hand from solid rock.

"Come here, son," the old man called out.

The miner who had tossed Art down the shaft was now standing beside him and nudged him forward. The knight extended his arm and Art reflexively extended his hand. The knight grabbed Art's forearm just below the elbow.

"I am Kerr Shalerunner, leader of Clan Fargrave. It was our duty to protect you. Instead, you had to save a foolish old man."

"Our King," the dwarf next to Art corrected.

"Quiet, Duncan," the old man said, "you'll get a chance to say your piece. You saved my life, son, the life of a king. It is not a debt I intend to forget. Ever. You have proven yourself worthy far beyond how you were described to us. As the last act of a King ..."

"No, father!," Duncan cried out.

Shalerunner smiled. "I'm not dying. Except from shame." He looked at his son. "An old man's pride put all of us in danger. It should have been Duncan who led us to protect young Arthur. Let the word go forth from this place and on this day that Duncan Shalerunner is now the King of Clan Fargrave." The old man handed his son his sword.

The mass of miners bowed their heads reverently for a moment and then let loose a hearty cheer that echoed up and down the tunnel. They clapped Duncan on the back.

"Then, as my first act as King, I decree that Zefrom Arthur Williams the Fourth is a full brother in our clan, entitled to all of our rights and responsibilities."

Duncan handed the sword to one of the other miners. "Eori, I must get our new brother back to his own world for now. Take care of our father and our sword and I will meet you at the rendezvous point in two hours."

Eori and the others bowed to their new king and set to work making a stretcher to bear old Shalerunner. Duncan led Art up a long and winding tunnel.

"How far down are we?," Art asked as they continued their rise to the surface.

"About five hundred feet by your measurements."

"How many years did it take you to dig this?," said Art, who was beginning to feel a bit winded.

Duncan laughed. "Years? We did this in a week. One hundred dwarves on each shift working 'round the clock."

They finally stopped in front of a crude wooden ladder. The backs of Art's legs burned from the climb.

Duncan turned to him. "When you go up, you'll be in the thicket of trees in the southeast corner of the grounds.

I'm going to collapse this tunnel behind me. All they'll find is this area here and a tunnel just below the surface leading back to the basement of the house.

"It's very important that you tell no one what you've seen tonight. Not about us. Not about the Sidhe. Not about the Banshees, either. They probably wouldn't believe you if you told them. You must trust me, for I've taken an oath to treat you as kin. The more people who know of what you've seen here, the greater danger you all will face. You'll be protected when you're with your parents. You'll be protected when you're at your school. And soon all will be explained to you. Tell me you understand, Arthur."

Art nodded.

Duncan embraced Art tightly, even though his head only reached the middle of Art's chest. It felt as if his ribs were going to cave in from the strength of the new dwarf king.

"Till we meet again, Brother," Duncan said and moved swiftly back down into the tunnel and out of sight.

As Art mounted the ladder and was about to push through the final layers covering the opening, he heard Duncan's voice say, "Sorry about your stuff."

Art didn't know what Duncan meant until he pushed through a foot of dirt and rocks to the surface. When he crawled out and got to his feet, he could see that the dawn was breaking in the east. There were police vans and ambulances parked across the great lawn. A yellow crane was positioning itself into place, maneuvering its boom over the southeast corner of Winfield House. That corner of the mansion was where his room had been. That part of the mansion had been pulled into the earth below.

"Can't they work any faster?," Mildred Williams pleaded with her husband. "He could be down there, hurt."

The Ambassador and his wife, together with everyone who had been in the house, had awakened in the middle of the great lawn. Mildred had opened her eyes just as half of the mansion, the half where she thought her son was sleeping, collapsed with a great roar. A cloud of dust billowed out and covered her and everyone around her as she wobbled to her feet. Metropolitan Police, and fire and emergency crews poured onto the grounds of Winfield House within minutes. Floodlights were set up around the house and bathed it in pure white light.

When Mildred saw the men preparing to lower themselves down into the open maw of earth, she ran forward to David Wilkins, the head of Scotland Yard's emergency response team, with the Ambassador following after her, trying to get her to stop.

"I want to go down there," she insisted to Wilkins. "My son is down there. He needs me. He needs his mother."

Wilkins looked over at Mrs. Williams and then to the Ambassador. "Mum," he said, "my men are highly trained. We'll find your boy and we'll get him out. But my people can't do that and look after you. The rest of the house may still fall into this hole."

The Ambassador stood behind his wife and put his hands on her shoulders. "Mildred, we need to let these men do their jobs. Art's the only one unaccounted for. The quicker they work, the quicker they can find him."

Mildred nodded reluctantly. "I need to do something. What can I do? "

Wilkins patted Mildred on the forearm. "Say a prayer, Mum. Never underestimate the power of a mother's prayer."

As Wilkins turned to brief his men one last time before they lowered themselves on lines into the rubble, the three of them heard a voice calling from behind.

"Mom! Dad!"

Mildred turned and saw her son walking across the

great lawn, his hair even more of a mess than usual. In the dawn's light, she could see that he was covered in dirt from head to toe. She broke into a run, followed by her husband.

Wilkins signaled for the men to stay out of the pit, then pointed to one of the waiting ambulances and directed it towards Art and his parents.

Art felt his mother collide into him with the force of a linebacker, nearly knocking him to the ground. She hugged him as tightly as Duncan had. Her tears mixed with the dirt caked on his face, turning it to mud. His father was not far behind and he felt him embrace them both.

His mother let out a cry and Art could not tell if she was happy or sad.

"I'm okay, Mom," he said softly.

She nodded and tried to compose herself, and then started to cry like before. "I was afraid we lost you."

Art tried to relieve his mother's tension. "No such luck."

That made his mother's eyes overflow with tears once more. She held her son even tighter.

As the ambulance pulled up beside them, the Ambassador asked, "What happened to you?"

Art had a decision to make. He could tell his parents the truth or hide it from them, like Duncan made him promise. Was there a danger in telling them? Art was not going to risk it finding out.

"I was asleep in my bed when the whole building started to shake. I thought it was an earthquake. Then the lights went out and I could feel myself falling. I blacked out. When I came to, I started crawling and found a tunnel. It came out over there. What happened to you?," Art asked, already knowing the real answer.

"They're guessing that it was a gas leak and explosion in the laundry room," the Ambassador answered. "Caused the whole thing to drop into an underground cave that no one ever knew about. My guess is that the security team was overcome by the gas, but with their training still managed to get us out."

The EMTs alighted from the ambulance and pried Art from his mother's embrace. They draped a Mylar plastic blanket over his shoulders. One wrapped a blood pressure cuff over his right upper arm, while the other shined a penlight in his eyes, watching the reaction of his pupils.

"Are you cut?," the first EMT asked him.

"I don't think so," Art answered. "Why?"

"You've got blood all down your front." He lifted up Art's shirt and then ran his rubber-gloved hands over his scalp looking for a wound. "You're clean. But I think we'd better get you checked out at hospital. Just to be on the safe side."

"I'm fine, really," Art protested. He knew the blood belonged to the witch. He was not going to tell them that.

"Nonsense," his mother said, overruling him. "You're going and that's final."

FIVE
THE RAVENMASTER

Edward had come back to his flat in the Casemates, the apartments on the Tower grounds set aside for the staff and packed up his belongings. He was surprised at how little he owned. The furniture in the flat had been his parents'. After he went down to speak to the Chief Yeoman Warder, he planned to ring up the British Red Cross and donate the whole lot to them. They would get some good use out of it. Perhaps a homeless family might be able to use it.

Homeless. The word struck him. That was what he would soon be. He thought again. Perhaps not really homeless. He had inherited his grandparents' farm in Childwickbury. The annual rent on the farm was a tidy sum, which he had saved all these years. He could find a pensioner's cottage somewhere and finish out his days. His eyes became misty and he wiped them on his Ravenmaster's tunic. He knew it would be the last time he would be wearing it. He missed his ravens and he was already starting to miss his old life.

The shock of the morning had worn off. He did not

know what the creatures in the cages were, but he knew they were not dragons. There were no such things as dragons.

He looked at his wristwatch. It was nearly seven o'clock. The Chief Warder would be walking through the Tower grounds very soon. As he crossed the Tower Green, he heard a young voice cry out to him.

"Ravenmaster, the Chief Warder would like a word wiff' you." It was George Bailey, the new Warder who served as his unofficial Assistant Ravenmaster.

Edward turned in the direction of the voice and saw the young man holding the large stainless steel bucket, tossing bits of meat across the lawn. Behind him was the largest cage. Edward could see that the split in the bars had been repaired. The metal work was so fine, he could not make out where the opening had been. He looked in the direction where George was tossing the food.

Nine small black creatures waited patiently as the beef was tossed to them. With each pitch, they rose one-by-one and caught it in mid-air, swallowing it whole before they fluttered back down to the ground.

When Edward walked up to stand beside George, the black-feathered reptiles saw him and jumped up and down excitedly before hopping over to stand all around him.

"I've never seem them do that before, sir," George said.

"Them?," Edward asked.

"Yeah, the ravens. They never caught their food like that. They're usually such lazy birds. They wait to see where it lands and then they pick at it. And," he said pointing at the little dragons at their feet, "they've never been this excited to see you."

Edward stared as they stretched their black leathery wings and stared back up at him.

"They've never been this quiet before," George observed.

Almost as if on cue, the creatures looked at one

another and started to caw, perfectly imitating the ravens they had eaten the night before.

"Don't they look a little funny to you?," Edward asked.

George eyed them carefully. "Funny as in 'ha-ha' or funny as in not really funny? No, to either one. What you have here are nine fine specimens of *corvus corax*. You taught me that, sir. Genus and species. *Corvus corax*."

"Flummox-Jones," a voice called out, "where the devil have you been?"

It was Chief Yeoman Warder Humphrey Archer. Edward suddenly remembered that Bailey had told him that Archer wanted to see him. Standing next to Archer was a young woman in her early thirties, with straight black hair with the same blue highlights found in the shine of the ravens' feathers. She was dressed in a black Beefeater's tunic trimmed in red. Edward could see that the lack of seniority markings on her sleeve showed her to be a new recruit, just like Bailey.

"Ravenmaster Edward Flummox-Jones," Archer said, "this is Obsidia Hawkins. She's going to be your new assistant."

The young woman was standing at attention and then snapped a smart salute at Edward. He returned it without thinking.

"Sir," Edward protested, "I don't need a new assistant. George here is a quick study. We're getting on just fine."

"Nonsense. She's perfect for the job. She's a trained ornithologist and was an Assistant Keeper of the King's Swans for seven years."

"Sir," Edward said, "a word with you in private, if you please."

As the two of them stepped off a few paces, George tried to make conversation with Obsidia.

"So," he asked, "ornithologist? That'd be someone what studies 'orns?"

Obsidia smiled at him. "Birds. Ornithology is the study of birds."

"You'd think they'd call it bird-o-thology, then now, wouldn't you?"

Obsidia smiled as she lowered herself to get a closer look at the ravens.

"Sir," Edward said when they were far enough away so as not to be overheard, "I don't know if you've noticed, but Miss Hawkins is a ... female woman. There's never been a woman Beefeater in our 650 year history."

"I'm quite aware of it, Jones," Archer said uncomfortably. "Our new Queen became aware of it, as well. She thought that your little department might be the best place to start. You and your ravens will be helping to crash through the glass ceiling and all. Decisions been made, old boy, unless you'd like to take it up with the Queen herself."

Edward shook his head and sighed. "No, sir. This I do for Queen and country."

Archer beamed at him. "That's right, Jones. For Queen and country."

SIX
ER

It was only nine in the morning, but Art was already exhausted. He had been poked and prodded at the hospital all morning long. Needles had been inserted into him to draw fluids out and to pump medicines in. He had been given a tetanus shot to ward off lockjaw and antibiotics as a precaution to fight off infections they were not sure he had. He was now being forced to lie on a table while powerful magnets took digital slices of his insides and displayed them to the doctors in the little windowless room next door.

"Just a few more seconds, young man," the doctor said to him over the speakers.

"You're doing fine, honey," he heard his mother add.

Art gritted his teeth, but could not move. His head had been immobilized in a plastic helmet attached to the bed. He told her he did not want her seeing the images of him, especially if they were going to display him without his hospital gown.

Art said, "You promised you wouldn't be watching."

"Relax, sweetheart," she said, "its not like I didn't see

everything when you were a baby."

"Mom!," Art shouted as the thrumming of the machinery suddenly died.

The table slid silently out of the MRI scanner. The radiologist stepped into the scanner room, with Art's mother trailing close behind, and unlocked the mask holding his head in place.

"Everything appears to be where it should be," the doctor said. "No signs of internal bleeding or trauma. All things considered, I'd say you were a very lucky young man."

Art sat up and found his mother hugging him once more.

The door to the MRI room opened and a janitor slipped in. Art's bodyguard eyed the man's credentials that hung from a lanyard around his neck and nodded for him to come in, without questioning him. Apparently, the agent was willing to overlook the fact that the man was only four feet tall with arms like tree trunks and a waist length beard that had been collected into four long braids. Or more likely, Art thought, he could not see him like Art could.

The dwarf, out of everyone else's line of vision except Art's, raised his index finger to his lips. The little man then stepped into the control room and emptied the garbage can into the larger container on his pushcart.

"Doctor," Mildred said to the doctor sweetly. "Do you think it would be all right if Art were to go out this afternoon? You see, we've been invited to have tea with the Royal Family and I wouldn't want to disappoint them."

"Madam," the doctor said, eying Mildred, "I'm sure Her Majesty would understand if you begged off. After all, a house did just fall in on the lad."

"I know," she answered, "but you said everything was all right."

The doctor looked up from his chart. "There's nothing wrong with you, young man. If you feel up to it, I don't see that it would hurt anything."

"Then it's settled," she said triumphantly. "Our things arrived on an Air Force transport this morning. We're going to be staying at the Tower Hotel for the present. The State Department booked the Presidential Apartment for us."

His mother looked down at the bag she was holding. "The staff pulled this out of the things that were on the transport."

She also handed him a small box that was gift-wrapped.

"It's a small present, as a way for your father and I to start to make it up to you for ruining your birthday."

He opened the wrapping paper. Inside was a new iPhone to take the place of the iPod Touch that had vanished down the hole with the dwarves.

SEVEN
PROTOCOL

The Tower Hotel sat right on the River Thames next to the Tower of London. There were no sharp angled corners on its surface. Instead, it looked like a long, thin egg with a fine latticework of steel on its surface holding diamond wedges of thermal glass into place.

The Presidential Apartment took up half of the uppermost floor. There were three bedrooms, each with their own bathroom. Art claimed the bedroom on the far side of the apartment, away from where his parents slept. Next to his bedroom was a door that connected into the next suite. When circumstances demanded it, the entire floor could be turned into one large suite with as many as nine bedrooms.

At 11 a.m., he went into the apartment's formal dining room as his mother had instructed him.

A little woman in a tweed suit watched Art critically as he walked into the dining room. The table next to her was set with fine china and it overflowed with small sandwiches and cakes. Steam vented from the spout of a dainty porcelain teapot.

Art kept his hands in his pockets as he approached her. "What's up?," he asked as he took an earbud from his right ear.

Mrs. Chillingsworth winced as she heard the music blasting from the small speaker that was now dangling at chest height. She plucked the other earphone out and pulled the iPhone from his front jacket pocket. Without looking away from him, she snapped her fingers and a butler stepped forward and took the device and disappeared behind a swinging wood paneled door.

"Hey," Art yelled out to the man, "where are you going with my iPhone?" He looked down at the woman. "Where's he going with my iPhone?"

Mrs. Chillingsworth did not answer him, but instead looked Art over from head to foot. He had a noble face, she thought, good bone structure. He got that from his mother. She looked at his clothes and shook her head.

"Master Williams, I told you to dress for an afternoon tea party."

Art looked down at himself, stretching out his long arms. "I wore what I always wear to parties. My leather jacket, my Levi's, my boots, and a shirt from my favorite band."

She motioned for him to open his leather jacket so that she could see.

"Drowning Armada?," she said through pursed lips.

"They're fantastic," Art said, nodding. "That's who I was listening to when that guy took my iPhone." Art looked over at the door. "I know you're back there. I want my iPhone back."

"Pay attention to me, Master Williams. You can't wear that t-shirt again in public."

"Why? Do people in England hate Drowning Armada?"

"In 1588, the Spanish Armada was driven back by the British, preventing an invasion intent on deposing Queen Elizabeth I. Bad weather, I suspect a hurricane, really, drove what was left of their fleet onto the rocks off the Irish coast where most of the sailors drowned. Wear that shirt in public and you risk offending both the British and the Spanish."

"1588?," Art pondered. "You'd think they'd be over it by now."

Mrs. Chillingsworth shook her head. "In any case, one does not wear dungarees and a leather jacket to see the Royal Family."

She snapped her fingers once more and the butler who had carried off the cell phone walked back through the swinging door holding a suit on a hanger, a button-down shirt, a tie, and a pair of dress shoes.

"I thought you might not grasp what I was asking you to do, so I asked Mr. Davis to bring me something appropriate for you to wear. I'm going to step outside while you change and then we're going to have tea. Won't that be nice?"

The long, black Cadillac limousine stood out among the tiny European cars as it wound its way west out of London on the M4.

"It'll be good to see old Stinky again," Ambassador Williams said as he looked out the window at the English countryside rolling by.

"I wish you wouldn't call him that," Mildred scolded.

"Why? That was his nickname at Fillmore Academy. We were roommates. He was Stinky and I was ..."

Mildred cut her husband off. "I know what they called him. You can't call him that. Not now."

The Ambassador shook his head. "Why? What's changed?"

Mildred stared at him for a long moment. "What's changed? You're the American Ambassador to the Court of St. James and he's the Queen's consort."

Art snickered.

"What's so funny, Art?," his father asked.

"Consort?," Art said and laughed out loud. "Do you know what that means? He's like a drone bee, there to get the queen bee preg —"

"Zefrom Arthur Williams the Fourth," his mother said, cutting him off, "so help me if you embarrass me in front of the Queen of England, I'll lock you in the dungeon!"

"We live in a hotel now. No dungeon."

"I'll borrow one if I have to," she said coldly. "It's quite an honor to be invited to have tea with the Queen and her family. I will not have you ruin it or embarrass us."

Art looked over at his father for support, but the Ambassador only shook his head.

"Listen to your mother, son. You're not only here as our boy. Think of yourself as an unofficial ambassador of America."

"Sit up straight while we go over the rules for tea once more. I promised the embassy's protocol officer that you'd be a perfect gentleman."

The last thing that Art wanted to do was to be drilled again on how to drink tea and eat terrible tasting food.

Art tried to loosen his tie, but his mother leaned forward and tightened the noose around his neck. He wished he had his iPhone back so he could tune out his parents. Mrs. Chillingsworth said whether he got it back depended on how he "performed" at tea.

"Stop fidgeting. We'll be there soon," his mother said. "Now remember, speak only if spoken to first. You're to refer to Queen Caroline as 'Your Majesty' and Prince Francis as 'Your Royal Highness'." She turned to her husband. "Does he have to bow?"

The Ambassador looked back from gazing out the window. "I don't think so. We're Americans. We don't bow. We don't curtsy. I wish we brought Chillingsworth with us. She'd know the answer."

Mildred tightened her son's tie once more and Art could feel his eyes begin to pop out from the pressure.

"Oh, and you have to call Princess Guinevere 'Your Royal Highness' or 'Ma'am'."

"She's a kid. I'm not calling her 'Ma'am.'"

"She's royalty. Oh, you probably don't remember when the two of you first met. It was when Caroline was only a princess. They came to our place for dinner when they were in the States. You were three. Guinevere was two. You hugged each other. I have a picture of it somewhere. It was so adorable."

She turned to her husband and grabbed his arm.

"Do you think we could get another picture of them together? It would be so cute. Who knows, maybe one day, our boy could marry a princess."

"Guinevere's not going to marry our son."

Mildred moistened the tips of the fingers on her right hand and smoothed down her son's unruly hair.

"Why not? She'd be lucky to have him. Has Stinky ... I mean the Prince, said anything?"

"No," the Ambassador said. "But face the facts. She's royalty and he's not. Art's not even British."

The glass divider in front of them slid down. Chief Diplomatic Agent Kent Kidd, seated next to the driver, said, "Mr. Ambassador, Ma'am, we'll be at Windsor Castle in five minutes."

"Thank you, Kidd," the Ambassador replied.

Mildred patted her son on the knee. "Don't you listen to your father, dear. If you want to marry a princess, you can."

If this had been an occasion of state, the arrival of the Ambassador and his family at Windsor Castle would have been overflowing with pomp and ceremony. There would have been a band from the Foot Guards Battalion from the nearby Victoria Barracks there to play both the American national anthem and "God Save the Queen".

But this was not an occasion of state. The Embassy

limousine pulled up to the guest entrance to the State Apartments in the Upper Ward. Chief Usher Hugh Hyde stood in the January afternoon chill as the car came to a stop and waited as Agent Kidd hopped out of the front seat and opened the passenger door. Ambassador Williams emerged and extended his hand to help his wife out. Art exited on the opposite side.

"On behalf of Her Majesty Queen Caroline and his Royal Highness Prince Francis, I bid you welcome to Windsor Castle, Your Excellency," Usher Hyde said and then bowed his head as a sign of respect.

"Thank you," Ambassador Williams said formally.

By now Art had come around the back of the limousine and stood next to his mother and father.

"May I present my wife, Mildred Harrison Williams and my son, Zefrom Williams the Fourth."

The Usher acknowledged them both. Art had been briefed on how to conduct himself during tea, but did not remember any instructions for meeting anyone other than the Royal Family. He decided to wing it and grabbed the Usher's hand.

"On behalf of the President and First Lady, we accept your welcome and invite you to visit America."

Art saw that his mother was glaring at him.

"Land of the free and home of the brave," Art said as he quickly released his grip on the Usher.

Usher Hyde was still stone faced. "Very kind of you, Master Williams. Now, if you all would be so kind as to follow me, Her Majesty and His Royal Highness await."

As the Usher turned, an attendant opened the Guest Entrance door and they moved towards it. Prince Francis, with Prince Gregory astride his shoulders, galloped through the open doorway.

"Binky!," Prince Francis cried in delight. "When I heard about what happened this morning, I was relieved that all of you were all right. I couldn't wait any longer. I just had to come down to greet you myself. All this protocol be dashed."

"Stinky!," the Ambassador answered reflexively as they embraced.

Prince Gregory was balanced on his father's shoulders and let out a loud laugh. The crowd that had been following the two princes poured out of the door.

Prince Francis reached up and took his son under his arms and plucked him off his shoulders. As he said, "Would you mind terribly?," Gregory's nanny stepped forward to receive the child. Instead, Francis handed the boy to Art.

"*Ab incunabulis*," Prince Francis said, extending his right elbow.

The Ambassador answered, "*Ut sepulchrum!*," twisting so that his right elbow touched the Prince's.

Francis tucked his arms underneath his armpits and flapped. "*A Fillmore vir!*"

"*Est usquequaque fortis.*" The Ambassador did the same and they both laughed and shook each other's hand.

Little Prince Gregory smiled in Art's grasp and clapped for his father.

"Stinky," a voice from the back of the pack said, "aren't you worried that your son could catch his death of cold out here?"

The crowd parted suddenly. The Queen, with the baby's sweater in her hands, walked to Art and the little prince. She held her arms out and the baby practically leapt to her. She wrapped the sweater around her son and smiled at Art.

"I was so relieved to hear that you weren't hurt. How are you, dear?," she asked Art, squeezing his forearm.

Art was flustered. He had practiced formalities with Mrs. Chillingsworth, but it had not prepared him for this.

"Fine. Ma'am. Your Queenness. I mean Highness. I mean Your Royal Highness. And you?"

Art gritted his teeth. One of the things that Mrs. Chillingsworth had practically pounded into his head was that he was not to ask a question of the Queen. He was certain that he'd never see his iPhone again.

"Wonderful, now that you and your family are here." She looked over at Art's mother. "Mildred, it has been far too long."

The Queen extended her hand, while Mildred attempted a half curtsy. Art thought it made his mother look like she was dodging sniper fire.

"Why don't we all go inside and catch up?," the Queen asked. "Stinky," she said to her husband, "lead the way."

EIGHT
THE GARTER THRONE ROOM

Art tried hard not to let material things impress him. His parents lived in a big house in Back Bay Boston, in what was once a grand mansion that had been split into apartments. His mother had taken it upon herself to make the building a single home once more. Including the attic and the basement, it had six floors and more room than his small family would ever need. Windsor Castle went far beyond anything he ever experienced in the States, and Art had visited the White House.

Twice.

"It is the largest castle still occupied by royalty," Mrs. Chillingsworth had instructed him. "First settled by William the Conqueror, it has been home to almost every British monarch since. Henry VIII is buried there."

When they came into the Crimson Drawing Room, the sun had come out for the first time since Art had arrived in England. Now, great shafts of sunlight poured into the room. The light bounced off of mirrors and reflected from crystal walls and a ceiling that was covered in gold leaf. He winced and fought hard to keep his eyes open through the glare. He wished that Mrs. Chillingsworth had not confiscated his shades before he got into the limousine.

The Queen handed off Prince Gregory to the nanny as they entered the room and directed them to sit down at the round table that had been set in the center of the chamber. There were six elegant place settings of fine porcelain china, the kind his mother only let him eat off of when they had important company. Steam rose from the two pots filled with tea and coffee next to the flowers in the center of the table. There were trays of food arranged on the table, as well.

Art felt a little more at ease. He had been through this with Mrs. Chillingsworth and remembered most of what she taught him. He recognized the food. There were little cucumber finger sandwiches, blueberry scones, plus cakes and pastries. Mrs. Chillingsworth explained that the white stuff in a small bowl was "clotted cream", which was a name that grossed Art out. She had insisted that he try everything on the table and the clotted cream turned out to be surprisingly good, kind of a mixture of cream cheese and whipped cream.

A butler poured tea for them all and Art waited last before taking a small sandwich from a tray on the center of the table. He would have given everything at that moment for a can of Mountain Dew and a plate full of Buffalo wings.

While his parents and the Royal Couple talked, Art downed his cup of tea in a single swallow. Wordlessly, the butler refilled it and then went back to his station. Art's eyes wondered about the room, from the two full body portraits of a king and queen from long ago, then to head portraits of ancient royals. Every one of them, Art concluded, was too pasty and all could have benefited from at least a weekend in Miami.

As he tried to make out the portraits at the far end of the room, a young woman about his age in a blue silk dress and pearls entered and stepped into the light. Her form disappeared for a moment in the sudden, radiant flash of a sunbeam. Both the Ambassador and his wife stood. Mildred had to reach down and tug at her son's elbow to signal for him to rise.

"Darling," Prince Francis said, "you've met before, but you might not remember. This is Ambassador and Mrs. Williams and their son, Art."

The Princess extended her hand to Art palm down and looked at him with reservations. When Guinevere had walked into the room, all of Art's careful rehearsal escaped him. On instinct, he gave her a fist bump.

"Charming," Guinevere said and looked over at her mother, hoping that she would see this as proof to support her early morning argument.

Mrs. Williams was offered Guinevere's hand, which she accepted with the lightest of grips. Art's father, when offered the same back of the hand, brought his face down and kissed the air just above it.

Art clenched his fists by his side. Kiss the hand, he remembered. He knew he would remember next time. If there was a next time.

Guinevere took a seat at the table next to Art.

"Darling," the Prince said, "the Ambassador was just telling us that the new President would love for us all to visit. He even suggested that Mummy address a joint session of their Congress."

Guinevere took a sip of tea and looked up from her cup. "I know just how she should start her speech."

The Queen cast her a wary look.

"Come back, America," she said with a sweet smile. "All is forgiven."

Prince Francis laughed uproariously and the Ambassador and Mrs. Williams joined in politely. The Queen merely raised an eyebrow.

Guinevere put down her cup. "Mother," she asked, "may I be excused?"

"I think that's an excellent idea," the Queen said.

"I've got an even better one, Gwennie," Francis said. "Art's never been to Windsor. Why don't you show him around while Mummy and I finish getting caught up?"

Guinevere flashed a look of horror at her mother and then her expression changed to one of quiet pleading.

The Queen nodded and smiled. "I think that's a wonderful idea. Don't wander off too far, dear."

Princess Guinevere walked so briskly that Art had trouble keeping up with her.

What was her mother thinking, Guinevere seethed to herself. Making her a tour guide to this loutish boy, this ... American! Of all the indignities she had been forced to suffer, this was one of the worst. She was being punished — punished for daring to express an opinion. One day, this would be her realm to command and when that day came ...

She stopped in mid-thought. That day would never come. She had been destined to be Queen, a great Queen, greater and more beloved by her subjects than even her mother would ever be. That was, until the birth of her little brother, Prince Gregory. If he had the decency to be born a girl, nothing would have changed. Now, instead of being the heir to the throne, she was pushed into second place.

"Excuse me," the voice from behind her said.

She turned sharply. "What do you want?," she asked Art.

"I think you're lost. We've passed that same suit of armor three times now. I think we're going in circles."

"Fine," she answered abruptly. "You want a tour? Follow me."

Guinevere's governess and Art's diplomatic bodyguard followed at a discrete distance and the Princess led him down a long corridor. She pushed open a massive door that yielded to her touch.

"Do you understand power?," she asked him. "Do you understand stagecraft, Mr. Ambassador's son?"

"It's Art."

"What's art?," she asked impatiently.

"My name. It's Art. Well, actually, it's my middle name. But I've always liked it better than Zefrom."

She ignored his babbling.

"Art, look around you. What do you see?"

Art stopped and looked at the long room they had entered. The walls were covered with light honey oak paneling. There was a royal blue carpet with an intricate pattern on the floor. There were two rows of five chairs facing each other. At the far end of the chamber, beyond a proscenium arch, was a single chair covered in red and gold silk beneath an elaborate crest.

Art motioned. "This part looks like a conference room, but they took out the table. Over there," he said, pointing to the red chair, "looks like a stage. Is this like a little theater? If you moved the chair, you could install a really wicked TV screen. You could turn this into a killer media room."

Guinevere started walking towards the front of the room and beckoned Art to follow her with the gesture of her index finger.

"This is the Garter Throne Room, just one of many throne rooms in the kingdom."

She stood to one side of the red silk-covered throne and directed Art to stand opposite her on the other side of the chair. The governess and the diplomatic agent stood at the very back of the long room and watched the two young people without interfering.

"Once, the word of the sovereign was law and a command issued from a throne like this had to be obeyed. It is easy to follow the command of your queen when issued in a shout," Guinevere said and leaned forward over the throne.

She motioned with her finger again, directing Art to move forward. When they were practically nose-to-nose, her voice softened.

"But sometimes, you get the most attention when you speak in a whisper."

She tilted her head to the side and back, parting her lips slightly. Art could smell the sweetness of her perfume and the heady warmth of her breath on his lips. He felt the room begin to spin as she closed her eyes and moved forward towards him ever so slightly.

Acting on impulse, he closed his eyes and moved forward to kiss the Princess.

She pulled back and watched as he advanced, his blind lips searching empty air for hers. He leaned too far over the throne and lost his balance, falling onto the arm of the chair and rolling off of it, landing on his back on the floor.

As he opened his eyes, he saw the Princess standing over him, her arms crossed in front of her, a derisive smile on her face. She just shook her head at him. Art looked to the back of the room and saw the governess and the agent coming forward to see what was the matter.

Art sprang up on his knees and extended his long arms outward. "I'm all right," he called out to them, trying to project calm and confidence in his voice. "Nothing to see here."

As she walked past him, Guinevere said, "You're right about that. Nothing to see here."

NINE
THE GREAT GOLDEN LADY

Art and his bodyguard followed a footman back to the Crimson Drawing Room, arriving just as his parents were rising to take their leave of the Queen and Prince Francis. The Princess had left him kneeling in front of the scarlet throne.

Art thanked the Queen for her hospitality, this time remembering everything that Mrs. Chillingsworth had taught him. The Prince was no slave to formality, putting his arm across the back of Art's shoulders and tightening his hold.

"Promise me," Francis said, "that this won't be the last we see of you. Right?"

Art smiled and nodded self-consciously, but then realized that this was the best moment of the entire trip. He suddenly understood why his father was so fond of the Prince.

"I promise, sir."

The Prince winked at him and smiled. "That's a good lad."

"So," his mother asked as soon as they were all safely in the back of the limo and headed out of the castle, "what did you and Guinevere talk about?"

Art was embarrassed and shrugged. "She just showed me around. I saw the Queen's throne. That was pretty cool. They've got a lot of old armor and stuff on the walls. Lots of swords, too."

"Do you want me to get you her phone number?," Mildred asked. "I could make a few phone calls."

"Dear," the Ambassador said, trying to run interference for his son, "leave it alone."

"I'm just trying to help," she said.

"Believe it or not," he replied, "there are some things a boy doesn't want to talk about with his mother."

Art saw his father open the top of the armrest console between his parents and pull out his iPhone. He nodded appreciatively.

"Son, you did good on your first diplomatic mission."

Art gratefully took the phone from his father and unwound the white earbuds. He plugged himself back into his music.

Princess Guinevere was finishing the last of her evening beauty rituals, brushing her long auburn hair in preparation for bed.

Long after the Americans left, her Mother found her and spared nothing in expressing her disappointment in her daughter's attitude.

"Being a member of this family does not give you the right to look down on any person. Art and his parents were guests in our home and you did everything you could to make them feel unwelcome," the Queen told her.

"I didn't invite them, Mother."

"You're right. Your father and I did. And you refused

to respect that."

"Why should I care what these people think?"

"Why? Because you're going to find that few people are prepared to accept you as you are. Most are going to try to think of ways to use their closeness to you to their advantage. I envy your father. He made friends, good friends, long before I made him famous. He knows who his good friends are, like Art's father. Gwennie, if your only use for people is to manipulate them, then you're going to be very lonely as you get older."

"Mother, are we done?"

"One last thing," the Queen said. "I understand that there was a little misunderstanding in the Garter Throne Room."

"Art tried to kiss me."

"You led him on."

Guinevere denied it. "No, I didn't."

The Queen raised an eyebrow and watched her daughter wordlessly. Guinevere had always hated the power of her mother's one raised eyebrow.

"What if I did? He had no right thinking he was good enough to kiss me."

"Do you know what my father once told me when I was your age? 'Around fifteen, girls get sneaky and boys get stupid.'"

"What's that supposed to mean?"

"I asked my father the same thing. He said, 'I think you already know,'" the Queen answered. "And I think you already know, too. It's getting late. We'll talk more in the morning over breakfast."

The Queen kissed her daughter on her cheek and left her alone with her thoughts.

Guinevere put down her brush. This was her room in Windsor Castle, but it was not really hers. It had been decorated a century before by people who were long dead.

It reminded her of the hotel rooms her family stayed in when they traveled abroad on state visits. Just like those hotel rooms, she was powerless to change anything.

There was a painting over the fireplace done by an artist named James Stark, who painted it in the 1860's. It was a picture of a stand of trees and a herd of deer in the Home Park, the vast royal acreage that surrounded Windsor Castle. She had been to that very stand of trees many times. They were taller and fuller now, but she could still pace off the exact spot where the artist had placed his easel.

Guinevere detested the painting, but her Mother refused to direct the Windsor Castle conservancy to change it. She stared at the painting for a moment and thought she saw the limbs of the trees sway as if blown by the wind. Something tiny looked like it ran into view from the side of the canvas towards one of the deer in the background. The entire herd of deer began to move, running beyond the edge of the picture frame and was gone. In a moment, two young does were back in view, with two small figures riding on their backs. The deer turned and started running straight towards her at a gallop. As they got closer, she could see the small figures slapping the does' flanks with their hands, demanding greater and greater speed. Then the deer, one by one, leapt forward, springing out of the front of the painting and landing with a crash in front of her fireplace.

Guinevere had barely leapt out of the way, missing being trampled by the two deer and their riders by no more than a second. She could now see a small man, no taller than two feet, on the back of each deer. The first had a grey mustache that wound round his face and connected to his sideburns. The second was younger than the first, with spiky orange hair. Both were dressed in black from head to foot and a brilliant silver dagger hung from both of their belts.

Guinevere scrambled to reach her dressing table.

There she would find her panic button and, with one push, castle security would come pouring in.

Both small men dismounted and tackled her before she could reach the alarm.

"We're not here to hurt you, Princess," the first one said. "We bring you tidings of great joy from the Great Golden Lady."

The second little man bowed his head reverently at her name.

"My name is Rockpocket," the first man said, "and this here is Gomyr. We are gnome messengers in service to our Lady."

Guinevere finally found her voice and spoke from behind the small hand covering her mouth. "What do you want?"

"Fair question. If I release you, do you promise not to scream?"

She nodded timidly and the gnome moved his hand away from her mouth.

"See?," Rockpocket said. "We're all friends here. A long time ago, an evil magician cast a spell on the whole world, spli'ing it in two. Your half, the ordinary world went on wiffout' magic, only 'membering it in your stories and fables and ..."

"Nightmares," Gomyr interjected.

Rockpocket gave him a dirty look. "Our half, the world of magic, remembered where we come from, where we belong. The Great Golden Lady is on the verge of defeating that evil magician in a battle that's been raging for thousands of your years, but only a few of ours. We've been sent ahead as, you might say, ambassadors."

"It's because of our size," Gomyr added. "Nothing too big can break through the barrier."

"I was just getting to that," Rockpocket said. "Our Lady wishes to speak with you, personally, through her son. Much has changed in your world. There is much the Prince wishes to understand before speaking with your mother, the greatest queen in your world."

Gomyr pulled a package from his backpack that was wrapped in deerskin. He opened it and held its contents out to Guinevere.

"For you," Gomyr said, his head bowed reverently, "great Princess."

She took it. It looked like a small dollhouse door in a frame, no taller than ten inches. She ran her fingers across the surface. It was neither cold nor warm to the touch. Although her fingers pressed hard against it, she could not feel anything.

"What am I supposed to do with this?," Guinevere asked.

"You will be given further instructions later," Rockpocket answered. "For now, keep it close at hand, but hidden from others. And, for the sake of peace between our two worlds, no one must know of its existence. No one."

The two gnomes stood up and bowed deeply to the princess. They then went about quickly straightening the room. The only thing they could not set right was the arrangement of half-eaten flowers the two deer had nibbled on.

"Farewell, fair princess," Rockpocket said as he turned his deer around. He drove his heels into its flanks and the doe leapt up and back into the painting. Gomyr immediately followed, waving to Guinevere as he disappeared from view.

Rockpocket and Gomyr landed back in the forest on the precise spot that James Stark had painted the picture hanging on the Princess' bedroom wall. They dismounted the deer and sent them back into the forest to find their sisters and their herd.

"That was easy," Gomyr said.

"Of course," Rockpocket said with a smile. "As the

Great Golden Lady once said to me, 'At fifteen, boys get sneaky and girls get stupid.'"

Gomyr and Rockpocket shared a laugh. They had shared little of the truth with the Princess. They did work for the Great Golden Lady, but they were not messengers. They had been trained as assassins, able to slip through the smallest cracks, delivering poison or pressing a blade between the ribs of their sleeping victims. This was the first time that either could remember when the heart of their target still beat after a late night meeting.

Rockpocket started to feel the tug of the air around him, moving like the tide receding from the shore. It was starting. They were being pulled, but not in any physical direction, but back through the rift that had opened allowing them to slip into this world. One half hour was all they were given and one half hour was all they had received. A jagged wound opened in the space around them and they were yanked back inside, the unseen forces of the universe snapping back like a taut bungee cord.

10
THE BUTCHER'S BILL

Edward Flummox-Jones arrived at Smithfield Meat Provisions, Ltd. in the long before sunrise. For years his usual habit was to take one of the small lories and lay in a supply of about 20 pounds of steak, enough to feed the ravens for at least two weeks. He did not need to sign for the meat. A bill was run up at the end of the month and forwarded to some far off financial office, which sent it up the line to other nameless and faceless bureaucrats who rubber stamped the invoice and sent it on to someone else who applied his seal and moved the paper forward again and again and again until, finally, a cheque was cut and dropped in the Royal Mail. The butcher's bill would be paid in six months and five more just like would be working their way through the system.

This morning was a little different. Edward brought one of the large open-bed trucks.

In just the first few days the little dragons had eaten the beef that would have fed his ravens for a fortnight. And in that time they had grown. In less than a week they had doubled in size and then doubled again. The little pinfeathers that made them look like baby penguins from the neck down had fallen out. Their bodies were now sleek and scaly and they were more confident in their ability to fly. When they first arrived, they moved like his ravens, flying unevenly. Now, they took turns watching for onlookers while one of them, usually Loki, darted into the sky and flew up and over the Tower's walls.

At first, Edward thought they were flying to get exercise. That was until he saw them all fly up together to the top of St. Thomas Tower, one of the towers that faced the River Thames over the Traitor's Gate. He climbed to the top of the tower and opened the trap door and stepped out on to the flat roof. The saw-tooth crenelated wall hid what the little dragons were doing from the tourists below.

They had arranged themselves in a circle. In front of eight of the creatures was a large, dead river rat. Edward heard a flutter of wings and looked up to see Loki slowing to land on the rooftop with a dead rodent in each claw. He dropped his prey and landed in front of Edward. The dragon looked at the vermin and then up into Edward's eyes and then back down at his kill. When Edward did not move, Loki pressed his snout against the back of one of the rats and pushed it forward to Edward's feet. He squatted back on his haunches, placed his small front claws on its knees, and gazed up at Edward and waited.

"Is this for me?," Edward asked.

The dragon did not reply, but got up soundlessly and made its way into the circle with his brethren, dragging its own rat with him. Each waited for Loki to nod and then bent forward and picked up the head of his meal in his mouth and tossed back his own head. The rats were downed in a single swallow, with the tails following like slurped spaghetti.

Loki looked over and saw that Edward had not touched his. He hopped over in two bounds and looked up at the Ravenmaster. His little front claws were extended and opened like palms. Loki moved them backward and forward, as if trying to gesture that the tenth rat was meant for Edward.

"Ravenmaster," a voice from behind him said, "I don't believe it."

Edward turned and saw Obsidia Hawkins stepping up through the trap door and onto the roof. The dragons all looked at one another for a moment and began to caw. They hopped away and moved up and onto the wall. Spreading their wings, they glided down into the center of the Tower grounds, making sure to fly as unsteadily as the ravens they had all replaced.

Obsidia bent forward and started to reach for the rat. Edward kicked it away with his boot.

"Stop that. You don't know where that's been," he said, wondering how much she had seen.

"This is fantastic. I know that some species of crows will hunt voles, but they typically weigh no more than 15 or 20 grams, less than an ounce. That rat has to be at least 600 grams, maybe more," she said. "Loki was carrying two of them. How does a raven that weighs, what, a kilogram carry its own body weight in flight? This is fantastic. And did you see how they ate them? A single swallow, like the way a snake devours its food."

"I think you're making too much of this."

"And the socialization. Loki brought you food. He offered it to you."

"He didn't gesture with his hands," Edward said.

Obsidia stopped for a moment and looked at Edward. "Birds don't have hands."

"I meant wings. He did not gesture with his wings."

"We've got to get them to do this again," Obsidia said, the tone of excitement rising in her voice. "I could write a paper for the International Journal of Avian Science. I mean we could write it together. We could videotape their behavior. We'll draw blood samples and send them out for DNA testing. Maybe this population of Tower ravens has mutated into some new species over the last 700 years. Oh, Edward, this is so exciting."

Obsidia next did something that Edward was not expecting. He would not have expected it if he had been the one and only Ravenmaster for the last thousand years. She hugged him. She grabbed him and held him tight and placed her head down onto the hollow his shoulder. Her hair brushed up against his nose and he could smell how fresh and clean it was. He tried, but could not remember the last time a woman embraced him. He felt his heart take wing, just like one of his little dragons.

When she released him, he cleared his throat and smiled. "Well, I guess we can work on that in our spare time. But it'll have to be our little secret. Even though you're really a scientist and all, I don't known if the Chief Yeoman Warder would be too keen on it. We'd best move carefully. All right?"

Obsidia beamed at him and nodded. He took out his handkerchief and picked up the rat and chucked it up and over the wall and into the river.

Edward was determined that Obsidia would never see the ravens, or really the dragons pretending to be ravens, devouring their kill again. To achieve that, he resolved to keep them well fed. In doing so, he was ensuring the safety of not only the rats of London, but also the cats and dogs, and maybe even the larger creatures of the city.

Edward's remembrance was interrupted by the sound of the large steel door of Smithfield's rolling up and out of sight. Edward was Smithfield's first and only customer this early in the morning. Kevin Blonson, the morning manager was surprised to see him.

"Edward," Blonson said, "you're here bright and early. The usual? Twenty pounds of sirloin for your birds?"

"I was thinking a little more."

"If you buy a couple of stone, I could shave the price 20 pence a pound."

"I was thinking even more," Edward responded.

"How much more?"

"I was thinking about a side of beef."

Blonson scratched his head. "That's 300 pounds. That'll feed your bloody birds for almost a year. We could cut it and wrap it for the freezer. Although I will miss seeing you so often," he said with a wink.

Edward shook his head. "I was thinking about a side of beef — a week."

Blonson slapped him on the back as they walked into the cutting room. "Edward, my boy, I think this is the beginning of a beautiful friendship."

11
THE FIRST DAY

The American School in London would have been just a five-minute walk from Winfield House. Art recognized what would have been his neighborhood.

The black Ford Escape pulled up to the entrance to the school. The kids of a number of diplomats attended the American School and a small separate parking lot with its own security guard had been set aside for them. It was filled with cars bearing diplomatic plates. Given what Art had been through, his father insisted that Agent Kidd, the Embassy's chief of security, be the one to act as his bodyguard, at least for today. The two of them made their way into the school's office.

When Art stepped into the building, he was instantly relieved. The place had the look and feel of an American public high school. He was afraid that the school would issue everyone striped ties and funny hats. Or worse yet, long robes. The students he saw in the hallways were dressed just like him, like normal kids.

There was a girl his age behind the counter in the main office. Her jaw was working a huge wad of gum. She slid a pad of attendance forms to Art without looking up. "You need a late pass. Fill out the top form and have your father sign it."

Art looked around and realized that she was talking about Agent Kidd. "That's not my father."

The girl looked up and rolled her eyes. "Your stepfather, then. Whatever."

Agent Kidd leaned forward. "This is Zefrom Williams. He's starting here today."

The girl's eyes widened. "Oh, my God. I saw the story on TV. I thought you'd died or something."

Art shook his head. "No died. No something. Look, I just need my schedule and directions how to get to my next class."

The girl secreted the gum from her mouth into a piece of paper and held up her hand. "Wait right here."

She disappeared for a moment into the back part of the office. A plump woman with short-cropped grey hair led the counter girl back to her station. She was holding a manila folder in her hand.

The woman addressed Art directly, ignoring Agent Kidd, and extended her hand. "Art, I'm Tatiana Garvin, the headmistress of the American School. I'm glad to see you're all right. The news on Sunday morning gave us all quite a shock. I frankly thought we wouldn't see you for weeks, at least."

Art shook her hand. "Thanks. It was really no big deal."

The school bell rang and the sound of students emptying out into the hallways could be heard just outside the office.

Mrs. Garvin looked up at the clock and then opened the folder. "That's the end of the first period. You'll go next to your third subject which today is," she said, scanning a yellow sheet of paper, "Advanced Placement English with Professor Merwin. He's very good. I think you'll like him."

"You put me in AP? I'm not the best student. Maybe something more ... basic?"

Mrs. Garvin flipped over a few pages in the folder.

"No mistake. You did very well on our entrance test. You show a real aptitude for language ... and math ... and science ... just about everything. It looks like you're going to be having Professor Merwin for just about everything. We have a few students like you." She paused for a moment, thinking about it. "They're all children of diplomats, too. Why hadn't I noticed that before? In any case, Melissa here will be happy to escort you to Mr. Merwin's class, won't you dear?"

The girl had been sneaking several pieces of fresh gum into her mouth while Mrs. Garvin was speaking to Art. All she could do now was nod enthusiastically in agreement, hoping the headmistress did not notice the bulge in her cheek.

The crowd in the hallways had begun to thin, but several students remained, refusing to spend any more time in their next classroom than they had to. Some students nodded to Melissa, calling her by name. A few others stared at Art as he passed. Almost no one took any notice of Agent Kidd walking a few paces behind. Art guessed that he was not the first American Ambassador's kid to be followed by a large, hulking shadow.

After they walked what seemed like a mile, through twisting corridors and up and down stairs, Melissa stopped at a door marked "AP Lab 1."

"Here you go," Melissa said. "Good luck." Then she whispered, hoping that Agent Kidd would not hear. "Professor Merwin's kind of weird."

Before Arthur could say anything, the door sprung open. On the other side was a tall, thin man with a short white beard and black bushy eyebrows. He was dressed in a tweed jacket with suede patches on the elbows, a striped shirt, and a bow tie. A pair of gold-rimmed reading glasses were perched on the end of his nose. He held a paperback in one hand, but continued reading, motioning Art and Agent Kidd to come inside as he continued reading aloud.

"While I nodded, nearly napping, suddenly
there came a tapping,
As of some one gently rapping, rapping at my
chamber door.
'Tis some visitor,' I muttered, 'tapping at my
chamber door -
Only this, and nothing more.'

"So begins Edgar Allan Poe's 'The Raven'," the man
said in a refined British accent. He looked up from his
book. "Thank you, Melissa, I'll take it from here."

"You see what I mean?," Melissa whispered as she
turned to leave. "Weird!"

"Welcome, Zefrom Arthur Williams the Fourth. I do
note for the record that you are late."

Art was embarrassed. "Well, I had to register in the
office …"

"I wasn't talking about this morning, Mr. Williams. I
meant this year. Our school year starts in September."

"Yeah, but we didn't move to London until a few days
ago."

"That's the problem with youth," Merwin said as he
walked to the podium, "living in the present, while old age
lives in the past. You should have known what was going
to happen and planned in accordance. Why don't more of
us live in the future?" He dismissed the thought with a
wave, as if wiping a chalkboard clean. "Take any seat in
the first two rows."

Arthur did as instructed and Agent Kidd sat in the desk
immediately behind him.

"And you are, sir?," Merwin asked peering over his
glasses at Agent Kidd.

"I'm Agent Kent Kidd, Head of U.S. State Department
Security for the American Embassy. I'm detailing Mister
Williams today."

"Understand something, Mr. Kidd. If you sit in my
classroom, I will expect you to do the same work that my

students do. Otherwise, you can wait outside."

"No, sir," Kidd answered from behind his mirrored sunglasses.

"Let me ask you something. Your embassy checked the safety and security record of this school did you not?"

"I'm not at liberty to confirm or deny."

Merwin looked at the other students. "That is American for 'yes.' I'm also going to assume that you did a background check on me, the other instructors at our school, and the administration. I accept that. You think we live in a dangerous world. Less dangerous than in centuries past when brother set upon brother to gain the throne, where enemies were dispatched without the least pang of a guilty conscience. Look around you, Mr. Kidd. There is only one door into this classroom and it has no windows. I assure you that Mr. Williams will be perfectly safe. The only battle he's likely to be engaged in is a battle of wits. Whether he's heavily armed is entirely up to him."

Merwin stood at the podium glaring at Kidd over his reading spectacles.

Art was certain Agent Kidd could break the teacher in half if he wanted to. This was a standoff that was going to last all day.

Agent Kidd stood and Art tensed. Here it comes, he thought.

The agent leaned down and said to Art in a low voice, "I'm going to stand guard outside." Then he looked at Merwin and pointed a finger at the teacher. "Nobody comes in or goes out during class. Understand?"

Merwin smiled and nodded. "I wouldn't have it any other way."

Once Kidd was standing outside and his shadow fell on the frosted glass panel in the door, Merwin said, "I believe introductions are in order. Mr. Williams, as the new kid on the block, as you Americans would say, you get to go first. And we stand when we address the class."

"My name is Art Williams. I'm from Boston,

Massachusetts." He sat down.

Merwin motioned for him to stand up again. "Not good enough, Mr. Williams. You're cheating on the details. At least tell us why you're here."

Art shrugged. "My dad was just appointed the American Ambassador and my mom and I came with him."

Merwin smiled. "I suppose that's good enough for now. We'll get more information from you as the year goes on, I'm sure. Mr. Wilcox, you're next."

There were only four other students in the class. The first one stood. He was at least a head taller than Art. He had bright red hair shaved into a crew-cut. His upper body and arms were massive, almost as if someone had scaled up one of the dwarves he met in the laundry room yesterday morning.

"I'm Angus Wilcox. I'm originally from Toronto, Ontario. This is my third year at the American School. I'm here because my father is the Canadian High Commissioner to London."

A girl with long brown hair parted down the center and gathered loosely in a ponytail just above her neck stood next. She had large hazel eyes and her lips were the color of coral. Her forehead was adorned with small dot, a bindi, the same shade as her lipstick.

"My name is Dipeka Jaswinder. I was born in Kolkata, India, but I've spent most of my life in London. My father presently holds the position of the Indian High Commissioner."

Art raised his hand, but did not wait to be called on. "High Commissioner? What's that?"

"India, Canada, Australia, and even Hong Kong were all part of the British Empire at one point, just as America once was," Dipeka answered. "Although all of our countries have achieved independence, some of us send 'High Commissioners' to London rather than Ambassadors."

"Not all of us," a young man to Art's left countered.
Merwin directed him to stand.

"I'm Henry Ying. I was born in Hong Kong, which is in a special administration region of the People's Republic of China. Like America, China has an ambassador."

"Hong Kong was part of the British Commonwealth until 1997, when it reverted back to China," a blonde girl interjected. She saw Merwin direct her to stand. "Amanda Keating from Quilpie Station, Queensland, Australia. I'm here because there are no Aussie schools in London. And, for your information, Art, my father is the Australian High Commissioner to London."

"Australia? Cool," Art said. "Kangaroos and dingoes, 'ay mate?"

Amanda rolled her eyes.

"The British stole Hong Kong from China during the First Opium War through the Unequal Treaty of 1842," Henry replied. "It was only through shrewd negotiation and the patience of the Chinese people that Hong Kong returned to China."

Merwin tapped the wooden podium with his fountain pen. "We're going to be debating Britain's role as a colonial power in a few weeks. Mr. Williams and Mr. Ying will be on the side against colonialism and Mr. Wilcox and Ms. Keating will be on the side of the Empire. Ms. Jaswinder may choose whichever side she wants."

Merwin took a deep breath. "The rest of you know me, probably too well." There was a wave of gentle laughter. "But for Mr. Williams' information, my name is Willard Merwin. I was born a very long time ago in Caerfyrddin in Wales. Our new little prince, Gregory, is the Prince of Wales, so my homeland seems in both capable and tiny hands. I speak seventeen languages. In addition to the most popular tongues in Europe, I speak ancient Greek, Latin, Hebrew, and a number of dialects you have never heard of. I have six doctoral degrees and taught at Harvard University in Cambridge, Massachusetts, next to your Boston, Mr. Williams, for 20 years. Upon retirement several years ago, I moved back to the UK and accepted this position with the American School."

The class spent the next 45 minutes dissecting Poe's *The Raven* before the bell rang again.

"Mr. Williams, we take an hour for lunch," the Professor said. "When you return to this room at 12:45, we will be continuing a unit we started on Friday in Chemistry dealing with carbon nano polymers. I will see you all then."

Angus Wilcox and Henry Ying threw their backpacks over their shoulders and left together, sharing a joke.

"Do you have plans for lunch?," Dipeka asked Art as she passed his desk.

He shook his head.

Amanda slapped Art on the back. "I 'eard how you dug your way out of the basement of your 'ouse, mate. That was blonza'. When I first turned on my telly yesterday morning and saw you'd gone a gutser, I thought you were cactus. Then I saw you walking out of the bush and I thought, good on you, mate. Well, come on, shake a leg. I brought a Tucker-bag my oldie packed and there's enough to share."

Art nodded politely and then looked at Dipeka. "What'd she just say?"

"You'll get the hang of it soon enough. She can speak English well enough when she wants to, but she likes to pull the Australian bush woman on new people. As near as I can tell, she thought you'd died in the accident and was pleased that you did not. She brought food from home and she's offering to share it with you."

Art leaned over to Dipeka. "How do you say 'yes' in Australian?"

"Say 'Yes, thanks heaps,'" Dipeka answered.

"Then, yes, thanks heaps."

Amanda winked at him. "An American bloke with a sense of humor? You're all right, mate."

TWELVE
THE KNOCK

Princess Guinevere awoke that Tuesday morning in her own space. She was in her dormitory room in Norris House at the Benendon School, surrounded by her own things. The only history here was the one that she made for herself. It was designed to be a double study bedroom, but she did not have a roommate, which is just as well, because she could tell that all the other girls, even those she considered to be her friends, were secretly jealous of her. She was, after all, The Royal Princess.

The small room directly across the hall was occupied by one of three agents who worked in shifts, following her around by day, and sitting with the door open in the other dorm room at night, listening for any signs of trouble.

Guinevere heard a knock at the door.

"Who is it?", the Princess called out.

There was no response, but the knock continued and got louder.

"Who the hell is it?," she demanded, flinging her dorm room door open.

There was no one in the hall. She looked across to the

room where her security agent was sitting. The man nodded to her, but did not say anything.

"Who was knocking on my door?," she demanded.

The man stood, stretched, and shook his head. "No one, ma'am. It's been very quiet since about midnight."

She slammed the door. As she turned, she heard the knocking again, this time coming from the floor in front of her. More precisely, it was coming from her suitcase on the floor.

She had been too hurried when she got in to unpack the few things she brought back from Windsor Castle with her. She tossed the case on the bed and opened it. Inside, on top of her clothes, was one of the pillows from her room. She had zipped the miniature door into one of her pillows in order to smuggle it past her governess. If asked, she was prepared to tell her that the pillows at school were too hard and she wanted to bring this one.

She pulled the pillow out of its case, unzipped its side, and reached in. The little door was wrapped inside a towel and, as she pulled it out, she felt the force of something knocking from within. The sound of the knocking was instantly louder and Guinevere grabbed the remote and turned the telly on, increasing the volume to mask the sound of someone rapping on the little portal. She set it down on the nightstand beside her bed. She looked it over, front and back and even twisted the tiny doorknob. It opened. There was nothing behind it, but the knocking did not stop.

"Hello," she whispered. "Who is it?"

The knocking continued. It was not a steady cadence, but a series of beats followed by a pause before the pattern repeated. Where had she heard that same rhythm before? Then she remembered. Her father was a great fan of American movies and had forced her to watch *Who Framed Roger Rabbit?* with him over and over when she was growing up.

When the evil judge pounded out the same rhythm in

the movie, the mad rabbit burst through the wall, yelling, "Two bits!"

Guinevere waited for the pattern to repeat and then answered the call by tapping the door with her knuckle twice.

Although there was nothing on the other side of the door on her nightstand, a green glow began to pulse from behind it. The light became so intense that Guinevere had to look away. What followed was the sound of a hollow creak of rusty hinges. When she could again open her eyes, the small door had opened inward and a bright green mist poured out onto the nightstand and over the edge before evaporating. Beyond the door was a small room about a foot square. A wooden chair rail wrapped the inside of the room like a belt. Below it was dark walnut paneling and Victorian wallpaper spread upward to the pressed tin ceiling. She looked over the top of the door. From that angle there was nothing behind, just the open wooden door. Viewed head on, she could see into the little room. There was even a set of glass-paneled French doors on the opposite wall.

She stuck her hand into the room timidly, withdrawing it rapidly at first. She tried again, tugging at the tiny knobs on the French doors, but they would not open. She peered over the door again with her hand inside. The opposite side was as before. Her hand was not sticking out of the open doorway on the other side. As she pulled her hand free, she felt something she had not noticed before. It was a small suede leather bag with a drawstring top. When she pulled it free, the little door slammed shut with a thunderous boom.

She opened the leather pouch and poured the contents into her hand. A stream of liquid metal, the color of the purest gold, pooled in her palm. It solidified into a golden heart-shaped locket with the initial "G" engraved on its rounded surface, surrounded by a circle of fifteen tiny perfect diamonds. The remaining liquid metal flowed off her palm, transforming itself into the most delicate gold chain she had ever seen. There was a catch on the side of the locket and Guinevere touched it, curious to know what lay inside. As the heart opened, a small translucent figure of a young man, not much older than herself, appeared like a ghost, hovering above her hand.

"I bring you greetings, your Royal Highness, from my mother, the Great Golden Lady herself." The figure took a deep respectful bow.

"Who are you?," Guinevere asked.

"My name is Prince Mordred. I know that you have many questions. We cannot speak directly. An evil warlock has placed a curse on my people. Time in your world passes differently than in mine. Therefore, I have sent this locket to you so that I can communicate with you. And with it, you will be able to send it back through the doorway to communicate with me.

"You must wear the locket by day. It will draw the energy it needs from you. There is nothing as magical as a young girl's heart," the apparition of Prince Mordred said with a smile that radiated charm. "On the night when the moon is new and completely black, open the locket and speak from your heart. It will record you as it has recorded me. Place it back in its leather pouch. Then tap on the door and, when it opens, place the pouch back inside. The magician I speak of is hell-bent on first destroying my world before unleashing his great black powers on yours. We must work together, in secret for now, to stop him." The Prince paused and looked down. "I have heard of your great beauty, Princess. I cannot wait to see it for myself. Until then, *adieu.*"

The figure faded from view. Guinevere snapped the locket shut. She hefted it in her hand and thought about what to do next. She stood and walked to her dresser. She opened the top of her nightgown and looked at her long graceful neck, one born to wear the jewels of an empire. She grabbed both ends of the locket chain and brought them around her neck. The chain closed itself without a clasp, the two ends joining like a snake biting its own tail. She watched as the locket fell against her chest, admiring it for a moment. Then it disappeared. She reached for it, and could feel it beneath her fingertips and was aware of the gossamer weight on her neck. When she pulled it away from her body and willed it, it winked back into view.

There was another knock on the door, this time from the hallway. Guinevere let go of the locket and it dissolved from sight, but she could still feel it on her. She snatched up the little door and stuffed it back inside its pillow-hiding place. She then flung the door open. It was Eugenia Cavendish, a distant cousin who one day would be known as The Countess Eugenia, but for now was known simply as "Genie."

She was a tall, thin blonde, more bone than beef. Genie was wearing the Benendon uniform of a blue and green woolen plaid skirt, a white shirt with a Peter Pan collar, and a thick navy sweater with the embroidered crest of the school on the front.

"Look at you, Gwennie," Genie scolded. "We've got to be in class in ten minutes and you're still in your jim-jams." She tossed her book bag on the bed. "You get dressed. I'll do ya' hair."

Guinevere passed her dresser mirror as she headed to the closet to pick out her own uniform. Her hand went to her neck and she touched the cool, invisible metal heart resting inches from her own and smiled.

Like Joan of Arc, she thought, she was going to be savior of her people.

THIRTEEN
BLINDED BY SCIENCE

Obsidia's frustration was growing day by day. The ravens had not repeated their feeding behavior. Several times a day they all repaired up to the top of St. Thomas Tower. She would follow them, stealthily climbing to the roof and cracking open the hatch to spy on them. She saw them mingling about. When Loki, the leader, spotted her in her hiding place, he would begin to caw strangely and bring one wing forward, as if it was pointing. If it had not been a raven, she thought, she could have sworn that it was pointing at her and laughing. The other ravens turned to where Loki indicated with his wingtip and, when they caught sight of Obsidia watching them over the edge of the trapdoor, seemed to join in on the laugh. Each time her observations would then get interrupted by the sound of someone banging on the side of a metal rubbish can. With that, the ravens would take off as one and glide away.

Her goal was to film the birds eating their prey like they had done several weeks before, swallowing the large river rats whole. With that footage, she knew that she could make a mark for herself in ornithology. Without it, nobody but Edward would believe what she had seen.

In the last few weeks she had grown terribly fond of Edward. When they were on duty, she called him by his natural title, "Ravenmaster." Off duty, or when no one was within earshot, he insisted she call him "Edward."

Edward had enthusiastically embraced the journal article that Obsidia had proposed, almost as if it was his idea. He insisted on weighing the birds himself. He even went to the extreme of getting a new digital scale to weigh the birds on. She had been a bit perplexed when it arrived, was unpacked, and installed.

"Ravenmaster," she said to him, "this is a veterinary scale."

"That's right," Edward nodded. "One of the most accurate made. Complete down to a tenth of a gram."

"It's a livestock scale, used to weigh horses and cattle. Much too big for our purposes."

Edward shrugged. "The tenant on my farm up in Childwickbury sent it to me. He was replacing it with something better. Didn't cost me a pence or a pound. Since it was free, we might as well use it. I'll figure out how it works and weigh the birds so you can focus on more important things."

Edward had waited until Obsidia had climbed up to the top of St. Thomas Tower each day before he swung into action. He had moved the beef that Smithfield Provisions delivered before dawn into a walk-in cooler that had been installed in his work area. When Obsidia was across the Tower grounds, Edward wheeled a large cart overflowing with meat cut into five-pound chunks, two large masses for each of his dragons. He fed them in the back alley, one of the few blind spots at the Tower, away from the view of tourists and beyond the apartment windows of the families that lived at the Tower.

Edward banged the lid of an aluminum rubbish pail with a hammer. The dragons had been conditioned to come to his workshop door whenever they heard that sound. Edward knew that it would take Obsidia at least ten minutes to gather up her film and video cameras and climb down the tower and come here directly. He had developed a rhythm so that he could feed the creatures and weigh them in five.

In a moment, he heard their wings flapping as they banked around the building. One by one, the dragons dropped down in the gap between the buildings and lined up. Edward had brought out the portable scale he had told Obsidia was donated to the Tower by his tenant. That was a lie. He knew he could not tell her the truth – the real reason he needed a livestock scale was he suspected that his flying reptiles would soon reach the size of livestock. He had never raised dragons before. He reckoned they might grow to the size of hogs or maybe even cows. He hoped the legends about dragons thirty feet long and weighing several tons was the stuff of myth.

Obsidia had explained how to chart a growth curve. He kept one set of records for what the real ravens should have weighed and those he shared with Obsidia. He had a second set he kept for himself.

He motioned for Loki to come forward. The dragons no longer hopped, but moved with a kind of slinky, almost feline grace. Loki stepped onto the pad, which was four feet long and three feet wide.

"Tail up," Edward said and Loki dutifully raised his tail so that his weight was fully resting on the scale. "One hundred seventy five point three pounds," he read off of the small device in his hand.

It was no larger than a pocket calculator and received the weight and size information transmitted wirelessly from the scale. Each creature had been assigned its own serial number so Edward could track his or her progress.

After Loki's information had been recorded, Edward reached into the cart and pulled out two large chunks of animal flesh and tossed them to Loki, who caught them and swallowed them whole. The others never fought each other for food and once, when Edward threw it over Matilde's head and it landed at Ajax's feet, he nudged it on the ground back to her, retaking his place in line and waiting his turn.

After all nine of his dragons had been fed, Edward pushed a few buttons on the remote and watched the most recent data displayed as a graph. The male dragons, Loki, Ajax, and Apollo, were all still about 20 percent larger than the six females, a difference that showed up from his first weighing.

What troubled him was that dragons were still growing at an accelerated rate. The remote projected a trend two months forward. At this rate, they each would weigh more than a thousand pounds. Even though they each got around ten pounds of food each morning and afternoon, they were gaining almost as much as that a day.

Obsidia had explained metabolization to him. She put it in terms that Edward could understand. A growing bird holds onto only a little of the food that passes through it each day. Some of it gets turned into energy, some gets turned into new bone and muscle, while most of it is dropped out the other end. Edward compared the growth curve to his feeding records. Either his dragons were converting almost all the food they were eating into new tissue or they were getting food from some other source. He was sure they were feeding, but he had no idea on what. He watched the news for stories of animals missing in London, but had not seen any.

He had already upped his order from one side of beef per week to two. Soon, the dragons' food demands would go beyond that. Edward was not sure that he could keep ordering an ever-increasing supply of food for the dragons without it being noticed by some accountant in the Queen's employ.

"Ravenmaster," Obsidia called out to him as he tucked the scale's remote into the pocket of his tunic. The dragons had stood around Edward, watching him concentrate on his calculations. They were each the size of a full-grown German Shepard. When they saw her coming down the alleyway, they took off, flying up and over the Beauchamp Tower to the Tower Green on the other side.

Edward pulled the sheets of paper off of his clipboard and handed them to her. He had handwritten weight and food data for the ravens earlier, being careful that they showed, within reason, what Obsidia was expecting to see.

"I just got done weighing the lot of them," he told her. "You should have seen it. All healthy as horses."

Obsidia took the sheets from him. "I feel bad," she said. "You're doing all the work."

Edward shrugged as he bent down to pick up the scale base and put it away. "You've got the hard part. You've got to write the bloody article and make sense of it all."

"I know, but I've been stalking the ravens ever since we saw them. And they haven't done it again. Have you changed what you've been feeding them?"

Edward tried to sound as convincing as he could. "Me? No. Everything is in the sheets you're holding."

Obsidia seemed crestfallen. "Maybe we should forget the whole thing."

"What say we both doff our uniforms tonight? We'll go out and grab a bite to eat and maybe a pint or two. Let's take a break and maybe you'll have a better idea in the morning. What'd you say? My treat. We can be back before midnight, 'cause that's when I turn back into a pumpkin."

Obsidia laughed. "I'd like that. But it's not a date."

Edward frowned. "That would be, how did they say it in the di-versity training? Inappropriate behavior. No, not a date. Just two colleagues popping off to dinner."

"Two friends," Obsidia corrected him.

Edward smiled at her. "Two friends. I like the sound of that."

FOURTEEN
THE DARK SIDE OF THE MOON

It had been three weeks since the tiny door had opened on Guinevere's nightstand. She had been wearing the locket since she first put it on, hoping that she was recharging its energy with her own. She had not been home to visit her parents in all that time. No royal duties beckoned her back to London. She considered her subjects like bad food at a never-ending banquet. In small servings, she could tolerate them.

She did have fond memories of her tour of the Aston Martin factory in Warwickshire with her mother at summer's end, not long after the coronation. Although the Queen had reservations, the workers encouraged her to take a new DB9 Volante out on the test track. She was still a year and a half from being able to get her driving license, but this was a closed course, not a public road. It was exhilarating to drift through hairpin turns like she had seen them do at the cinema. She ignored the factory's chief engineer seated beside her and his repeated directions for her to "slow down, Ma'am." It was only a five-minute ride, but it was the most intense period she had ever experienced. The car's top was down and the sunlight beat upon her face and the wind flowed through her long hair. When Guinevere and the engineer returned to where they had started from, her mother, the officials from the factory, and the press were all waiting. She bore down upon them at high speed, causing them all to scatter.

All of them, except her mother, who stood her ground, waving off her security staff. Guinevere hit the brakes hard, as she had planned, and the car came to a fishtail stop, the back of the DB9 rotating around so that the driver's side rear wheel came to rest just a few feet from her mother.

The press was close enough catch her mother's upturned eyebrow on tape and in pictures, and clearly overheard her say, "That was very reckless, Gwen."

Reckless? Just because she wanted to have a little fun? And her mother had been no great shakes on the jet ride back to London. Her mother kept repeating that she was especially disappointed in Guinevere's failure to consider the consequences of her actions.

When they arrived in London a little over two hours later, a full-page picture of her behind the wheel of the DB9 was on the front page of extra editions of every trashy little tabloid so beloved by the masses. Every one of them had rechristened her as "Wreckless Gwen."

Wreckless? She would show them all. She would save this world and the people would have to adore her. They would have to.

Guinevere pulled the door out of the pillow she had hidden it in and placed it back on her nightstand. She looked at her clock. It was 9:43 p.m. She had called the Royal Astronomer himself at the Greenwich Observatory to confirm the moment when the new moon would be the opposite of full, at its blackest.

"Taking into account the latitude and longitude of Benendon School, I calculate the height of the new moon will be at 9:50 p.m. on the 2nd of March."

She had thanked the man sweetly, knowing full well inside that it was his duty to answer her questions without pause or hesitation.

She had just seven minutes to go. Guinevere reached behind her neck and felt for the chain. Since it had no clasp, she gently tugged at it and it parted cleanly. The locket and the chain winked back into view. She brought the ends of the chain around her neck and they rejoined as soon as they were close enough to touch. She laid the locket flat on the palm of her hand and popped the catch on its side. It sprung open, laying flat. She cleared her throat and brushed her hair off her shoulder.

She had spent two hours getting ready to record her message to Prince Mordred. She had done it all by herself, both her hair and makeup. She was at an age when her mother's stylist would give her just a light touchup when they appeared together. No one could have even a hint that she planned to send a message to Prince Mordred, or that the Prince even existed, for that matter. Although the image of the Prince had projected itself as an iridescent blue, she took the effort of applying the full range of cosmetics. Her lips were outlined, glossy, red, and full. The shadow and liner around her eyes made them appear clear and inviting. The color she applied to her cheeks gave them depth and definition. She was surprised how much older than 15 she looked.

Guinevere even wore perfume, not knowing whether the locket would carry back more than just the sight and sound of her. Mordred was very handsome and he had mentioned he had heard rumors of her beauty. She did not want to disappoint him.

She licked her lips and then started speaking.

"Prince Mordred, I welcome your extension of friendship to our people, both on my behalf and as the daughter of Her Royal Highness, Queen Caroline. We send our warmest regards to you and to your mother, the Great Golden Lady.

"I have done as you asked and have worn the locket for these last three weeks. Whether born of technology or magic, or perhaps both, the locket is amazing. I look forward to many exchanges of messages using it.

"You know I must proceed cautiously. However, if your people have been placed under a curse, I would like to help lift it, if lifting is the right term. Please tell me what we can do to help on our end." Her voice became a little huskier without her realizing it. "I look forward to seeing you again."

She snapped the locket closed and exhaled. She hoped that it worked and that her first contact with a foreign people would be successful. She found the suede leather pouch and dropped the locket inside it. She squeezed her fingers and felt the jewelry return to its original liquid metal state. Guinevere eyed the clock on her nightstand. It was 9:49. She sat on the edge of her bed with her knuckle poised over the surface of the door, waiting for the last minute to slowly ebb away.

The clock's digital face changed to 9:50. She rapped on the door in the rhythm she had originally heard.

Bom-bom-ba-dumb-bom.

From behind the door, there was an answering knock.

Bom-bom.

The edge between the door and doorframe began to glow, this time in crimson, and intensifying so much that it hurt her eyes. When she could open them again, the door was open and this time a red mist flowed out from the floor of the little room. It looked like it had before, except the small candelabras on the walls were lit, casting a flickering orange light. She gently placed the suede bag on the floor of the little room into the swirling mist.

When she withdrew her hand, the door slammed with a sound that echoed through her room. When she opened the door again, the room on the other side was gone. The locket was away. She wondered how long it would take for Prince Mordred to craft a response.

The door to Guinevere's dormitory room opened suddenly. She had forgotten to lock it. It was Genie Cavendish dressed in a thick robe over her flannel nightgown. She held up a bag that was steaming.

"Gwennie, fancy some microwave popcorn?," she asked. Genie surveyed her friend from head to foot. "Look at you, dressed to the nines."

Genie realized that her friend's guardian was across the hall and closed the door. She dropped her voice to a whisper.

"I know what you're doing," Genie said slyly. "You're going to scarper off and see that boy."

Guinevere stood, trying to block her friend's view of the door. "What boy?"

"You know. The one who tried to snog you. The one you left on his knees, begging for more. The American."

"No!," the Princess responded sharply, "What makes you think I have the slightest interest in him?"

"I don't know. You're always going on about how you showed him up. I figured that if you weren't interested in him, you'd have forgotten him by now. I must have heard that story a hundred times if I've heard it once."

"I didn't know I was boring you, Genie."

"Well, if not him, who then? I don't think you'd get dolled up like that for yourself." Genie thought about it for a moment. "Have you taken a shine to ...," she motioned with her head to the door, indicating where the Princess' Royal Protection Squad bodyguard was stationed.

Guinevere winced and shook her head. "If you hadn't noticed, tonight Officer Amelia Gladstone is keeping watch over me."

Genie shrugged and then spotted the little door on the nightstand. She threw herself across Guinevere's bed to get a closer look, a shower of popcorn escaping from the top of the bag. "Hey, what's that?"

The Princess grabbed it and held it away protectively. "It was a present."

"Oh," Genie said with a wicked smile. "You've got a secret admirer. What kind of a boy sends a girl a door? Is he trying to say he's opening his heart to you? That could be very romantic."

"All you think about is boys," Guinevere scolded.

"That's not true," her cousin answered and stuffed a handful of popcorn in her mouth. "Sometimes I think about men. So who gave it to you?"

"It's not what you think," the Princess said, stalling while she thought of a plausible lie. "You know the big doll house on display in Windsor Castle? Queen Anne's dollhouse?"

Genie nodded her head while straining to get a better look at the door that Guinevere was holding behind her back.

"Mr. Chamberlain, the curator of the dollhouse, noticed that I was very interested in it and how I always stop off to see it when I visit. Well, he had one of the carpenters build a door and frame for me. To remind me, he said, that new doors and opportunities are always opening themselves to young people."

"Oh, so he's sweet on you, is he? An older man. I think I'm going to fall for an older man one day, just like your mom fell for your dad."

Guinevere wrinkled her face in disgust. "First, Mr. Chamberlain's got to be at least seventy and he's practically a hunchback. Second, as for my father, that's doubly disgusting."

"You're his daughter, so I wouldn't expect you to see it. I think he's very handsome."

The Princess walked over to her dresser and tucked the door beneath her panties. "Its talk like that that makes me wonder whether you really want to go with me to Balmoral this weekend."

Genie regretted saying anything. She was looking forward to visiting with the Queen and Prince Francis. What she was anticipating more were the long horse rides through the Scottish countryside and what necessarily came with them, a chance to chat up the Scottish stable boys.

She sat up on the Princess' bed saying, "I promise I won't every say that ever again."

Guinevere was pleased. "I'm going to hold you to your promise."

FIFTEEN
THE CHUNNEL

The Toyota Prius Plus pulled into the belly of the Euroshuttle train at dawn and kept driving forward. The train cars built for hauling autos were open at both ends and they rode up the length of the train on the inside, like riding through the inside of a snake. Art counted as the car click-clacked across the threshold dividing one carrier wagon from another. They were in the front train car now, ten carriers forward of where they had entered the train.

Art was in the front passenger seat. He checked the rear view mirror next to him. The black Ford Explorer from the Embassy came to a stop close behind them. Agent Kidd was behind the wheel. In the past month, the assignment to provide Art with a bodyguard had usually been tasked to one of the less senior agents. But today was different. His class was on a field trip to France, about to speed beneath the English Channel through the tunnel uniting Great Britain with the whole of Europe.

In the month since he started at the American School, Art's class had gone on four extended field trips around England. At least one day a week they went off to various parts of the city. They spent the day looking over the collection of the British Museum, from the earliest stone tools and fertility totems to suits of armor and steam engines.

They had explored Whitehall where the British Parliament meets and climbed the staircase to the top of the clock tower to see Big Ben, the thirteen ton bronze bell that chimes every hour. They reached the top at noon, just as the wrench hammer dropped on the outside of the bell a dozen times, once for each hour. The noise was deafening and Art swore that the vibrations were going to rip his heart loose. From there they walked across the Westminster Bridge to Jubilee Gardens. There, right on the River Thames, was one of the largest Ferris wheels ever built, the London Eye. It rose to a level of 443 feet and its circumference was studded with enclosed passenger capsules, each large enough to hold twenty-five people in air conditioned comfort for its half hour rotation.

"Professor," Art asked as they began their ascent above London. "I'm not complaining, but why so many field trips? Back in Boston we rarely left the classroom."

"And your education has suffered for it, Mr. Williams. Look out as we rise above the city. Across the river you can see where Parliament meets. That's both history and political science. Understand the buildings beneath us. That's architecture. How the buildings are grouped in different boroughs is sociology. London has been the backdrop of some of the great literature of your Western world. Arthur Conan Doyle's Sherlock Holmes mysteries, Stevens' *Dr. Jekyll and Mr. Hyde*. H.G. Wells set *The War of the Worlds* here, as did Neil Gaiman in the *Neverwhere* series. The river flows beneath us, draining the south of England. That's meteorology, hydrology, and geology. See the boats plying up and down the river? Business and commerce. What's in the water? That's chemistry and biology."

The Professor paused to look at all five of his students as the ovoidal pod moved higher. "I have no doubt that each of you will go back to your native countries and become the leaders of your people. If I do nothing else, I want you to realize that all knowledge is interconnected. You can't understand law without understanding history. You can't understand business without understanding science. You can't comprehend politics without a grasp of your people's customs and literature."

"All right, then," Professor Merwin said as he ratcheted the parking brake up on the Prius. "You can stretch your legs, if you like. We'll be at the terminal in Coquelles in forty-five minutes."

Although the Prius Plus seated seven, it was still a tight fit. As they went to originally get in the car, Art called out "shotgun." None of the others had heard of that American custom.

"What do you mean, shotgun?," Henry asked him. "Is this a threat?"

"No," Art answered. "I called 'shotgun'. You know, the shotgun seat. On an old stagecoach out west, the guy who held the shotgun sat next to the driver."

"Very good, Mr. Williams," Professor Merwin said with a smile, "you've taught us all some American history."

Art was sure that when they emerged from the tunnel on the other side of the English Channel that Angus would claim the shotgun seat after practically having to fold himself in half to fit in the last row.

Agent Kidd got out of the Explorer and stood next to the car, keeping Art in sight.

There were small windows on the sides of the train car and the English countryside began to race by in a blur.

"First time in a tunnel?," a voice next to him said.

Art turned, recognizing the voice. It was Duncan, the new king of Clan Fargrave.

"Pretend we're strangers, Art," Duncan said softly out of the side of his mouth.

"Where'd you come from?," Art asked, still looking out the window.

"We're in the car in front of you. I drove."

"Really?"

Duncan shrugged. "I steered. Eori worked the pedals on my command. It took some practice, but we're not bad."

"Aren't you afraid someone will recognize you?"

"No. We're all under an enchantment, for your safety. Everyone who looks at us sees what they'd expect. A normal Brit on a motor holiday to Paris. A man and wife and three kids."

Art had to look and turned to the Range Rover parked in front of the Prius. There was a female dwarf sitting in the passenger seat. Or what Arthur took for a female at first glance. With a longer look, he could see it was one of the miner dwarves, his beard trimmed down to rough stubble, wearing a bright yellow wig and fluorescent pink lipstick. Art could feel the dwarf's anger from this distance, no doubt because he had drawn the short straw and lost, forced to play the wife and mother. In the back seat there were three more dwarves with long braided beards, all of whom Art recognized from that first morning in the laundry at Winfield House.

The dwarves in the back had t-shirts from Disneyland Paris, Stonehenge, and Legoland Windsor covering their leathers. All three of them waved enthusiastically to Art. Art looked over at Agent Kidd, who only smiled. All he could see, Art guessed, were three children waving to their father. Art smiled and waved back at the dwarves.

Art turned back to the window as the train was plunged into darkness. "Why start following me now?"

Duncan shook his head. "Understand that unless

you're at your school, there are at least four of us within twenty feet of you at all times. Brother, you have no idea how dangerous the world is becoming and important you are. That's why we're sworn to protect you. But you're leaving England. The mystical forces that protect you and that shield us will begin to weaken. Since you're returning to London tonight, it will probably be all right. But be careful."

"All right," Art nodded. "Why me? I'm nobody special."

"It is your destiny, Art. You will be the one to help save your people."

Art motioned with his head over his shoulder at his classmates, who were on the other side of the train car looking out the opposite window.

"Look at them," he said. "Angus is strong as an ox. Dipeka's the smartest person I know. I don't think Amanda's afraid of anything. Professor Merwin is always trying to get us to see how everything is connected. Henry gets that. I'm having a hard time keeping up with all of them. Maybe destiny should make a new plan and choose one of them."

"Destiny makes its own decision. And once its mind is made up, it cannot be changed. Besides, each of them, and each of us, have our roles to play."

"Do I have a choice?," Art asked.

Duncan shrugged. "No. None of us really do. Stay focused and learn as much as you can."

Art tried to change the mood. "I'll bet you don't have anything like the Chunnel where you're from."

"Aye, you're right. A thirty-two mile tunnel under the sea?," Duncan said and smiled. "Not bad, for amateurs. Maybe one day you'll get a chance to see Vanwalanthir, our capital city. We have tunnels fanning out for hundreds of miles in all directions."

"Why aren't you there protecting it?"

Duncan thought about it for a second. "Not to put too

much pressure on you, Brother, but when you save your world, you'll save ours as well."

A car horn beeped behind them. When Arthur turned he saw the passenger window on the Range Rover was down and two of the t-shirted dwarves were leaning with their bodies half way out, fighting.

"Barster. Hargren. Stop that," Duncan bellowed.

"He won't stay on his side," Barster said as he cocked his first for another blow.

Hargren tightened his grip on Bartser's throat. "You're the one who's on my side."

From the far side of the backseat, Boldin called out, "Are we there yet?"

"You better stop it. They're going to kill each other," Art said in a loud whisper.

"Nah," Duncan replied. "I've seen the two of them fight for days without more than a few bumps and bruises. That's how dwarves let off a little steam."

Barster took a swing at Hargren and missed, but punched a hole through the car door. Art's classmates, the Professor, and the other passengers riding in this carrier car seemed not to notice yet.

"That's not what humans do and if you want to fit in unnoticed, you better get them to stop it now."

"Aye. You're right." Duncan walked over to the car and banged on the door with his fist. "Break it up, you two. That's it. If you don't stop it right now, I'm going to turn this train around and we're going back to London. I'll ban you from Disneyland Paris for the rest of your lives. Don't make me do it. I will, if I have to."

Barster and Hargren stopped fighting and settled down.

"He started it," Hargren muttered.

"Did not," Barster answered under his breath.

The train came up through the earth and back into the sunlight.

"Art," Professor Merwin called out, "the train'll be stopping very soon. Come on."

Art could see that Angus had already claimed the shotgun seat. He would have to squeeze himself into the back row.

SIXTEEN
GREEN EYES

Guinevere was having a horrible day. She threw her book bag on her bed in disgust. She had a half hour before lunch downstairs and knew she had to use her time wisely. She was going to sulk.

She failed her geometry exam and forgot that her short story for English composition was due. Now she still had two more classes this afternoon and then had to study for a make-up exam tomorrow while trying to write a story showing two characters in conflict just from their dialogue. She did not care about obtuse or acute angles and as for conflict, she could usually end it with a curt, "Because we say so." That was all the conversation a Royal Princess needed to win an argument.

She had been especially on edge because she had not heard back from Prince Mordred. It had been a week. Why was he torturing her like this? She wanted to see him again. She unconsciously patted the front of her sweater, looking for the locket that once graced her neck. Then she remembered that she had sent it through the doorway back to the Prince. She almost felt a sense of hunger, but was not sure whether it was for the locket or for the sight of the Prince. Perhaps it was both.

In the days since she had sent her message through she had been anxious that she had done it wrong, that the Prince would not understand her. Deep down, she was concerned that she would not measure up to the stories of her beauty that the Prince had heard. What if he decided to find someone else to help him? She began to think about her competition throughout Europe.

There were the twin princesses of Monaco, Anisette and Lucinda. Monaco was a mere postage stamp compared to England. All they had was a harbor for yachts and an old casino. Home Park outside her bedroom window at Windsor Castle was ten times larger than Monaco. She checked the puny principality off her list. There was Princess Isabella from Spain, but she was almost as old as her mother. She doubted that Mordred would want some old wrinkled prune. She settled on Princess Anne-Britt of Sweden as her only real competition. Anne-Britt was several years older than she was, closer to Mordred's age, she was sure of it. She was a tall, leggy blonde. For some reason, boys seemed to go crazy for blondes.

That was it.

Mordred had probably already found a way to send those two little gnomes through a picture at the Drottningholm Palace. The next new moon was on March 30th, three weeks from now. He would be sending her a locket through her doorway soon and Anne-Britt would be sending her answer through on the 30th, she was sure of it. She wondered if there was enough time to convince her mother that Parliament should declare war on the Swedes. Guinevere wanted nothing more than to toss Anne-Britt, shaved of her golden hair, into a dungeon, and throw away the key. Who did that girl think she was?

Guinevere was so caught up in her fevered plotting of the downfall of the Swedish princess that she almost did not hear the knocking coming from the top drawer of her dresser. When she heard it, she leapt off her bed and yanked the drawer open. She sent her panties flying into the air as she searched frantically. Finally, her fingers found it and she pulled it free, unwrapping it from the towel that concealed it. She placed it on the top of her dresser and waited for the rhythm to break.

Bom-bom, she rapped with her knuckle.

There was the familiar green glow around the edge of the door. Guinevere hid her eyes for a moment and, when she opened them, the door was open. She could see the top of the small suede leather pouch sticking up above the bright green mist. She grabbed it free of the little room and ignored the door as it slammed shut. Her hands shook as she tried to unloose the drawstrings at the top of the pouch. She had to force herself to stop and take a deep breath and calm down. She widened the throat of the pouch and turned it over, pouring its liquid contents into her hand.

When the metal hit her palm, a dizzying feeling overcame her. The sensation was more intense than the fragrance of a hundred hothouse roses in the dead of winter, more vibratory than a thousand violins bowing Mozart, more relaxing than a mouthful of chocolate after a stressful day. For a moment, she vowed that she would put it on her neck and never take it off. Until she had it back, she did not fully understand how incomplete she had felt without it.

Then she realized that there was probably a message inside. She slowly opened her fingers. When she saw the locket, all the doubts she had about Mordred and all the plots she had hatched to take her revenge on Princess Anne-Britt faded. The fifteen diamonds surrounding her initial, a stylized scripted G, were now twice as large as before and the fire within them burned with ten times the brilliance. The reflection of light off of each facet was a like a rainbow of lasers burning her eyes, but she did not care. Mordred would not be sending her something as magnificent as this if he were planning to toss her aside for that Nordic witch.

She took a deep breath and tried to steady her hand as she touched the catch on the side of the locket. The locket opened and the glowing image of her prince appeared in front of her.

He took a deep bow. "Guinevere, my dear, the rumors of your beauty seem like slanders because they fail to fully extoll your visage. They damned you with faint praise. On opening the locket, I almost wept because a man is lucky if catches a fleeting glance of something so rare and pure and lovely. I was able to gaze upon you longingly at my leisure. My soul was made wealthier because you looked into my eyes and I could look deeply into yours. I will admit that I played your message over and over and over again, each time more overcome than the last."

Guinevere felt her knees start to shake and she took a step back to the edge of her bed and slowly lowered herself onto it, not wanting to risk interrupting the message.

"I am told there is a way that we can meet in person," the Prince continued, "if only for a few minutes, but that may be time enough to save both our worlds. On the evening of Friday, June 3rd by your calendar, our two universes, our two dimensions, call them what you wish, will be aligned so that I alone will be able to cross the rift that separates us. As good fortune would have it, it will be in London itself, on the very grounds of Buckingham Palace. After that time, I will be pulled back across the rift. That will give us enough time to give your mother our respects and ask her, as the leader of your world, to help us."

The Prince's expression became one of grave concern. "The battle between my mother and the necromancer is about to come to an end. They are trapped in a bottleneck that separates our two worlds. If he succeeds, first he will destroy all of us, then he will come for your world. The outcome still hangs in the balance. With your help, I know our two worlds will be saved."

She reached out with her fingertips, hoping to stroke his strong, smooth face, but her fingers passed through particles of light suspended in place.

"What I seek is a momentary repast with your family. It is a lot to ask of one so young and fair as you, dear Guinevere. But I pray that I must. You are the vessel through which I must pour my message. I do not know how you can do it. All I know is that love always finds a way."

The image in her hand faded. She felt warm and flushed. She fanned her face with her free hand. Love always finds a way, he said. Could the very sight of her have made him fall in love with her? She had to admit that it was possible. She knew that many royal couples throughout history had found each other through an exchange of portraits traded by messengers and then went on to rule their lands together happily ever after.

How was she going to do it? How could she get her mother to arrange the sort of royal ball that had not been thrown in Great Britain for at least a half century?

She would let it percolate in the back of her mind until the morning. Then she would call up her mother and ask if she could come home this weekend. She had a lot of work to do if she was to maneuver her parents into giving her what she wanted.

SEVENTEEN
WE FEW, WE HAPPY FEW

It took half an hour to get the car out of the terminal at Coquilles and then another hour driving on countless back roads.

"Professor," Art called out from the last row of seats in the Prius Plus, "don't the French know how to build highways?"

Merwin caught sight of Art's reflection in the rear view mirror. "Mr. Williams, don't focus so much on the destination that you neglect to enjoy the journey. Besides, we are here."

The car slowed to stop on a two-lane road that separated two large fields and pulled off onto the north shoulder. Agent Kidd, in the black Ford Explorer pulled off the road and parked behind them.

All along the south edge of the road were figures of fifteen soldiers, cut from plywood and painted in bright primary colors of red, blue, and yellow. Each figure was an archer, holding a curved long bow at least six feet in length. The bowstrings were represented as being pulled back and the arrows were pointed high so that, if fired by real men, they would land in the middle of the field.

"All right," the Professor said when all the students had gathered around him, "anybody know where we are? Remember, I told you it was no fair to use the GPS on your phones or to Google an answer."

Dipeka raised her hand. "There was a sign in the last town we went through that said 'Canlers' and there was another sign pointing the way we came that read 'Tramecourt'."

Merwin pointed off to the east. "All right, if Tramecourt is to our east, what's to our west? Mr. Ying, do you know?"

Henry shook his head. "You usually give us the readings to do a few days before one of our trips. You didn't tell us anything this time, except we were going to France."

"Fair enough, Mr. Ying, but life doesn't always allow you to read ahead. Ms. Keating?"

"I'd be guessing, but maybe something to do with where Joan of Arc fought?"

"You're getting close, but Jeanette d'Arc was born on January 6, 1412. What I'm looking for happened on October 25, 1415, St. Crispin's Day, so Joan of Arc, as the West calls her, would have only been about three. Mr. Wilcox, you've already got some clues. Can you enlighten us?"

Angus shook his head. "My mother's from Quebec so I speak a little French. I could walk over to that farmhouse and ask."

"*Sage tâcher, mon jeune amie,*" Merwin chided him and then translated for the others, "Nice try, my young friend. Mr. Williams, its up to you. If you don't get it, then we'll all go back to London."

Art took a moment to reflect before answering. Tramecourt. St. Crispin's Day. 1415.

Last year his English teacher gave out extra credit for attending a performance of a Shakespeare play put on by the Commonwealth Shakespeare Company. It wasn't a comedy. But then again, his parents once took him to one of Shakespeare's comedies and he did not get a single joke. His old teacher told them that what they would be seeing was a history. One of the Henry plays, but which one? There were two plays about Henry the Fourth, three about Henry the Sixth, and one each for Henry the Fifth and Eighth. He decided to guess.

"Henry ... the Fifth," Art said with some reservation.

Merwin nodded. "Very good. Although I suspect it was a lucky guess. I already see Ms. Jaswinder has her hand in the air."

With Art's clue in place, Dipeka pointed to the west. "Over there is the town of Agincourt. The field in front of us is where King Henry V defeated a far superior French force." She turned and pointed across the road at the plywood archers. "The victory came in large part because of the English use of longbows that could rain destruction down on the French from a safe distance."

"Very good, Ms. Jaswinder. And credit to Mr. Williams, as well. We're standing on a road that cuts through the battlefield where the Battle of Agincourt was waged during the Hundred Years War, the *Rue Henry Sanc.*"

Art looked around. Except for the plywood archers, there were no markers, only dormant agricultural fields. "Why haven't the French set this aside like the Gettysburg battlefield in Pennsylvania?"

"Two reasons," Merwin answered. "First, the French lost and lost badly. The second reason is that with thousands of years of recorded history, there are few places in Europe that have *not* been the site of a major battle at some time. You can't lock away the entire continent."

Merwin crossed to the south side of the road and the class followed behind and as he gestured with a sweep of his arm.

"Picture it in your mind. King Henry V brings an army

across the English Channel to Harfleur to the west of here and lays siege to the town. The Hundred Years War was started with his father, Henry IV, and ended during the reign of Henry VI, who was crowned as an infant when Henry V died.

"After finally taking Harfleur, Henry V and his army decided to march across the north of France, where we are today, which was territory that England claimed as its own. The French disputed this and were finally able to amass an army that would have gathered to the north of us in that field. The French army was at least six times the size of Henry's. Surrender was not an option for the British. The common soldier prisoners would be killed. The nobles would be held for ransom and the king would be held for ..."

"A king's ransom!," Henry called out.

"Exactly," Merwin said. "That's where the saying comes from. A king's ransom could bankrupt a country and many times throughout history, it did.

"Now back in 1415, there were large thick forests on either side of the field to our north. In fact, it narrowed like an hourglass, so that any troops coming south would have to squeeze together to make it through the tight fit. It had rained for a week before the battle. Since it was October, the crops had been harvested and the fields plowed to ready them for planting in the spring. Henry chose his battleground well. But there was no guarantee of victory. Remember, the French outnumbered the English six to one. Think about that for a moment."

Merwin paused as his students looked around.

"Let's take a detour into literature. When Shakespeare wrote *Henry V*, he imagined how a king, facing likely capture and ransom, inspires his men, noble gentlemen and illiterate common soldiers, to fight even though they're greatly outnumbered. It's a long soliloquy that the King gives, but he ends it by saying, 'We few, we happy few, we band of brothers.'"

Art remembered this speech from the play that he had seen with his class the year before and then later studied in class and joined the Professor in reciting it.

> "'For he to-day that sheds his blood with me
> Shall be my brother; be he ne'er so vile,
> This day shall gentle his condition;'"

Merwin stopped speaking and watched as Art delivered the last lines with the force and intensity that would have made any Shakespearean actor proud.

> "'And gentlemen in England now-a-bed
> Shall think themselves accurs'd they were not here,
> And hold their manhoods cheap whiles any speaks
> That fought with us upon Saint Crispin's day.'"

Merwin applauded Art's performance, making his blush. "Very good, Mr. Williams. I'm impressed."

"I didn't think I remembered it," Art said, "but I did."

"Professor," Angus asked, "what happened in the battle? Did Henry win?"

"Win? Oh, yes. The English stood their ground in the center, making the French cross the muddy field to them. The armored French knights did not put armor on their horses. Their riders were thrown and many sank into the waist deep mud and drowned. Each wave had to climb over the bodies of the previous charge. The battle was a rout. After the best of French nobility were killed, the rest of the army fled. Henry was able to march north to Calais, near where we got off the train, and sail back to England.

"Later this year, we'll be reading *Henry V* in class. But for now I want you all to follow me."

They walked south across the open field to where the Professor had indicated that King Henry had his camp. A small grouping of striped and brightly colored tents seemed to shimmer into existence like a mirage in the middle of a desert.

"I made an arrangement with the farmer who owns this field and a troupe of Renaissance players to set up here so that you could see what life was like during King Henry's time."

Merwin looked over his shoulder at the black-suited figure following them. "How are you holding up, Agent Kidd?"

"Don't worry about me, Professor. Carry on."

There were six small tents arranged in a semi-circle, with a seventh larger tent erected in the center. A side of mutton was roasting on a spit over an open fire as a boy, dressed as a 15th century peasant, slowly turned a crank, rotating the meat above the fire. Art took a careful look at the boy and saw that he was a dwarf, the miner who had come into his MRI room at the hospital.

A small forge was set up in front of the tent furthest from the center of the grouping and a blacksmith swung his massive hammer down on a piece of white hot steel and shaped it on an anvil. Sparks flew. The smith worked without protective eyewear or even a leather apron and did not flinch as the pinpoints of heat and light hit his flesh. He, too, was one of the dwarves that been in the basement of Winfield House. He looked up at Art and nodded, and then went back to his work. With just a few rapid strikes of his hammer, the steel was already taking shape as a sword, about half the length of Shalerunner's weapon. The two dwarves had no doubt infiltrated this group in order to stay close to him. No one else seemed to notice their true forms.

"They have armor that should fit you all," Professor Merwin said. "Ms. Keating, Ms. Jaswinder, you go into the blue tent. Men in the red. I'll wait out here."

"Professor," Dipeka said, "women of this era didn't fight. Wouldn't that be a little anachronistic for a Renaissance fair?"

"You can dress up as a maiden in distress," Amanda said, "I wouldn't mind a good tussle." She entered the tent.

"True enough," Merwin admitted. "But our purpose here is to understand what it was like to fight with King Henry during the Battle of Agincourt, not tend the fires in the camp while the battle raged."

Dipeka shrugged and went inside.

Art, Henry, and Angus went into their own tent. Inside, five men were ready to assist them donning their suits of armor. All of them, as Art expected, were also dwarves. They worked from the ground up, first fastening sabatons on their feet, armored boots with spikes on their toes. Next came the greaves and cuisse pieces for the fronts and backs of their legs. Each was then given what looked like an articulated skirt to cover them from waist from mid thigh. They put on a quilted vest before being strapped into their breastplates and back pieces. Metallic sleeves were assembled and they were fitted with pauldroons, large shoulder plates. Finally, visored helmets were lowered onto their heads.

Through the small louvers cut into his visor, Art could see Angus and Henry fully dressed for battle.

"I'm glad they had my size," Angus' muffled voice exclaimed.

"It must be 8 degrees outside, but I'm already sweating and I haven't done anything yet," Henry said.

Art did a quick mental calculation. Eight degrees Celsius was about 45 degrees Fahrenheit. Regardless of which scale it was measured on, Art was getting warm, too.

The three of them tottered out of the red tent, their vision obstructed and hearing limited. Each suit of armor weighed at least 75 pounds.

The two girls were already out of their tent waiting for them. Their armor was made of the same polished steel, but clung to their forms. It was easy to see who were the boys and who were the girls. Art, however, could not tell which of the two was Amanda and which was Dipeka. He noticed that three female dwarves followed the girls out of the tent, the first he had ever seen.

"I see you've all suited up," the Professor said as he exited the large main tent. He had a leather tabard on his chest, the front of which had been divided into fourths.

Two of the quadrants were fixed with the stylized British lion and two were adorned with a trio of *fleur de lis*, the ancient symbol for France. He wore green woolen leggings and a solid gold crown ringed his head. "I, as you have probably guessed, am playing the part of King Henry V. Please follow me."

He took them over to a long rectangular area outlined in chalk powder. There was a rack that held swords and another that held shields.

"Choose your weapons," Merwin said.

Kidd stepped forward. "Professor, I don't think giving them swords is safe."

Merwin walked over to the rack and picked up a blade. "Neither do I." He held out his open palm and drew the edge of the blade across it. There was no blood.

"You made me spoil the illusion. There's an iron bar running through the center of the blade to give the sword weight and balance. The outer covering is hardwood, painted silver. If you rubbed two swords together, you might start a fire, but you won't cut anything."

Kidd took a step back and let the lesson continue. A tall figure in a suit of armor came out of the boys' tent and a female knight, her face likewise covered, exited the girls' dressing area. Both were normal sized, much taller than the dwarves.

"You're each going to face off against an experienced knight. This exercise is similar to fencing. You want to touch the tip of your blade to the metal circle on the center of the other knight's chest before he can touch your target with his sword. But just surviving for two minutes means that you've won, as well. Mr. Wilcox, you go first."

Angus stepped onto the back of the rectangle while the other knight took his place at the opposite end.

"Ready, set, go," Merwin said and slashed his hand through the air.

Angus was at least eight inches taller than his opponent and easily weighed 70 pounds more. He kept his left shoulder and his shield towards the knight. The shield became a weapon in its own right and Angus used it to both block strikes and to hit the other knight with full body bashes. With his last charge, Angus knocked the knight to the ground and stepped over him, first tapping the target on his chest and then pointing the tip of his sword at the other man's neck.

"Yield," Angus commanded.

"Technically, you won, Mr. Wilcox," Merwin said. "Would you look below your waist for me?"

When Angus did, he saw that the knight's sword tip was poised at a gap in his armor, ready to run through the inside of his thigh. A real blade would have opened his femoral artery, guaranteeing death in a matter of seconds.

"Although you would have won, Mr. Wilcox, the price of victory would have been your life. Step back. Ms. Keating."

Amanda brandished her sword, bringing it through a full circle spin, and stepped into place and the female knight did the same. The Professor signaled and the match began. She was more cautious than Angus was, testing her opponent with small jabs that were deflected while fending off similar strikes. The two women proceeded like that for most of the match, until Amanda seemed to drop her guard. The other knight took a chance and lunged for the circle on Amanda's chest, but her blow was deflected. Amanda brought her sword up quickly and tapped the target on the other woman. Before anyone could react, she spun around and tapped the target again.

"Well done, Ms. Keating," Merwin said. "Do they use swords a lot where you grew up?"

"Nah," she said as she brought her visor up to get some air. "But I've got an older brother on the fencing team at the University of Sydney. He's shown me a thing or two."

"Mr. Ying, you're next."

Henry moved to the arena and watched as the other

knight stepped in. He reasoned that he would probably be tired from his match with Angus — two minutes of full-on exertion with only a two-minute rest while Amanda fought her challenger. The physical effort would have left him with an oxygen deficit and a build up of lactic acid in his muscles. He now wished that was not wearing the armor. Without it, he could outmaneuver the other man, get behind him, and throw him off balance. Instead, he had to go face to face with a taller and heavier opponent. Balance, Henry decided, was the key.

When the Professor signaled for them to begin, Henry sprang forward at a run. The knight hesitated for a moment, and then brought his sword forward. While just beyond the sword's tip, Henry dropped and slid into his opponent, like a baseball player trying to steal home, and bowled him over. As the knight toppled over him, Henry bought the tip of his sword up and tapped the other man's chest target. He then pushed the knight off of him and struggled to his feet.

"Unorthodox," Merwin said, "but if you tried that in battle, you'd be helpless on the ground."

Henry pulled the helmet from his head, his hair soaked with perspiration.

"Professor," Henry countered, "that is beyond the parameters of the test. The goal was to defeat a single opponent by hitting his target with the tip of the sword. Additional combatants were not mentioned as variables."

"As well argued as any grade lawyer I faced at Harvard, Mr. Ying. Your victory is noted. Ms. Jaswinder."

"I don't think hand-to-hand combat is where my strength lies. I'd rather not," Dipeka said as she removed her helmet.

"Are you afraid you'll fail?," Merwin asked.

"Not afraid. Accepting of the fact that I will fail."

"It is one thing to know your limitations. It's another to accept them. Any alternatives?"

Dipeka pointed to a bow and a quiver of arrows next to

it. Out in the field, at least 25 yards away, three hay bales were stacked on one another with a cloth target fastened to them.

"All right," Merwin challenged her, "get one bull's eye out of three shots and you don't have to have a sword fight. Fail that and you face the lady knight for three minutes instead of two. Agreed?"

Dipeka nodded. The three female dwarves helped her out of the armor that covered her chest and her arms. Once free of it, she slung the quiver over her shoulder and picked up the bow. She drew back the string just to test it and then reached over her shoulder and pulled out an arrow. With one fluid motion she fitted the notch in the back of the arrow onto the bowstring, drew the string back, and raised it into her line of sight. Closing one eye, she held her breath and waited for a fraction of a second before letting the arrow fly. It found the dead center of the target and buried itself halfway into the bale. Without waiting for a word from Merwin or the other students, she drew a second arrow, aimed, and fired it. It hit just an inch to the left of the first. A third arrow found a spot directly between the first two. She turned and placed the bow and quiver where she found them. The only clue as to the pride she felt was the half skip she took while walking back to the where her classmates were waiting.

"Whoa," Angus said. "Its like you were born to do that."

"Almost," Dipeka said, finally breaking into a broad smile. "My father was on India's first Olympic archery team that competed in Munich. He taught me."

"Well played, Ms. Jaswinder. All right, Mr. Williams, you're our final champion."

Arthur went over to the rack and looked at the swords arrayed there. Angus had chosen the largest sword, probably because of its size and Henry chose the smallest. As he looked his choices over he noticed that the last sword to his right looked familiar. It was just like King

Kerr Shalerunner's sword, the only one he had ever used. Even so, he'd managed to kill the cat-witch with it. Perhaps something like it would work against this knight. He grabbed the sword by the pommel and pulled it from the rack. It had the same weight and balance as the old dwarf's sword. He tapped his boot with the tip. It rang like a bell instead of having the dull thud of wood. It *was* the same sword.

"Good, you've found your weapon," Merwin said. "Now take your place."

Art knew he should have said something, but he did not. Instead, he took the sword and got into his fighting stance. Duncan obvious left the sword for him to use. But why? Why give him a real sword when all they were doing was play-acting? Then he saw the knight tap his sword on his grieves, his shin plate, and heard the same metallic ping. The mystery knight was now armed for real, as well.

Professor Merwin signaled for them to begin. The other knight came forward, making a wild slash at him. It missed Art. His opponent stepped outside of the chalk outline boundary of their arena and took another broad swing. Art dodged that one as well, but he saw the knight drifting towards Dipeka, who was back in her street clothes after demonstrating her archery skills. Art stepped between the knight and Dipeka just as the warrior brought his sword around. Art blocked the blow using the chest plate of his armor when he could not bring his shield up quickly enough. There was a large clang as metal collided with metal. The armor and the padding underneath absorbed much of the blow, but Art grunted in pain nonetheless.

Art was sure that the knight was no longer pretending, but was out to harm them. But why didn't he attack Angus and Henry, Art thought. Angus had simply overpowered him with brute force and Henry never gave him a chance. Or maybe the reason was that Dipeka was the real target. The lady knight did not get a chance to fight her, so this might be their only chance. More likely, this knight was Dipeka's cat-witch, someone sent to destroy her.

Art borrowed a little from what he learned from watching Angus fight him. He used his shield as a battering ram, while his sword crossed the knight's blade, pushing the warrior away from Dipeka.

"Back in the arena, both of you," Merwin said, but the knight ignored him.

Art was not going to obey either, if it meant giving his opponent a chance to harm his friend.

"You're no match for me," the knight said. His voice was deep and hollow.

"Really?," Art taunted back, "I've killed something scarier than you before breakfast."

His classmates cheered at his bravado, not realizing that it was true. They also did not realize the danger they were in. He poked and prodded with his sword, hoping to find an opening. He was not looking to just tag the knight's chest target — he wanted to run him through. He deflected two thrusts and saw his chance. He jabbed his blade, aiming high above the target, looking to separate the knight's head from this shoulders. The knight recovered and blocked with his shield, sending Art off balance. He fell on his back, his sword dropping from his hand. The knight stood over him, repositioning his sword so that it pointed downward to the center of Art's chest with both hands on the pommel, ready to drive it through him.

"Time," Merwin called out.

The knight tensed and drew the blade upward, gathering his strength. Then he heard a click and looked up. Agent Kidd was standing just beyond reach, his semi-automatic pistol raised to eye level, the barrel pointed into the eye line of the knight's helmet.

"He said, 'Time,'" Kidd declared in a voice colder than the weapon in the knight's hand.

"We can finish this another time," the knight said. He sheathed his sword and stepped away, then turned and walked into the same dressing tent he had emerged from.

Art struggled to his feet and went after him, Duncan's sword back in his hand. He flung open the tent flap and peered inside. There was no one inside the tent. He could not have gotten away. Art was standing in the only entry into the tent and was only ten seconds behind the knight. He could not have just vanished into thin air, Art thought. Then he remembered that he could have.

The Banshees and the cat-witch appeared out of thin air. Why not this knight? And where was Duncan? Why hadn't the dwarves, his brothers, stepped in to help him?

He stepped out of the tent, ready to demand answers but was met with applause.

His classmates pressed around him.

"Well done, mate," Amanda said, slapping her gauntleted hand against his back plate.

"If I ever get in a fight for real, I want you to have my back," Angus said banging his fist on Art's shoulder.

"It was very sweet the way you tried to protect me," Dipeka said.

"Bravo," Professor Merwin said.

Art looked over at his teacher, who was standing next to the knight. Without his helmet on, Art could see that he was a young blonde man in his twenties with a narrow face and large eyes. He extended his hand.

"Art," the young man said, "I hope 'zer is no hart feelings. Your teasher asked me to change 'zis on you. Throw, how you say, a curve ball? *Oui*?"

"You weren't pretending out there, Mr. Williams," Merwin said. "You showed real bravery. I hope all of you now understand what Shakespeare wrote a little better. 'For he to-day that sheds his blood with me shall be my brother.'"

One of the female dwarves stepped over and announced, "Lunch is served."

They filed into the large tent, four of them still dressed in their armor. A round banquet table was positioned at the center of the tent. Merwin guided Art to the largest wooden chair at the table and directed him to sit. He also took off the crown he was wearing and placed it on Art's head.

"Courage demands that you wear this crown, Mr. Williams," Merwin said.

Angus grabbed one of the filled tankards from the table and held it aloft. "Three cheers for King Arthur!"

His classmates laughed and then joined in, "Hip-hip hooray! Hip-hip hooray! Hip-hip hooray!"

Art accepted their cheers and downed his tankard with delight.

Roasted lamb was brought into the banquet tent already carved and ready to serve. There were a few root vegetables on the table, but no potatoes. There was also ham and a dark bread and fresh churned butter.

"The potato is a product of the New World and did not reach England for almost 200 years after King Henry's death," Professor Merwin commented, not one to waste a opportunity to teach. "So none of the Europeans were meat-and-potato men. If this were an authentic royal meal, there'd be grilled beaver tails. Oddly, the church considered the beaver a fish, so it was safe to eat on Fridays. We'd also be enjoying whale meat, a roasted peacock with its beak covered in shiny gold leaf, a roasted boar's head, black pudding, and roasted swans. We'd finish off the meal with almond cakes. Oh, and of course, wine and beer. All we've got is ginger ale, I'm afraid. But with all of that meat, you can see why Henry VIII suffered from gout, as well as a number of other health problems."

"Did they eat like that everyday, Professor?," Angus asked.

"Quite. A man in Henry's court might consume 5,000

calories a day, more than twice what a man needs today. If you were work as hard as they did, you needed all that food to survive. And the water back then was nearly undrinkable. It was common to give children water that had been mixed with wine or beer. The alcohol killed the contaminants. Safe drinking water was at least 400 years off in the future."

Merwin looked around. Only Angus had asked for a second plate of food and, the teacher knew, he was capable of finishing a third, as well.

"I've got a few more things I want to show you before we head back to London. Change out of your armor and meet me over by the scarecrows."

The dwarves helped the students remove their steel suits. The sun was now a little lower in the sky. It would be twilight in a few hours.

"Swords weren't the only close combat weapons," Merwin said when they all were gathered around him. "A battle axe, wielded by someone powerful enough to swing it, could stun a knight in full armor and then find the gap in his protection and eliminate him as a battlefield threat."

There was a rack with a number of large double bladed weapons. Merwin picked up one of the smaller blades.

"This is a single handed axe. A knight could use this in his right hand while blocking with the shield in his left." He put the axe down and picked up one that had a head twice its size with a much longer handle. "This is a two handed axe. Just like a baseball or a cricket bat, the power of the blow comes from the swing of whole upper body and not just the arms."

Merwin looked over at Angus. "Mr. Wilcox. You play football, don't you?"

"Yeah, both Canadian rules and what the British call football - soccer."

He handed Angus the two handed axe and pointed to two parallel lines of scarecrows that snaked across the barren field. "Punch through that line."

Angus hefted the axe, moving it from his left hand to his right to see where it fit right. Unsatisfied, he picked up a second axe. He held them so the wooden handles crossed at chest height and then slashed downward.

"Okay," he said, nodding, "this feels right."

Angus charged at the line of wooden and straw figures draped in rags, a two handed axe clutched tightly in each fist. The two rows of scarecrows were staggered four feet apart. As he reached the first figure, he cut it in half with the axe in his right hand and spun, continuing to move down the line. As he finished the turn, he brought his left arm up and took off the head of the second avatar with a backhand motion that would have made a Wimbledon champion proud. He continued down the line without wasting any motion until all twenty scarecrows were reduced to splinters. He jogged back to where his classmates waited, a light beading of sweat on his forehead.

"That was fun," he said, just a little out of breath. "Can I do it again?"

"Alas, Mr. Wilcox," Professor Merwin said as he took the two axes from Angus and replaced them on the rack, "it seems you've taken out the opposing army all by yourself."

EIGHTEEN
THE DEATH OF ARTHUR

The trip through the French countryside was uneventful. This time, Dipeka had called "shotgun", but at least Art did not have to ride in the very last row of the Prius Plus.

Duncan and the other dwarves were nowhere to be seen. Although, Art admitted to himself, it might have looked a little conspicuous to be driving a Range Rover with a hole punched through one of the doors. They probably ditched the car and found some other mode of transportation. But he was sure that the new dwarf king was true to his word, that they were still following him.

When Art looked back, he could see Agent Kidd tailing them in the black Ford Explorer. At first, it bothered him that none of his other classmates had bodyguards from their embassies shadowing them. He had found out that there were many more sons and daughters of high diplomatic officials attending the American School than just his friends. None of them had their own security details, either. At first, Art was afraid that all of the students in his school would resent him. After a few days, most of them ignored his shadow.

When they drove the Prius into the train car, Art was

convinced that the dwarves would be in one of the autos near them. He walked up and down the train car looking into each vehicle, but did not find them. What if the enchantment that prevented everyone else from seeing the dwarves in their true form was now working on him? He supposed that they could turn it on and off they wanted to.

As the train neared the end of its journey, Merwin called them all to the back to the car. He opened the hatch and pulled out a canvas tote bag. He rummaged around inside and pulled out copies of a paperback book and began handing them out to his students.

Art looked at the cover of the book he was handed.

"*Le Mort D'Arthur*? I can't read French," Art said.

"Only the title is in French," Merwin said with a smile. "Change of plans. On Monday, we're going to be discussing Sir Thomas Malory's *Le Mort D'Arthur*. As you might suspect, the story of King Arthur, his Knights of the Roundtable, and the tales of Camelot are an important literary touchstone for the English-speaking world. The stories have been part of the tradition of the British Isles for over a millennia.

"The first mention of King Arthur can be found in the *Historia Brittonum* written in the 9th Century. Malory collected the stories in the 15th Century. John Steinbeck, who won a Nobel Prize for literature, reinterpreted the Arthurian cycle, as T.H. White did in *The Once and Future King*."

The students grumbled at the thought of having to give up their weekends. They knew that, with such a small class, they could not afford to be unprepared. Every one of them would be called upon, especially since King Arthur appeared to be the only topic they would be discussing the entire day. None of them would be saved by the bell.

"Its a quick read, I assure you," Merwin said. "Who knows? You might enjoy it."

NINETEEN
PLEASE LOOK AFTER THIS BEAR

It was late Friday afternoon when Princess Guinevere arrived at Buckingham Palace. Her mother, the Queen, would be back from an inspection of a military base in Herefordshire within the hour. She was going to have to move quickly.

Her father would have normally accompanied her mother, but since he hosted a luncheon for business leaders at the Palace, he had to stay in London. His schedule was clear now and she found him where she suspected he would be, playing with her dear little brother.

The Buckingham Palace Gardens were directly behind the Palace. It consisted of a great open lawn that was ringed by a thick forest of trees. There was no hiding the fact that the Palace sat in the middle of what Guinevere considered to be the greatest city in the world. The trees screened the Gardens from the streets that bounded the royal residence.

Despite all the grandeur and history of the Palace, her father had the royal architect erect a wooden fenced area in a small clearing among the trees. It was both quaint and sentimental. It was the same size as the back garden of the little house where her father grew up in Surrey, only about 40 feet on each side. There was room for a set of swings and a slide and a bench. A couple of rose bushes, homely little things, had been transplanted from her father's old house and planted along one of the walls. None of these common plants, Guinevere thought, could compete with the roses in the Queen's formal garden. Her father gave strict orders that the gardeners were not to clip, trim, or prune his roses. He would raise them like his mother had.

Gregory was seated on his father's lap, holding a stuffed Paddington Bear. Guinevere had been given the same stuffed toy as a child. Hers was now balding in patches and had lost one of its plastic eyes. Hers was naked, as well. Its blue duffle coat and shapeless red hat were long lost. Gregory's bear was new. It still bore the yellow tag with the handwritten note reading, "Please look after this bear. Thank you."

She smiled, remembering all the good times and secrets that she and her Paddington had shared together.

Her father looked up over his reading glasses when she entered his secret garden and smiled.

"Gwennie, welcome home. Please sit with us. I picked up a picture book for Greggie this afternoon. *Paddington Bear in the Garden.*"

As Francis read the title, he pointed to each word for the benefit of his son.

Gregory was not speaking yet, but he held up the Paddington Bear for his sister to see, and then snatched it back in a tight embrace. Nothing was going to separate the boy from his bear.

"Father, he's a little young to be reading," Guinevere said as she took her place on the bench. She stroked her brother's head without thinking.

"Nonsense," her father said. "You were reading *Winnie the Pooh* to me at three."

"You read it to me so many times, I was reciting it by

heart. You only thought I could read," she said laughing.

"Its nice to hear you laugh, Gwennie. It's been a long time."

"I don't know what you're talking about, Father."

Francis put his hand behind Paddington's back, animating him for Gregory while he talked with his daughter.

"The last few years, I feel we've drifted apart. We used to be so close, Gwennie. You couldn't wait to see me when you got home from school. We'd sneak off and have our little adventures together, just you and me. When I look in your eyes now, all I see is disappointment. It's as if you convinced yourself one morning that I wasn't good enough to marry your mother."

"Father, that's not true," she said, but started thinking. How much had her mother told her father?

He just did not understand, Guinevere thought. She could not help it if the people expected the Royal Family to act a certain way. He was older than her mother and came into his royalty late in life. He was a prince by a decree of her mother, not because of any birthright. Perhaps, one day, she could be brutally honest with him. But not today.

Her father made a growling noise and moved Paddington in close, pretending to nip at Gregory's nose. The little prince giggled with delight.

"Did you know that I had a last name when I married your mother? Stone. I was Francis Joseph Stone. Stinkie Stone they used to call me at school. When I married your mother, she didn't take my last name. I lost mine. I'm now My Royal Highness Prince Francis, Duke of Dorchester, Earl of Westbury, and a list so long I have to read it off a card I keep in my wallet.

"Your mother knew I was not high born when we met," he continued. "My father served as British Consul in Boston when I was a lad. That's how I met Binkie Williams. We had them over for tea. You showed his son,

Art, around Windsor. You remember the boy at least, don't you?"

"Vaguely," she answered.

"I love your mother and I've always tried to do what I can to make her happy."

She reached over and took her father's free hand in hers.

"I'm sorry, Father. It's not your fault. It's mine. I guess after Grandfather died and Mother became Queen, it felt like the whole world fell in on me. I knew that the whole world was watching me, now more closely than ever."

Francis squeezed his daughter's hand. "Your mother told me almost the same thing when her father died. That the world had fallen in on her. But you're not going through this alone. I'm here. Your Mum's here."

"I know, Father."

"When did I become 'Father?' When you were little, I was 'Daddy.' When you got a little older, I became 'Dad.' I still called my father 'Dad' until the day he died when I was thirty-five."

"All right, Dad."

Francis beamed. "That's the stuff. I'm your Dad and don't you forget it."

They shared a laugh, which Gregory joined. He handed his sister his Paddington to hold, but just for a moment.

"I wanted to talk with your about something, Dad. I'm worried about money for university."

Francis winked at her and whispered. "I hear your mother's got a few quid stashed away in a cookie jar somewhere. I think we'll be able to cover your books and tuition. Although you might have to get a job after classes for spending money."

"No. Not for me. For other girls. The economy's been really bad for the last few years. The cutbacks at the Ministry for Universities are making it impossible for a lot of girls to get an education. I'd like to set up a fund to help deserving girls. We might not be able to pay a lot of full scholarships, but we could give a little help to a lot of girls who might not be able to study otherwise."

Francis looked at his daughter and smiled. "Who are you and what have you done with my Gwennie?"

Guinevere laughed. "I'm serious, Dad. I realize that I've been very fortunate. So have a lot of people in our country. Perhaps its time we all gave back a little."

"I'm impressed. Why education?"

"I want to do it because it's right. You're a businessman," she said.

"Was a businessman," Francis corrected her.

"If you need a sound business reason, how about the fact that an educated workforce can adapt to the changes that face Britain today?"

"When were you planning to do this?"

She bit her lip. The date was the crucial part. "June 3rd. It's a Friday. I've already checked. There aren't any big events planned here at Buckingham and Mother's calendar is open that evening."

"Ba-ba-ba-bah," Gregory chimed in.

"You've convinced your brother and you've got me on board. How do you want to raise money?"

"I was thinking of a grand ball," she said pointing to the great lawn, "out here, under the stars. It'll grab the attention of the press and the public. We present a group of young college-bound British women to society. There hasn't been this kind of magical royal ball since ... I don't know when."

Francis smiled. "We could make it a real knees up affair, couldn't we? A way to let your hair down. We'll get a couple of great rock bands. Disco balls. That could be fun."

Guinevere clenched her teeth and winced. "I was thinking a traditional ball, not a disco. Elegant gowns. A symphony playing waltzes. I also put in a call to Sir Henry

Addington, the President of the London Symphony. He said they'd be willing to do it for my new charity. Not that your idea isn't great, Dad. Maybe for the second big fundraiser. I'd like to see if we could make this work my way."

"You're as headstrong as your mother, I'll give you that. How can I help?"

"Things have been a little strained between ... Mummy and I for a while. I'm afraid if I come straight at her she'll say no. I need you to break the ice for me. To soften her up. Would you do that for me, Daddy?"

"All right, Gwennie. Anything for you."

She ran her finger through her brother's curly blonde hair and smiled at him. She leaned over and kissed her father on his cheek. "Thank you, Daddy."

"See you at dinner," he called out to her as she walked the gravel path back to the Palace.

That was easy, she thought. Getting her mother to bend to her will was going to be much harder.

TWENTY
A CURIOUS DRAGON

Art stood on the open-air balcony of the Presidential Apartment of the Tower Hotel. It was shaped like a giant egg sitting on its broad bottom, a fraternal twin to another egg shaped structure about a half mile north of the Tower Hotel, The Swiss Re Building.

"The Swiss Re is not egg shaped. It looks more like a gherkin," Dipeka had told him when his class had come over to work on a project after school one day.

"They wanted it to look like a pickle?," Art asked.

"Oh, yes," Dipeka assured him. "The shape allows it to withstand wind-loads better and to use energy more efficiently.

Dipeka had told them that afternoon that she planned to become an architect and remake the skyline of Kolkata. Amanda had a different goal.

"I know it sounds cliché and all, but I plan on returning to Quilpie Shire in Queensland. My family has a sheep farm there."

"Forty acres and a mule?," Art asked, jokingly.

"More like 600,000 hectares," Amanda responded, then

119

seeing that the metric measurement was lost on Art, she added, "Its about the size of your state of Delaware. We've been sheep farmers for generations. I don't know what got my father interested in politics, much less international relations, but here we are."

"I'm planning to go to the Royal Canadian Military Academy when I graduate the American School," Angus told them. "I'm going to study engineering and be commissioned as a first lieutenant in the Royal Canadian Army."

Henry had grand ambitions as well. "My father owns a textile factory in Guangdong, China. I'm going to take it over after I get my business degree. He makes a fabric better than American Kevlar."

"He makes bulletproof vests?," Angus asked, impressed.

"The fabric is stronger than steel," Henry said. "It's used in automobile tires, ship sails, roofing materials. It has a lot of other uses than bulletproof vests."

When the conversation turn to him, Art tried to distract the group by pointing over the balcony edge.

"See that below us?," he said, "that's the Tower of London. A couple of British queens bought it there." He made a slashing motion across his neck and a sound like an axe taking a single swing.

"Come on, Art," Amanda said. "Whatya' going to do when you graduate? Off to university? Harvard's in Boston, right? Off to Harvard?"

Art knew that even with his family's connections that Harvard was probably out of reach. He had no desire to be in the military like Angus, but he supposed that his father's relationship with the President could get him an appointment to West Point or the Naval Academy. His parents did not own vast acreage like Amanda's family.

"I was thinking of taking a year off after high school and bumming across Europe. I'm already here, so I don't think that's going to be my plan now." He finally admitted, "I don't known what I'm going to do next."

"You could always go shear sheep for Amanda in Quilpie," Angus said, laughing and sharing a fist bump with Henry.

"Don't pay them no never mind," Amanda said. "We're all still little nippers, really. You've got a lot of time to figure out what you want to do with your life, mate."

He had a good time with his friends in France earlier in the day. He wondered what prompted him to remember that conversation from a few weeks ago. Maybe he was just tired. It had been a long day.

His parents were at a reception that the Australians were giving.

"You really ought to come, dear," his mother had told him. "The lobby of Australia House was used as the set of the goblin bank in one of the 'Harry Potter' movies."

As fascinating as that sounded, he told them that he was too tired.

He peered over the edge of the balcony at the Tower of London below. From the 40th floor, he had an eagle-eyed view of it. The White Tower in the center was brightly lit and shone like a diamond against the night.

His father kept a set of binoculars on the patio and had shown him the little black birds that flew about the Tower's grounds. He even described an old legend to him.

"The ravens guard the Tower. If they leave, the Tower will crumble into the Thames."

"Dad," Art had said, "we're right next door. If the Tower falls into the river, won't we go with it?"

The Ambassador thought about it for a moment. "Maybe. Let's hope they stay healthy until we can move back to Winfield House."

Art took the binoculars now and trained them on the Tower below. It was late and it was dark and he knew his chances of being able to pick out the black birds in the night were slim, but he looked anyway.

He could see people milling about on the Tower grounds below. It was a cool spring evening and the Tower would be open for at least another hour. His parents kept insisting that they were all going to visit the Tower together, but they never found the time.

While he was spying below, the images in the ocular lenses went black for a second. Then it happened again. And again. And again. Art pulled the rubber eyecups away from his eyes and stared down. Below him were what looked like five gigantic vultures. There were buzzards circling his giant egg shaped hotel, he thought.

Art brought the binoculars up to his eyes once again and focused on the birds. When the image cleared, he saw they were not buzzards. They were not the Tower's storied ravens.

They were dragons — black dragons the size of ponies — their inky leathery wings rowing against the nighttime air. Two of the creatures were clearly larger than the other three. Except for the swish of air that their wings made, they were completely silent. They were flying about a hundred feet directly below him, keeping station over the Tower. One looked up. Art was sure it had made eye contact with him. Its eyes were the color of dried blood and, when it opened its mouth, he could see two sets of sharp teeth. This was a carnivore, Art thought, the dominant predator in its ecosystem.

And it had seen him.

Art ducked down below the edge of the balcony. The balcony was really a room whose window curtain wall retracted like an overhead garage door, opening the space to the outside. The patio space was two stories high and twenty feet deep. Art expected that all five of them could land here, have him for a late night snack, and be gone before what was left of him was found by the hotel maids.

His first thought was to close the opening, returning the glass to its original position. There were people on the other floors behind glass, obviously in plain view of the dragons. The Tower Hotel must have looked like a sandwich vending machine to the dragons. He wondered why they had not gone after anyone below. The hotel manager once told him that the hotel was cloaked in thermal glass. Maybe the dragons used heat vision to see and their vision could not penetrate the special glazing.

The controls were at shoulder height on the far wall. He would have to stand up to activate them. Where were the dwarves?, Art thought. Some much for Duncan's promise that no harm would come to him when they were around.

Art had to close the window. He steeled his courage and counted to three.

One.

Two.

Three.

He went for the control panel, moving sideways and low, like a fiddler crab, hoping that the edge of the balcony would shield him. As he got to the sidewall, he sprang straight up and reached for the button that would bring the glass panels back down into place. Looking out of the balcony, he suddenly found himself face to face with a large black dragon.

It was hovering in place. It tilted its head from one side to the other, keeping its gaze focused on Art. Art was certain that it was calculating his calorie content, figuring out whether he was going to be a take-out meal for one or whether there was enough of him to share with his flying buddies.

Art had seen a scientist in a movie claim that dinosaurs could not see things that were not moving. He doubted it was true, but for his sake, he hoped that the man was right. He froze in place.

The other four dragons rose into his field of view, elevating straight up like helicopters. Now all five of them were staring at him. Art began to relax a little. They had not made any aggressive moves towards him. He held their interest. He edged back one step and the other four dragons moved a step closer to him. He moved to his left and all five of them kept their positions relative to each other, but moved as a group three feet to the left. He moved back to his right and they all followed in unison. He jumped up and down. All five of them matched his height and speed, bobbing in the air as long as he was jumping.

Then Art heard the clanging of metal against metal. The five dragons all looked down at the Tower below at the same time. One by one, starting at the back of the group, they peeled off and dived away, like buzz bombers in an old war movie. The last dragon, the first one that confronted Art, looked down again and back at him. The dragon opened his mouth and Art took a deep breath, realizing that they were nose-to-nose.

A big, pink, wet tongue came out of the creature's mouth and licked him across the face. The dragon hovered back from the balcony and wheeled in the air and started to glide down to the Tower grounds.

Art stood for a moment, unable to move or even to process his thoughts. He was covered in dragon spit and reeked of stale meat. When he gathered his wits, he grabbed the binoculars and refocused them back on the Tower below.

Art could count a total of nine dragons, not just the five that had visited him. They were all lined up in single file, like customers at the counter of a fast food restaurant. He could see what looked like an old man standing between two buildings, tossing huge chunks of meat to the waiting dragons.

Art had to get down there, to find out how the dragons and the dwarves, and the Banshees and the cat-witch, and all of the other craziness that had invaded his life since coming to this country were related. He was sure that the old man with the dragon food held all the answers.

21
A VERY DISTURBED YOUNG MAN

Art had slipped out of the hotel once before without his bodyguard and managed to slip back in without being detected. There were two smaller suites that interconnected to the Presidential Suite. Art had lifted a key card from one of the maid's carts that opened the interconnecting door near his bedroom into one of the smaller suites.

The center of the circular floor housed the maid's utility room, the garbage chute, the elevators, and the stairs. There were closed circuit television cameras on the passenger elevators, as well as in the stairwell. His midnight explorations led him to two discoveries. The first was that the maid's key that opened the door into the other suite also opened the door to the service elevator vestibule. The second was that the service elevator did not have an onboard camera.

On his way out, Art managed to change his shirt, pulling on something that may have been dirty from his laundry pile, but at least it was not covered in reptile saliva. He also splashed some cold water on his face and wiped it clean with a towel. He did not welcome the possibility that the lizard spit might be pre-digesting his face.

Thankfully, the other suite was empty. In the months since they had moved in, it had only been rented out a few nights. The lights were out and Art moved across it cautiously, his way illuminated by the glow of the city lights reflected off a layer of clouds.

He pulled the lever handle on the front door down and the lock let out a loud, metallic click, which echoed across the empty suite. Art held his breath and listened, but only heard the sound of his own heart thundering in his chest. He slowly pulled the door open a crack and looked down the hall at the entry to the Presidential Apartment. All was quiet. Just inside the door to his suite was a young State Department security agent who was supposed to be "babysitting" him. Agent Kidd and another security officer from the Embassy had picked his parents up to take them to Australia House.

He slipped out of the suite and headed down the hall. Art would have to move quickly and be back very soon. His parents rarely stayed at a diplomatic party past eleven o'clock and usually returned well before that. He would have to get to the Tower, find the old man and talk to him, and be back upstairs before his mother came home. Art knew her habits. Checking in on him would be her first priority.

Art edged his way down the hall to the elevator lobby. He listened intently, trying to hear elevator cars moving towards this floor. Once his feet moved off of the carpeting and touched the marble flooring, he would enter a no-man's land. The lights next to an elevator door came on and the chime pinged. He hurried across the floor, the rubber soles on his trainers squeaking. He could not stop or slow. Instead, he ducked around the corner into the room that the service elevator emptied into.

What if it was his parents? He could wait until they got in the front door of the Presidential Apartment, and then make a mad dash down the hall and into the suite next door. With luck, he'd be able to get into the bathroom of his room and turn the shower on before his mother could drop in on him.

A bellman got off the elevator, pulling a luggage cart. He was followed by a second bellman with a cart filled with even more designer suitcases. Then a fat bearded man in a white flowing burnoose stepped off the elevator. Three women whose veils covered the lower halves of their faces joined him.

Art watched with a rising sense of panic. If they turned left, they would be heading down the hall to the suite he had escaped through and would need to reenter in order to get back undetected.

"Turn right. Turn right. Turn right," Art whispered.

But they turned left.

Art did not know what to do now. He had never tried to use the maid's key on the other suite's door or on the interconnecting passage back into the Presidential Apartment. Even if it did work, the door was next to his parent's bedroom. If he walked from that end of the suite back to his own bedroom, the State Department agent would surely see him.

"Sorry," Art heard a voice say from down the hall. "The Emperor's Suite is the other way."

In a moment, the caravan of luggage, bearers, and travelers from Saudi Arabia crossed the end of the elevator lobby heading in the opposite direction. Art gave a sigh of relief. He just hoped the sheik did not have more wives who would be moving in and blocking his escape route.

When the service elevator came, it dropped down so quickly that Art had to swallow to equalize the pressure in his ears. In less than 15 seconds, he made his way through the "back of the house" and into the lobby. He walked calmly, hoping not to draw attention to himself. Once outside, past the front drive and the valets, he sprinted to the street, rounding the corner where the All Hallows by the Tower Church sat. He jogged up Byward Street until it turned into Tower Road. After about a hundred yards he came to a sign directing him back towards the river, indicating the Tower entrance.

He ran down the path until he came to a ticket kiosk. The woman inside looked surprised to see him.

"We'll be closing in about 20 minutes. I've got to charge you full price. Come back early tomorrow and you can spend the whole day for the same amount."

"No," Art said, gasping. "I need to see it now."

"All right then. That'll be nineteen eighty."

He pulled out a twenty pound note and gave it to the woman and grabbed his ticket, not waiting for his change. He sprinted through the Middle Tower and across the wooden footbridge that covered the now empty moat. He handed his ticket to the attendant at the Byward Gate and moved inside, pushing himself through the current of tourists who were leaving the Tower. He passed under what was labeled "The Bloody Tower" and the crowd seemed to thin. There was a small green lawn to his left and a low stonewall to his right.

Art stopped for a second to catch his breath and to get his bearings. He had looked down on the Tower every day and night for months. It looked different at ground level. Then he figured out where he was. There was a chapel in the corner ahead of him.

He was in the wrong place.

The Tower had a large outer wall that surrounded the entire complex. Inside that wall were apartments and work areas. He had entered the inner ring of the Tower when he meant to find the old man in the outer ring. Art fought his way through the departing crowd to the area by the Byward Gate that nested between the two walls. He jumped over a low chain fence with a sign warning visitors that the area was off limits.

He ran up the open area to where he remembered the old man feeding the dragons had been. Luck was with him. The man in the black Beefeater's uniform was pushing the big blue cart that had been filled with meat just a few minutes ago, but was empty now.

Ravenmaster Edward Flummox-Jones was annoyed that a tourist had ignored the signs that were as plain as the nose on his face. This was some high school kid who was probably dared by his mates to jog through the outer ring. During the streaking craze back in the 1970's some of these blokes ran starkers around the Tower. At least, Edward thought, this one had his trousers on.

"You, sonny," Edward yelled, "you can't be back here."

"I saw you feeding the dragons," Art said.

Edward looked and was relieved that there was no one around. The volume of his voice dropped to a normal level.

"I don't know what you're talking about. Dragons? Have you been drinking, young man?"

Art pointed to the top of the Tower Hotel looming above them. "They flew up to my balcony. There were five of them. They watched me. Then they heard you banging on a garbage lid and they flew down here. I know what I saw."

"I can tell you're a very disturbed young man, you are. There are no such things as dragons."

As Edward said this, all nine of the dragons dropped down, forming a circle around the two of them.

Art pointed over at the largest dragon, Loki.

"You don't see this? It must weigh 800 pounds. It's shiny black with red eyes. It has feet like a hawk's and little tiny arms on the front of its chest like a T-Rex."

There was no question that this boy could see his dragons, Edward thought. But why him after all this time? He could not have him arrested for trespassing. Maybe his telling people he could see the dragons would open their eyes and they would see them, too. Who knows what would happen then. He would be sacked for sure, but that was not Edward's concern at all. He was worried that the

Army or the police would come and would try and take his dragons. Loki, Matilde, Atlas, and all the others could get hurt or killed. Or he might lose control of the dragons and they would start hurting people if they felt threatened.

Edward looked around again not knowing what to do. George Bailey, the young Yeoman Warder who was his assistant before Obsidia, was walking towards him. He would get George to escort this boy out quietly, no questions asked.

"Ravenmaster," Bailey asked, "is every thing all right?" He walked into the circle that the dragons had made around Art and Edward, oblivious to the creatures.

"It's fine," Edward said. "This young man came back here, probably on a dare. He's leaving now. Aren't you? You don't want any trouble. George here will escort you out. And I don't want you coming back to the Tower. Ever."

"Not until you explain about the dragons," Art said, a tone of anger rising in his voice. Without thinking Art had started poking Edward in the chest with his index finger for emphasis.

A low-throated growl emerged from the dragons. Art felt something grasp his wrist and turned, expecting it to be the young Beefeater who had just joined them. Instead, it was the largest dragon that was holding his wrist in its small three-fingered hand.

"Art, what are you doing here?," a voice asked.

Art recognized it. When he turned he saw King Duncan standing where the young man had been just a few seconds before.

"So, George," Edward said, "you know this young hooligan?"

Edward looked over at George Bailey and then stopped. George was a lanky lad of about 22. Standing in his place, wearing a small Beefeater's uniform was a man no taller than four feet with long blonde hair and a chest length bristly beard.

"Who the hell are you?," Edward asked feebly. "Where's George Bailey?"

"Ravenmaster, I know this is going to be a shock. This is Art Williams. His destiny and yours are both tied to these dragons. He wasn't supposed to learn of them, not yet anyway. But he can see them now, just as plainly as you can. You can also see me. My name is Duncan Shalerunner. There is no George Bailey. That was me all along."

Edward felt light-headed for a moment and leaned on his empty meat cart for support. Matilde and Athena each extended one of their small arms to try to steady him.

"Everyone else, for the time being, will continue to see the dragons as ravens and me as George Bailey."

"What about Obsidia?," Edward demanded. "Is she just an illusion like you? Is she even ... human?"

Duncan nodded his head. "I can assure you that she's very real. And very human."

"All right then," Edward said as he felt the strength surge back into his legs, "what is my destiny? I don't even know this boy. I'm old enough to be his grandfather. From the sound of him, he's an American. How is my destiny tied up with his?"

"I can't tell you that now, Ravenmaster," Duncan said. "Keep doing what you're doing. You've raised these dragons almost as well as their mothers could have. The butcher's being paid and the Queen's bookkeepers are none the wiser. In fact, you should double your meat order again." Duncan patted Loki on the belly. "They need to get up to their fighting trim over the next few weeks."

Duncan took Art by the arm and walked him towards the front gate.

"I know you've got a lot of questions, Art. Get out on the balcony at midnight and I'll explain what I can."

22
DINNER WITH THE QUEEN

The Queen's Apartment in Buckingham Palace was just that — an apartment. The Palace had over 800,00 square feet of floor space, over 19 acres inside. There were grand ballrooms, several throne rooms, picture galleries, rooms named for colors, and rooms named for years that famous rulers from other countries visited.

The Apartment had bedrooms for the Queen and Prince Francis, a nursery and playroom for Prince Gregory, and a suite of rooms for Princess Guinevere. There were two dining rooms, a large one for entertaining guests and a small one for use by the family. Dinner this night was being served late in the smaller dining room because fog delayed the Queen's flight back to London.

Guinevere was waiting anxiously in the dining room for her mother to arrive. This had to work, she thought to herself. If her father did his part, he would have already sold her on the idea of her charity ball. She nearly jumped out of her seat when the door to the dining room opened and her parents entered.

"There she is," Francis said. "Our little girl is ready to

take on more responsibilities."

Guinevere stepped forward and kissed her mother on the cheek. Then, to the Queen's surprise, she kissed her father on the cheek, as well.

"Mother...Mummy, how was Herefordshire?"

"Lovely," the Queen said. "I saw a demonstration of how the RAF trains helicopter pilots for combat."

"The next time you go, you must take me with you," Guinevere responded.

"You said you hated that sort of thing," said the Queen.

"Maybe I did in the past, but no more. I realize that I've got certain duties that fall on me as your daughter. Duties which I gladly take up. In fact, if you'd like, I could speak with the headmistress at school and see if I can be available every weekend for these kind of events."

"You need to focus on your school work, darling. If you'd like, we can schedule a few things during your next holiday week."

"That would be brilliant." Guinevere tried to smile appreciatively at her mother.

She could detect some skepticism in her Mother's eyes. Without consciously thinking, her hand went up to the area below her neck and she felt the heart-shaped locket under the fabric of her shirt. That calmed her.

They took their seats at the table and the staff brought out their food. Francis said grace over the meal.

"Your father tells me you'd like to hold a charity ball. Is that right?"

Guinevere swallowed quickly. "Yes. You're no doubt aware of the state of the economy..."

"Yes," Caroline interrupted. "The Prime Minister and I spend a good part of our conversations each week talking about it."

Guinevere waited to make sure that her mother had finished. "Then you know of the cutbacks to universities. There are a lot of girls who won't be able to afford college anymore."

"Gwennie, I'm sure that all of your friends will be going off to university."

"No, Mother...Mummy. I'm talking of the ordinary British girl, the one with not enough savings or aid, who's going to miss out on a better life for herself."

"But a ball? Your great-grandmother put a stop to all the debutante nonsense. The idea of aristocratic girls with ostrich feathers in their hair, curtsying and staging a backwards walk was silly, really. You don't want to bring that back, do you?"

"No. But perhaps Father ... Dad didn't explain it quite right. Yes, there would be girls from society invited. But I also want to include girls from all levels, especially the girls who would benefit from the program."

"Just girls, then?," her mother asked.

Guinevere could feel the end of her mother's eyebrow begin to rise. She touched the locket again and her anxiety went away.

She shook her head and smiled. "No, not just girls. The program would be just for girls, but you can't have a grand ball without boys."

Francis jumped in, trying to help. "You know, we could give this thing an international flavor. There are quite a few members of the diplomatic corps that have children Gwennie's age. We could include them on the guest list."

The Queen smiled. "That would be a lovely thought. Those girls you're so concerned about could meet all sorts of interesting people. We could invite Art Williams over with his parents. That might the perfect time for you to apologize to him."

This was not going at all the way she had planned it. It looked like she was getting her ball at the Palace, but at a terrible price. She would have to be nice to that American boy. She would have to do something that she fought at every turn — admit that she was wrong. Just before the screech of protest rose in her throat, she remembered the vision of Prince Mordred. She was doing it for him. She would even be nice to that Williams boy if that meant she could get what she needed to save Mordred's world and her own.

"You're right, Mother," Guinevere admitted. "I did behave badly at Windsor Castle and I would be happy to ask Williams for his forgiveness."

The Queen smiled. "We'll start making the arrangements in the morning, darling."

Guinevere got up and hurried over to her mother and kissed her on the cheek. She then turned to her father and embraced him warmly. "Thank you, Daddy."

Caroline felt triumphant. The distance between them felt like it had closed. Her daughter was finally beginning to take her royal responsibilities seriously and she was also showing signs of humility. Perhaps the days of Wreckless Gwen were finally behind them all.

23
THE HUNT ROOM

Edward returned to his flat, shaken. Somehow, caring for the dragons over the past few months started to feel normal. It seemed just as normal that he was the only one who could see their true forms. He enjoyed taking care of them. They were far more intelligent than the ravens ever were. All of this was now threatened. That boy could see the dragons. Maybe the magic that protected them was breaking down. How long would it be until everyone could see them?

He sank into his recliner, lost in thought. He had a destiny, the little man had told him. His destiny had always been to be the Ravenmaster. He obtained that over a half century ago, when his father passed away. Since then, he never had to worry about the future. He always figured that the future would take care of itself.

A knock on his apartment door lifted him out of his fog. He opened it.

Obsidia was standing there. She was in a black cocktail dress and her hair was pulled up high on her head. She also wore a light jacket to ward away the chill. She frowned at him.

"Edward, did you forget?", she asked.

He winced. It had slipped his mind with everything that had happened this evening.

"I'm sorry, it did. Just give me a few. I'll be ready in two shakes of a dragon's tale."

Obsidia laughed. "What was that? Two shakes of a dragon's tail?"

"Did I say dragon? I meant to say lamb. Lamb's tail." He motioned for her to come in. "I'll just be a moment."

He went into his bedroom and closed the door. How could he have forgotten? It was his birthday and Obsidia insisted on taking him out for dinner. Someplace fancy, she told him. No fish and chips wrapped in a newspaper tonight.

He emerged from his bedroom wearing a suit with narrow lapels and a skinny tie. It was so old that its style had become fashionable again.

"You look dashing, Edward," Obsidia said with a smile.

Edward blushed. "This old thing? I can't remember the last time I wore it. Where to?"

"I thought I'd take my favorite birthday boy to the Hunt Room at the Tower Hotel next door. It's a nice night. I thought we'd walk, if that's alright with you."

He smiled. "I can think of nothing I would like more."

Art picked up the house phone in the lobby and asked to be connected with the Colony Suite on the 40th floor.

"I'm sorry, sir," the operator told him. "No is staying there at the moment. I can look up your party by name, if you'd like."

"No, thanks," Art said, relieved.

The suite was still empty. He could use the keycard to get back into the Presidential Apartment without anyone being the wiser. Getting back to the service elevator would be trickier than getting onto it. He had traveled a lot with his parents. Leaving an area where you were not supposed to be drew fewer questions than going into one. Plus, there was the question of timing. When the elevator hit the ground floor it was easy to charge off and head for the exit. It was another thing all together to stand in the open and wait for the elevator to arrive.

Still, Art managed to slip into the back of the house and call the service elevator. No one came off it when the doors opened and no one came to the vestibule to board the car while he was waiting. So far, so good.

As the door of the elevator opened on the 40th floor, Art was awash in the sound of Drowning Armada's most recent hit, "Serious Fantasies". The sound was coming from the right of the elevator lobby, in the direction of the suite that the sheik and the veiled women were now occupying. Maybe one of the women was a daughter his age and not a wife, Art thought. In any case, the noise would provide sonic cover for him as he made his way down the hall and through the other suite.

He held his breath as he passed the door to the Presidential Apartment. Art crouched low out of instinct. He made it to the door of the Colony Suite without being detected and pulled the key card from his pocket and slid it into the handle slot. The red light above the slot blinked twice, but then came on a steady red again. He pulled the card out and tried it again.

Two long red blinks and a steady red once more.

This was not working, Art knew. What if they had discovered that the card was missing? What if they changed the electronic combinations randomly and his card was now obsolete? He took a deep breath and concentrated, as if the force of his will could alter the universe. When he dropped the card into the opening again, it blinked red twice again. Then the light changed to green. He was in.

He opened the door cautiously and slipped inside, then held the door handle to slow its speed. It closed without the loud click.

For the first time since stepping foot back into the hotel, he relaxed. He was less than 100 feet from the interconnecting door and safety — his home base. He tapped the dial on his wristwatch and it illuminated. It was 10:13. He had made it back with time to spare. His parents would be home in a few minutes, but by then, he would be in his room with his copy of *Le Morte d'Arthur* opened in front of him. His cover was a scholar, but his true calling seemed to be spy. He wondered whether his father could help him get a job at the C.I.A. after college.

As he made his way through the black, Art noticed that the suite was much darker than before. The curtains were drawn. Someone beside himself had been in the suite. Just as he was about to enter the hallway that led to the interconnecting door, one of the lamps in the living room came on.

"Good evening, Art."

He jumped back. Agent Kidd was sitting in a wing chair, watching him through the lenses of his mirrored sunglasses.

"Out for an evening stroll, I see," Kidd said with a calm in his voice that made Art very uneasy.

"Yeah, I just needed some fresh air."

Art tried to walk past.

"Sit down," Kidd directed and Art knew he could not ignore him.

He took a seat on the couch opposite Kidd.

"Do you have any idea how much trouble you've just created for yourself and your parents?," Kidd asked.

"And for you, no doubt," Art said with a small tone of defiance.

"What? You think I'm going to get in trouble because you slipped your collar? You think you're first Ambassador's kid who stepped off the reservation? Dream on. I've been doing this for 25 years. This is my third tour of duty in London alone."

"Let me just say...," Art began, but Kidd did not let him finish.

"Zip it, kid. You know how dangerous this world is? You think that because you're in London and not in the middle of some war zone, that the rules don't apply to you?" Kidde got up and stood over Art. "Bombings happen in London. Kidnappings happen in London. Murders happen in London."

"Nothing was going to happen," Art protested.

"You think my people like following you around? When I found out you weren't here, I had to leave your parents. I had hotel security back up the video feeds. I was one minute from calling in a stage one alert when I saw you walk back into the hotel lobby. You were gone forty-five minutes. If somebody snatched you off the street, you could be hidden in a million places in less than an hour. Then a phone call from your kidnappers blackmails your father into betraying your country or they start shipping pieces of you back to your mother in the mail. What the hell for? I shouldn't be having this conversation with you. I should be on the phone right now with my superiors in Washington. Your butt would be on an Air Force transport back to the States in an hour and your father would be fired. Is that what you want?"

Art was stunned. He had not considered the consequences of his actions.

"No," he said quietly.

Kidd sat back down. "I don't want to make that call. I like your father. He's a good man. But I'm not going to let our national security be compromised, not again."

Kidd looked up and touched his earpiece. "Roger that." He looked over at Art. "Your folks are pulling up to the hotel driveway right now.

"Do they know?", Art asked.

"No, if they did, I'd have to make that call to Washington. For right now, this is going to stay between you and me. We're not going to have this conversation ever again. Are we clear on that?"

"Yes, sir," Art answered.

Kidd walked Art to the interconnecting door and took out his own keycard to open the door. He held out his hand and Art surrendered his.

"I'm tightening security so this can't happen ever again," Kidd said. "From now on, the rules are different. I'm shortening your leash. My people are going to stick so close to you, that if you sneeze, they're going to be the ones to hand you the tissue."

"I'm sorry," Art offered.

Kidd nodded. "I think you are. Goodnight, Art."

The Hunt Room was a contrast in red and black. The chairs were all upholstered in red leather, while the walls had been painted the kind of black that not only refused to reflect light, it stole it from its surroundings. The restaurant's wine cellar was actually a small glass enclosed chamber in the center of the dining room. Thousands of bottles were arranged in neat racks that spanned from floor to ceiling. The maître d' confirmed Obsidia's reservation and escorted them to their seats. Without even ordering, a waiter brought a stand that held a large steel bucket filled with ice and a bottle of French champagne.

"What's the occasion?," Edward asked as the wine appeared.

"Its your birthday, silly," Obsidia said.

The bottle was opened with a loud pop. The waiter presented Edward with the cork. Not knowing what to do he looked it over and handed it back.

"That's a real cork, alright."

Two fluted goblets were filled.

Obsidia raised her glass and offered a toast. "Edward, I wish you a happy and hearty birthday. I look forward to many more years of working together. You're not only my boss, but my mentor and my friend."

They clinked glasses and Edward took a sip. The bubbles tickled his nose. He looked over at her through his thick glasses and was suddenly filled with a feeling of warmth. He was touched that a young girl like her would want to spend time with an old man like him. Edward knew that every man in the room must be envious of him. She was smart, funny, and beautiful. He liked her smile. He liked her laugh. He liked her violet eyes.

"Thank you, Obsidia. You make an old man remember what it was like to feel young again."

Obsidia shook her head. "You're not old. Age is just a function of mind over matter. If you don't mind, it doesn't matter. At least not to me."

Edward accepted her compliment and took another sip of his champagne. It felt like the bubbles were going straight to his head.

"I need to say something. All the time, we've worked together," she said, "you've never made any sort of move. I just have to come right out and ask whether you have any sort of feelings for me."

Edward spit out his wine, feeling like someone had punched him in the stomach. He did not know how to answer and just fumbled words in his mouth until his mind re-engaged.

"Well...well...I...uh. Feelings? Look at me. I'm an old man. Look at you. You're young. You're beautiful. Any man in this room would be proud to be with you. You don't need to waste your time on an old, deft codger like me."

She reached forward and put her hand on his. "Then just look me in the eye and tell me you have absolutely no feelings for me. That's all. Just do that. And if you can truthfully say that you don't, I won't ever bring this subject up again."

His eyes locked onto hers, cut amethysts that sparkled with fire. He could not deny it. But he could not admit it, either. He could not let her throw her life away by being with him. He withdrew his hand from her and took the napkin off his lap and laid it on the table.

"I need to get back to the dragons...ravens. I meant to say ravens." He stood. "Thank you for a wonderful birthday."

Edward walked out of the hotel and back to the Tower. His mind was swimming. He wondered if he was stupid. This was the first woman who ever expressed the slightest interest in him. He was old enough to be her father. Older, he thought, but he would not let the word "grandfather" be uttered, even by his subconscious. He decided that it could never be and the thought made his heart sink.

He went back to his flat and changed into a pair of work coveralls. The Ceremony of the Keys was long over and no visitors would be present. He filled a bucket with meat scraps and headed out to the Tower Green. He knew the beasties had already been fed, but he felt a need to be with them.

He saw the dragons up on the different towers that surrounded the Tower of London. They had gotten into the habit of taking up separate stations, like gargoyles on a church, keeping watch when they were not circling overhead. He brought a steel spoon out and banged it against the side of the bucket. He could see that all nine dragons looked over at him, but only Loki on the Bloody Tower spread his wings and glided down to him.

"Guess the rest of your mates aren't hungry tonight," Edward said as he pulled out a chunk of meat the size of his fist and tossed it at Loki.

Loki did not snatch it in mid-air with its jaws, but caught it in one of his front claws. Edward had seen that the arms of the dragons were becoming longer and more developed.

"You're not hungry either, I see," Edward said. "I haven't got much an appetite, myself. I got some shocking news tonight. Did you know it was my birthday? One more trip around the sun, as my Dad used to say. I just took one more trip around the sun. Well, I went out to dinner with Obsidia. You know who I'm talking about, of course?"

It was a rhetorical question, one that Edward did not expect an answer to, but he thought he saw Loki nod his head. He decided to ignore it. This big lizard could not understand him, he was sure of it.

"She up and tells me that she has feelings for me. That's a woman for you. Anyone who's sane and logical would see that there's no future for us. I had to do what's right. What's right for her, anyway. Don't you understand?"

Loki tossed the meat that he was holding back into the bucket.

Edward shook his head. "My heart tells me one thing and my head tells me another. What am I supposed to do?"

Loki balled up his right claw into a fist and beat it twice against his chest and then looked into Edward's eyes and sighed.

Edward reached over and scratched Loki under his jaw. "I wish I was 40 years younger. There'd be nothing from stopping me from sweeping her off her feet. It's hopeless."

Loki closed his eyes and a contented rumbling emanated from his broad chest.

Edward patted him. "You're a good listener, you are."

24
LITTLE VANWALANTHIR

The last thing Art wanted to do was to risk his father's appointment as the Ambassador to Britain. He had promised Agent Kidd that he wouldn't do anything stupid anymore. He had also sworn a brother's oath to Duncan. He could not tell Kidd about the reason that the mansion collapsed. Any talk of dragons would have him tossed on that Air Force transport in a straight jacket. He was not sure what to do.

It was nearing midnight. His parents had come in after the party at Australia House to say goodnight.

"You should have come," his mother had told him. "Amanda from your class was there. She was so disappointed you didn't come. I had a chance to say hello to Beverly Ying with the Hong Kong Trade Office. She wants to have you and your classmates over for dinner sometime next week."

"Anything exciting happen here while we were gone?," his father had asked.

Art wondered whether Agent Kidd went back on his word.

"No," Art said, the upbeat tone in his voice sounded a little forced even to him. "Just hanging out here, trying to get a start on Monday's assignment."

He had held up his copy of *Le Mort d'Arthur* for his parents to see. Art had bent back the spine half way through the book so that it looked like he had been studying it all night.

"Look at that, the death of Arthur," the Ambassador had said with a smile. "I read this when I was a boy. I always loved the tale of King Arthur."

"It's true," his mother had said. "When you were born he wanted to name you just Arthur, but I figured if there was a Zefrom Williams the third there had to be a Zefrom Williams the fourth. But since everyone calls you Art anyway, I guess that's just as good."

Art now tossed the book aside. He was halfway through it. Professor Merwin was right, it was a quick read. He stood and stretched. It was 11:55. He walked across the suite, nodding to the agent seated in foyer. He opened the French doors leading out to the enclosed balcony and went to the control on the far wall and opened the curtain of glass. The sounds of the city came rushing up to him. Cars were moving below and honking their horns. Boat traffic plied the River Thames and a helicopter flew by the hotel, following the path that the river had laid down.

He pulled a chair close to the balcony's edge and stared up into the sky, trying to see a few familiar stars. He suddenly missed Boston, his old school, and his old friends. His life was easier there. His teachers and his friends did not expect much from him, and he met their expectations. Before he came to London, Art had not expected too much of himself, either. Back there, he knew he had been just strolling through life. Here, it was much harder. Professor Merwin expected so much from all of them. It took everything Art had to keep up with Dipeka, Henry, and Amanda. They were far brighter than any of the kids he went to school with. Even Angus had a greater understanding of the world than he did. Then there was all the weird stuff that had been happening to him since he arrived in England. Witches were trying to kill him and his family, a clan of dwarves had sworn to protect him, and just tonight, a dragon gave him a big wet kiss. All of a sudden, his boring life back in Boston did not seem so bad.

Art looked up again at the sky and saw that the stars were beginning to fade. A London fog was rising off of the river and was working its way up the height of the building. He stood and looked out. He could see the top of the clock tower at Whitehall, where they had felt the vibrations of Big Ben rip through his chest. He could see just the top few capsules of the London Eye, the giant Ferris wheel they had ridden. Across the cityscape, just a handful of buildings popped up through the upper fog deck. Art liked the sight of it. A few feet of snow softened the edges of Boston, but a few hundred feet of thick fog made London look like it belonged on another planet.

The mass of fog about a hundred yards out from the balcony began to agitate and swirl, as if something was boiling beneath it. In a second, two dragons popped up and flew past the balcony opening, with a rider on the back of each. They circled the top of the egg-shaped tower and then banked in, flying into the large patio area. The dragons hovered for a moment before dropping to the floor.

Across the back of each dragon was a large leather saddle, with a number of straps that crisscrossed beneath the creature's belly. Duncan was riding on the back of one dragon, while the dwarf who had been forced to play the mother on the Eurostar train got off the other. Both were wearing leather harnesses across their chests that buckled onto their saddles.

Duncan extended his forearm in greeting and Art took

it. The other dwarf did the same.

"Art, this is Kol Founderson, one of my most reliable men."

Art nodded, but was distracted by the saddled dragons. "You can ride them?", he asked.

"Of course you can ride them," Duncan said. "Didn't you just see us fly in here?"

"No, I mean, they let you. They're tame enough to be ridden?"

"I don't know about tame," Duncan said. "If you got one of them mad, they'd have no problem letting you know it. And by the way, the dragons look at the Ravenmaster at the Tower below like their adoptive mother. They've agreed to help us protect you by promise, but they think of the old man as blood. I'd advise against poking him like you did this evening. You're lucky Loki was in a good mood and didn't bite your arm off."

"I'm sorry," Art answered.

"Don't tell me," Duncan said with a tone of admonishment. "Tell them."

"I'm sorry," Art repeated, feeling a little foolish talking to a pet like this.

The two dragons watched Art carefully. The first nodded his head, while the second held out her arms with her paws opened, gesturing as if to say, don't worry about it.

"Can they really understand us?," Art asked Duncan without breaking his gaze at the two dragons.

"You're an awfully rude young lad," Founderson scolded. "They're right here. They can hear you."

"I'm going to take that as a yes," Art said, still unable to look away.

"Aye," said Duncan, "they can understand you."

"Can they speak?"

"Yes, but they've never learned Dresch, their native tongue. They came through the rift as eggs, when they were small enough to fit."

"How can you communicate with them?," Art asked.

"Trust me," Founderson added, "when a dragon's unhappy about something, you'll know."

"Art," Duncan said, "I need to take you on a little trip. We'll only be gone a few hours."

"No," Art said emphatically, "I was gone for forty-five minutes tonight and it almost got my Dad fired as Ambassador. I'm not going to mess this up for him."

"I know what happened earlier tonight. But no one will ever know you're gone," Duncan said.

"Somebody's going to check on me. I'm sure. When I'm not in my bed or in the suite, they're going to sound the alarm."

"If they do, they'll see you."

"How?"

Duncan pointed to Founderson. "To everyone else in the world, he looks just like you, just like I still look like the young Beefeater."

Founderson took his harness off and pushed Art down into one of the chairs and strapped him in.

"I'd much rather pretend to be you than a mother of three children," Founderson said as he cinched the last buckle. He gave the harness a tug in several places to make sure that it was secure.

"And now, I'm off to bed," Founderson said and slipped in through the French door.

Even through the closed door, Art could hear Founderson's voice, talking to the security agent at the door.

"Hello," Founderson said in a voice that still sounded like the dwarf's to Art. "I'm going to bed now. Bed is where I'll be, if you need me. That's where you can find me. In bed. If I'm not in bed, I may be in the bathroom. Or I may be getting a snack in the kitchen."

"Fine, sir, whatever," was the agent's bored response.

"See?," Duncan said with satisfaction. "We'll be back

before your parent wake."

Edward fell asleep that night like he did on so many nights, in his reclining chair in front of the television with the remote control in his lap. He had not taken out his dentures to soak or tucked away his eyeglasses. He was snoring softly until he felt like something was choking him. He coughed and sputtered and gagged and then sat up quickly. When he opened his eyes, the room was a blur. His hand went instinctively to his face, but he felt his glasses still resting on the bridge of his nose.

He put his hand to his mouth and could feel his dentures, but his mouth felt like it was being pried open, as if his gums had swollen to five times their normal size. The feeling of choking was getting worse. He reached into his mouth and was able to wedge his thumb under the front teeth of his dentures. He pulled forward with all of his might and the upper plate came flying out of his mouth. He spat out the lower set and leaned against the front door to his flat, panting for breath.

Edward's eyes were watering, so he took off his glasses and wiped them on the sleeve of his coveralls. He blinked and looked around his apartment. He could see.

Perfectly.

He had gotten his first pair of glasses in the third grade, but now he could see without them. He could read the titles of all of his books on his bookshelf from across the room, even the smallest line of print.

He reached up to check his gums with his thumb and was surprised to feel teeth, real teeth. He'd lost all of his when he was in his fifties. He ran his thumb across the top and bottom of his mouth. They were all there, all of his teeth. He looked over at the mirror hung next to his door and did not recognize for a moment who was staring back at him.

It was a familiar face. But there were no lines or bags

or jowls. There were no deep creases or liver spots on the forehead. He stared at his hairline. The tide of hair had rushed back in. It was thick and full and dark. His temples had just a touch of gray. It was his face, the one he remembered from four decades ago.

Edward straightened up. The small hump that had been developing between his shoulder blades, causing him to stoop, was gone. He felt his chest. His skin had tightened and his muscles had gotten back their tone.

The most important thing of all was that Edward no longer felt like an old man. The hundred little pains that dogged his every step were gone.

New. He felt new again.

He knew exactly what he had to do. He threw open the door to his flat and ran down the stairs. He felt like he could run for days without stopping.

As a lifelong member of the Tower staff, Edward had one of the larger apartments. He ran around the outer ring to another apartment block in the Casemates and found the door he was looking for. He started knocking on it, surprised at his newfound strength.

"Obsidia," he yelled out. "Open the door."

"Hey," an angry voice called out from an apartment above him, "some of us are trying to get some shut eye."

Edward ignored the man. Windows around him suddenly appeared lighted. It seemed that everyone was listening except Obsidia.

"Obsidia, please open the door."

With bleary eyes that looked like they had been crying, Obsidia opened her door.

Half asleep she asked, "What do you want? Who are you?"

Edward grabbed both her hands. "Its me! Edward!"

She widened her eyes and looked at him, confused by the sight of this stranger. Then she recognized him, mostly because of his smile.

She looked at him again. "What happened to you?"

"I don't know," Edward said in a giddy laugh. "I woke up and I had changed. I don't know how it happened. But it did. I ran right over here to apologize to you for how I acted tonight. I'm sorry if I hurt you."

He squeezed her hands and waited for her to say something, but she was still in shock.

"You asked me tonight if I had feelings for you," Edward said. "I wanted to scream 'yes', but I couldn't. I'll say it now. Yes. Yes. Yes. Yes! I love you."

He waited for her to say something to him, but she just stood there, looking him over from head to toe. People started popping out of the doorways of the nearby apartments, watching to see who had come pounding on the door in the middle of the night. He was beginning to feel a little self-conscious with so many eyes on him.

Quieter now, Edward asked, "Is there anything you'd like to say to me?"

She shook her head and Edward felt embarrassed for the first time. He had done it. He had put his heart out there.

"Actions," she whispered, "speak louder than words."

Obsidia pulled him close to her and wrapped her arms around him. She kissed him twice, gently and sweetly.

"Marry me," she said.

"What?," Edward asked.

"Before you can change your mind."

"For God's sake, man, marry her so we can all get some sleep," one of Obsidia's neighbors called out.

"When?," Edward asked.

"Tomorrow morning, as soon as City Hall opens."

Edward shook his head. "No. How about now?"

"Now? We don't have a license," Obsidia said.

"We don't need one," Edward said, pleased of his knowledge of Tower history. "An Act of Parliament gave the Chief Yeoman Warder of the Tower the power to perform civil marriages in 1617. It was so the condemned could marry. Its never been revoked. What do you say?"

Obsidia smiled. "I say let's wake the man up."

Obsidia did not bother to dress, but walked in her sleeping gown and robe with Edward to Chief Yeoman Warder Humphrey Archer's flat. A growing crowd of Obsidia's neighbors followed them, curious to see what was going to happen next.

Edward and Obsidia pounded on Archer's door together.

Archer opened the door dressed in a nightshirt with a sleeping cap on his head.

"Hawkins, what's the matter? Is there something wrong with Flummox-Jones?"

"This *is* Edward Flummox-Jones, sir," Obsidia said, holding Edward's hand tightly in her own.

"Who? This?," Archer said, trying to focus his sleepy eyes on Edward. "My God, man, it is you. What happened? I dare say, you look like a chap half your age."

Edward beamed. "I know."

"Should we call you an ambulance?," Archer asked.

"No, sir," Edward said. "We want you to marry us. Right now."

"Marry you? It's the middle of the night. Can't this wait until morning?," Archer said.

Obsidia was insistent. "No. I want to him to say 'I do' before he comes to his senses."

The crowd that had trailed them across the Tower grounds laughed.

"Go on," one of them called out, "marry them."

"Do it," a woman yelled.

"If you'll let me go back to my bloody bed, fine," Archer said. "Right here, in my doorway then?"

Both Obsidia and Edward nodded.

"Fine. Do you have a ring, Flummox-Jones?"

Edward did not wear jewelry, so he could not give her a ring of his own. He fished in the pocket of his coveralls and pulled out a metal leg band that bore the Queen's seal, one that he had made to fit the dragons' legs a few months before. It felt about the right size.

"Will this do until I can you a proper ring?," Edward said holding it up for her to see.

She smiled. "That will do forever."

Archer cleared his throat. "Do you, Obsidia Hawkins, take Edward Flummox-Jones to be your husband till death do you part?"

"I do," Obsidia said.

"Good," Archer continued. "Do you, Edward Flummox-Jones, take Obsidia Hawkins to be your wife till death do you part?"

"Yes, I do," Edward said.

"By the power vested in me by Her Majesty, Queen Caroline, I now pronounce you husband and wife. Now both of you, go to bed right now."

The crowd around them laughed loudly.

"That's not what I meant," Archer said, but his voice was drowned out as the crowd cheered as Edward took Obsidia in his arms and kissed her.

Duncan had made sure that Art's harness was securely fastened to the saddle.

"I didn't think your people were leather craftsman," Art said.

Duncan laughed. "Don't assume you know everything about us. Not everyone can be a miner. Our society's not much different from yours. We've got farmers and teachers. Dwarf jewels are prized for their cut. Elves claim that their jewelry is more beautiful than ours, but no self respecting dwarf would wear something that dainty."

"Elves?"

"Aye," Duncan said as he mounted his own dragon and strapped himself in. "The universe is grander than your human mind can comprehend. Watch and learn."

Without warning, Duncan's dragon elevated straight up in the air and darted out the opening. The fog had risen to cover the Tower Hotel. Art was not ready, but his dragon shot into the air and followed Duncan's. Art could not help letting out a scream as he was thrown back as his dragon careened into the night.

The fog enveloped them both. Art could see Duncan flying about 20 feet ahead, but nothing beyond. It was deathly quiet, the mist seeming to absorb all noise. Once their dragons reached what Art assumed what their cruising speed, it only took a few wing flaps a minute to keep them moving.

"How do dragons see in the fog?", Art called out to Duncan.

"How do bats see in the dark?," Duncan answered.

"I don't know," Art answered.

"Neither do I."

With that, Art clung a little tighter to the straps on his saddle. There was a glow up ahead, which kept getting bigger with each swish of the dragon's wings. The circular yellow radiance soon filled the entire sky. They could not be this close to the moon, Art thought, and it was too early for the sun to be up. Duncan and his dragon darted to the right, cutting deeper into the fog bank. Art and his ride proceeded for half a wing beat, until the glow resolved itself into the face of Big Ben. Just as the clock began to chime the quarter hour, Art's dragon finally turned, but not before being able to run along the face of the clock on the minute hand, which was pointing straight at three.

Duncan popped out of the fog to ride beside him. "Twelve-fifteen. We've got plenty of time."

"How fast can they go?," Art called over to Duncan.

"A full grown dragon can go a couple hundred miles an hour without a rider. But these are teenagers, like you. They've still got some growing to do." Duncan patted his dragon's neck. "Ajax, feel like racing your girlfriend?"

Ajax roared.

"I forgot to introduce you," Duncan said. "You're riding Margaret."

Ajax shot forward and dove down into the fog bank.

"We don't have to race them, Margaret," Art said, trying to reassure her. "Let's just get there in one piece."

Art saw his dragon shake her head from side to side just before they dropped down into the fog. Art leaned forward to cut his wind resistance, grabbing onto spikes at the base of the dragon's neck. The fog blinded Art to any reference point. He did not know whether they were still flying north or even right side up. They could have been a mile in air or just a few feet above the ground.

After Art's watch told him that they had traveled fifteen minutes, they shot free of the fog. The half-moon light revealed that they were flying over a patchwork of farms and fields. Duncan was riding beside him so close that their dragon's wingtips nearly touched when they were fully extended.

"Where are we?," Art asked.

"Beacon's Bottom. Nothing but flat farmland and forest. Not our first choice. A dwarf's not truly at home unless he's either deep in the earth or high on a mountain."

Duncan pointed to a small encampment in the middle of a square mile of woods. Art recognized the tents from the field near Agincourt.

"This isn't going to be our permanent home," Duncan said. "But it's close to the M40."

"You commute into London?"

"Who can afford the rents in London?," Duncan said with a laugh.

They circled once around the camp and landed on the edge. The Renaissance fair in the French farmer's field had only seven tents. The dwarf's camp had hundreds.

Two young dwarves ran out to them as soon as they landed. As they removed Margaret's saddle, Margaret leaned forward and nuzzled Art.

"Ha!," Duncan exclaimed. "She's taken a shine to you, she has."

Art ran his hand down her long neck and he could feel her almost purring inside.

Eoli ran forward and dropped to one knee in front of Duncan. "Your Majesty, we were not expecting you tonight. Should we wake the Dogent?"

"No," Duncan said, "let my father sleep. I will see him in the morning."

"No," a big, booming voice called out, "you'll see him tonight."

"Father," Duncan said and moved forward to embrace Kerr Shalerunner.

"Welcome, Arthur," Shalerunner said when he turned to young man, "to Little Vanwalanthir."

Arthur bowed respectfully. "Thank you, your Majesty."

Shalerunner leaned on his walking stick. "No, we'll have none of that. Duncan is our king now. I am the Dogent, the most senior member of Clan Fargrave after the King. Come, let us sit and talk." He called over his shoulder, giving orders in a voice that made him still sound like a ruler. "A pot of slateberry tea and honey for our guest and a tankard for the King and I."

Art followed Shalerunner and Duncan into the largest tent and was directed to sit in a chair that looked like it had been hewn out of a solid granite boulder. The seat conformed to his back and thighs and was surprisingly comfortable. An older dwarf woman came in bearing the teapot and two lidded steins. Art stood as soon as she entered.

"Oh," she said, "this one's got manners. I like him."

"Art," Duncan said, "this is Barbryn, my mother."

The woman was a little younger than Shalerunner. Her red hair was streaked with long strands of gray. Her face was plump and her figure was full. She wore a green fabric dress with an embroidered pattern that looked like crystals. The lines around her eyes showed that she had much to smile about throughout her life.

STEPHEN CODY

More royalty to meet, Arthur thought. He hoped he could get through this experience with breaching protocol so badly that he started a war. When Barbryn extended her hand to him, he kissed the air just above the back of her hand.

"It is an honor to meet the mother of the King and the wife of the Dogent," Art said.

She smiled and slapped him on his upper arm. "No need for formality here, Arthur. You're not only a member of Clan Fargrave, but a brother to my son. Think of me as your ..." She paused for a second and then spoke to Duncan. "What's the English word I'm looking for?"

"*Dul famm wah?*," Duncan said searching his mind, "Godmother is as close as we can get."

"Your dwarf godmother," Barbryn said proudly, "that's what I am. You not only saved the life of our king, but you made sure that my husband made it back home to me, safely."

"Safely?", Shalerunner growled. He put his foot up on a square block of stone that served as a coffee table for the collection of chairs in the front of the tent and tapped the marble cast that his foot was encased in with his walking stick. Arthur could see him flexing his toes out the open end. "It'll be another fortnight before this comes off."

Art looked at Shalerunner's foot for a moment. He was wearing a boot made of stone. There was a fine seam that ran down the side, but no sign of the glue or mortar holding it together.

"In my world, we use plaster for casts," Art said, hoping to make conversation.

"Plaster?," Shalerunner said. "Only elves would use plaster and fairies use spit and wishes. I wouldn't trust a fairy healer. He'll take your gold up front and leave you sitting there waiting to see him all day."

Barbryn directed Art to sit and poured him a mug of sweet, fruity hot tea. It did not look as if the tea customs of the dwarves were as formal or rigid as the English.

Duncan and Shalerunner hoisted their tankards.

"*Addoed at 'r banon chan 'r dylwyth teg,*" Duncan offered.

"*Mai c bori 'i enaid,*" Shalerunner responded before they clinked vessels and took a long swallow.

Barbryn looked at the two of them with a scowl. "You shouldn't say such things, not in front of Arthur. He'll get the wrong idea about us."

Art said, "I have no idea what you said."

"We said that the person responsible for what's to come should ... ," Shalerunner started.

Duncan patted his father's arm. "We wished ill health on the enemy whose presence brought us so far from our home."

Shalerunner looked at his wife and grumbled. "I guess that's accurate enough ... for now. That reminds me, we need to teach Arthur to speak proper Orrak."

Art tried to stifle a yawn. The tea had relaxed him, but he did not dare fall asleep.

"The boy is tired," Barbryn said, "you should get on with it."

"Aye, mother," Duncan said. "There's only so much I can tell you now, Arthur. June 23rd by your calendar is a date that has been prophesied. You and your four classmates will play pivotal roles. If we succeed, both your world and ours will be safe. Should we fail, the universe itself will unwind. The stars, one by one, will go dark. Matter will dissolve into energy and energy will flicker and fade into nothing. All that ever was will never have been."

Art was now wide-awake.

"Starting Monday," Duncan continued, "you and your classmates will travel here to be given the training you need to succeed, to stop the scourge that would destroy everything. Learning to fly on the dragons is but one part of it. You need to learn weapons, tactics, and strategy."

Art held up his hands to stop Duncan. "Whoa. Whoa. Whoa. Look at me. I'm just a kid. Call the Army. Call the Navy. Call the President. You want his number? I'll give it to you." Art fumbled in his back pockets, looking for his iPhone, but could not find it. "Okay, I can get it for you. Let's call the American Embassy. I met the Queen. Let's call her. You need to get some adults involved, right now."

"No," Shalerunner said roughly, "we need you and the others. It is you five who will turn the battle."

"Bullets are no match for magic," Duncan added. "Remember what happened when you shot the Sidhe with the pistol? You might as well have been firing mosquitoes at her. You need to fight magic with magic."

"Let's give the army some magic, then," Art argued.

"No, your people would never believe," Duncan said. "You, Dipeka, Henry, Angus, and Amanda are all still of an age when you yearn for magic, you believe that anything is possible. Years don't just harden hearts, they stiffen the imagination. A vortex will open between your world and ours on June 23rd. On that day, the forces we are fighting will be able to push through a small squadron here in London that will capture what they need most to tear down the barrier between us. If they succeed, the consequence will be that time itself, from the moment that Mighty Begom dreamed this world, and the dream of a god was made real, to today and all the tomorrows will cease to be."

Shalerunner tried to put it in simpler terms. "You must be there, because he who has already seen it saw you there. Our people have a saying, *'Choegddyn ddymuniadau allai chyfnewid 'r heibio i a 'n brudd ddyn chnotiau e nacht chyfnewid 'r ddyfodol.'"*

Shalerunner nodded satisfactorily, looking at Art as if he should understand.

"It means," Barbryn said, "A fool wishes he could change the past, but a wise man knows he cannot change the future."

Shalerunner crossed his arms over his broad chest and sat back. "That's what I said."

"We're not warriors," Art said. "We don't know how to fight."

"You have the heart of a warrior," Shalerunner challenged. "The rest is just technique. We can teach you."

Duncan tried to be more conciliatory. "Arthur, why do you think that all of this has happened you? It's because you were chosen. Not by us. But by the hand of destiny. Now is when your training began, so now is when your training must begin."

Art felt like he was running head first into a stone wall. He tried another tactic. "The security at the Embassy is ready to ship me home in a box without air holes. I can't disappear for even a few hours without them noticing it."

Duncan relaxed. "That should be the least of your worries. It is already being taken care of."

"Professor Merwin's going to notice if his entire class is missing for weeks. He's going to tell somebody."

"Who's Professor Merwin?," Shalerunner asked.

Duncan kicked his father's marble encased foot with the toe of his boot, causing the old man to grunt in pain.

"He's their teacher," Duncan said, talking slowly and emphasizing each word through his teeth. "You remember. We've talked about him. Many, many times."

Shalerunner finally caught on. "Oh, yeah. The Professor."

"You're not going to do anything bad to him, are you?," Art asked.

Duncan looked puzzled at first. "No. Of course not. We couldn't."

Art stood and extended his forearm to Duncan. "Swear to me as your brother and your kin."

"You doubt our honor?", Shalerunner bellowed.

Duncan stood as well and extended his right forearm and touched his father's shoulder with his left hand. "I know no insult is intended and," he said, looking down at his father, "none is taken. I swear on my oath as King of

Clan Fargrave and as your brother and your kin that we will allow no harm to come to Professor Merwin. Satisfied?"

Art only had a few seconds to think, to run the words back through his mind, to see if Duncan was trying to be a lawyer and leave a loophole for himself to betray Art in spirit, but not by words.

"Satisfied," Art said and pulled Duncan towards him, forearm to forearm. "I need you to tell me everything. You must answer every question that I and my classmates have."

"Agreed," Duncan said. "First thing Monday morning."

Art nodded. "Agreed."

25
RUBGY

It was not yet dawn, but Edward had not been able to sleep. Slumber found Obsidia shortly after their return to his apartment. The dragon leg band was secured on her ring finger. Her left hand was on his chest, her head rested on his shoulder. Just a few hours before, he would not have been able to stay in one position for long, but the burning arthritis he had suffered from was gone. He wished this moment could last forever.

"We're going to have to do this up proper, you know," he whispered. "A real wedding in a church. And a honeymoon, not some old codger's flat. I've always wanted to see the south of Spain. Maybe we could do something brilliant. We could see the world together. I once read that there are four kinds of penguins that breed in Antarctica — the Adelie, the Emperor, the Chinstrap and the Gentoo. I don't know why I remember that. You're an ornithologist. Maybe you'd like a bird honeymoon on at the hindquarters of the world."

"Shhh," Obsidia whispered. "I had a dream that I married the most wonderful man in the world. Don't wake me up."

"We could check into the hotel next door until we can make travel arrangements. It's not right for you to spend your wedding night here."

Without opening her eyes, she kissed his cheek. "Silly man. Don't you know that wherever you are is my home?" She squinted at the clock on his nightstand. "It's almost time to feed the ravens."

"There's something that I've been wanting to show you. Get dressed. I want you to feed them with me."

They both dressed and walked around the outer ring to the Ravenmaster's workspace. Because the people who worked at the Tower also lived in the apartments within the Tower walls, it was like a small town set in the center of one of the largest cities on the planet. It was a Saturday morning and the children of the Tower staff were already up and playing, and their mothers were up as well, keeping an eye on their broods.

Before last night, Obsidia only had a nodding acquaintance with the women of the Tower. She was one of the few female employees and the only woman Beefeater. This morning something had changed. The women of the Tower either witnessed her midnight marriage or had heard about it over their morning cup from their neighbors. Nearly every woman she saw rushed up to speak with her, to offer her congratulations.

"Best wishes, Luv."

"You make such a handsome couple!"

"When are you going to start filling your nest?"

"I cried. There in me jim-jams and curlers in the middle of the night and I cried. And my Wesley, he asks me, 'What're crying for?' And I tells the big lout, 'Because I'm happy for her.' It was so romantic."

Edward's youthful transformation was noticed, but hardly discussed.

One wife pulled her cellphone from her pocket and

held it up to her eye. "Let me get a picture of the two of you. This'll have to do as your wedding photo."

They stopped and posed, arm in arm, both wearing their Beefeater's uniforms. The only distinction, besides the shape of their bodies, was the silhouette of the raven's head on his sleeve. Edward was going to have to be re-measured and refitted for his uniform. His did not properly fit his now younger body, but it would have to do for a few more days.

Edward opened his workshop door with his key. Inside was the massive walk-in cooler. Obsidia had never been inside this warren, only the smaller space next door. In fact, none of the Tower staff had been in here.

"What's this, then?," she asked.

"This is where I keep the food." He opened the cooler's heavy door and she saw packages wrapped in butcher paper arranged on the shelves, tied up with salmon colored adhesive tape.

"There must be enough meat here to feed the ravens for a year," Obsidia said as she walked into the cooler.

"You'd think that, wouldn't you?," Edward said as he rolled the deep plastic cart in and started pulling packages off the shelf. He handed her one so that she could feel its weight.

"This must be ten pounds," Obsidia said.

"Ten pounds on the nose," Edward said and started counting bundles of meat. "15...16...17...18. That's 180 pounds. That'll do for breakfast. C'mon."

He walked over to the gap between the buildings, where passersby would not see them. He grabbed the steel spoon and the large metal rubbish can lid on top of the pile of meat and started banging it.

"That was you?," Obsidia said, feeling her face begin to redden. "All the time I was trying to film the bloody ravens and you had trained them to come to you? I can't believe you did that. I thought you wanted to help me with my research."

"I did, my love. Just wait, please."

Obsidia saw the ravens round the corner one by one, flying fast and sleek. When they saw her, they started to fly unevenly and erratically, as if the cut edges of their wing feathers suddenly threw them off balance. When they landed, they jumbled up in a group, looking at each other.

"You lot know the drill, line up," Edward commanded.

The ravens looked at Edward and moved their heads as one to look at Obsidia and back to Edward. When he said nothing further, they arranged themselves in single file and waited. Edward pulled a package of meat off the top of the heap in his cart and unwrapped the waxed craft paper.

Edward said, "Loki, bottom's up," and threw the beef in the air.

"Careful," Obsidia said, "you'll crush him."

The raven jumped up and opened its beak. The two pound bird managed to swallow a chunk of flesh and bone five times its own size. Edward tossed a second mass of beef and Loki caught it again and devoured it whole.

"How...how did it do it?," Obsidia asked in astonishment.

"They're not what they seem," Edward said. "Take a close look at them. Don't just look at them with your eyes."

Loki walked over to Obsidia and held out his feathery wings and then slowly turned in place until she had been able to examine all sides of him.

"I don't think there should be secrets in a marriage," Edward said. "That's why I need to share this with you. What do you see, my darling?," Edward softly asked.

"A raven ... with a monstrous appetite."

"No. Here, watch." He waved his hands in the air. "Reveal. Remove your disguise. Take your true form for Obsidia. Okay, on the count of three. One. Two. Three."

Obsidia saw the ravens looking uncomfortably at Edward and each other.

"Edward, perhaps the past 24 hours has been too

much a strain. Why don't we both go lie down? You'll feel better."

Edward began to feel anger rising. "I'm not crazy. I just wish you could see these as I see them."

"Darling, I know you're very attached to them, but ..."

She did not finish her sentence. The visages of the small black corvids began to inflate. The wings on nine small birds stretched and grew. Feathers turned to leather. Tiny thighs and tarsi lengthened longer than her own legs. Small arms and claws seemed to sprout from the bird's breasts. Sharp little bills drew into snouts and little beady black eyes swelled and reddened.

"My God," Obsidia screamed as she realized that the heads of all nine creatures were inclined towards her. She grabbed for Edward and pulled him closer.

"Shhh. Tell me, Obsidia. What do you see?," Edward asked.

"Dragons. I see dragons. They're hideous," Obsidia said.

Loki pulled his head back, no longer interested in showing himself to Obsidia. All of the creatures took a step back, their half expanded wings drooping with disappointment.

"It's all right," Edward said in a voice that was soothing as he stroked Obsidia's shoulder, "she's scared. She didn't mean it."

"Edward, who are you talking to?"

"The dragons, of course."

"They talk to you?," she asked, now watching her new husband with caution.

"No. They don't talk. But they are awfully smart. They can communicate. Let me introduce them to you. Once you get to know them, you won't be frightened. This big one here is Loki."

The largest of the nine dipped his head below the level of hers. Edward reached up and stroked the dragon's face, then brought his fingers beneath Loki's jaw. The dragon began to softly rumble and his tail wagged from side to side.

"He likes it when you do this," Edward said. "You try it."

Obsidia brought her hand up timidly and touched the dragon's skin. She expected it to be slimy, but it felt smooth and slick, like finely tanned leather. The animal's red eyes were closed and it was still thrumming, purring like a kitten. When she reached under his neck and scratched with her long nails, Loki's right foot began to tap up and down and the purring became louder. Obsidia could have sworn that the corners of his mouth bent upwards into a smile.

"Oh," Edward said, "you've found his sweet spot. He's a good lad. All right, Loki, let's give your brothers and sisters a chance to officially meet the missus."

Loki opened his eyes and brought his long head down on Obsidia's shoulder for a second before stepping back and out of the way. The introductions went on. Obsidia met Aphrodite, Margaret, Apollo, Ajax, Matilde, Boudicca, Helena, and Victoria with similar success. Victoria, the smallest of the brood, embraced Obsidia with her tiny arms, holding her tightly as she rocked back and forth, singing snatches of dragonsong.

Edward was beaming. "She's never done that before with me."

"Where did they come from?," she asked when Victoria finally released her.

"I don't know. The night before you arrived I went down to feed the ravens. This lot was just chicks then, I suppose, no bigger than the ravens and covered with fine downy fluff. They broke into the cage and ate them. Didn't you?," Edward said, looking at Loki, who refused to return Edward's gaze.

"Nobody else could see they were dragons," he continued. "So I kept them. I fed them and they kept growing. From the growth charts you gave me, I figure that they'll grow to be a good half ton each."

"My word," she said. "We can't tell anyone. They wouldn't understand."

"Exactly," Edward agreed.

"All right, Edward. I appreciate you're telling me this. Are there any other secrets you'd like to share?"

George Bailey turned the corner and walked over to where Obsidia and Edward were standing. "Excuse me, mum," he said, "might I have a word 'wiff the Ravenmaster?"

Edward could see Duncan's true form now.

"There still might be a thing or two more, my love," Edward answered.

Mildred Williams knocked on Art's door. "Are you awake? You're leaving for the stadium in Twickenham in 20 minutes."

"Tutire," Art mumbled from beneath his pillow.

Despite Duncan's promise, he did not get back from the dwarf's camp until almost five in the morning. He then had to maneuver past the security agent at the door of the suite to get to his bedroom, wake Founderson and get him to slip out to the balcony so he could ride off with Duncan. With all that, it was six before he finally fell asleep. He had gotten only a few hours of sleep and now his mother wanted him to go to some rugby match.

Without waiting for further acknowledgment or permission, Mildred came into her son's room.

"Can't I watch it on TV?," Art asked.

"Come on, sleepyhead, you know you promised your father you'd go with him. An American rugby team is in an exhibition match with the UK team and you and your father have got to show the flag."

She started rummaging through his closet, looking for something appropriate for him to wear.

"Your father tells me that Prince Francis and Princess

Guinevere are going to the game," Mildred said as she pulled a pair of khaki trousers and a blue buttoned-down shirt from his closet. "You're going to be sitting in the Royal Box for a couple of innings or halves or however they keep time."

"Princess Guinevere?" He sat up and took a whiff. He did not know if what he smelled was from his own exertion last night or the leather saddle or dragon musk. He was not going to risk it. He grabbed the clothes from his mother and took them into his bathroom and started a hot shower.

When he emerged, he was wearing the clothes his mother had chosen for him. She had also hung a solid navy blazer on his bedroom doorknob and a necktie.

His father was waiting for him in the living room, dressed like he always did for work, in a dark suit and a striped tie.

"Ready, sport?," his father said when he saw him.

Arthur nodded. "Let's go."

Agent Kidd and two other bodyguards were waiting in the foyer of the Presidential Apartment. Art nodded to Kidd, who did not acknowledge Art at all.

He's probably still ticked off about last night, Art thought.

"Mom's not coming?," Art asked.

The Ambassador shook his head. "No. Some friends of hers flew in last night from Boston. She's meeting them for lunch."

Art was relieved for three reasons. First, anytime his mother got near British royalty, she became a quivering mass of insecurities. Second, she wanted to play matchmaker with him and the Princess. There was as much chance of that happening as him getting elected President one day. Finally, he had stuffed the necktie she picked out for him in his dresser drawer. Now she would never know. After all, who would wear a necktie to a stadium to watch a ball game?

Art was surprised to find Mrs. Chillingsworth sitting in the back of the limousine waiting for them when they got downstairs.

"Glad you could make it, Chillingsworth," the Ambassador said as they got in.

"My pleasure, sir," she answered briskly, and opened a leather folder on her lap. "It is good to see you as always, Master Williams."

"Mrs. C, how are you?," Art said with a smile.

She reached into a small shopping bag on the seat beside her and pulled out three silk neckties and held them up, seeing which one would go best with Art's blazer. She handed him the red regimental rep stripe.

"I thought we understood that one does not meet a member of the Royal Family half-dressed," she said. "At least you're not wearing your Drowning Armada t-shirt."

Chillingsworth looked down at her leather folder once more and pulled out an envelope bearing the royal seal. "There are a few matters. First, you and Mrs. Williams have been invited to attend a Royal Ball at Buckingham Palace on June 3rd on the occasion of Princess Guinevere's new college charity. You both have been invited to a private dinner with Her Majesty and His Royal Highness earlier that evening."

"Good," the Ambassador said, "Mildred loves a good party. Although, I suppose that this is all she's going to talk about for the next few weeks."

Art was relieved that he seemed to have been left off the invitation. Then Mrs. Chillingsworth pulled out a second envelope with his name clearly written in the finest calligraphy hand.

"And you, Master Williams, have been invited to attend the Ball itself. It's a white tie affair. I don't suppose you've got your own set of tails, do you?"

"Tails? Like pin the tail on the donkey?," Art asked.

"No," she responded, not knowing whether Art was serious or not. "Formal dress. To put it in terms that you will understand, it makes a tuxedo seem like a pair of grubby dungarees. And there will be ballroom dancing."

"I know how to dance," Art said confidently.

"When I was young, if we saw someone moving the way people your age dance, we would have assumed they were having a fit and summoned a doctor." She pulled a photocopy of a newspaper clipping from her leather folder and handed it to Art.

The article was from thirty years ago. The large photograph to the side showed a woman in a tight ball gown dancing with a man wearing what Art assumed to be white tie and tails. The woman in the picture was clearly a much younger Mrs. Chillingsworth. The headline read, "Chillingsworths Sweep U.S. National Ballroom Championships Third Year in a Row."

"My late husband and I made quite a splash on the dance scene," she said, lost for a moment in nostalgia.

"You want me to take you to the dance?," Art said as he handed her back the clipping.

Chillingsworth looked over the Ambassador, who was looking out the window at the scenery.

"No, Master Williams. I am going to teach you how to dance. Remember, you're a representative of the American government. We can't have you embarrassing us or yourself, for that matter."

Art tried to get his father to intercede. "Dad, do I have to?"

"'Fraid so, son. Not preparing? Wouldn't be prudent."

Chillingsworth smiled. "Very good. Now let me give you a rundown of who's going to be in the Royal box today."

Twickenham Stadium was far larger than the Gillette Stadium where the New England Patriots played in Foxboro back home. His father's hedge fund had one of the luxury boxes at Gillette, but it was nothing compared to the suite they were ushered into. The outside glass edge of the box was lined with two wide rows of spectator seats. Inside, there were several tables where the lucky fans could sit and eat, watching the game on flat screen monitors around the room. There was also a buffet line across the back wall. Instead of hot dogs and burgers and fries, like they served in his father's box, waiters were circulating with silver trays filled with fish on crackers.

"Smoked salmon with dill on crostini," one of the waiters corrected Art when he called it fish on a cracker.

The waiter told Art that at the half there would be lamb shanks on a bed of creamed spinach with sweet potato fondant and a red currant *jus*. Art assured the man he was looking forward to it, but had no idea what either a fondant or a *jus* was.

There must have been at least fifty people in the suite, but there was no sense of crowding. His father worked the room, meeting and greeting dozens of men and women. Art was introduced to them all. A few remembered him by the name the British tabloid press had christened him with the day after his house collapsed: "Tunnel Boy".

Prince Francis was seated in the row of seats directly in front of the floor-to-ceiling glass. With so many other people present, the Prince and his father shared a much more restrained greeting.

"Your Excellency," the Prince said, offering his hand.

"Your Royal Highness," the Ambassador responded, "thank you for inviting us. It was very kind of you."

The rules of diplomatic engagement meant, however, that the Prince could be less formal with Art.

"Art, good to see you again, lad. How've you been?"

"Fine, your Royal Highness. This is all so magnificent, sir," Art said.

"Happy to have you. Are you a fan of rugby?," the Prince asked.

"No, sir. This will be my first game."

"Tell you what, when the game starts, you sit next to me here and I'll talk you through the first couple of scrums. You'll be a fanatic in no time." The Prince looked over to his right. "Gwennie, you remember Ambassador Williams and his son."

Princess Guinevere nodded at them both, but did not rise. She offered her hand to Art, who remembered to kiss it lightly. She smiled to herself. Perhaps with enough treats and rolled newspapers, he could be trained after all.

"Darling, I'm going to step off for a moment to talk to the Ambassador. Art, would you keep my seat warm while I'm gone?"

The Prince did not wait for a reply, but moved up the steps with Art's father.

Art sat next to the Princess and smiled nervously at her. Chillingsworth had reiterated to him that one does not address royalty first, one waits to be addressed. He waited. And waited. And waited.

When Guinevere decided that she had made Art feel as uncomfortable as he was going to get, she spoke to him.

"Art?"

"Yes, ma'am?"

"You might not believe it, but none of my friends at school call me 'ma'am'," the Princess said.

It was partly true. Genie Cavendish and a handful of the Princess' classmates could address her less formally. For the rest, she insisted that the royal protocol established when Queen Victoria's daughters attended boarding school be followed. To those outside her circle, she was still "ma'am."

"I'd like to think of us as friends, Art. You needn't call me that. If I can call you Art, you can call me Gwen." She rested her hand on his forearm.

Art was instantly aware of her touch. He remembered that she had left him kneeling on the floor in front of her mother's throne. He also remembered the broken promise of her kiss.

"I'd like you to think of me as your friend, ma'...
Gwen," Art said.

"Good. I wanted to apologize to you for the way that I
acted the day we met. I was simply horrible to you. I don't
blame you if you hate me."

"Hate?," Art said. "I don't think I could ever hate you."

Guinevere was pleased and little puzzled by this boy.

"I don't know if you've heard, but I'm throwing a
grand ball for a new college fund I've set up for girls in the
UK. I sent your invitation to your father's embassy. I do
hope you'll consider coming."

"I just found out this morning. I was going to RSVP
today."

"I'll put you down as a 'yes'. The first dance is going to
be a Viennese waltz. Would you be my first partner?"

Art spoke without thinking. "Yes. Of course."

"You know how to dance?," she said.

"Oh, yes," Art lied. "The Vietnamese waltz is one of
my favorite dances." Art hoped that Mrs. Chillingsworth
could teach him the Vietnamese waltz in time for the ball.

"Really?," Guinevere said with a knowing smile. "It's so
hard to find a boy who knows how to move like that.
Maybe we could cause a stir with a tango or a samba?"

"Those are good, too," Art said. "You decide. How
about right now? You tell me which one, right now."

She laughed and squeezed his arm. "Art, I didn't
realize how funny you are. Why don't I surprise you on
the dance floor?"

Art sat next to the Prince when the match started, with
Guinevere on his other side. Francis tried to explain the
game to him, how it was similar to American football and
how it was different, but Art could do little but nod.

His mind was focused on the dance floor at
Buckingham Palace. In about seven weeks he would be
dancing with a real princess in front of hundreds of

people. What if it went up on YouTube? Millions of people would see he had two left feet.

Great, Art thought. If he did not die of embarrassment on the 3rd of June, he was still going to risk death on the 23rd. He did not know which he would rather face.

There were only a few time-outs in the match and it was over in less than two hours. Art had no idea if the Americans or the Brits won. At that point, he really didn't care.

The Prince and Guinevere were the first to leave the luxury box.

The Princess made it a point to remind Art of his promise, saying, "I'm saving my first dance for you, Art."

All Art could get out as a response was a nervous, "Too."

Art was never so happy to see Mrs. Chillingsworth waiting for them in the back of the limo. Rather than taking his place next to his father, he sat on the backward facing bench next to Chillingsworth.

"Do you know how to dance the Vietnamese waltz?," Art asked her.

"The what?," she responded.

"The Vietnamese waltz. The Princess asked me to be her first dance partner at the ball."

"Master Williams, there is no 'Vietnamese' waltz."

"Are you sure?"

"Quite sure," she told him. "The people who live in Viet Nam are not known for their waltzes. There is a Viennese waltz."

"Crap. Yeah, that's the one. She also said that she was going to surprise me. It could be a tangle or a stambo. What am I going to do?"

She patted him on the hand. "Rest assured, Master Williams. We will see you through this. Perhaps our first lesson today could be on getting the names of the dances right."

26
A REINTRODUCTION IS IN ORDER

When Art took his seat in the classroom, Amanda and Dipeka were smiling at him.

"How was your weekend, mate?," Amanda asked. "Do anything special?"

"No," Art said and shrugged. "Just a boring weekend at home."

"Too right," Amanda said with a sarcastic laugh.

Dipeka brought out a copy of the London Daily Comet and unfolded the tabloid. There was a black and white picture of Art talking with the Princess at the rugby match, taken with a long telephoto lens. The portion of the photo showing Guinevere's hand on his forearm was blown up in a box to show detail. The large headline read, "Wreckless Gwen & Tunnel Boy", and the smaller one said, "Is This Yank Trying To Dig Into The Royal Family?"

"According to this paper," Dipeka said with a smile, "you're practically engaged to Princess Guinevere."

Amanda held up her copy of the paperback they had been assigned. "Arthur and Guinevere? The last time it happened it didn't turn out so well. Better luck to you this time."

While his classmates were cajoling Art, Professor Merwin spoke with the young Embassy agent. "We aren't going to be taking any breaks today and I do not wish to be disturbed. Is that understood?"

The agent nodded and took his place outside in front of the classroom door.

With the door closed and locked, Merwin wrote the words "Le Mort D'Arthur" on the blackboard behind him.

"'The Death of Arthur,'" Merwin said, turning to the class. "Thomas Malory actually starts us off before the birth of Arthur. Here's something about the author. Malory fought in France in the War of the Roses and was knighted in 1442. In 1450, he was accused and convicted of armed assault and other crimes and spent most of the 1450s in prison. He started writing this book in prison and finished it shortly before his death in 1470. What did you think of the story?"

"Pretty unbelievable," Henry said as he stood, ticking off topics from his fingertips. "A magic sword. A wizard and a witch. A hunt for the Holy Grail. A king who dies and is destined to return."

Angus stood. "Don't forget that Arthur was both father and uncle to Mordred, Morgan Le Fey's son."

"Eww," Amanda said, "I missed that part."

"Yeah," Angus said. "She put a spell on Arthur, who was her half-brother and had a baby with him."

"Sounds like a new reality show on MTV," Art said.

"Professor," Dipeka asked with a raised arm, "is there any truth to the story or is it all fiction?"

"Some of it is true," Merwin said. "Most of it was made up. The story actually takes place about 500 BCE by your calendar. That should immediately tell you that there was no hunt for the Holy Grail because the events all took place before the birth of Christ. But there was a king. There was a sword. There was a wizard. And a witch, Mr. Ying. And there was magic. The world was full of magic."

"You're pulling our legs, right?," asked Angus.

"No," said Merwin. "I know because I was there."

The class, with the exception of Art, laughed, convinced that their teacher was playing a joke on them.

"Mr. Williams, do you believe in magic?"

Art stood. "Well, I don't know." He remembered his promise to the dwarves.

"Really? After all you've been through, Mr. Williams, and you still have doubts? You faced down and killed a Sidhe, a cat-sith for the rest of you. You saved the life of a dwarf king. You heard the wailing song of the Banshees and lived to tell about it. Two nights ago, you rode on the back of a dragon. What more proof do you need?"

How did he know all of that, Art thought to himself. He looked around him. His classmates were no longer smiling, but watching him carefully.

"I don't want to talk about it," Art finally said and sat down.

"Once again," Merwin said, "a non-denial denial. That's American for 'yes'."

"What do you mean," Dipeka challenged, "that you were there?"

"Look at the back wall of the classroom and I'll explain," Merwin directed and then recited, "*Agor 'ch dendio. Agor 'ch asgre.*"

The back wall, covered with cabinets and bookshelves dissolved. There was supposed to be another classroom behind them, but that was not what was on the other side of the wall now. Art was looking out onto the central clearing of Little Vanwalanthir, the dwarf camp. All of Clan Fargrave had gathered in the clearing. Shalerunner and Duncan were dressed in polished steel armor and stood along side Barbryn. The rest of the dwarves were also dressed in their finest.

"A re-introduction is in order," the Professor said, "My name is really Merlin."

27
WRECKLESS GWEN
AND TUNNEL BOY

Guinevere walked to class in one of her moods. Genie had failed to come by this morning to get her and, as a consequence, she overslept. Her cousin had a fever of 103 and had spent the night in the nurses' infirmary. Guinevere was going to be late to class and Genie had not helped her with her hair. Why did everything bad have to happen to her?

She touched the locket underneath her shirt and its presence gave her strength. She would soon see Prince Mordred in person. She had seen to it. Her mother had demanded that she swallow her pride and apologize to Art Williams for whatever mistaken slight he had imagined. She had asked her father for a few moments with Art when he arrived so that she could express her sorrow and seek his forgiveness. It was a humbling experience. She was learning that humility left a bitter taste in her mouth. Her father was aware of her efforts and she had no doubt that he conveyed every detail back to her mother.

"I appreciate your taking time to speak with Art to

straighten everything out," the Queen had told her when they got together for dinner.

"He's actually very charming," Guinevere had told her mother deftly. "I asked him to dance the first dance of the ball with me."

"What did he say?," the Queen asked.

"What could he say?," Guinevere replied. "He was enchanted."

She could tell that her mother was pleased with her.

She had departed her life in the palace and the planning of the ball with her mother's staff on Sunday night and returned to her life of schoolwork and drudgery.

Her first class was English composition and Genie was normally her buffer with the rest of her classmates. When she walked in, a few of the girls who sat behind her were gathered around a newspaper and laughing. The Princess' sudden presence made them laugh louder and harder. One of them turned the paper over so that Guinevere could see the photo of her and Art at the rugby match.

"Wreckless Gwen and Tunnel Boy," the three girls said in unison and then burst out laughing.

Guinevere's face reddened. She grabbed the paper from them and crumbled it into a ball, then turned and stormed back out of the classroom. She looked over her shoulder and saw the woman from the Royal Protective Service following four paces behind her. Why had that woman done nothing? She had been humiliated in front of everyone and her bodyguard let it happen. If Guinevere had had her way, the three of them would have been arrested for treason and shut up the Tower of London until they were old and toothless and gray. That would serve as an example to the others.

She ignored the bell announcing that the first period had begun and went back to her room. She flung her book bag on her bed and grabbed her telephone off of her nightstand. She had memorized her mother's private number. Wherever the Queen was, this call would be routed directly to her, not to her secretary or staff. Even the Prime Minister did not have this number. The call was picked up after the first two rings.

"Gwennie, what's wrong?," the Queen asked.

"Mummy, did you see the front page of the Comet this morning?"

"Yes. I was hoping you wouldn't see that, darling."

Her eyes were beginning to water. "Do you see how they treat me? To them I'm a fifteen-year-old joke. I'm trying to change. I'm trying to do my best. It is so unfair."

"I know it is, sweetheart," the Queen said. "I wish I could tell you that I went through the same thing when I was a girl, but the press was much more restrained back then. Now, everything we do is front page gossip."

"I'm going to get my revenge on them, Mummy. I swear I will."

"Gwennie, calm down."

"I'm not going to do anything stupid. I'm going to raise a ton of money for 'Gwen's Girls', more than they could ever imagine. Daddy once told me in business that success is the best revenge. Tell them all to look out because Gwen's coming. And warn Art Williams that when the orchestra strikes up, we're not just going to take to the dance floor. For his sake, I hope he can keep up with me. He'd better be brilliant. I'm going to make all those doubters choke on their own words."

"Darling, are you going to be all right? I can't remember when you've been so upset."

Guinevere touched the locket again. She did not know if talking with her mother had calmed her down or the locket had worked some kind of influence on her, but she was beginning to feel at peace. She wiped her eyes on the sleeve of her sweater and sniffled, and then laughed softly.

"I'm okay. I just needed to talk with you. I'm sorry to bother you."

"Gwennie, you're never a bother. That's why you have this number. I wish you'd call me more often. Promise me you will, all right?"

"All right," the Princess said. "I will."

"What are you going to do right now?"

"I'm going to wash my face and go back to class."

"That's my girl," the Queen said.

28
A MATTER OF DESTINY

"Everyone follow me," Merlin said as he walked to the back of the classroom and then out into the forest clearing.

Angus, Henry, Dipeka, and Amanda seemed overwhelmed as they moved slowly. Henry extended his toe forward at the classroom's edge, like a bather testing the temperature of his bath water. Satisfied, he jumped across and landed on ground that was covered in old, fallen leaves. As if almost by instinct, the two girls clasped each other's hands as they walked out of class, relying on each other's strength. Angus was on guard, not knowing if the mob of little men and women were friend or foe. Art walked past them all and presented himself to Duncan and his father.

"Your Majesty," Art said, taking it upon himself to make the introductions, "and Dogent Shalerunner, I am pleased and humbled to introduce you to my friends. This is Henry Ying of Hong Kong, Amanda Keating of Quilpie Station, Dipeka Jaswinder of Kolkata, and the big fellow back there is Angus Wilcox of Toronto. And our teacher is Willard Merwin. Or, as he just told us, Merlin."

"This is an illusion, right?," Henry asked.

"Pulling a rabbit out of a hat is an illusion, Mr. Ying," Merlin said. "You just go along with the magician and accept his misdirection that the rabbit was not there the whole time. This is no illusion. You are in a forest about 45 miles from London."

"Class," Art continued. "This is King Duncan of Clan Fargrave and his father, the Dogent Kerr Shalerunner. Standing next to them is the Dogentess Barbryn." He turned to Duncan. "Can we make further introductions as we go?"

"Aye," Duncan said with a smile. "Let us offer you the hospitality of the King's tent. Art, you know the way, lead on."

Art entered the large tent at the center of the clearing and held the flap open.

"Enter first," Duncan directed the young people, "for you are our guests."

When they all were inside, Duncan and his father moved to the same seats they had taken early Saturday morning when Art had flown in. The rest of the class was directed to sit in the surrounding chairs. Merlin and the other dwarves who followed into the tent remained standing.

Barbryn and two other dwarf women brought in two great steaming silver samivars of fruit and herb tea.

"In our world, sixteen is old enough to enjoy a stonecutter's brew," Shalerunner started, preparing to apologize for offering nothing stronger than tea.

"But the lean half of the day is no time to be drinking like an idle man, regardless of how fair or feeble you are," Barbryn interrupted. "We respect your customs that say you're too young to drink."

Shalerunner looked at his cup of hot tea. "I'll have you know that it must be the fat half of the day somewhere on this planet."

"Yeah, its five o'clock somewhere," Angus said.

Shalerunner roared with laughter and clapped Angus on the arm. "Aye, boy. You heard him. Its five o'clock somewhere." Shalerunner motioned for them to bring him something stronger.

Barbryn glared at her husband. "But its not five o'clock here."

Shalerunner stared back at his wife and then down into his tea. "It can't get here quickly enough," he muttered.

When all the cups had been filled, Duncan rose and offered a toast. "To old friends and new; and to faith, hearth, and home."

"And confusion to the enemy," Shalerunner added and then tossed back his tea in a single swig.

"*Add buchedd*," Duncan finished.

"*Add buchedd*," the other dwarves in the tent called out and they all downed their tea.

Art and his classmates joined the toast. This brew was not the relaxing, sweet slateberry tea that Art had drunk on his prior visit. This one had a kick like a triple shot espresso.

"Merlin," Duncan said, "I think you have something to say to your class."

Merlin stepped forward. "I offer a half apology to you for my deceit. If I had told you who I truly was at the beginning of the school year, I'm sure you would have thought me mad."

"The jury's still out on that one," Angus said, then realized that his joke was met with silence and disapproving stares from the men and women gathered in the tent.

"That's quite all right, Mr. Wilcox. The situation we face is grave. Humor may prove to be a comforting refuge. I guess I should begin at the beginning."

As Merlin stepped back, he waved his hand and his clothes rearranged themselves. His bow tie was gone and his tweed jacket had lengthened into a robe.

"Don't you need a wand to do magic?," Angus asked.

Merlin turned and smiled. "There's nothing magical about a stick. The magic comes from here." He tapped his temple with his forefinger. "You first have to understand the universe.

"As I was saying in class," Merlin continued, "the fable that Thomas Malory tells contains some truths. There was a king whose name would translate in modern English as Arthur."

At the sound of his name, the dwarves in the tent repeated it, almost like a choir repeating prayer.

"Arthur *was* tricked into having a child with his half-sister, Morgana."

"I still say, 'Eww'," Amanda said.

"Let him finish," Art said.

"Morgana was a minor sorceress. I made the mistake of teaching her."

"Aye," Shalerunner said. "You taught her everything you know."

"No," Merlin shouted in a voice that boomed like a thunderclap. "I taught her everything she knows, but I did not teach her everything I know."

"Same thing," Shalerunner said with a shrug.

"There's a world of difference," Merlin replied and then turned back to his students.

"When I was born, I found that I both understood the workings of the universe and I could unloose myself in time, moving forward and backward at will."

"That's impossible," Henry said.

"Really?," Merlin answered and then faded from view. He was gone no more than ten seconds, then winked back into existence in the same place he had been standing before. "I jumped ahead in time and waited for all of you to catch up."

He went on. "After I lost the *'Llyfr Chan Chwnselau'*, a book of secrets I was using to teach Morgana, I traveled forward in time five thousand years. I had done it many times. This time, there was no future. There was no universe. Everything had ceased to be. Before my trail was cold and I was forced to drift in a void of nothingness, I slid back towards my point of departure, feeling for the spot in time when everything was destroyed. I found it. Morgana had attempted to cast the *Sillafa Chan Gwneud*, the spell of creation. Her mistake brought the universe to an end."

"If her mistake brought the universe to an end, why are we still here?," Dipeka asked.

"Very good question," Merlin said. "Because I stopped her. The world at one time was different. Man and magic lived side by side. Man and beast were on one side, magical folk, fey, and mystical creatures on the other. Arthur, you can tell them you've seen dragons."

Art looked over at Duncan who nodded his head, releasing him from his oath.

"I have," Arthur said. "I've ridden on the back of one of nine that now live in the Tower of London."

"Once the skies of Earth were thick with dragons," Merlin said.

"What happened to them?," Art asked.

"I created a pocket universe into which all the magic of the world was poured. That was the only way that man and magic could both survive."

Shalerunner pounded the arm of his stone chair with his fist. "And you sent us there, too. To be lorded over and ruled by Morgana. For five years, we've been fighting a war against her and her bastard son. A war we may very well lose. You abandoned us, Merlin," the old dwarf yelled in anger. He stood, balancing on his good leg. "I ought to take his marble cast and kick your a..."

"Father," Duncan said, interrupting the Dogent. "Enough. When Merlin contacted us from this world, we gave our oaths that we would assist him."

"Its only because the gnomes were already in Morgana's pocket and the elves were too large to bring through the rift," Shalerunner said defiantly.

Duncan urged his father to sit, agreeing with him. "There is some truth in that."

"Too much truth, I'm afraid," Merlin admitted.

"Five years?," Dipeka asked. "I thought you fought with her thousands of years ago."

Merlin nodded. "Both are true. Time in the pocket universe moves at a different rate than in yours. I wanted humanity to be able to grow and develop in case the barrier between the two worlds was ever destroyed."

"Five or twenty-five hundred," Shalerunner grumbled, "you still abandoned us."

"Before I could close the spell *and seal myself inside*," Merlin said emphasizing the last part for Shalerunner's benefit, "Morgana began an attack on me. We've been battling in the bottleneck between the two universes ever since."

"Who wins?," Angus asked.

"It's going to be a draw," Merlin said.

"How can you know?," Amanda asked.

"Because it's already happened."

"Wait," Art said. "You just told us that the battle is still raging."

"It is," Merlin said with a tone of exasperation in his voice. "On June 23rd, the bottleneck between the two worlds blows open at both ends. Beings from the other side manage to get through, including Mordred, Morgana's son. I need your help to defeat them, so that I can close it forever."

"And you know this how?," Henry asked.

"Because when I was blown out of the bottleneck into this world, it was June 23rd. I met myself. I told myself the date. Well, I will meet myself. The present me will meet the past me, which to you is the future me. I will tell me that the bottleneck will open on June 23rd. The other me will slip back 25 years in the past to rest and recuperate and prepare, which I have already done."

"How do we fit into all of this?," Art asked.

"You were there in my past, so you must be there in your future."

"That is the destiny that I spoke to you about," Duncan said to Art.

"That is why you must commence your training now," Merlin said.

"In your past, we've already had the training, right?," Henry reasoned.

"Yes," Merlin said wearily.

"So shouldn't we already be trained?," Henry followed up.

"No, it doesn't work that way, I'm afraid. You're going to have to take up arms, aided by magic."

"Why not be ready with rifles and bombs?," Angus asked.

"Bullets don't work," Art said. "I killed a witch in my basement the morning my house collapsed. Bullets didn't affect her at all."

"When Mordred and his minions come through, they will be protected by a magic that will defeat any earthly weapon," Merlin said.

"Do we have a choice?," Amanda asked.

"You do," Merlin said. "But since you were there on the 23rd, you've already made that choice."

Amanda stood up. "Well, if this is what we're meant to do, we better start doing it, right? Somebody get me a sword to fight with."

29
THE LAST NEW MOON

Guinevere had gotten the date and time of the next new moon from the Royal Astronomers at Greenwich and was now counting down the moments until she could send the locket back through.

This was to be her third and likely last message to Prince Mordred. She had sent a brief message on the new moon on March 30th, telling the Prince that the ball had been arranged. It would commence at seven o'clock London time on June 3rd. She had begged and pleaded with her mother, who had agreed to appear with her entire family, including her little brother, Prince Gregory. She had also folded a map of the area surrounding Buckingham Palace and tucked it beneath the leather pouch holding the locket.

Prince Mordred's response was just as swift as it had been the last time.

When the locket came back through to her, after several agonizing and anxious days, he gave her a message that she desperately wanted to hear.

"I am so overjoyed at the thought of holding you in my

arms," Mordred's image had told her, "if only for the lifetime of a brief song. My heart will carry each second, holding tender the memory until the day I die. Thank you for sending me the writings that you did. I must confess that I do not speak your language."

Guinevere had been shocked, because the Prince spoke with such an elegant tongue.

Mordred had then held up the article she had printed from Wikipedia on Buckingham Palace.

"However, the locket translates my feeble attempts to speak with you and to praise your beauty into your language. Unfortunately, it cannot translate the writings you sent. When our two worlds were driven apart, there was no English and the language I speak has, I'm afraid, faded into obscurity on your world. I could, however, understand the pictures you sent to me. So clear were the images. I must meet the artist who painted it. He has a talent for capturing life."

Mordred had pointed to the picture of the Palace.

"If you could give us more of these wonderful paintings of your castle and show us where the ball will be held. I want to make sure that when the rift opens between our two worlds, that it will be far enough away from your guests so that no one is injured. The last thing that I want is for the relations between us to be affected by an unintended harm. I hungrily await your response, dearest Guinevere."

The Princess had played that recording so many times that she could recite it by heart, even duplicating Mordred's continental accent.

In the three weeks since she had received that message, she had done as she was asked. There was a growing pile of photographs, diagrams, and floor plans of Buckingham Palace in the back of her closet at school. She had annotated each, with arrows and markings, laying out where the dance floor would be, the orchestra stand, and even where her family would stand before descending the garden staircase.

To simplify matters, she included the most recent official photo of the Royal family, drawing a unique symbol over the heads of herself, her mother, her father, and her little brother. She had been required to give a presentation similar to this in her public speaking class, so she felt prepared.

It had taken almost as long to do her hair and makeup as it had to arrange the pictures she wanted to show Mordred. If he was as smart as she knew he was, he would catch onto her system and would be able to understand her message.

She pictured herself standing on the edge of a lonely beach shore in the dead of night with only starlight to illuminate her way, with an empty bottle in one hand and her message in another. Soon she would toss her message and her heart into the cosmic ocean and the power of fate would drive it to Mordred's shore. That is what the locket and the doorway represented to her: her bottle and the sea.

She had made an outline this time and had the photos and diagrams she needed on her lap. As the clock neared the time when the moon was nigh, she removed the locket from around her neck and opened it. Now knowing that the locket had to translate her speech, she spoke more slowly than before.

"Good Prince Mordred, brave Prince Mordred, my heart overflows with warmth and happiness with each message we exchange. I have done as you have asked. The doorway will soon be filled with a stack of pictures that I have written on to tell you of all the events planned for June 3rd. But first, I must tell you of the numbers and symbols you will find."

She had asked her math teacher how a pre-Roman era Brit would have written numbers.

"The numbers we use were developed by the people of India and brought to Arabia," Mrs. Finnegan had told her. "That's why they're called Arabic numerals. They didn't come to our shores until about the first millennia. Before that there were Roman numerals, starting in about 43 AD."

"And before that?," Guinevere had asked Mrs. Finnegan.

"Well, ma'am, the Celts used a numbering system based on twenties. Forty-two would be 'two and two twenties'."

When Guinevere found out that ancient Brits did not have clocks or marked the hours like they did today, she gave up on trying to translate everything for Mordred. Maybe the locket could help her make it clear enough.

She held up flash cards towards the locket. On each were a numeral and a corresponding number of dots. That is how she conveyed one through twelve and an overview of how the hours are marked. Then she held up an aerial photo of the back of Buckingham Palace on to which she had drawn a rectangle on the lawn to site the dance floor.

"The dance will begin at seven o'clock when I and the girls being helped by my charity will make our entrance. I will have a dance with a boy. He means nothing to me, trust me. He's an American, after all." She paused. "They didn't have Americans back then, right? Well, he means nothing to me, in any case.

"At eight o'clock, precisely, my mother, the Queen, my father, and my little brother, will exit the back of the Palace here and will walk to the top of these steps. Its going to be well past his bedtime, so don't expect him to be a perfect angel, because he won't be. My parents will be in a receiving line. I can introduce you to my mother right then."

Guinevere put down the last aerial photo and looked at the locket. "I hope this has been helpful. There may be time for one last message after this one. Send me your response quickly."

On impulse she brought her first two fingers on her right hand to her pursed, reddened lips, and then moved them to the locket. She closed the locket and took a deep breath. What had compelled her to practically blow him a kiss?

She put the locket into the suede pouch and placed that on a stack of papers and included the flash cards with the rest. She waited for her nightstand clock to count down. When the exact hour and minute of the new moon arrived, she knocked on the little door. As it had before, the edges glowed red and it opened, spilling out a cardinal fog. She hefted all the materials that were resting on her lap through the open doorway. It closed with an immediate slam.

Guinevere kissed her fingertips again, this time knowing exactly why, and pressed them against the door.

Ufor polished the tiny doorway in his master's chambers. He was its keeper, its sworn protector. It was his duty to unload it when a message arrived. He received the glory of telling his master that the girl has sent him a response. He would also receive the pain if something were to go wrong.

He was short, even for a gnome, standing about one and a half feet tall. His head was bald and he had big, rounded ears that stood out from his head, which matched his large, bulbous nose. His brothers were all either assassins or engineers. They either dispatched the enemies of the crown or designed the great fighting machines that Mordred and the Great Golden Lady used to subdue her enemies. He lacked the aptitude for killing on either a small or grand scale.

He had served the Master and his mother for years before the Cleaving, when the humans and everything else that was not magical were ripped from this world. The Cleaving also took all the stars and the other planets, leaving just the sun and the moon. Before the separation of the mystical from the mundane, Ufor had shown his child the great backbone of the Milky Way that spread across the sky at night, but it had been five winters since that time. The night sky was dull and empty and featureless now.

There was a knocking behind the door and he answered the pattern with two raps of his knuckles. With a flash of green light, the door opened. The little room that the Master had created was filled almost to overflowing with hundreds of small sheaves covered with pictures and writing. There was a picture of a family. One them had a face that he recognized, the young girl who sent the messages to his Master in the locket. The girl looked serious in this paper portrait and had a nose that was slightly upturned in the air. There was a woman wearing a full bejeweled crown, where the girl only wore a thin tiara. On the woman's lap was a child, whose eyes and smile were both wide. Standing next to them was a tall man with graying hair, who looked like he was struggling to keep a serious expression. Ufor was sure that after the artist who created this lifelike portrait had finished, the man had burst out laughing.

The leather pouch was on the top of the pile. Ufor removed it all and the little door creaked shut with a slam. He jumped down from his workbench and ran to give the news to his master.

30
THE RIGHT HAND MAN

Prince Mordred was brooding in his throne room, spread out on one of two massive chairs placed side by side. The chair he was sitting in, the smaller one, had been assembled from bones of different creatures. The knobs on the ends of the arms of his throne were skulls of gnomes with jaws agape and open, hollow eyes. Higher up on the back of the throne were two dwarf skulls, notable for their thick foreheads and even thicker jaws. The expression on both sets of faces mirrored astonishment, an all too late understanding that life was over. The larger throne, cut from black volcanic glass, belonged to his mother and had sat empty for the past five years.

Mordred was nineteen and had a face that favored his father. King Arthur of All the Britons was no mere legend in this world. He had united all the tribes of the English isles, both man and mystic. But then Mordred also bore an amazing resemblance to his mother, Morgana. It was no shock that he favored them both since they were half-siblings, the result of a cruel spell that Morgana had cast on her brother. His genesis did not matter to Mordred. All he cared about was his future.

When Arthur learned of Mordred's true lineage, he cursed the boy and called him a monster. Arthur refused to acknowledge Mordred as his sole and rightful heir and Mordred killed him when he turned fourteen. Excalibur, the Sword of Destiny, returned to the hand of Nimue, the Lady of the Lake. With his father's sword, Mordred could have claimed the right to rule the entire world. Instead, he was forced to battle to capture each hill and hamlet. Without the aid of his mother's magic, it was proving nearly impossible.

There was one battlefield on which Mordred could not tread. During the time of the Cleaving, when Merlin had separated magic and mundane, his mother had flown alone to Birnham Forest to stop him. Merlin managed to trap them both in a kind of purgatory, halfway between the two worlds.

There was a small crack in the fabric of reality through which Mordred could look and see the ongoing struggle between the two. Watching it did little good. Time within the capsule moved slowly. Just as a tree's growth is too slow to be observed directly, so too was the action within the bottleneck. Mordred returned each month to try to gain a new perspective on the clash, but there was no way to tell who was gaining the upper hand.

His mages, his practitioners of petty magic, had calculated that, although five years had passed on Mordred's Earth, only five days had ticked by inside his mother's battlefield. The few dark incantations that his mother taught him were of no use in freeing her. Individually, the mages could do little in the way of real magic. On the other side of the bottle, where the real Earth lay, twenty-five centuries had passed.

Everyone Mordred knew, including the countless girls that he had promised to marry, was dead. Even their bones had turned to dust by now. Worse, far worse, Merlin had exiled him into a world with no other humans. His incantation had robbed men of all certainty of magic, leaving only dusty cobwebs in their memories, weak stories that might cause their young children to hide under their covers, but nothing else. His own name, he was sure, had faded. How else had the girl not recognized it?

Guinevere's name had obviously survived. Mordred was amused that his princess in the other world had been named for his father's unfaithful wife. How fitting that a new betrayer to her crown be named for an ancient traitor.

Mordred's black meditation broke as he looked around the throne room at the assembled members of his court. There were the Dark Elves, his paranoid statesmen and advisors, always playing the other races against each other to their own advantage. They seemed the most human-like of all the races. Their long pointed ears and double hearts proved them to be impostors of mankind, not their kin.

The generals of his Orc armies were also before him, large greenish brutes whose only battle tactic was to charge the enemy and overwhelm them with blunt weapons and bared canine teeth. A battle was only declared won when the armies stewed the meat off their enemies' bones.

There was also a small group of gnome engineers present, ready to demonstrate their latest technological creation. They always had to be reminded to scale back their designs so that even the stupidest of Orcs could operate them.

The last gnome chief engineer, Folwick, responded to the Prince's criticism once by saying, "Our designs are perfect. Maybe how you train your Orc armies is to blame. No offense, Sire."

"You needn't worry, Folwick," Mordred had told him. "You'll always be my right hand man."

Mordred stroked the gnome skull on the right arm of his chair. He had kept his promise to Folwick.

"We have succeeded far ahead of schedule, Sire," Dwifae said with an unctuous smile. He was a Dark Elf who acted as vizier, the Prince's chamberlain. Mordred kept Dwifae close to him in his palace, knowing the Elf had his own designs on his mother's throne.

STEPHEN CODY

"The pens are near bursting with the ten thousand prisoners you directed us to gather," Dwifae continued. "It wasn't easy to remind the Orcs in your army to take the enemy alive."

"I have seen your report," Mordred said. "How many of them are women and children?"

Dwifae looked down at the parchment. "A little over half, Sire."

"How much life force is there in a dwarf infant?," Mordred yelled, bring those attending his court to utter silence. "You scoop up fairies? I could squash them between my fingers. Where are the dwarven warriors?"

"They would rather fight to the death than surrender to you," Dwifae said cautiously.

Mordred slammed his right fist down, shattering Folwick's skull. "Their deaths on the battlefield may grant them honor and a place in the Halls of Kaldemar, but they do me no good. Go now to the wilderness and gather up five thousand of your cousins, the Thadans."

"The forest elves?," Dwifae said. "Sire, you signed a treaty of neutrality with them. They are neither aligned with the dwarves or with you."

"The time for neutrality is over. Since they have not chosen to side with us, they have proven they are our enemy. Or would you rather I had my generals sweep into the desert and pick up five thousand of your Oreme brothers?"

Mordred watched Dwifae to see if anger flickered across his face. For someone whose people lived in a desert, the Dark Elves had hearts made of ice. Mordred toyed with the idea for a second as he looked at Dwifae. The Oreme, the Dark Elves, were tall and almost painfully thin. Physically, they were no match for the Orc's massive strength and size. But they were cunning and cruel. Since time had begun to be measured, they had not lost a war. Mordred decided that he would rather have the forest elves as his enemy than Dwifae's people.

"We will burn the forests to the ground, if we must, Sire," Dwifae said finally. "I swear to you that five thousand Thadans will soon fill your dungeons."

Ufor ran into the throne room.

"Sire," he said not waiting on any formality or recognition, "the girl has sent a reply. It awaits you in your chambers."

Mordred stood. "Dwifae, Vabur, come with me. The rest of you, leave my sight. You all disgust me."

Mordred walked quickly down the stone hallway to his quarters, followed by his vizier and his highest-ranking Orc general. The room was lit by dozens of large lamp wicks, which gave the air an oily, black taste.

Ufor arranged the items on the table for Mordred's review.

The suede leather pouch was there and he would attend to it soon enough. It took all of Mordred's patience not to call Guinevere an idiot girl. She was ready to sacrifice the safety of her people and her world for a few empty promises. She had included a picture of herself and whom Mordred assumed was her family. The Prince ran his finger over her face, his long nail scratching the photo paper's plastic coating. In the proper light, she was companionable enough, Mordred thought, if only she could be taught to keep her mouth shut. Still, she was young and presentable and, most of all, human, something he could not say about any of the females in his world.

Ufor had climbed up on a bench on the opposite side of the table to assist his master as he was going through the pages that had just arrived.

"Very beautiful," Mordred said, studying the picture as Dwifae and Vabur looked over his shoulder. "This will do quite nicely."

"The girl is lovely and seems quite smitten with you, my Lord," Ufor said.

"Not the girl, fool, the infant. We can hasten the reuniting of our two worlds if I can perform the *Chrau*

Blentyn Breneen. The missing ingredient is the blood of a human infant king."

"Is the child their king?," Ufor asked.

"He will be instantly upon the death of his mother, their Queen."

"How will we know when his mother is dead, Sire?," Ufor asked.

Although Ufor was a middle-aged gnome with a child of his own, Mordred rubbed his head as one might soothe a pup.

"Because, my little fool," Mordred said, smiling, "we are going to kill her before we return here with the child."

Mordred's mood changed abruptly. He wheeled about and handed the sheaf of papers to Dwifae.

"Put our cleverest gnomes to work. Have them design a practice area that directly duplicates the back of the girl's palace and gardens. We will develop a battle plan accounting for each moment when we are in the other world. We will meet their Queen and take her off her guard, then strike. Our objectives will be to kidnap the baby and kill the Queen.

"You know how much energy we will be able to generate. Figure out the best and largest possible force we can take through the rift. Time to employ your cunning at its best, Dwifae," Mordred said with a wry smile. "I known you've always wanted to kill a queen. Here's a chance to do it and be rewarded handsomely for it at the same time."

Mordred hefted the leather pouch containing the liquid locket before handing it to Ufor. "Have my scribes write a new speech for me to say to the girl. Make sure that I sound even more enraptured by her beauty. This should be the last time I have to speak with her, thank the Maker. Tell them I need to sound even more..." Mordred struggled to find the right word.

"Sincere, Sire?," Ufor questioned.

"Precisely, fool. Let it ooze with sincerity."

31
THE METEOR HAMMER

Henry said, "Professor, I have something I want to show you." He held up five heavy black canvas duffle bags. "Its that thing I told you about the other day."

Merlin nodded and muttered the incantation and the back wall of the classroom dissolved. They were not in the middle of Little Vanwalanthir, but on the weapons range to the east of camp.

They had been going at this for three weeks now, and Art was beginning to feel weary. He was pleased when he first heard that Shalerunner would be training them. He knew he could outpace an old man. He was wrong. Once the cast came off his foot, Shalerunner proved to be more driven and more demanding than any Marine Corps drill sergeant had ever been to a platoon of raw recruits.

Shalerunner was impatiently waiting for them to arrive. "Merlin, did you let them sleep in? They've wasted half the day."

"Kerr," Merlin said, "it's only eight-thirty in the morning. We're half an hour early. Mr. Ying is going to give us a demonstration of something that may be useful.

A different kind of weapon."

"New weapon?," Shalerunner sputtered. "A true warrior uses a sword," he said with a nod to Art and Amanda. "Jaswinder's proved to be the master of the bow and Wilcox can handle two bloody axes at the same time. There's no need for anything new."

"I don't think I'll ever be a good swordsman," Henry said.

"I promised Merlin I'd make you deadly," Shalerunner said.

"I'm more concerned about being dead," Henry answered. "I don't have time to get to be even good. But I did learn to use this a few years ago when I spent a summer with my great uncle in China."

Henry reached into one of the duffle bags and pulled out a canvas sack. He opened the drawstring top and began pulling out yards of a thick, flexible cord.

"So," Amanda said, "you're going use a whip, eh? Very Indiana Jones of you. All you need is a Stetson hat and two days of beard stubble."

"A whip?," Shalerunner yelled. "You're going to take on Mordred's army with a whip? They'd go through you before you could draw it back. Let's see how your whip fares against my bastard sword."

The old man reached over his shoulder and drew a long sword from the scabbard strapped to his back. He gripped the pommel of the sword in both hands. The blade was three feet long, almost as tall as the former king. It was ugly and battle tested, a lot like Shalerunner, Art thought.

"C'mon," Shalerunner commanded, "whip me. Whip me good. Or are you afraid I'll show you up?"

"I don't want to hurt you," Henry said as he reached into the sack.

"You should worry about yourself. Best me," Shalerunner said, "and you can take your toy into battle."

Henry looked over to Merlin. "I don't want him to get hurt."

Merlin smiled. "It would be hard for you to seriously injure a dwarf, even one as old as Kerr." He raised his hand and waved it towards Henry. "This is your first time fighting with real weapons. I'll make sure you won't get hurt."

"What about him?," Henry asked.

"He won't get hurt," Merlin answered as he stepped aside, "much."

Art figured that there was at least fifteen feet of cord coiled at Henry's feet. At the end of the rope was a ball made of cast bronze. It looked like a small round pumpkin. Henry swung the ball quickly in a circle.

"What is that thing?," Amanda shouted to Henry over the sound the cord made as it cut through the air.

"A meteor hammer," Henry said, "a weapon of ancient China."

"Maybe if you fanned me with that thing, I'd catch my death of cold," Shalerunner said and lowered his sword.

Henry could tell that old man had no idea of the capability of the hammer. He changed the momentum and swung the hammer, sending the ball squarely into Shalerunner's chest. It knocked the wind out of him, making him gasp for breath. Henry switched hands, rotating the other side of the chain. With a snap of his wrist, he made the coil wrap securely around Shalerunner's sword. Henry tugged and the sword was pulled free from the old man's grasp. It spun once high in the air and plunged blade first deep into the soil.

When he could finally speak, Shalerunner breathlessly said, "I wasn't ready. Let's go again."

"But you said ...," Henry protested.

"I know what I said. But the rules changed. There are no rules on a battlefield." Shalerunner jogged ten yards and pulled his blade from the soft earth. "On three. One. Two."

The old man started to charge Henry, trying to get inside the diameter of the hammer's arc.

"Three," Shalerunner said with a devious laugh, figuring that he was now too close to Henry.

Henry was ready. At the first sign of the Dogent's feint towards him, he reeled in the line just as the cord reached Shalerunner's head. The bronze pumpkin was pulled in, smacking the old man on the back of the head from behind.

Shalerunner shook off his new concussion and brought his sword up, trying to cut the line as it flew by. The cloth sleeve actually covered a metal chain inside. The fabric was uncut. Henry pulled the hammer back to him and Shalerunner was able to advance two steps. By then, the hammer was airborne again, this time sweeping low. The chain caught its target at the ankles and the meteor bound Shalerunner's feet together. The old man fell face first into the dirt.

Henry rushed forward and freed his battle coach. "So can I use this?," he asked the Dogent.

There was a bruise underneath the old man's eye and his hands were bleeding from the force with which the sword had been ripped from him. He rejected offers of help to pull him to his feet.

"We'll talk about it later," was the only answer he would give.

Shalerunner limped off to the edge of the training field to a large water cask, where he pulled off the lid and plunged his head inside. Then he called over to Kakdon, the camp's weaponsmith, who had watched the match between Henry and the Dogent with amusement.

In a low voice, he asked Kakdon, "Do you think you could make me one of those things."

"Aye," Kakdon said. "At least the metal parts. If you want a cloth that can't be cut by blade, you'd better talk to Merlin. That's powerful magic."

Henry's classmates crowded around him.

"Well done, Mr. Ying," Merlin said.

"Where did you get this?," Dipeka asked.

"This one is a new old weapon," Henry said. "The chain inside the fabric is titanium, much stronger and lighter than iron. A Kevlar sleeve protects the titanium. The sharpest blade will not be able to cut or tear it."

Art felt the weight of the ball-shaped hammer and understood what it could do at high speed. He could see why Shalerunner was limping.

"Hey," Angus said, "how come you never told me you were a lean, mean, killing machine?"

Henry felt a little embarrassed. "My great uncle learned it from a group of Shaolin monks before the Revolution. He taught it to me when I visited home two summers ago. I learned to use it as a favor to my great uncle, who wanted the knowledge of it to be passed down to future generations." He looked over at Merlin. "May I show them what else I brought?"

"By all means," their teacher said.

Nobnocket hoped that Prince Mordred would be pleased. He had replaced Folwick as the Prince's chief engineer. Fifty gnome engineers had examined the pictures of the human female's palace and listened to her speaking through the locket. They assumed that the human males in the photographs were approximately the same height as the Prince. With that, they were able to calculate the dimensions of the back of the palace and the gardens.

A suitable meadow was found and the serfs toiling the land were thrown off of it. A thousand lumbermen, carpenters, and joiners toiled ceaselessly to construct the gnome's design. Painters had decorated the wooden sheeting so that it looked like stone. Captive Thadans were brought in to coax rapid growth from young trees planted around the space so that the forest surrounding the staging area was an exact duplicate of one shown in the pictures. He had made all of it in six days, and Nobnocket knew that it was good.

The engineer looked out to the west and saw a cloud of dust rising from behind a far hill. The Prince and his army were coming.

"Sound the alarm," he said. "The Prince will be here in moments."

The workers present finished their tasks and rushed to assemble in lines to greet the son of their ruler. Nobnocket put on his red woolen coat, the symbol of his office as chief engineer and smiled as the multitude swept towards him. He fell to his knees as the Prince's horse neared him. Mordred dismounted and towered over Nobnocket.

"Sire, we have duplicated the area where the girl's ball will take place."

"Show me," the Prince commanded.

They walked to the steps leading to a platform that ran the length of the wooden wall they had constructed. There was a working door at the center of the wall, where the girl indicated that her mother, father, and brother would exit the palace. All the other features were painted to fool the eye into thinking that there were actual doors and windows. Below the steps was a wooden platform on which people could dance, surrounded by a number of round tables and chairs. Nobnocket even constructed a raised venue for where the orchestra would play.

"What to you think?," Mordred asked his vizier.

Dwifae studied the area before giving his answer. "I am constantly amazed with gnome ingenuity. One would think that with brains that small, they would not be able to remember what they had for breakfast, yet they design and build the most fantastical devices."

Nobnocket bowed deeply, more to hide the scowl in his face. That condescending Elf, he thought. One day, he would have his brother, Rockpocket, slip into Dwifae's bedchamber in the dead of night and put a few drops of tincture of monk's hood in his ear. It would not kill him, but it would surely drive him mad. Nobnocket would bide his time. He knew what had happened to Folwick and he had no desire for his skull to become part of the castle's furnishings.

"Thank you, your Eminence," Nobnocket said on rising, a stiff smile on his face. "We gnomes live to serve."

"All right," Mordred said, "the stage is set. What's your battle plan, Dwifae?"

"Sire, we will be able to pry open the rift for only about twenty-three minutes with the energy we have available to us. If you were to go alone, we would be able to give you several days. But with the force necessary to carry out the mission, the time will be much shorter."

"Can't we just sacrifice more dwarfs and Thadans?," Mordred asked as they walked to the dance floor mock-up.

"We could sire, but we reach a point where each hundred new lives grants us only a few more seconds. Besides, if the goal is to enter the human world, take the child, kill its mother, and return here to perform the rite, it does not make sense to linger too long in that world."

Mordred nodded. "I suppose you're right. Walk me through the mission as you see it."

Dwifae and the Prince moved to the edge of the forest that had been landscaped around the meadow.

"We will be able to have the rift open here, in these woods. We will actually open several small rifts, with each separate unit taking its own place and hiding until called out."

Dwifae pointed to a small area enclosed by a wooden wall.

"That appears to be the child's playground. You will enter there. The walls will hide your arrival. I would expect that young humans haven't changed that much in two and a half millennia. They will be sneaking off into the cover of the forest to ... How shall I put it? Be alone with each other. You can drift back to the dance and make your way over to the Princess."

They walked the path between the tiny playground and

the dance floor.

"Here, Sire, you will meet the Princess. It will be approximately five minutes until her mother is scheduled to appear at the top of those steps. You will have those five minutes to gain her trust and to make her fall in love with you. The locket has done much of the work for you already. By the way, you have to record your response to her tonight and we will send it back through the doorway."

Mordred laughed. "Even without the locket, I could make her fall in love with me in two minutes. Go on."

Dwifae raised an eyebrow, knowing that the Prince's confidence was perhaps unwarranted.

"The girl will introduce you to her mother and her family. When you are close enough to the child, you will grab it. You must neutralize anyone who is a threat around you and you must kill the Queen. When the twenty-three minutes expire, you will be pulled back into the rift and will return here, regardless of wherever you happen to be."

"And the child?," Mordred asked.

"So long as it is held by someone who crossed the rift, he will be pulled back as well."

Having seen the broad strokes of the plan, the Prince was satisfied. "Once I get the child, can we close the rift early?"

Dwifae shook his head. "No, Sire, the rift will open once to deliver us, close, and then open again to pull us back. Once we begin, the timing cannot be altered."

"We? You make it sound as if you are going with us."

"I had planned to, Sire. I cannot send you so far into that world without someone to protect you nearby. With a little effort, I can be made to look passably human, at least for a while."

He pointed to the contingent of Orcs that had accompanied them. They stood and scratched themselves, or stared off vaguely into space. For most of them, their vocabularies consisted of little more than their understanding of the words "kill" and "stop".

"They cannot pass as human. But twenty of them will be hiding in the woods and will move forward on the people at the dance. Most of those attending the dance will be unarmed. They will flee and the confusion will slow the response of the Queen's army and protectors. We will also have cover from the air."

Dwifae stuck two bony fingers in his mouth and blew, letting loose a high-pitched screech of a whistle. From over the hill, six winged creatures took flight climbing sharply into the air. The sun was behind them as they flew. Mordred squinted.

"Dragons?," Mordred said in delight. "You brought the dragons over to our side?"

"Sadly, no, Sire. They remain as stubborn in their opposition to you as the dwarves."

"What are they then?," Mordred said, just as he got a good look at them. "Oh. You know how I feel about those creatures."

"Manticores? Yes, Sire. But the Orcs can only move so quickly. They are brutal, but not fast. I feel we need these in order to succeed."

The six riders set down ten yards in front of where Mordred and Dwifae stood. Mordred tried to tamp down his revulsion at the sight of the winged mounts. Each had the body and paws of a red-furred lion, but was large enough to carry two riders with ease. Each had a great flowing mane on its head that fully framed its face. It was the face that made Mordred uneasy.

He and his mother were the only humans that had been exiled to this world by Merlin. However, they were not the only things with human faces. From chin to forehead, the manticores looked like old men. They were stupid creatures, no smarter than a pig or a horse. It was the combination of a small sliver of humanity and their servile beastly nature that repulsed him.

"There's one more thing, Sire," Dwifae said with a tone

of reluctance. "You're going to have to learn to ride one of them."

"Ride?," Mordred exclaimed sharply. "Why?"

"Sire, after you take the child, the safest place for you to be would be far from their forces and their weapons until the rift reopens. As the Orcs charge and the people scatter, one of the riders will swoop down and pick you and the boy up."

"How safe will we be?"

Dwifae smiled. "Very safe, Sire. There are no dragons in their world. We can easily handle anything mechanical."

Mordred smiled at Dwifae. "I see you have anticipated every contingency. We are very pleased."

Dwifae led him around the back of the wooden wall. There was a village of tents.

"Sire," Dwifae said as he led Mordred into the largest tent that bore the Arthurian crest on its side, "your tailors await. They have finished the costume you will be wearing when you meet Princess Guinevere."

"I heard of and interesting practice that goes on in the lands south of here. It's called a 'harem.' It's a place where the many wives of a ruler are kept. When our worlds are reunited and my mother and I rule them both, I should like a harem of my own."

Henry looked at Art and Angus excitedly. "Gentlemen, do you remember when I took you to that shop to be fitted for your rented suits?"

"Yeah," Art said, "so?"

"They took a lot more measurements than they had to fit you for a tux."

"I thought that guy was getting a little too adventurous with his measuring tape," Angus said.

"My fault," Henry said. "I needed all of those measurements so that I could have these made."

He opened the duffle bag with the name "Ying"

written on one side followed by several Chinese letters. Each of the students had their names written on the side of one of the bags. Henry pulled out what looked like a set of black coveralls.

"You got us leotards?," Art said. "This isn't a ballet dance."

"No," Henry said, frustrated that they did not understand. He stepped forward and encouraged his classmates to touch the fabric garment in this hand. "Its outer shell is made from carbon nanofibers and its inner lining is made from Kevlar. It has an underlayment that disperses force energy over a wide area."

"What's that supposed to mean?," Amanda asked.

"It means that it can resist anything short of a cannonball," Angus said. "I've read about stuff like this. It can't be burnt. It can't be cut. It's supposed to be about five years away from being put into use. How did you get this?"

"I told you once that my father has a factory in China that makes advanced fabrics. Professor Merlin came with me to China last weekend. He persuaded my father to help."

"Put a spell on him and his factory, no doubt," Dipeka said.

Merlin smiled. "There are many forms of persuasion. I just happened to find the right ones."

Henry reached into his duffle bag and pulled out what looked like a hard black plastic breastplate.

"Carbon nanotube armor. That stuff we wore in France gave me the idea. It weighed about thirty-five kilos and it was hot, even on a cold day. For someone Angus' size, this stuff is still only about eight kilos. Its light and it's cool."

"So, you had a set made for each of the boys, eh?," Amanda said. "What about us sheilas? We didn't give you our measurements."

"True, for that I had to rely on Chinese intelligence."

"What," Dipeka said with outrage, "you had your government spy on us?"

Henry laughed. "Not that Chinese intelligence. My Chinese intelligence. I called your mothers and asked for the name of your dressmakers. You both said you were having something custom made for the Princess' ball. They gave me your measurements."

Amanda scolded him. "Mate, I consider that to be a violation of my privacy."

"If I hadn't," Henry said as he picked up one of the duffels and handed it to her. "I couldn't have made this for you. I want to make sure we all get through this."

Amanda pulled back the zipper and poked around inside, finding her own bodysuit, armor, gloves, and even boots and a helmet.

"It's really bonzer, Henry," Amanda said with a smile. "Thanks, heaps."

"Why don't we all try them on now," Henry said.

"Here?," Dipeka said. "There's no place to change."

"We have to be ready at a moment's notice," Henry said. "We can't spend the twenty-third of June geared for battle. Our secret will slip out."

Amanda looked at Henry through narrowed eyes. "Just when you do something special and nice, you have to go off and act like a stupid boy. You'd like to see us change out here, wouldn't you?"

"That's not what I meant," Henry stammered.

"Let me be of some assistance, Mr. Ying," Merlin said. "You're right, you can't walk around with a bag filled with armor, much less your weapons. I have conjured up a solution."

Merlin reached into the pocket of his robe and pulled out five small jewelry boxes. He took care in sorting them out, handing one to each of his students. Inside were five high school class rings.

"Students don't usually get theirs until the end of their junior year, but I had to find an inconspicuous way for you to be able to change into your armor. Slip the ring on your right hand. Then I want you to press the center stone with your left hand three times quickly and then hold it."

"Hold it for how long, Professor?," Art asked.

"You will know, Mr. Williams. On the count of three. One. Two. Three."

Each of them did as they were told, holding the white diamond on the face of their ring. The air around them began to swirl rapidly and darken.

Art felt like he had been hit by an electrical shock and his vision went dark for a second. He moved to touch his head, but felt a helmet through a gloved hand. There was a tinted shield across his face. His sword was now firmly in his right hand.

Art looked over at the others. All of them were no longer in their street clothes, but were wearing the same style of armor. Dipeka had her bow in her hand and Amanda held her sword. Angus held a large axe in each hand.

"This is fantastic," Angus yelled, although the helmet muffled his voice.

"Two things," Merlin said, whose voice could be clearly heard. "Only you can activate or deactivate your suits by pressing your rings. If anyone else tries, the ring will know. The rings have a range of about fifty miles, so you don't always have to have your armor bags with you, but it has to be relatively close."

"A few pointers," Henry said. His voice was clear. "The helmets have a radio comm system so we can keep in touch. And don't worry about washing them."

"They're going to get pretty grody after just one wearing," Amanda said.

"Not to worry, Ms. Keating," Merlin said. "When the suits are deactivated, they clean themselves. The next time you put them on, they will be as fresh as they are today."

They all touched their rings again and the armor vanished, replaced by the clothes they were wearing before.

Shalerunner walked over to the group. Art noticed that the swelling beneath his eye had already started to heal. He suspected the only thing that really got hurt was the old man's pride.

"If you're through goofing off," Shalerunner said. "I've got a five mile stretch of pavement I want to introduce you to. Let's go, double time!"

32
VOICES OF SPRING

Art dragged himself into his room at the Tower Hotel and threw himself on his bed. He was exhausted.

After their five-mile run, they continued with their weapon training, this time wearing their new armor. Art felt the back of his ring with his thumb. The ability to summon the armor with the ring was an amazing bit of magic, the first one that he had been able to keep. He did not like jewelry normally. The ring felt heavy on his hand, but he was certain that he would get used to it.

Art knocked his shoes off his feet with his toes. He did not even have the energy to sit up and loosen the laces. It was 3:45. From the first, Mrs. Chillingsworth scheduled the lessons so that she would be over at six in the evening. Art had quickly agreed, since it meant that he would be able to get another half hour's rest after his training with the dwarves, instead of being hustled off to some dance studio. He set his alarm for five-thirty and quickly dropped off to sleep.

The next thing he remembered was being shaken by his shoulder.

"Hey, sport, Chillingsworth's here," his father said. For once he had come home early from the Embassy. He got a whiff of his son. "Why don't you wash up and change your shirt? I'll tell her you'll be right out."

Art splashed water on his face to wake himself up and grabbed a new shirt from his closet. He had intended to wake up early and shower, but had slept through his alarm.

As they had done every afternoon for weeks, the hotel staff had cleared away the furniture from the patio, giving them ample room to practice. This lesson was going to be a bit more crowded. His mother was on the patio, but she was not the only one.

"There you are, dear," Mildred Williams said as he stepped out. "Mrs. Chillingsworth suggested that you might enjoy practice with someone more your own age."

Standing next to his mother were Angus, Dipeka, Henry, and Amanda. Art looked over to the side and saw that two of the tables were still out, set for dinner. The first table was empty. At the second were all of his classmates' mothers. Art was introduced to each of them and could see where each of his friends got their personality and looks.

Mrs. Wilcox, Angus' mother, was almost as tall as he was. She seemed a little reserved, which was how Angus struck him, at least until Art got to know him. Henry's mother was tiny in comparison to Mrs. Wilcox, but she carried herself with an easy grace.

Amanda's mother was just as blonde and had a sun-freckled face and a broad smile. She took Art's offered hand and shook it with obvious delight. "My Amanda's spoken quite highly of you, Art. Amanda and I are spending August at our place in Australia. You're welcome to come visit us anytime."

Mrs. Jaswinder was a stunning beauty with coal black hair and high cheekbones. Art's father had once advised him that if he wanted to know what a girl was going to look like in twenty years, look at her mother. If that were true, Art contemplated, Dipeka would still be breathtaking for decades to come.

"Master Williams and Miss Jaswinder here and Master Wilcox and Miss Keating there," Mrs. Chillingsworth directed. "Master Ying, watch and learn. You'll get your chance soon enough."

The two couples took their places on the floor.

"The Viennese waltz is perhaps the most graceful and elegant of all the ballroom dances," Mrs. Chillingsworth continued. "Buckingham Palace was kind enough to provide me with a list of the dances and the Viennese waltz will be the first dance of the evening. You will not be expected to dance every dance, but you will be expected to dance this first one."

Chillingsworth moved about, repositioning the two couples. Art felt a little more comfortable, having practiced with Mrs. C. for the last three weeks. It would be nice he thought, to try it with someone his own age.

"We will walk through this without the music first. When we begin, you each open to the side. Right side for boys, left side for girls. The gentlemen make a graceful bow and the ladies answer with a polite curtsy. Let's try that, shall we?"

Art's moves were more polished and precise, but only because he had been practicing. Angus was going to have to pay attention. This was one physical exercise that he could not just barrel through.

"Very nice," Chillingsworth said. "Men, now step to your partners. Place your right hand on her left shoulder blade lightly. Ladies, rest you hand on his upper arm, ring finger and pinkie extended."

Dipeka flowed into Art's arms as light as a spring breeze.

Amanda swatted at Angus' chest with her hand. "My shoulder blade isn't down there."

"Sorry," Angus said, suddenly aware that Amanda's mother, his own, Mrs. Chillingsworth, and the rest were staring at him with disapproval. He blushed. "Sorry. Force of habit."

"It's all right. But don't let it happen again, or I'll break your arm," Amanda said.

Art was certain that she meant it.

"You are supposed to be a gentlemen, Master Wilcox," Chillingsworth said. "Think of yourself as a chivalrous knight. Would a knight put his hand on the ... hindquarters of a lady of the court?"

"No," Angus said in a low voice.

"It would be beneath him. It is beneath you. Let's move on," Chillingsworth said. "You're going to do a simple box step. Men, step forward on your left, ladies backward on your right. Then step to the man's right, the lady's left, then men step back and the women step forward. Again, step to the man's right and the lady's left and you should be back where you started. Understand?"

Both Art and Dipeka nodded confidently, but Angus looked as if he was struggling with the concept. He tried to work it out in his head, making little half gestures with his body.

Chillingsworth saw him struggle. "Your mother tells me that you're a football player. If you don't tense up, it's no harder than a football play. Imagine it as a short down-and-out with a reverse."

Angus smiled. "You're a football fan?"

"My late husband was. We never missed a Baltimore Colts game when we were stationed in D.C.," Chillingsworth said kindly. "All right, we're going to walk through it. Ready? One, two, three. One, two, three. One, two, three. One, two, three. And you're back where you started. Very good."

Although Art was supposed to lead, he and Dipeka moved effortlessly together. Angus started off with a confused stutter step, but then corrected, eventually falling into rhythm.

"Very good," Chillingsworth said and put her hand on

a portable CD player. "Now we're going to try it with music. The first song they will be playing is Johann Strauss' 'Voices of Spring'. Keep dancing until I tell you to stop."

The music began to play. It was not the dull music that Art had been practicing to before with Chillingsworth. Played by a real symphony, this would be a joy to dance to, he thought. Although he was supposed to look away from his partner, he could not help but to steal a glance at Dipeka. She caught him more than once looking at her.

"Hold your position," she whispered. "If you're less than perfect, I'm sure that Wreckless Gwen will have your head."

"She's not that bad," Art answered, still able to keep in perfect rhythm, "once you get to know her. I'll introduce you at the ball."

"I'm looking forward to it," Dipeka said and turned her head as they swung around to face Mrs. Chillingsworth.

The song ended.

"Very good. Master Ying, you take Master Wilcox's place and Master Wilcox join Miss Jaswinder. You sit out the next dance, Master Williams."

As the two couples started 'Voices of Spring' again, Art sat down at the table next to Mrs. Jaswinder and poured himself a glass of water.

"Honey," his mom said, beaming, "you and Dipeka looked radiant out on the dance floor."

"Yes," Mrs. Jaswinder said. "She is quite graceful. You are very good, too, Art."

"Thank you, ma'am," Art said. "They're both very graceful. Both Amanda and Dipeka."

Mrs. Keating heard him and gave Art a smile.

The lesson continued to nearly eleven, interrupted briefly by a light dinner served by the embassy chef. By then, the exertions of the day began to catch up with all of them. They started making little mistakes and stepping on each other's toes.

"I think we've made excellent progress tonight," Chillingsworth said, congratulating them all. "We'll get together again in two nights. See you then."

Art walked his friends to the door, but was happy to see them leave. He was bone tired. But there was one thing he had to do before going to sleep.

He stepped into his bathroom and closed the door. Art squeezed the diamond on his class ring and his tech armor suddenly appeared. He squeezed his ring again and it disappeared. He did it twice more.

This, he thought, was never going to get old.

33
THE PRICE OF WISHES

Guinevere was awakened just before midnight, but she did not mind. There was a familiar knocking coming from her top dresser drawer and she anxiously flew to it. She pulled the little doorframe from beneath her clothes, careful this time not to send her things flying into the air. Prince Mordred had answered her message.

She set the door on top of her dresser and answered its knock with her own. It opened as always. She retrieved the small leather pouch and saw there was something else inside the little room, a gold picture frame. When she brought it out, she saw that it was a small oil portrait of her seated on a chair that was not quite a throne, but had throne-like qualities. Standing behind her in the portrait was Mordred. Her heart started to melt when she thought of all the trouble he had gone through for her. It was too much to expect that he had painted it himself, but she appreciated the gesture.

When she remembered she was holding the leather bag in her hand, she quickly opened it and poured its contents into her palm once more. When the locket formed this time, the fifteen diamonds were now quite large. Perhaps, she thought, it was a sign of how much his affection for her had grown. When the chain solidified, she opened the face of the locket hurriedly. The image of Prince Mordred appeared suspended in the air above her palm. He was dressed differently.

"Dearest Guinevere. I was overjoyed to receive your last message. With your brilliant teaching, I know how I will act when I cross the rift and get to finally meet your parents. I know where you get your beauty. I am sure that your mother is as benevolent as she is beautiful. I also had my tailors examine the images you sent me. From that, they were able to create this. I hope it is to your liking."

Mordred turned so that she could see both his front and back. She could not believe it. Somehow, they had managed to put together a full set of white tie and tails. The black cutaway jacket was perfect and the ebony trousers looked as if they had been run up on Savile Row. Mordred wore a wide ribbon sash across his chest under his jacket, but Guinevere could not tell what color it was. It was a symbol of royalty, like the one that her mother would be wearing. A small medal hung from a ribbon around Mordred's neck, dropping just below his white bow tie. Guinevere made a mental note to tell him how elegant he looked in her next message.

"Everything has been arranged" Mordred continued. "I will be able to cross the rift just before eight o'clock your time. We will only have twenty-three minutes before I must return. I want to meet not just your mother, but your father and your little brother, as well. I cannot speak to the customs of your people, but honor demands that I meet your entire family." He paused. "Not only for diplomacy's sake, but for the sake of my intense feelings for you."

Guinevere covered her mouth with her free hand. He had intense feelings for her.

"I must ask that you wear the locket when I meet your

family. I will not be able to speak with them directly, but with the locket, you will be able to translate for us."

Us, Guinevere thought. We are now an "us".

"It saddens me to tell you that this will have to be our last communication until I see you at the ball. The battle between my mother and the evil wizard has grown so intense lately that the stray magic will prevent us from communicating. But fear not, my beauty, nothing will keep me being by your side on that fateful night. I will rip open the fabric of space and time with my teeth if I must just to be with you for a few precious seconds. *Adieu*, Guinevere, *adieu*."

The Princess fell back onto her bed, clutching the locket to her chest. If she died right now, she would be the happiest girl on Earth. No, check that, she thought. If she died after meeting Prince Mordred, she would be the happiest girl on two Earths.

"Obsidia," Edward called out. "I'm not feeling well."

Obsidia felt for the light switch on the nightstand. She flicked it on and turned over in bed. Her husband, her beautiful husband, was not just sick. He appeared to be dying. The skin on his face had gone slack and was wrinkled. His dark full hair was coming out in patches. To her horror, Edward's teeth were falling out and blood oozed from the corner of his mouth.

"My dear Lord!," she cried. "We've got to get you to hospital." She felt his pulse. It was weak and thready. She reached over him to get to the phone on his nightstand, but he grabbed onto her wrist.

"No. There is nothing that doctors can do for me. Take me to the Tower."

"Edward, this is serious. You need medical attention."

"No," he repeated. "I need to go to the Tower. I need to see the dragons. Have them bring the car around. Please, my love."

Obsidia did not know why he needed to see the dragons, but against her better judgment, she called downstairs and asked that the valet have her car at the door in three minutes.

This was supposed to be the first night of their getaway honeymoon. She had resisted the idea of leaving the Tower until they could arrange their trip, but she allowed Edward to talk her into a single night of luxury in the Tower Hotel before they were to board a flight at Heathrow Airport for a week on the Spanish Riviera.

Obsidia was able to change into a pair of dungarees but was only able to get Edward into his bathrobe. She put his weight on her and they moved to the elevator. He closed his eyes and leaned against the wall as they descended towards the lobby.

"Edward, stay with me," Obsidia said.

"I'm with you, my love. I'm just resting my eyes."

The car was running in the driveway and she put Edward into the passenger seat, bypassing the valet's outstretched hand that was waiting for a tip. Next time, she thought, not now.

She bolted down the driveway, screeching onto the street. Several cars had to brake hard to keep from hitting her. She came down the Tower's back drive and blasted her horn, motioning the guard to get out of the way. She was not going to slow down until her car was sitting in the middle of Tower Green.

She came to a stop in front of the entrance to the Queen's House. Before she could run around the car to help Edward out, he opened his door and leaned over, falling to the ground.

"Edward," Obsidia yelled out in a fright.

"Loki," Edward whispered. "Get Loki."

Obsidia did not know what to do. She did not know where the dragon was.

Out of panic, she started yelling. "Loki, Edward needs you."

In just a few seconds, Loki dipped down out of the sky and landed next to Edward's shoulder. The other eight dragons landed around them, but kept back out of the way.

Loki bent down and rolled Edward over gently with his small arms.

"I know what you are," Edward said quietly.

Loki looked at him and shrugged.

"Don't play coy with me, old boy. I know it was you. I made a few wishes and you granted them. That night you arrived, the bird cage was broken into by you lot. I wished it was fixed and it was. I wished I could keep my job. To everyone else in the world, you look like my ravens, so the Ravenmaster kept his post."

He looked over at Obsidia and smiled. "I wished that I was younger so that I could be worthy of her and it happened."

"Edward," Obsidia said, "age never mattered to me."

"It did to me, my sweet. I wanted to be the man you deserved." He turned back to Loki. "You did that, didn't you? You granted my wishes."

Loki watched Edward's eyes and then nodded.

"I knew it," Edward said, satisfied. "Thank you all for granting me a little bit of happiness."

Duncan walked into the circle that the dragons had formed around Edward. "Ravenmaster, get up."

Obsidia turned on who she still thought was George Bailey. "George, he's not well."

Duncan looked over to Edward. "It's time she knows everything." He touched his finger to the side of his nose.

Obsidia saw George shrink down before her eyes. He was now a very short man with long blond hair and a beard in a Beefeater uniform. The man held out his hand.

"My name is Duncan, Mrs. Flummox-Jones. I'm the head of Clan Fargrave. I'm the one who brought the dragons to the Tower." He turned to Edward. "Yes, the dragons granted your wishes. They've formed a special bond with you. They're like children, anxious to have their parents' approval. But the wishes they grant always come with a price. Your wish for youth was a very big wish. The price is that the magic only works within the Tower walls. If you stray from here for more than twenty-four hours like you just did, the wish breaks down."

"So he's going to have to live in the Tower for the rest of his life?," Obsidia asked.

"Yes," Duncan said, matter-of-factly. "You got back here before the spell was completely broken. It's been able to repair itself. C'mon, Edward, stand up."

Edward realized he was feeling better. As he got to his feet, he caught sight of himself in the car's outside mirror. His hair had almost fully grown in.

"Ow," Edward said and rubbed his thumb across his sore gum line. New teeth were already pushing out to replace the ones that had fallen away.

"You can't stray very far," Obsidia said. "It'll be like you're in prison."

Edward found the strength to embrace his wife. "I could be in the coldest, dankest cell. But if I know that I am yours and you are mine, then no paradise can compare."

She laughed. "You sometimes say the stupidest things." Then she kissed him.

"I know," he whispered. "I love you, too."

"Why here? Why did you have to bring the dragons here?," Obsidia asked Duncan.

Duncan looked straight up. "On the night of June 23rd, a vortex will open just above the Tower. A battle has been raging for over twenty-five hundred years by your calendar. It ends that night. The vortex will open a gateway from our world to yours. All of the evil in our world will come pouring into yours, if we don't stop it. The breach has to be sealed. The dragons will play an important role. Come," he said, "there is something I need to show you."

"My car," Obsidia said, "I've got to move it."

"Don't worry," Duncan said.

Obsidia saw two men, no taller than Duncan get in her car. One man sat on the floor to work the pedals. The other stood on the seat to steer.

"Can they do that?," she asked.

Duncan smiled. "They have a system worked out."

The car started up and jumped into reverse, swung around, and then headed off in the direction of where Obsidia normally parked.

They climbed to the top of Wakefield Tower. There were more little men there. Loki landed and the men immediately got to work fitting a leather saddle across his broad back.

"The dragons are still growing," Duncan said. "We made the saddles so that they can be adjusted as they get bigger. Tonight is the first time that we're putting saddles on most of them. Ajax and Margaret are experienced mounts, but some of the others haven't been harnessed yet."

"Do you steer them with a bit in their mouths like a horse?," she asked.

"No," Duncan said. "We consider that to be cruel. A dragon's mouth isn't like a horse's. If you tried that, they'd throw you off their backs and stomp you."

"They'd be just as likely to eat you," one of the saddle makers commented.

"Is that true?," Obsidia asked.

"No," Duncan said, giving the talkative dwarf a glaring look. "Edward did an excellent job raising them. They're imprinted with humans. They think of you as part of their families. Edward, especially, and you as his mate."

"His what?," she said.

"That's how dragons think," Duncan said. "It's not me. It's like bringing a baby to a home that already has a dog.

229

The dog accepts the child as a part of the pack, not as a threat or competition."

"Or a food source," the saddle maker said, once again without thinking.

"We're fitting all nine dragons with saddles," Duncan continued. "But not all nine will be flying on the twenty-third. My people will be here every night, training the dragons to accept riders and training ourselves to saddle them. We need to be able to saddle each dragon in two minutes. With three teams of stable mates, we can get the entire flight airborne in six minutes. When the breach begins to open, we'll need to be ready."

Edward craned his neck to stare straight up into the sky. The dragons were flying in a tight formation, two-by-two at an altitude of about a thousand feet.

"I've watched them do that for weeks now," Edward said. "Why do they keep circling above the Tower in that one place?"

Duncan took off his tiny Tudor bonnet and stared up as well. "Can't you feel it? They can. They can feel the universe begin to weaken right there. They're on the prowl. They're protecting their Tower, Edward. They're protecting you."

34
THE LADY OF THE LAKE

Art wiped the steam off of his bathroom mirror and took a good look at himself, standing with a white hotel towel wrapped around his waist. His training had put him the best shape of his life. He had muscles. He had never had those before. It used to be that, if given a choice being exerting himself or not, he chose not.

He flexed and took a weightlifter's pose and then started to laugh, seeing how stupid he looked. He was no body builder. His muscles had not swelled to look like big, rounded tumors that had attached themselves to his body. He was a warrior, though — a warrior training for a war that was out of date. He knew that bullets could not stop the threat looming ahead of them. It would take swords and arrows and axes — and Henry's swingy thing.

When he looked at it objectively, it did not make sense. A world filled with tanks and planes and missiles should be able to stop the universe from collapsing. Not now. It would take five students, hundreds of dwarves, and an old man who could slip the bonds of time to keep everything from unraveling.

There was a knock on his bathroom door.

"Honey," his mother said, "Agent Stallings is here. Are you ready?"

"I'll be out in five, Mom. Thanks."

He felt for the class ring on his right hand with his thumb. He was still getting used to wearing it. It took everything he had not to press the diamond in public, just to show off or to demonstrate it to his parents so he could explain the danger they were all facing. He had promised Merlin that he would not. His parents were safer not knowing and he intended to keep them that way.

He dressed quickly and said goodbye to his mother. The agent walked behind him a few steps. Stallings was the bodyguard that he knew the least. After his "escape", Agent Kidd had been very cold and distant to him, only speaking when it was needed to give Art directions. In the past few weeks, he had begun to lighten up. Art was sure that he saw Kidd crack a smile when he told a joke the other day, if only for a second or two. Stallings was all business, all day, every day.

They made their way to the American School. As they walked into the building, Art looked around and saw so many faces he did not recognize. It was his own fault. He and his classmates had become academic hermits, keeping to themselves all day. Maybe after June 23rd, everything would be back to normal.

"Good, you're here," Merlin said as Arthur was the last to arrive. "Today, we won't be visiting Little Vanwalanthir."

"I guess the dwarves need a break from us," Angus said.

"Perhaps," Merlin said. "But today I want you to meet some other allies that we have in this world. I perhaps overstated the case when I told you that I was able to move all of the magic in the world into its own universe."

"You left behind the memory of it," Amanda said.

"Indeed," Merlin said. "I could not wipe men's and

women's minds. I could not erase their cultures. No one has enough magic to do that. Facts, though, became legends. Experiences became myths. There were some forces too powerful to move, however, and which remained behind."

The back of the classroom dissolved and opened onto a pool, set in the middle of a cavern. There was a hole at the top of the chamber, an oculus, which allowed light to stream in. The bottom of the cave was really a giant lake with a small island of stone and sand rising up in the middle, directly under the opening. They stepped out onto the island.

"Where are we?," Dipeka asked.

"We're in Derbyshire, in the East Midlands of England. A part of the Speedwell Caverns that have still not been discovered by man." Merlin looked around at his students. "That is until now."

"How could it be undiscovered? Somebody must have come across that hole in the roof by now," Henry said.

"Not unless she wanted you to. And she wouldn't want it. She values her privacy," Merlin answered.

"Who?," Art asked.

The water in front of them forming the shore of the little island began to move. A column of water rose out of the surface and solidified, taking the form of a beautiful woman. She was dressed in fine white linen. Her hair was long and curled and black. She had golden eyes and her ears rose to sweptback points. She walked on bare feet across the surface of the water, stepped onto the dry land, and stood directly in front of Merlin.

"Nimue, that's who," the woman said to Art. She then turned her attention to their instructor. "Good to see you again, Merlin." She slapped him as hard as she could across the face. "That's for ignoring me for the past twenty-five hundred years."

"Who's Nimue?," Angus whispered to Dipeka.

Before she could answer him, Nimue turned to Angus.

"You might know me better as the Lady of the Lake."

Edward was awakened in his favorite way — with a morning kiss. A man could get used to this, he thought.

"You're awake?," Obsidia said, and handed him a cup of coffee. "I let you sleep in because we're officially on our honeymoon."

Edward looked around, confused. They were in the bedroom of his flat. This was no place to have a proper honeymoon.

"We can't go anywhere. That's not much of a honeymoon for you," Edward protested.

"Just get dressed," Obsidia said. "Put on your swimming trunks. And don't forget your sunscreen. I reckon something as white as you doesn't tan. It crisps."

Edward did as he was told, putting on the bathing suit and Hawaiian shirt combination he had bought for his wedding trip. Obsidia put on her bathing suit, a bikini, and a beach jacket and sandals. No one seemed to take notice of them.

"They can't see us," Obsidia said, noting Edward's confusion. "Just like they see the dragons as ravens. They think we're off on holiday in the south of Spain. So that's what they see."

She led him over to the Salt Tower, which was right on the River Thames.

They climbed to the top and popped up through the hatch in the roof. There was a thick layer of beach sand on the top of the tower, two reclining beach chairs, and an umbrella.

"How did this happen?," Edward asked. Then a terrible thought crossed his mind. "You didn't wish for this from the dragons, did you?"

She smiled and shook her head. "No. Only your wishes get granted. Not mine. Duncan and the boys felt bad about our honeymoon getting ruined. They did this up. Said we deserved to sun ourselves on a sandy beach by the water's edge." She pointed to the Thames. "There's the water and here's our beach."

As they settled onto the beach chairs, Duncan came up through the roof hatch bearing a tray of long champagne flutes.

"Mimosas," Duncan said. "Orange juice with a splash of champagne." He was dressed in a white linen waiter's jacket. "We're making a nice Spanish paella for lunch. Tonight, you're taking a dragon flight to Beacon's Bottom, where you'll dine on a saddle of roasted venison with red currant jelly, asparagus, and pureed turnips with horseradish whipped cream."

"Whoa," Edward said, "that sounds like a feast fit for a king."

Duncan smiled. "You're right about that, Edward. For now, sit back and relax. Enjoy the sounds of the beach." He hit the remote control for a small music player he had hidden on the top of the tower, and the soundscape of a Mediterranean beach washed over them. "Listen to the cry of the seagulls hovering in the sea breeze above your head."

On cue, the dragons began to call out. They cawed like ravens.

"I said, listen to the cry of SEAGULLS," Duncan said much louder.

The dragons went silent for a moment and then began to screech and yammer like shore birds.

Edward donned his sunglasses and took a sip of the mimosa. He smiled and laid back, reaching for Obsidia's hand.

"Paradise," he said dreamily, "Like I said, I'm in paradise."

"I take it you two know each other," Dipeka said as Merlin rubbed his reddened cheek.

"Know each other?," Nimue said. "He told me I was the one true love of his life. To think the Queen of the Water Nymphs got taken in by a magician."

Merlin bristled. "You can call me a lot of things, Nimue, but I'm not a magician."

"Ha," she cackled. "You've probably been playing some tacky little room at a hotel in Las Vegas. Who are these, your children?"

"No," he said, "my students."

"You know about Las Vegas?," Henry asked.

"Of course I know about Las Vegas, young man, I'm a water nymph. Wherever there is fresh water, my nymphs and I are nearby." She turned and spoke to Merlin. "They're your students and you never told them about the Naiad?"

Merlin massaged his red-hot cheek with his hand. "The subject hadn't come up until today."

"So," Nimue said to the students, but kept her eye on Merlin, "I'm on today's lesson plan, eh? I see you've brought your classroom with you, too. All right, gather round, let me tell you a few things about ethereal magic."

"I'd much rather hear about you and Professor Merlin," Amanda said.

Dipeka and Amanda both stifled a giggle at that.

"Would you, girls?," Nimue said. "Well, perhaps it will serve as a lesson to you about the fickle nature of men. You might not make the same mistakes I have."

"Nimue, I don't think this is the time or place for it."

"Really? When will be the time? You've had twenty-five centuries to come up with an excuse."

"I can't offer you an excuse," Merlin said.

"Mark this date in your calendar, girls, a man's being truthful. How can you normally tell when a boy is lying to you?" She gave Merlin an icy glare. "It's when he speaks."

"Morgana Le Fey stole my book. I had to stop her before she could perform the spell of creation. I had been to the future where she had succeeded. There was no

Earth. There was no sun. There was no moon. There was nothing. The universe ceased to exist. All light, all hope, all magic was gone. You and the Naiad would never have been. So I created a pocket universe for Morgana and her son, Mordred, and when I pulled them into it, everything that was magical went with them, including myself. For those twenty-five centuries you spoke of, I have been battling her on the border of two dimensions, that one and this. The battle will be ending soon. You have something I need so that we can defeat her."

"The battle is still ongoing? Yet, you are here," Nimue said. "How can that be?"

"Its a whole time and space thing," Amanda said. "I had to work it out on a piece of paper after he told us before I really understood it."

"The bottleneck that Morgana and I were stuck in," Merlin said, "or are stuck in, will open on June 23rd. I will be there to rescue myself and send myself back twenty-five years in time so that I could recover and lay the groundwork for what needs to be done. I've had a lot to do, Nimue. And there is still even more to do. So I would appreciate it if you could cut me some slack!"

As Merlin spoke storm clouds formed inside the cavern and, with his last sentence, lightening bolts began to strike the water's surface.

"I accept your apology," Nimue said as she stepped forward and kissed him lightly on the cheek.

The redness on Merlin's face departed.

"Why didn't you come to us, Merlin? We could have seen to your physical recovery."

"I knew that if I came to you, if I called out your name, I would be so obsessed with you, as I was before, that I would soon lose all memory of anything but you. I would forget Morgana. I would stop caring about the end of the universe. That kind of love is not healthy, Nimue."

She nodded in agreement. "Perhaps, but it was fun while it lasted. How can we help you defeat Morgana?"

Angus looked around. "We?"

As he said that, the waters around them began to shimmer and roil. At least a hundred Naiad took form and walked onto the small island, crowding around them.

"Yes, young man. These are my people, the Naiad."

Art looked around. Each of the Naiad was female, each of them was about his own age, and each of them was, in her own way, as beautiful as Nimue.

"These are my girls," Nimue said proudly.

"Why weren't you all swept into the other universe with the rest of the magical world?," Dipeka asked.

"Clever girl," Nimue said to Merlin. "You did like to surround yourself with clever girls, didn't you? I guess that's where your problem with Morgana started. She was a student of yours, too — the cleverest of girls. To answer your question, dear, we Naiad only take a physical form when it suits us."

"Nimue," Merlin said, "you can guess why I've brought them here."

"Oh, I knew the moment you stepped out of your little magic classroom. You're interested in the sword. Am I right?"

"Arthur's sword?," Henry asked.

"No," Nimue answered sharply, "my sword! Merlin asked me to lend it to Arthur. Upon his death, it returned to me. It is a weapon of great power. Ultimately, Arthur proved unworthy to be its keeper."

"Arthur was like a son to me," Merlin said.

"I say this with all love for you and respect for him as well, but perhaps you should have raised your son a little better."

The storm clouds above them in the cavern began to rumble as flashes of light raced within them.

"Merlin, keep your temper in check," Nimue said. "Arthur was too hot-headed. He broke Excalibur once by invoking its power unfairly. I should have kept it after that. You told me that he could unite the worlds of magic and man."

"He came very close," Merlin said.

"In the end, he failed. You think that one of your students is worthy to wield Excalibur?"

"That is why I brought them here. To see."

Nimue looked the five students over. "Are any of you princes or princesses? Are you of noble birth? Are you gentlemen or gentle ladies?" She looked at Art. "Or are you, perhaps, a peasant prince?"

"That doesn't matter," Art said. "Who our parents, or grandparents, or any ancestors were tells you nothing of who we are. History is full of examples of purebred kings who brought their lands to ruin and of common men and women who were able to lead with wisdom and strength."

"What's your name, child?," Nimue said, eyeing Art carefully.

"Zefrom Arthur Williams the Fourth."

"The Fourth?," Nimue said with a smile. "That sounds like a royal line. And one of your names is Arthur." She turned to Merlin. "You've found another Arthur! Was it for sentiment's sake or a coincidence that you included another Arthur among your followers?"

"Leave the boy alone," Merlin said.

"If you think he's worthy to wield my sword, don't I have a right to know a little bit about him? Arthur, do you believe that a king has a right to rule his people?"

"No. An accident of birth won't make you a leader."

"Merlin," Nimue said, "what have you been teaching your pupils? How can he wield the sword of a king if he doesn't want to be one?"

"You misunderstand me, Lady," Art said. "I don't wish to be king, but I am in this fight to defeat Morgana and Mordred. When that threat is gone, I expect that I will return to my old life."

"Do you think that?," Nimue said. "You've changed. Just knowing Merlin changed you. Knowing these people all around you has changed you even more. You can't go back to what you were. The Zefrom Arthur Williams the Fourth you were in the past is gone. You're a man now. Are you prepared to take on the full responsibilities of a man, or do you want to go back to being a carefree boy?"

"I stand ready to fight for my world, for my family, for my friends," Art said.

Nimue walked past Art and encircled the others as she spoke. "What about the rest of you? If you're prepared to fight, are you prepared to die for what you believe in?"

"We don't have a choice," Dipeka said. "Merlin told us we were in the thick of the battle when he entered our world. We can't change that."

Nimue wheeled and stared at Merlin. "You told them that? Merlin is wrong. Your future has not been cast. You are free to accept the responsibility that he has insisted you take. But you are also free to reject it. You can see if Excalibur finds you worthy to wield her. If she claims you, then there is no turning back, no room for second thoughts. You will meet Mordred in battle. To what end, I will not tell you. If you test yourself, you also set yourself down that same path. It is only if you decline the test that you will reserve all of your options. You can still choose to fight with Merlin or you can stay home and let others fight for you. Arthur, how do you choose?"

"I choose to be tested," Art answered.

"As single-minded as your namesake," Nimue said. "I like that. And you?," she said pointing to Henry.

"I also choose to be tested," Henry answered.

"And you?," she said, indicating Angus.

"Test me. The sword will be mine," Angus said.

"Overconfidence? Also an Arthurian trait. Fine, the three of you may try."

"What about us?," Amanda demanded. "We have the same right as them."

"In my day, women did not battle," Nimue said.

"Yet, you lead your people, a race of women," Dipeka challenged. "Do you need men to protect you? To fight for you?"

Nimue smiled at Merlin. "I told you she was clever, using psychology on me. Do you think I've spent eons in this cave by myself? I am in every river in the world, every lake, every reservoir. I have seen the progress of man. I know that women of your day do many incredible things. But I am reluctant to put you in battle."

"All it means," Amanda said, "is that we've got to be quicker and smarter than they are. Merlin's taught us to be quicker. We've always been smarter." She looked over at Art, Angus, and Henry. "No offense, boys, but it's true."

"I like them both, Merlin," Nimue said, inclining her head to Dipeka and Amanda. "Understand that I will not be making the decision. Excalibur has a mind of her own."

Art was anxious to get started. "Where is the sword?"

"Your classroom landed on it. It's on the other side of this island."

"Allow me to shut the door," Merlin said.

With a wave of his hand, the opening into their classroom faded from view, allowing them to see the other half of the island. There was a large boulder on the sand, just at the water's edge. A long blade stuck out of it, its surface gleaming from the light that poured down from the oculus above.

Nimue led them over to it, followed by even more Naiad who waded out of the water to observe. One of Nimue's daughters stood close to Angus and brushed up against him as he moved to get a better look at the sword.

"What's your name?," Angus asked.

"Jardana," the girl said. She had light blue eyes and the longest eyelashes that Angus had ever seen. Her fiery copper red hair fell down below her waist. Above her full lips was a little button nose.

"Do you have a number? Of course, you don't. You can't use a cell phone underwater. How do I call you?"

"Stand by a body of fresh water and call my name three

times. I will come," Jardana said.

"All right, big fellow," Nimue said. "I can see you're a risk taker. Hitting on my daughter while I'm standing here proves that. You go first."

"All I have to do is pull it out?," Angus said.

"That's it," Nimue said.

Angus winked at Jardana. "Piece of cake. Watch this."

Excalibur stuck out at a slight angle to the right. Angus grabbed the pommel and tugged, expecting it to slide out easily. It did not budge.

"I'm just getting warmed up," he said as he tightened his grip on the sword.

Angus started to strain as he pulled, causing the veins in his arms to pop out. His face reddened and sweat began pouring off it. Blood vessels in his neck came to the surface and Art could see his rapid heartbeat in the throbbing of the arteries in his forehead. Angus put his weight behind the sword and tried to bend it away from the water's edge as he pulled. Art was sure that the blade would snap in half. Perhaps that was Angus' strategy. He would make the sword surrender to his will.

The blade did not snap, but it swung back, knocking Angus into the air. He landed in the lake ten yards out with a splash. Jardana leapt out after him, changing into water as she flew through the air. A huge wave picked Angus up and washed him down the side of the island and onto the shore where they first stepped out of the classroom. The wave that broke over Angus formed into Jardana, who started administering mouth-to-mouth resuscitation to him. Angus turned his head and spat out a mouthful of water, then fell back on the sand dizzy. Jardana went back to administering aid to him.

"Jardana!," Nimue called out. "Jardana! You can stop now. He's breathing."

Angus opened his eyes dreamily and smiled at her.

"That was great," Angus whispered to her. "Can I drown myself again?"

"You," Nimue said to Dipeka.

Dipeka walked all around the boulder, examining the sword from every angle. She dropped to her knees and examined where the blade entered the stone, trying to divine some clue as to what was holding it inside. Unable to figure it out, she decided to try something that Merlin had done.

"*Agor 'ch dendio. Agor 'ch asgre*," Dipeka said as she pulled. The sword did not move. She lost her grip on the handle and fell backward into the lake. None of the young Naiads helped her make her way back onto shore.

"You have been teaching them magic!," Nimue accused Merlin. "Did your experience with Morgana teach you nothing? The test is over."

Nimue turned and all of her daughters followed her out onto the lake. Jardana looked sad as she left Angus' side and joined her sisters. Nimue gave Merlin a last angry look and shook her finger at him. With that, all of Nimue's daughters and the Lady of the Lake turned to water and dropped into the pool.

Merlin looked at Dipeka and shook his head.

"I'm sorry," she said as she dropped to the sand. She started to cry. "I remembered that's what you said the first time you took us to the dwarves' camp. I thought the words had power. I thought they could help me."

"Dipeka," Merlin said, taking his handkerchief from his jacket pocket and lowering himself on one knee, "when you think, what language do you hear in your head?"

Dipeka was in shock. She expected Merlin to be angry. His tone was gentle. He had also just called her by her first name for the first time ever.

"Sometimes English. Sometimes Hindi," she said with a sniffle.

"You don't speak the ancient Celtic tongues and you don't think in them, either. To you, the words were just noise. They had no meaning, so they had no power."

"The only power they had was to get us kicked off this

island," Amanda said bitterly. "No one's going to use Excalibur. You screwed it up for everyone."

"I'm sorry," Dipeka said with a sob as the weight of what she had done and how she had disappointed her classmates and her teacher pressed down on her. "How can I make this right?"

"How do you think?," Merlin asked.

"I don't know. If I did ... I'll do anything."

Art knelt down beside her. "Come with me. I have an idea."

He held her hand to steady her as they walked out until they were knee high in the water. Art whispered something in her ear.

"Do you think it will work?," Dipeka said.

"Try," Art said.

"Jardana, Jardana, Jardana," Dipeka said.

They stood there for what seemed like forever, waiting. Dipeka heard a far off drop of water hit the surface of the lake from above with a "plop."

"I don't think it's going to work," Dipeka said.

"Wait," he told her and squeezed her hand.

They heard the sound of thunder. But it did not come from Merlin's low hanging clouds. A sun shower had moved above them and a fine mist began to fall on Dipeka and Art. She started to move, to turn back to the shore, but Art held her hand tighter.

"Look," he said.

The rain was coming down with greater intensity now, each drop exploded as it hit the surface of the lake. Where the light touched the water, the rebounding raindrops created perfect balls of prismatic light.

"They're beautiful," Dipeka said.

"They are, aren't they?"

The water around them began to slosh about. Jardana's form sprang up.

"Jardana," Art said, "Dipeka would ask if you would do her the favor and the honor of relaying a message to your mother, the Lady of the Lake." He looked at Dipeka and then nudged her with her shoulder.

"Would you please tell your mother that I am sorry that I offended her. Merlin did not teach me that magical phrase. I overheard him say it once and I remembered it. Ask her not to punish Amanda, Henry, and Art because I was so stupid."

"You were trying to be too clever, weren't you?," Jardana said, but it was not Jardana's voice.

Jardana took on additional water so that she was taller and older and had dark hair. It was Nimue.

"I told Jardana to stay below." She pointed to Angus, who had joined the others at this end of the island. "Seems she's infatuated with the big one over there. I didn't want to send her up without a chaperone."

She looked at Art. "How did you know that in my anger I might not pull you under and drown you both?"

"You have daughters, my lady. You know that death is not an appropriate punishment for selfishness." Art looked over at Angus. "Any more than it would be fitting for inconsideration."

"You understand compassion. That is the first step towards wisdom, a much needed quality in a leader." Nimue looked over at Merlin. "There is a lot of Arthur in him, after all." She looked back to Art. "Try the sword, Arthur."

Art walked cautiously to the boulder and grabbed the pommel. A hum ran through his body, an electricity that he could feel and taste. The sword felt right in this hand. He pulled slowly.

Nothing happened.

Then he felt the vibration running up the blade as the metal scraped against the granite that had held it tight. It was moving. He pulled on it more and it came free. He held the point to the light for the first time in an epoch.

"You did it," Dipeka said crying, but this time for joy.

"You did it," Angus said and rushed over and lifted Art

and Excalibur into the air.

"You did it," Merlin said, amazed that he had lived to see another wield the Sword of Destiny.

All of his friends gathered round him and they cheered and laughed together. When they calmed, Art looked over at the Lady of the Lake, who seemed both pleased and concerned.

He walked to her and dropped to one knee. "I promise you when the crisis ends, I will return Excalibur to you."

"Arise, Arthur. There is no need for you to kneel to anyone. The sword has chosen you. I think she has chosen wisely."

35
A BEAR OF VERY LITTLE BRAINS

"**S**ix tickets. One adult and five students, please," Merlin said as he slid his credit card to the woman in the kiosk.

"Just to warn you, sir, the Tower will be closing in an hour."

"That's quite all right," Merlin said as he scooped up the tickets. "My students are very quick learners."

Merlin handed the tickets to Henry, who passed them along.

"Agent Stallings," Merlin said, "I'm certain there's enough room in your State Department's budget to cover the cost of your getting in."

Stallings went to the ticket kiosk and passed a twenty pound note to the woman inside, but never took his eyes off of Art.

"Art, do you know what to do?," Merlin asked.

"Yeah."

Stallings joined them with his ticket in hand and they proceeded inside. Just as they crossed under the Bloody Tower, Art grabbed his abdomen.

"I think I'm going to be sick," he said and sprinted to

the men's room.

Kol Founderson, the dwarf who had substituted for him the night he flew with the dragons, was waiting in an empty stall for him. He was sitting on the tank of the toilet with a child's paperback book in his hand.

"Art," he whispered, "good to see you, lad."

"Thanks," Art said hurriedly, knowing that Agent Stallings would be no more than thirty seconds behind him.

Founderson held up his paperback, *Winnie the Pooh*. "Been teaching myself to read your language. Listen to this, 'I am a Bear of Very Little Brains, and long words bother me.' The bears of your world are very wise, much like the bears in mine."

"Are you ready?," Art said frantically.

"Aye," Founderson said and jumped down off the tank. He tucked the book into his jacket and picked up a large jug of water.

"Art," Stallings called out as he entered the men's room, "are you okay?"

"Hold on," Art called out and then made a retching noise. He cued Founderson, who tipped the jug over, emptying half its contents into the toilet bowl.

Art coughed and sputtered and then they repeated the process. Founderson gave Art a thumbs up and stepped out of the stall, pulling the door closed behind himself.

"You do not want to go in there," Founderson said. "It is a mess. It will require much cleaning. Do you have any hand sanitizer with you?"

Stallings could not see through the mystical disguise that the dwarf was projecting.

"No," Stallings said. "I think I should get you back to the hotel. You don't look too good."

"I concur with you," Founderson said. "I am feeling vomitus and dyspeptic. I obviously need at least four hours of uninterrupted rest in my room. Where I will be. In my room. Unless I am in my bathroom. Tell me, have you studied much about Winnie the Pooh?"

Stallings shook his head. He hoped the kid was not going delirious on him. "Let's get you home."

Art waited two minutes after Founderson and Stallings left before exiting the men's room. Merlin and his friends were waiting for him with Duncan.

"Good," Duncan said, "follow me."

They wound through the Tower, avoiding the guards and the sentries. Duncan led them all to the top of Wakefield Tower. It was a bit crowded with the two saddle mates who were already present. They quickly strapped the students into rider's harnesses.

It got even more crammed when Margaret touched down.

"You weren't kidding, mate," Amanda said excitedly. "It's a dragon, a real bloody dragon."

The students all moved forward to touch her. Surrounded by so many people she did not know, Margaret became skittish. As she turned, her long tail swished behind her, knocking Angus back.

"Margaret," Duncan said sternly, "stop that."

Art stepped towards her and held his hand to her muzzle, letting her smell his scent. She focused on Art and calmed.

"Hello, girl," he said to her quietly. "It's been a while. I come out onto the patio up there," he said pointing to the top of the Tower Hotel. "I watch you and your brothers and sisters circling over this place all night. I can always pick you out. I always say to myself, there's Margaret."

She rubbed her snout against his hand and opened her mouth.

Dipeka gasped when she saw her gleaming teeth. She strangled a little cry in her throat when she saw Margaret's big pink tongue lick Art's hand.

"Shhh, Dipeka," Art said. "You can't treat her like a beast. She's quite smart. She's a clever girl, like you. Isn't that right, Margaret?"

Margaret started to purr.

"What does she eat?," Henry asked.

"Beef," Art said. "Lots of beef. I met the Ravenmaster. He keeps all of them very well fed."

"Ravenmaster?," Angus said. "These aren't ravens."

"Funny thing," Art said. "Everyone sees them as ravens. You don't now. I suspect that Professor Merlin had something to do with that."

"No, Arthur," Merlin said, "the dragons control who sees them and who doesn't."

"So that first night when I saw them?," Art said.

"It was the dragons, not me. I told them you were one of my students. I told them that you would be working together. I even pointed out to them where you lived. They chose the time and place of your first meeting. You made a good impression on them. They were willing to meet you all after that."

Art looked over at Dipeka. "Margaret's calmed down now. Would you like to meet her?"

Dipeka nodded and let her hand be guided by Art to a spot where her chin met her throat.

"You have long nails," Art said. "Give her a good scratching right there."

"Won't it hurt her?"

"No," Art said. "Dragon skin's pretty tough. If we had more room up here, I'd have you rub her belly. She really likes that."

As Dipeka stroked and scratched, Margaret closed her eyes and started to purr.

"I see you've got a double saddle on her," Art said to Duncan.

Duncan spoke to the class. "I thought your first flight should be a tandem flight. I'll be taking you up tonight. Starting tomorrow, we'll have several of the dragons at Little Vanwalanthir. You'll study advanced dragon flight and then we'll cover airborne combat."

"Dipeka," Merlin said. "Since you've established a

rapport with Margaret, you get to go first."

The two saddle mate dwarves helped secure Dipeka's leather harness and then strapped Duncan in front of her.

Art patted Margaret on her side and said softly, "Give her a gentle flight, Margaret."

The dragon looked back at Art and nodded her long head and then stepped off the Wakefield Tower with her long, leathery wings fully unfurled. They dropped a few feet before the air caught them. Dipeka yelled for a second and then started to laugh as her dragon starting climbing away.

Ajax and Boudicca landed next on the crenelated wall that encircled the Waterloo Tower's roof. Merlin addressed his students.

"Since Arthur has already had his maiden flight, I'm going to take him up. I would appreciate you all staying together on top of the Tower until the last of you has your turn. Then we will leave as a group and I will get you back to your parents."

Ajax hopped down off of the wall and Art was secured into his saddle. The dragon lifted almost straight up, making room for Boudicca to take Merlin on as a rider.

"Follow Boudicca," Art said to Ajax. "Professor, you're not wearing a safety harness," Art called out.

"I've been riding dragons since before your great-great... I've been riding dragons a very long time."

"Where are we going?," Art yelled.

"I want to show you a few things," Merlin said, his voice now perfectly clear in Art's ear. "No need to shout, I can hear you."

They flew eastward, following the Thames until the vast expanse of Battersea Park was on Art's right. Boudicca banked left and they headed north.

"There's Buckingham Palace," Merlin said, pointing off to his right.

The Palace sat wedged between St. James Park to the east and Green Park to the north. With three days to go before the Princess' ball, there was a flurry of activity on the open green behind the Palace. It looked like they were building the staging for the orchestra.

"How's your dancing?," Merlin asked.

"Great. Want me to teach you some moves?," Art said with a smile.

"When this is all over, I'll look forward to it."

They flew a little further north, passing over Grosvenor Square, a small open park that the American Embassy sat next to. He recognized it from the times he had gone to visit his father. In a way he wished that Agent Kidd was standing at one of the windows and could see him flying by. Then he would understand that he was not just an irresponsible kid. They traveled another mile north and were above Regent's Park. Art strained to see Winfield House below.

The mansion was still under reconstruction. Almost half of the house had been demolished. The wooden framing was gone, replaced by thick steel girders. They were engineering it so that the mansion could never collapse again.

Boudicca pulled back and began to lose altitude. She was aiming to land on the Winfield House lawn.

"Professor," Art said. "There are State Department security people all over the place. They'll see us."

"No, they won't," Merlin said.

When the dragons landed about fifty yards from the house, Merlin hopped off of Boudicca's back. It took Art a few seconds to work the clips that kept him secured to the saddle.

"I wanted to explain something to you," Merlin said, walking towards the house, "and this seemed the best place to do it."

Merlin sat on the treads of a boom crane, now idle and quiet. He directed Art to sit down next to him. He pulled a tattered moleskin diary from his inside jacket pocket and handed it to Art.

"This is the book I gave myself when I fell out of the vortex," Merlin said.

Art turned it over in his hands. It was tattered and burned. The writing on the pages was in a symbolic language that Art did not understand.

"What happened to it?," Art asked.

"It was damaged in the battle before I slipped back into the past. I attempted to write a future history for myself. There was a lot that I either did not include in the book or was destroyed."

Art looked at the damage. "Were you injured when you gave it to yourself?"

"I don't know. For me, that's still my future. The only facts in the book are those written a few weeks before I gave it to myself. I know the vortex opens. I know that we battle Mordred in the skies over the Tower."

"Who wins?"

"That, I don't know. That is where your skills come in, Arthur. You are the leader of the group."

"Me? Just because the sword is letting me use it?"

"No, you would still be the leader without Excalibur. You saved Shalerunner and the dwarves made you one of their own. They accept you now as a brother to their king. I can't remember the last time that happened to an outsider. You took the initiative and made peace with Nimue. That wasn't easy. I've seen her when she's angry. Your friends look up to you."

Art laughed. "Even Angus?"

Merlin smiled. "Even Angus. Your courage and leadership can inspire them to do great things. I've had to put a lot on your shoulders since you arrived in London."

"That's okay," Art said. "You've always had my back, right?"

He looked over at the Winfield House construction site.

"I've tried. The attack on you was one of those things where I failed. It wasn't in the diary. Those pages must have gotten burned or were torn away. I had recruited the dwarves to act as your protectors, even without knowledge that a Sidhe would be sent to kill you. Being a dwarf, Shalerunner decided that tunneling was the way they could get close to you without being detected."

"You have dwarf teams shadowing Dipeka, Henry, Angus, and Amanda, don't you?," Art asked.

Merlin was surprised at Art's power of deduction. "Yes. How did you suspect?"

"Except for when all of the dwarves were at Little Vanwalanthir the first time you took the class there, their numbers were always small for the size camp they built. Accounting for Duncan and the other dwarves who work at the Tower, I guessed that you had at least four of them watching each of the other students at all times."

"A-plus for you, Arthur," Merlin said with a smile.

"I don't think I could have worked that out before I joined your class."

"Half of knowledge is not knowing facts, it's being aware of the world around you," Merlin said. "If I've helped you with that, I am pleased."

"Have you always been a teacher?"

"Off and on, yes. I had other students before Arthur. Centuries' worth of students. I must say, there are none I have enjoyed teaching more than you and your classmates."

Art looked at the book. "Will you be giving this to yourself?"

"Not that copy, no. I've purchased the blank diary, but I haven't written in it yet. I will write it over the next few days."

"Why not just use this one?," Art said. "Or better yet, why not write it on something that cannot be burned?"

"I can travel through time as easily as you can cross the street, but I can't change my own past. I must do what I did. I would like you to keep that book safe for me."

"Why?"

"Call it a favor," Merlin said. He pushed himself off the crane's tread. "The others should be finishing their test flights. Ajax will take you to your hotel and pick up Founderson."

They mounted their dragons.

"Ever since I got Excalibur, you've been calling me 'Arthur'," Art observed.

Merlin smiled. "Call it an old habit. Goodnight, Arthur."

36
JUST ONE REHEARSAL

It had been a month and a half since their wedding and Obsidia had made a list of things she had to pick up at the market. She was going to make Edward a special dinner. He was an old fashioned fellow, which was one of the things she loved most about him. For him, it would be roast beef and Yorkshire pudding. He had once asked her for a "drowned baby", which she found out was a dessert pudding tied up in a cheesecloth bag and boiled. She couldn't bring herself to make anything called a drowned baby, but she knew how to make her mother's apple crumble by heart. That would have to do.

Edward had gone off to tend to the dragons, giving them their morning feeding. They had grown. All of them were larger than racehorses. At their size, they could easily hold two riders. The dwarves had fitted three of the dragons with double saddles, for a rider and a passenger. They had not told her who the riders would be.

She had enjoyed their trip to the wooded camp of the dwarves on the back of one of them. She had ridden on Victoria, who refused to dart about like the dragons that

Edward and Duncan rode. It was a smooth glide up and back.

The dwarves had treated them like royalty. They had dined alone, but when the last dish was cleared, the walls of their tent dropped and they were treated to a cavalcade of songs and dance. Obsidia learned that there was a certain universality of women. Like her friends, the dwarven women were curious as to how she and Edward had met, when she knew she was in love, and how he proposed.

Men, Obsidia had come to realize, were really just boys regardless of their height. They offered loud boastful toasts and challenged each other to games of physical prowess. Even Edward joined in, arm wrestling a few and tossing a hand axe at a target.

"They *are* boys," Barbryn, Duncan's mother, sighed to her. "But they're our boys. We're the ones that have to plan ahead. We're the ones that bring the next generation into the world."

As Obsidia buttoned her tunic, she was suddenly overcome with a feeling of nausea. She ran to the bathroom just in time. After she had unwillingly purged herself of her breakfast, she dabbed her face with a cool cloth.

As she walked out of her flat, she ran into Charlotte Callaghan, the wife of one of the other Yeoman Warders.

"Is everything all right?," Charlotte said. "You look as white as a sheet."

"I've been feeling nauseous for the last few mornings. I just threw up. I think it's passed."

"Are you put off from drinking coffee and tea?"

"Yes, how did you know?," Obsidia said. "I can't even stand the sight of it. I had to leave the room when Edward had his coffee this morning. Do you think it's serious?"

"Sounds like it. I think you've got a case of the nine month flu," Charlotte said with a grin. "Same thing happened to me. You're preggers."

Obsidia was stunned. "What? How?"

"I'm betting it happened in the usual way. Just to be sure, step inside."

Charlotte took Obsidia to her bathroom and took out a box from her medicine cabinet.

"This is a home pregnancy test," Charlotte said. "My Johnny and I are trying for our second, but no luck so far."

Charlotte waited while Obsidia used the test behind a closed door.

Obsidia came out of the bathroom staring at the small grey digital window. "It's not doing anything," Obsidia said as she started shaking the test stick.

"Relax, it takes three minutes. Here," Charlotte said handing Obsidia a handful of saltine crackers. "Chew these while you wait. It'll settle your stomach."

Obsidia set the test stick down on the table and watched the little clock symbol blink. It took forever for the seconds to click by. Just when she was sure that the test was broken, the clock faded and a word appeared: "Yes."

"Yes!," Charlotte screamed and hugged Obsidia. "I'm so happy for you."

When the initial shock wore off, Obsidia embraced Charlotte in return.

"You can't tell anyone. Not even your husband. I'm going to tell Edward tonight. You have to promise me."

"Cross my heart and hope to die, stick a needle in my eye," Charlotte said as she made two slashing motions with her finger over her heart. She then broke out into a mad grin. "A baby!," she squealed.

"I know!," Obsidia answered.

It was not nice to keep a princess waiting, Guinevere thought to herself. She had told him to be here at three o'clock. She checked the time on her watch. It was 3:01.

She had received word that he was stuck in London traffic, but that was no excuse. He should have left earlier.

"They've just pulled through the gate, ma'am," one of the ushers told her. "They'll be here in a moment."

She was giving him one rehearsal to prove himself. The Vietnamese waltz! He didn't even know the name of the dance. Was she expecting too for him to learn it, much less be able to master it, in just a few weeks time? Her plan at first was to humiliate him on the dance floor, to show him for the cloddish American boy he was. Then when that awful picture showed up in the newspaper, she could no longer afford for him to be embarrassed. Now, he had to be more than good. He had to be brilliant.

An usher entered the State Ballroom, followed by Art and an older woman. Had Williams brought his grandmother, Guinevere wondered.

"Presenting Zefrom Williams the Fourth and Mrs. Katherine Chillingsworth," the usher announced as the two entered.

Art inclined his head. "Your Royal Highness, it is my pleasure to introduce to you to Mrs. Katherine Chillingsworth, chief protocol officer to the United States Embassy in London and my dance coach."

"Ma'am," Chillingsworth said.

Good for you, Art thought to himself as he saw his mentor react with restraint. My mother would be beside herself, especially in this room.

Since his first encounter with the Princess, Art had become acutely aware of his surroundings and, like a good protocol officer, Mrs. Chillingsworth had briefed him on where they would be practicing their dance. They were in the State Ballroom, the largest room in Buckingham Palace. The room was white, accented in gold leaf. The floor was gleaming walnut parquet. There were large crystal chandeliers and an antique grand piano in the corner. At the far end of the room were the thrones, two golden chairs with scarlet and gold brocade cushions sitting beneath a canopy with the royal crest. This was a room meant to impress and awe both British citizens and foreigners alike. Art knew that the Princess could have had him meet her in another part of the Palace. He had read that there were 775 rooms in the Palace, but Guinevere's choice of this one told him that she still needed to try to intimidate him. It was not going to work, either on Chillingsworth or himself.

Guinevere acknowledged Chillingsworth, but did not bother to introduce any of her assembled staff. Art recognized the Princess' governess from his visit to Windsor Castle.

"Shall we get on with it?," Guinevere said.

Art smiled and politely asked, "May I have this dance?"

Guinevere was taken aback by his question. He was making it sound like he had a choice or, worse yet, that he was in control.

He held out his hand and escorted her to the center of the ballroom. The pianist started playing 'Voices of Spring'. Art did what had become second nature to him by now, after all the long hours of practice with Chillingsworth, Amanda, and Dipeka. He stepped to the side and bowed with a sweep of his arm. Guinevere answered with a curtsy.

I'm curtsying, she thought, to an American.

Art stepped forward and took her in his arms, placing his right hand on her back and extending his left. She put her hand in his and Art commenced to lead her. She was not used to this. The boys that she had practiced with deferred to her subtle direction. Art was guiding her, keeping time with the music as he stepped forward and back, sweeping her across the floor. When she tried to assert herself, he had the nerve to ignore her. His movements may have been flawless, but she was not sure that was how you treated a princess. For four minutes, they moved together.

As the music ended, he did something unexpected. He leaned her back and dipped her, holding her off-balance in his arms.

"Thank you, Gwen," he said to her softly. "That was lovely."

Guinevere felt her head spin. The room was moving about her. Then there was a burst of applause that came from the back of the ballroom.

"Bravo, bravo," Prince Francis said.

Art brought the Princess up into a standing position as the Prince approached them. He felt a little embarrassed that her father had seen them dance, especially that last part. The Prince, however, seemed genuinely pleased.

"Your Royal Highness," Art said, "I'm sorry. I didn't see you standing there."

"I was watching from the hall, Art. I didn't want to make you nervous. I don't think it would have mattered. Where did you learn to dance like that? Your Dad's got two left feet."

"Sir, may I present Mrs. Chillingsworth, my dance instructor?"

Chillingsworth came over and the Prince offered her his hand in congratulations.

"How long have you been teaching Art? Years, I fancy."

"No, sir, just a few weeks," Chillingsworth said.

"Really? Well then, the credit goes to both the student and the teacher." The Prince looked over at his daughter. "Where are my manners?" He kissed Guinevere on the cheek. "As always, darling, you were magnificent."

"Yes, sir," Art said. "A dream come to life."

"I've got to attend to something, darling. But promise you'll save a dance for me. Art, I'll see you this Friday night. Mrs. Chillingsworth, an honor and a pleasure to make your acquaintance. You can now add miracle worker to your list of accomplishments."

The Prince left and the two of them practiced some

more. Art requested both a samba and a tango and Guinevere had to work hard to keep up with him. After an hour and a half, they were escorted back to their waiting car.

Throughout their visit to the Palace, Mrs. Chillingsworth had been a model of calm and reserve. As Art climbed into the back of the Embassy limousine, she broke into a broad grin.

She held out her fist. "Who'da man?"

At first Art did not know what she was trying to communicate. Then he realized what she had intended and bumped his fist against hers.

"Who'da man?," she repeated. "You'da man."

Art just sat back and smiled and enjoyed the ride home.

Obsidia set the table with the fine china her mother had given her when she told her she had gotten married. She had had to apologize to her mother for not inviting her family to the wedding, but made it up to them by holding a church ceremony at the parish chapel on the Tower grounds, the Chapel Royal of St. Peter ad Vincula. It always struck Obsidia as ironic that the church's name literally translated to "Saint Peter in Chains", a fitting title for a church located in what was once the most notorious prison in the world. Her family all loved Edward, although none of them had a clue as to his real age.

Her shift had ended early and she had bought fresh flowers for the table. The roast had finished and was resting on the counter while the Yorkshire pudding baked. She had even bought a bottle of champagne. Since they did not have an ice bucket, she had filled one of the halves of the sink with ice and wedged the bottle into it to chill.

When Edward came in, she ran to him and threw her arms around him, giggling like a schoolgirl.

Edward looked around. "What's all this?" Then he realized. "It's our six week anniversary and I didn't get you anything, sweetheart. I'm sorry."

She kissed him. "It's all right. I didn't get you anything. Well, I did, but it didn't cost anything. Well, it will, but it didn't. Oh, go change and come out."

"I have no idea what you're talking about. But give me a few."

In a moment he was back in their kitchen, wearing a pair of khaki slacks and a polo shirt.

"Everything smells wonderful," he said.

She popped open the champagne bottle and poured Edward a flute. Hers was already filled with ginger ale.

"To our family," she said, raising her glass in a toast.

"To your family," Edward answered and clinked her glass. "How is your mum?"

"Not my family, our family. You and me and the baby."

"Baby? We haven't got a baby."

Obsidia broke into a wide grin and nodded. "We will!"

It took a second for Edward to understand what she was saying. It suddenly occurred to Obsidia that perhaps at Edward's age, he might not want a child. She need not have worried.

He whooped and picked her up and spun her around. Then he put her down and patted her abdomen, as if trying to smooth everything back in place.

"Sorry, sorry," he said.

"Edward, I'm not made of spun sugar. Just think," Obsidia said, laughing, "they're be another generation of a Flummox-Jones as the Ravenmaster."

Edward's look turned serious. "I wouldn't do that to my son."

"Or daughter?"

"Yeah, that's right. I was born into this. I was told I had no choice. I want my child to know that he or she can be anything they want. Being the Ravenmaster's been a good life for me. I can't complain. But it may not be enough for them. What if they want to do something else?

That'll be fine by me." Edward smiled. "So what do you want? A boy or a girl?"

"I don't know. What about you?"

"A healthy baby is enough of a miracle for me. All I want is someone with ten fingers and ten toes who can call me 'Dad'."

"The 'Dad' part may take a while," Obsidia said.

"That's all right. I've got all the time in the world."

37
BORROWED GIFTS

"**I** know you've all been invited to the Princess' Ball tonight," Merlin said. "I applaud you for your ability to put in a grueling day training here and then going off to learn to dance. My spies tell me that Arthur nearly set the parquet floor on fire in Buckingham Palace the other day. You're all scheduled for early release today so you can attend to the last minute details. But there are a few matters that we need to attend to."

Merlin waved his hand and the back of the classroom dissolved. He looked over at Dipeka as he did so. She blushed, but he just smiled at her. They were looking out onto the weapons range of Little Vanwalanthir. Shalerunner and Barbryn were waiting for them, together with Kakdon, the camp's weaponsmith.

"Girls," Barbryn said as they stepped out of the classroom, "I can't tell you how very proud I am of the progress you've made. I know that tonight is going to be very special for you. A night of dancing and maybe even a little romance. You both told me what you're wearing, so I looked through some of my things and thought you might like to wear these."

Barbryn opened two cases. In each was a set of matching jewelry: earrings, a necklace, and a bracelet. The diamonds and sapphires on one were just as brilliant as the diamonds and emeralds were on the other.

"They were gifts to me from the Thadans, the forest elves. Their work is very delicate. They fit your proportions nicely. Dwarf gold and gems would seem a little clunky on you."

"What she's trying to say is that you're both too skinny," Shalerunner said. "Kaldemar knows I tried to get you both to fatten up, but did you listen to me? No."

"Kerr," Barbryn said.

"I'm not embarrassing them," Shalerunner said.

"True. You're embarrassing me. Amanda, Dipeka, don't feel like you have to take these. I just wanted to offer them to you."

"They're for lending. Not for keeping," Shalerunner said sharply.

"Isn't it five o'clock somewhere?," Barbryn bristled.

"I do believe it is. Probably somewhere over China," Shalerunner said. "Have a good time at the dance."

As the Dogent walked off to find a mug of refreshment, the girls accepted Barbryn's generous gifts and hugged her.

"Now that that's out of the way," Merlin said, "Kakdon would like to share something with all of you."

The weapons master stepped forward.

"I've been working on your weapons with Merlin's help. We've made a few changes. Dipeka, can you come up, please?"

She stepped forward and took her bow from him. She looked it over quickly. Nothing appeared different.

"Would you try and hit the target downrange?," Kakdon asked.

Dipeka looked for her quiver.

"Where are my arrows?," she asked.

"Just draw back the bow string, if you would," Kakdon instructed.

She did and when the bow was at its maximum tension, an arrow appeared in firing position. Startled, she let the string go and the arrow went wild.

"Again, please," Kakdon said.

She pulled it back and fired, this time hitting the target dead center. She pulled back again and again, until five more arrows had been launched.

"This is amazing," she said. "How many shots can it fire?"

"It can fire as quickly as you can draw the string back," Merlin told her. "Henry, please step forward."

Kakdon handed Henry a thick bag made of the same material as his carbon fiber jumpsuit.

"This is new," Henry said as he strapped it to his waist.

"My concern was what would happen if you lost your meteor hammer in battle or in flight," Kakdon said. "Could you wrap it around the neck of that mannequin?"

The hammer went quickly around the neck of a mock-up of an Orc warrior.

"Now, let go, Henry," Kakdon said.

When he did, the meteor hammer dissolved.

"Look inside your bag," Merlin said.

Henry found his hammer inside.

"The weapon can't be lost or taken away from you," Merlin said. "It will always return to you if you lose it. Angus, step forward.

"The danger with a weapon like an axe is that you have to get close up to use it," Kakdon said. "Aim for the Orc's head, if you will and throw one of your axes."

With a grunt, Angus sent the two-handed axe flying. In mid-flight, it rolled so that it was on its side. It took the head of the artificial Orc clean off at the shoulders and then looped back, smacking itself firmly into Angus' hand.

"This way," Merlin said, "you can choose your mode of attack. Amanda, your turn."

Kakdon handed her her sword and a shield. Both felt comfortable in her hands.

"There is nothing that can get through your shield and nothing made that cannot be cut by your blade when they are in your hands," Kakdon said as she drew it out of its scabbard.

She held the scabbard to him. "How come it didn't cut this?"

"Okay," Kakdon admitted. "There's a short list of things it will not cut. You are at the top of that list. It can't cut you. It can't cut your armor. It can't cut any of your classmates' armor. Or them. Other than that, its unstoppable." He pointed her to a log that had been raised on a scissor jack stand.

She brought the blade down and it sliced through the log like a surgical scalpel.

"Let me see it," Kakdon told her.

She carefully handed it to him.

"See," he said after as he swung the blade down hard on the stump of wood and it stuck after only penetrating an eighth of an inch. "Now, stick out your hand."

"Are you crazy?," Amanda said.

"Try me," Angus said.

Kakdon brought the blade down on Angus' open hand.

"Ow," Angus yelled, bringing his jacket sleeve up to show that his hand was missing.

Both Dipeka and Amanda screamed, until Angus popped his hand out the end of his sleeve into view.

Amanda punched Angus in the chest. "Don't you ever do that again."

"I'm sorry," he said with a laugh. "I'm just messing with you."

Merlin looked at Arthur. "There is nothing I can do to Excalibur. Nimue has placed magic on it more powerful than I could ever cast. Starting tonight, your armor and weapon bags will be kept with your saddles at the Tower of London. The dwarves want to train the dragons, readying them to fly with a full load. When you use your rings to call out your armor, these weapons will come to you."

Merlin looked them over. "This is going to be your last free weekend until the 23rd, so have a good time and I will see you again on Monday morning."

38
GENERATIONS

Art's iPhone rang as he got in the Embassy's Ford Explorer with Agent Stallings. It was his mother calling.

"Hi, hon," she said when he answered. "I picked up your tails when I got your fathers'. My boys are both going to look so handsome. Now, yours is hanging in the bag behind your bedroom door. Your shoes are in the bag on your floor and I got new socks and underwear for you."

"Thanks, Mom. I gotta go."

"I'm getting my hair done and the agent is going to take you get a haircut."

"My hair is fine," he said.

"I know you think that, but listen to your mother. A trim is all I'm saying - a little trim to even out the back and to get it out of your eyes. That's all. A trim."

Art knew he could not win. She would stay on the phone through her own shampoo and haircut until he agreed with her.

"Fine," he said, surrendering.

"All right, honey. See you in a little while."

The trim did not take long. Art hated to admit it, but he was overdue. He no longer looked like a shaggy dog.

"Back to the hotel?," Stallings asked as they left the barber shop.

"Yeah," Art said. "I want to relax. This is going to be a long night."

Edward clambered up the ladder to the top of Waterloo Tower at sunset, taking two rungs at a time. He watched Duncan and his mates fit Aphrodite with a saddle. There was a large leather bag that was strapped to the back of each saddle, something that Edward had not noticed before.

"Evening, Edward," Duncan said. "Care for a ride around London once the sun goes down?"

"Thank you, Duncan," Edward said. "I can't take the risk, not any more. Obsidia and I are going to have a baby."

Duncan stopped what he was doing and extended a hand to Edward. "Congratulations. How soon is she due?"

"About seven and a half months, she reckons. She's got an appointment to see her doctor next week. They'll make it official. Give her a due date and everything."

Aphrodite leaned over and rubbed her face against Edward's.

"I can't wait to show my baby to you, Aphrodite. And you to my baby, for that matter." Edward looked over to Duncan. "Will the baby see them as dragons or ravens?"

"Good question," Duncan said. "It will be up to them. If I had to guess, since it's your child, I'd say dragons."

"That'll be grand. Just grand."

"How's Obsidia feeling?," Duncan asked as he got back to work.

"You know how pregnant women are. First thing in the morning, they're sick as dogs, then you can't keep up with them the rest of the day. I bought her a baby diary. She's got to write down something every day about her pregnancy. I figure, why not? If she could keep track of the weight of the King's swans, she can record what's happening, you know?"

Edward stopped for a minute and looked out. "Do you have any children, Duncan?"

"Two. They're both grown now. Still living back in our world."

"Grown? You look like an awfully young lad. How old are you, if you don't mind me asking?," Edward said.

"I'm eighty-four."

"Eighty-four, eh? Well, we're very close in age."

"Yeah," Duncan said, "but keep in mind that dwarves live to be about 160. My father's 143."

"Oh," Edward said, "can I come right out and ask you something?"

"Sure. What?"

"This change that I've gone through. Assuming that I stay in and near the Tower. How long have I got? I mean, is the change just on the outside?"

"Is what you're really asking me whether you're going to live long enough to see your child grow up?"

Edward nodded. "That's exactly what I was wondering. I want to be there through the first teeth, the first steps, the first day at school, and even, God forbid if it's a girl, through the first date. I don't want to be some old codger asleep on his porch while his children's life slips by him.

"Edward, you look like a man in his early forties now," Duncan said. "How do you feel?"

"Younger. I feel much younger than that."

"When the dragons granted your wish, they probably gave you another fifty or sixty years. From this point on, you're going to age normally. If you take care of yourself, you might even be around to meet your great-grandchildren."

"Whew," Edward said. "That's a load off my mind. Thanks."

"Anytime, Edward."

39
RINGTONE

Duncan's Bluetooth earbud rang just as Edward left the top of Waterloo Tower. He recognized the ringtone. He tapped it with his finger.

"Evening, Art," he said as he watched the two-man dragon ground crew finish putting the saddle on Loki, the last dragon on his list.

"Pitiful, guys," Duncan called to them. "We're supposed to be getting faster at this, not slower." He turned his attention back to the phone call. "What's up?"

"Nothing," you asked each of us to call in at this time so you could test your 'early warning system'. I'm in a holding room, waiting for the Princess. We should be using the comm system. Has anyone else called in?"

"The comm system in your helmet won't work when you're not wearing it. You're the first to call me."

Art was exasperated. "Figures. Henry was the one who insisted that you and your father and half your people get connected with mobile phones and he forgets to call in."

"Wait," Duncan said as the melody linked to Henry

played in his head. He hit the earbud again. "Henry?"

"No, this is Art."

"Okay." Duncan stabbed at the earbud again. "Henry?"

"No, it's still Art."

Duncan's earphone rang again. He answered it.

"Father?," Duncan said.

"Aye, I was trying to call your mother," Shalerunner said. "This bloody thing called you instead."

"Isn't she in camp with you?," Duncan asked.

"She is," his father answered, "but I want her to bring me another tankard and I don't feel like getting up."

"I have to go," Duncan said. He did not see that Merlin had come up onto the top of Waterloo Tower. Duncan punched his ear with his finger. "Art? I can't seem to connect to Henry. I'm going to have to call you back."

"Let me speak to Art," Merlin said, motioning for Duncan to hand him the earpiece.

Art heard an explosion of static in his ear. The connection was drowning in interference.

"Technology and magic don't work well together. That's why I can't use a mobile phone," Merlin said into the earbud.

"What?," Art said, unable to hear what was being said.

Merlin handed Duncan back the earpiece and wiped the side of his throat with his thumb and then pointed in the direction of Buckingham Palace. "I said that technology and magic don't mix."

Art clearly heard Merlin's voice, but it was not coming from his earphone, it was in his head. He pulled off his Bluetooth headset. "Hey, I can hear you."

"And I can hear you," Merlin said. "We'll get our communications issues ironed out Monday. Enjoy the dance."

Art felt the connection with Merlin break just as one of the Palace's ushers stepped in.

"Her Royal Highness is ready," he said to Art stiffly.

"It's about time," Art said under his breath.

He knocked on the door of the Royal Apartment as the usher stood behind him. This was the part of a date he hated the most: knocking on the door and meeting the girl's father. There was always that first momentary expression that every father gives when a young man comes to his door to pick up his daughter. Art had seen it before in the States. The father's face always wordlessly said, "Worthy enough to date my daughter? You're not worthy enough to empty her wastebasket."

Art took a deep breath when he realized that the Queen and the Prince were already in a dining room somewhere downstairs, having dinner with his parents and about a hundred other guests.

The Princess opened the door herself, which surprised Art. He expected more ushers and footmen and guards.

"Wow," was all he could say when he first saw her.

She was dressed in a white strapless gown. Its surface was covered with crystal beads that swayed down its length, following the curves of her body. The dress had a slit on one side that came up above her knee. She wore a diamond necklace, drop earrings, and a tiara. She looked a lot older than fifteen.

"You look like a princess," Art said without thinking.

She started to laugh, but suppressed it. "You look like a true gentleman." She had not known what to expect. A monkey in a monkey suit? She had to admit to herself that he was not handsome, but close. Handsome-ish.

A woman with a clipboard and a radio headset stepped from behind the Princess.

"Ma'am," she said, "they're ready for us downstairs."

Art presented his arm to Guinevere, who took it. They walked down a long corridor lined with oil portraits of the Princess' long dead relatives. When Art looked behind him, he saw that there was a crowd following them. He recognized some of the Palace security people from his last visit and Guinevere's governess.

At the bottom of the stairs were a group of about fifty young women, all dressed in long gowns. Some wore opera length gloves. Black seemed to be a popular color, but none of them wore white. None of them had a dress that could compare with the Princess'. These were just some of "Gwen's Girls".

In the past two months, there had been a concerted public relations campaign to promote Guinevere's new college charity, with the benefit that it had begun to recast the Queen's eldest in a new and better light. It had been weeks since any of the newspapers had referred to her as "Wreckless Gwen." She was now "Guinevere the Good" or "St. Guinevere."

As Art and the Princess walked to the head of the procession, one of the girls called out in a thick Cockney accent, "Any more like you at home, Luv?"

Guinevere patted his arm. "After tonight, girls, he's all yours."

The girls responded with "Oh's" and a couple of whistles.

The girl who had first called out said, "Look, he's blushing. It's so cute to see a boy who can still blush."

"Ladies," the woman with the headset said, trying to regain order, "we're going to be stepping out in just a moment. We're going to do it like we rehearsed yesterday. You're going to follow the Princess and Mr. Williams down the stairs and onto the dance floor. You will form a circle around them. Once they begin their dance, your partners will step forward and take you out on the dance floor. Are we ready?," she asked.

The Princess moistened her lips and nodded.

The woman spoke into her headset. "Cue the orchestra. We are out the door in five, four, three, two, one, and go."

She pointed to Guinevere who stepped forward,

tugging at Art. He got in step. As they crossed the threshold, it seemed like a thousand balls of light exploded in his face as professional and amateur photographers began snapping pictures.

They descended the staircase and walked onto the dance floor, which was crowded with people of all ages. A space opened up for the Princess and her retinue. Art took his place and saw his classmates standing in the crowd.

The music began. Art focused on Guinevere alone and it was as if all these people melted away. It was just he and the girl and the music. He bowed to her and then took her in his arms. They moved across the dance floor flawlessly, stepping and spinning in time with the music. As the song ended, Art dipped her back. She was not surprised by this, but was by what he said.

"I seem to remember the promise of a kiss you once made me," he said, his face close to her.

She did not know if it was the moment or the dance, but she pulled her lips together and closed her eyes in anticipation.

Art gently pulled her back into a standing position and whispered in her ear. "Play your cards right and after the next dance, I may just let you."

Before she could open her eyes or react, the Palace Gardens exploded in applause and cheers. He escorted her over to where her next partner was waiting.

"Gwen," he said, "I'll see you in half an hour for our next dance."

He walked through the crowd on the dance floor, accepting handshakes and blown kisses from people he did not even know. He eventually found his friends who greeted him like a conquering hero.

"You were brilliant, mate," Amanda said as she hugged him.

"There's an old saying in my country," Henry said, "'*Nee sho-sha ha*'. It means 'You clean up real good.'"

Dipeka laughed, "As long as we're dispensing hometown honors, let me say, '*De mous eh baklaud maudi.*' You kicked her butt."

Angus slapped him on the back. "You handled that perfectly. Leave the ladies wanting!"

"Or in your case," Amanda said, "just leave them wanting — wanting to be with someone else."

Dipeka and Amanda shared a laugh together.

"You both look stunning," Art said as he looked at both of them. Amanda did a catwalk turn just for laughs. She was in a long emerald gown with silver trim on the hem. It was slit higher than the Princess', to mid-thigh. The emerald jewelry that Barbryn had loaned her complimented what she was wearing perfectly.

Dipeka wore a traditionally shaped sari, with a long skirt and a top that would have exposed her midriff if not for the wrap that came across her body and up and over her left shoulder and arm. The material was anything but traditional. It was a sheer light blue that had been covered in rhinestones. She also wore Barbryn's sapphires and diamonds.

Although Gwen's Girls had been instructed to tone down their outfits, it was clear that Amanda and Dipeka's dresses both rivaled the Princess'.

Art looked around. "Where are your dates?"

"Well, after Mrs. Chillingsworth taught us how to dance so well ...," Dipeka said.

"It was hard to think of anyone who could...," Henry interjected.

"...keep up with us on the dance floor," Angus said.

"You guys came as each others dates?," Art said.

"Dates?," Amanda said with a snort. "No, not dates. Just dancing partners. We came separately," Amanda said, and then elbowed Angus hard in the ribs as he tried to put his arm across her bare shoulders, "and we're leaving separately. Right?"

When he could draw breath, Angus nodded and said,

"Right."

"What about you?," Dipeka asked.

"No. I'm just here to dance with the Princess at the opening, middle, and close of the ball. Mrs. Chillingsworth told me that it would have been bad form to bring a date or even to dance with anyone else."

"That hardly seems fair," Amanda said, looking out and seeing the Princess was dancing with other boys.

"They're the sons of big donors. Hey, her house, her ball, her rules."

The orchestra started a samba.

"That's our cue," Dipeka said. "Let's catch up in a bit."

As he watched the four of them walk out onto the dance floor, he called out in a half-mocking tone. "Go on, have a good time. Without me."

40
THE PANDORIUM

Prince Mordred stood in front of his full-length reflecting glass and looked at himself. How strange his people on Earth had become. The front half of his jacket was too small and the back half was too long. The little bow around his neck was something that a lap dog might wear, but only if the cur had no self-respect. The sash across his chest obviously meant that the wearer was a warrior, made to match the blood of the enemies the wearer killed. Mordred wondered what enemies of England had blue blood, the color of the Queen's sash. When his tailors presented him with the choice, he could have gone with either green to match the forest elves who would die tonight by the thousands, or red for the dwarves. He had chosen red.

"Our forces stand ready. We will be opening the rift in five minutes," Dwifae said as he entered Mordred's dressing chamber. His appearance had been altered. His pointed ears were bobbed to look more human and his eyebrows had lost their arch. His skin pallor was no longer ghostly white, but had taken on a deep tan. From a distance, he almost looked human.

The gnome servants, including Ufor, scattered.

"You look very handsome, my Lord," Dwifae said. "I'm sure the girl will have no choice to fall madly in love with you."

"Of course," Mordred said. "I was thinking of a change of plans."

"Change, sire?," Dwifae said cautiously. "Is it wise at this late hour?"

"Yes, I fancy it is. I want you on a flying mount. When I get near enough to the child, I will toss it into the air. You will catch it and keep it safe until we are pulled back through. I have decided that the girl may play another role. I intend to take her with me."

"Sire?," Dwifae said with alarm.

"Do you remember that I said I wished to have a harem?"

"Yes, sire, but..."

"She will be my first. She will be one of the mothers of my many children."

"Sire, you needn't look to another world. There are countless beautiful women in this world. My daughter, Drezella thinks you are ..."

"She's a desert elf," Mordred said, angrily cutting him off. "No offense."

Dwifae raised an eyebrow. "None taken, sire, I assure you."

"How would you react if I suggested that you marry a dwarf or a gnome?"

"Those can hardly compare to my people, sire."

"You're missing the point," Mordred said. "In any case, I intend to take the girl back with us."

"Sir, the gnomes accounted for the child's weight in their calculations. If we bring back the girl, someone will have to be left behind."

"Meaning?"

"Someone will have to die."

"So be it, then," Mordred said and walked off to the chamber from which they would launch their assault.

They had been led out of the Pandorium, Mordred's prison, in chains and shoved into deep pits with steep walls, too slick to climb. There were more than a hundred souls in each, adults and children alike. No babe was considered too young and no one was too old or infirm. There were a hundred pits in all. Large metal grates were laid over the openings and long metal cables were clamped to each. Like tentacles, they all snaked to a large machine the gnomes had built. When Nobnocket threw the switch, it would begin to extract the life energy from each living being in the pits. The energy would be gathered and focused, bypassing the bottle that held Merlin and the Great Golden Lady.

The life energy would trip the rift, forcing open several rips large enough for the strike force to get through. Those in the pits would not be killed, at least not immediately. The initial blast, siphoned from them, would open the door. It would deliver such agony that the victims would pray for death.

And then it would stop.

While the Prince and his warriors were in the other world, the agony would cease. A feeling of hope, misplaced and misleading, would soon fill those who were writhing in agony just a few moments before. Mothers and fathers would find the strength to check on their children, husbands would try to console their wives. The hope would give them enough energy to fuel the Prince's return. In the end, everything would be gone. Drained of their life's energy, their bodies would be consumed next. When the Prince returned with his child prize, the pits would be empty. No trace would be left of the ten thousand whose lives were extinguished like candle flames — no bones, no teeth, no clothes.

There was a flash at one of the windows of the castle, a mirror moved in the sunlight, the signal that it was time to begin.

Nobnocket moved a dial and used his body weight to pull a lever down into place. The machine began to hum.

"May the gods have mercy," the chief engineer said.

"I didn't known you cared for any of them," his assistant said to him.

"I was talking about us," Nobnocket replied.

41
THE SUDDEN STORM

The wind was beginning to blow, buffeting Merlin and Duncan on the top of Waterloo Tower.

"Sudden storm, Merlin?," Duncan asked.

The air had a familiar feel, a familiar taste. He looked up. The night sky directly above them was no longer black. Purple clouds were starting to form, moving like a cyclone churning on the summer sea. A bolt of lavender lightening stabbed down into the river below them.

"It's happening. It's happening now!," Merlin said.

"How can that be?," Duncan asked. "You told us it would be the twenty-third. Its only June 3rd."

"I don't know," Merlin said shouting above the wind that was beginning to howl, "something's wrong. Mordred's coming tonight."

"Your students aren't ready. They're off at Buckingham Palace at the ball," Duncan said. "They haven't finished their training."

"There's no time," Merlin said. "Call down the dragons. Keep Loki and Aphrodite here to guard Edward and the Tower. Have the rest follow me on Apollo. I've got to get to them now."

"I'm coming with you," Duncan said as the dragons dove down to the tower roof.

"Can you alert your ground crew?," Merlin said as they took off from the top of Waterloo Tower, followed by a flight of five dragons flying in a "V" formation.

"They're digging their way to the surface already. They should break through any minute now."

The air around the Prince shimmered. The stone walled room that he had been standing in dissolved away. He was surrounded by a small yard enclosed by a wooden fence. There were toys on the ground.

The baby's playground, Mordred thought to himself. He had made it. Now if his gnomes had been accurate, he should find the idiot girl quickly enough.

He stepped out of the playground and was confronted by one of the palace guards. The man spoke in a language he did not understand, but made no attempt to stop him. He only pointed Mordred in the direction of the dance, where the music was coming from. He nodded apologetically and moved on. The Prince was thankful that he did not have to kill this man, at least not yet.

As he moved forward, he saw hundreds of beautiful young women all adorned in diamonds and silks. When he conquered this world, his harem would be very large.

Then he saw her dancing with a boy, who was holding her against him, one arm outstretched in front of them, their other arms holding each other's backs as they moved forward across the floor. Once the battle and confusion began, Mordred hoped to have a chance to kill him. He would beat her for her infidelity when they returned to his world.

The Princess had not seen Art dance the tango with such fire and passion in their rehearsal. She felt herself getting swept away in the heat of the moment. He had mentioned something about a kiss at the end of their last dance, only to leave her hanging. He had paid her back for what she had done to him in the throne room at Windsor Castle. They were even now. She toyed with the idea of letting him kiss her now.

As Art spun her around one last time and leaned her back, she saw Prince Mordred's face step into view. He put his hand on Art's shoulder.

"No cutting in, my friend," Art said, disappointed that he had been interrupted once more. He should have kissed her when he had the chance.

"Tell him to get lost," Mordred said.

All Art heard was a garbled foreign tongue. The locket the Princess wore translated his words only to her.

Art extended his hand out our courtesy. He had already decided he did not like this fellow.

"Tell him that I do not touch peasants," Mordred said.

"He has a rash on his hand," Guinevere lied. "Would you excuse us? I need to introduce him to my mother."

With that, a voice over the speakers announced. "Ladies and gentlemen, Her Majesty, Queen Caroline, and His Royal Highness, Prince Francis."

With that, all eyes turned to the door leading out onto the deck. Queen Caroline stepped forward with the Prince, who was holding Prince Gregory in his arms. Amanda had gone back to join her parents to escort them out to the dance. She was a few paces behind the Royal Couple. The orchestra played "God Save the Queen."

When the song started, Art realized that the Americans had stolen the melody for "My Country 'Tis of Thee" from the English. All around him people were singing the British national anthem.

As it concluded, the people around Art sang in one loud, united voice, "God Save the Queen!" There was a roar of applause. The Queen waved appreciatively to her subjects. Prince Francis tickled his son's ribs and the boy laughed.

Art looked up at Guinevere and the rude fellow who had interrupted their dance. They were standing in front of the Queen talking to her. The Princess was translating. He was as pliant as a courtesan now. There was something familiar about him.

It was the language that he spoke. It was the same back of the throat clearing, garbled mess that Merlin spoke when he was casting a spell.

He was from Merlin's time. It was Mordred. *The* Mordred. He was here. He was early.

The Queen's staff was trying to get everyone on the deck to form a receiving line. It was expected that everyone who attended an event like this would have an opportunity to be introduced to Her Majesty.

"Mother, I'd like to introduce you to Prince Mordred."

"*Dydy eithaf bleser at chwrdd 'ch , 'ch 'n frenhinol huchelder,*" Mordred said and bowed his head.

"He says that it is an extreme pleasure to meet you, Mother," Guinevere said.

"Is that Welsh?," Francis said. "I do believe he's speaking Welsh. What about you, old boy," he said to Prince Gregory, "sound like Welsh to you?"

Mordred could see that Dwifae was diving towards him on the back of a manticore. Seizing his chance, Mordred plucked Gregory from his father's arms, spun, and heaved the child up into the air with all of his might. The baby, tumbling upward through space, cried out. Dwifae swooped in and caught Gregory by the ankle. They climbed into the sky, the baby struggling to break free and return to his parents.

As Mordred spun back around, he pulled a dagger from his sleeve and went to plunge it deep into the Queen's heart. A black shield blocked his blade. A female knight protected the Queen.

Mordred reached over and grabbed Guinevere, holding

the dagger blade to her throat.

"Come near me and she dies," Mordred said, but only the Princess understood his words. Everyone else understood his meaning.

Archers, seated aside the winged human-faced lions, started firing flaming arrows at the crowd, hoping to induce a panic.

The people did flee, especially after the twenty green skinned Orcs moved from the tree line and into the open. One member of the Royal Protective Service who had been stationed on the lawn took aim at one of the brutes and fired, emptying the clip of the weapon. The monster did not stop. He did not even flinch. He drew up his axe and, with one swift motion, split the man in two.

By now all of Art's classmates had summoned their armor and their weapons. The land at the center of the lawn erupted and one hundred-fifty dwarves armed with axes and swords spilled out, swarming the Orcs.

Mordred had backed up to the far edge of the deck. The Queen's protectors tried to move her to safety, but she was not going anywhere until her daughter was free and her son was returned.

A manticore and rider landed in front of Mordred. The animal's sharp claws and teeth kept almost everyone at bay. Art was still on the level of the Palace Garden. He dispatched two Orcs with Excalibur and then moved to the wall directly underneath where Mordred was standing. Art sprang up, climbing the sheer face of the garden wall to get behind where Mordred held Guinevere hostage. As he leapt over the balustrades, he saw that Mordred was on the back of a flying lion, his dagger still pointed to the Princess' neck.

"Sire, we're too heavy to lift off," the lion rider said.

"A pity for you," Mordred said and turned the dagger from the Princess' neck to the spine of the soldier. The desert elf arched his back in pain. Mordred shoved the body aside.

"*Gwsg*", he intoned at Guinevere, using one of the many minor spells his mother had taught him when he was a boy.

The Princess slumped over, not dead, but in a deep narcotic sleep. The manticore took wing before Art could get within striking distance.

As his dragon dove toward Buckingham Palace, Merlin saw the streets were filled with police cars, ambulances, and fire trucks. How had Mordred gotten through? He had always assumed that they would be coming via the bottleneck, but it was still closed.

Merlin could see the storm brewing over the Tower. The barrier had not broken, but it looked to him as if it was going to happen at any moment.

There were only two ways that the barrier between the two worlds could be breached. The first was by magic, but he was still inside the bubble with Morgana. The second was too horrible to contemplate, but it was the only answer. To move a group this large would require the life essence of hundreds, no, at least ten thousand for just the briefest time.

Merlin saw a light begin to glow in the trees. In a moment, all of the off-worlders would be pulled back across the rift. He was not going to let that happen.

"*Beth gwneir must bod andwyedig,*" he shouted. "*Chymer bacia 'ch buchedd.*"

The air around him began to fluoresce, the matter so excited by the magic he was releasing that it began to glow. A comet formed around him and then shot off towards where one of the rifts was opening. The energy that he had released entered the rift, closing it, and forcing all of the current that had come through back to its source. The glow faded.

Merlin looked back at the storm. The purple clouds were swirling fast and the center was beginning to glow white-hot.

"Your men can take care of the Orcs," Merlin said to Duncan. "The only way back for Mordred and his people now is through the bottleneck on flying mounts. Have Art and the others meet me at the Tower."

Duncan waved his acknowledgement and guided the dragons to the Palace grounds below.

42
THE UGLY PURPLE BRUISE

Amanda lifted the tinted visor on her helmet. "Your Majesty," she said, "are you all right?"

"Who are you people?," the Queen demanded. "Who has my son? Where's my daughter?"

Amanda sheathed her sword and took off her helmet, letting her sun bleached hair shake free.

"Amanda?," her father, the High Commissioner from Australia, exclaimed. "What's going on?"

"We don't have time to explain, Dad."

"Our rides are inbound," Art said.

With her helmet off, Amanda could not hear him.

"Majesty," Art said, lifting his visor to show his face. "We'll have to explain later."

Five riderless dragons touched down on the now empty dance floor. Art raced over and jumped on the back of Margaret. The saddlebag behind him bore his name.

High Commissioner Jaswinder recognized his daughter. "Dipeka, you get off that creature right now!," he called out to her in vain.

"Angus," Mrs. Wilcox shouted. "Where are you going?"

The Queen saw a sixth dragon set down as the five young people strapped themselves on. This was being flown by one of her very own Beefeaters from the Tower of London. He had better be prepared to give her some answers.

"You there, Yeoman Warder," she called as she ran down the stairs, "who has my children?"

"We're heading to the Tower of London," Duncan said as his dragon backed away from the Queen.

The Queen grabbed the edge of the double saddle. "I'm coming with you. No argument. Just fly." She shouted to the crowd that was moving down the stairs. "The Tower of London. That's where I'm going."

The Queen alighted the dragon as it were one of her prized horses and grabbed onto Duncan. As they leapt into the sky and banked right, the Queen saw the storm swirling down the river.

"Is that where my children are?," she asked Duncan.

"Yes, ma'am," he told her.

"Fly faster."

Nobnocket stood at the edge of the nearest pit, watching. He had thrown the second lever and the screaming had begun, but then it had stopped. The indicators on the panel in front of him were all wrong.

All of the life energy that he had taken from the wretches in the pits below was being returned to them. They had not started to fade into oblivion. They were getting stronger.

He had to stop it. He had no desire to end up as a trophy in the Prince's throne room. As he reached the panel on his device, there was an explosion. The walls between the pits started collapsing. The heavy metal grates shook loose and pivoted down into the pits and became broad ladders, allowing the Thadans and the dwarves, his fuel supply, to climb the sides of the holding pens. He

THE PEASANT PRINCE

panicked when he realized there were no guards here, only himself and a few of his gnome assistants.

He could see that the prisoners were helping each other and making a break for the forest. In a half-day, they would be safe with the Thadans.

Nobnocket tried to run as fast as he could, but his short legs were too small to be able to outrun even a dwarf. He was quickly cornered by five of them.

"Where do you think you're going, laddie?," the dwarf who tackled him said as his kin joined him.

Edward stood at the top of Waterloo Tower. It felt like he was in the middle of an amethyst hurricane. The wind whipped at them and lightening crashed all around. The roof hatch opened and Edward saw Obsidia climb out.

"Get down below where it's safe," Edward yelled to be heard over the wind.

"If the Tower is under attack I have just as much of a duty to defend it as you do."

"Not in your condition, you don't."

A desert elf on the back of a manticore rode by, firing a flaming arrow at them. The wind caught it and pushed it wide. It landed on the Tower Green harmlessly behind and below them.

"He doesn't care what condition I'm in," Obsidia said as the archer went by.

Before they could continue their argument, Duncan landed Aphrodite on the top of the Tower.

"Off you go, ma'am," Duncan said.

"Not until I have my children," the Queen insisted.

"Your Majesty, please," Obsidia said. "The dwarves know what they're doing."

"The dwarves?," the Queen said. "What dwarves?"

Duncan touched the side of his nose and the Queen saw him shrink before her eyes.

"Duncan Shalerunner of the Clan Fargrave at your service, ma'am." He tipped his Tudor bonnet to her. "Now, if you'll excuse me."

"It's all for the best, ma'am," Edward said as he helped lift the Queen off of Aphrodite's back.

Duncan and Aphrodite flew off.

Mordred did not need the girl who was tossed over the back of his mount like a pair of saddlebags, but he wanted her. He would only throw her overboard if he absolutely had to.

There were two things he did need. The first was the baby. Dwifae had him. The second was the death of the Queen. She was back at the palace, far out of range of the limits to his magic. With her death, he could have performed the rite his mother had taught him. All he needed was the blood drained from an infant king.

His only hope now was to hide from his pursuers until the bottleneck blew open. The ugly purple bruise in the sky told him that it would be a matter of minutes before it yielded. When it blew, he would ride his manticore up through it, gather his waiting armies and then return.

It was not a retreat. It was a tactical withdrawal.

His gnomes had figured out how to slow a falling body using nothing more than fabric and line. In just an hour, a hundred thousand Orcs would be the spearhead of his invasion. By morning, a million warriors would blanket the city and overtake this puny island. In a week, Europe would fall to his unstoppable army. In a month, the world would be under his control.

Mordred flew low, down streets at rooftop level, only popping up every few minutes to check on his surroundings. When he brought his mount up the last time, he was certain that he was being handed a present from the gods.

The idiot girl's mother was standing on the top of one

of the towers on the building just below the eye of the storm. He felt for his dagger. He still had it.

Mordred flew west and then cut south to the Thames. Flying at just above the water's height, he hugged the shore, trying to hide in the shadows. He pulled back on the manticore's reins as he neared the ancient prison's edge. The beast climbed sharply. As he passed the Tower, he let loose his dagger. It spun end over end towards its target.

"Oh, dear," the Queen said as she felt something sharp cut into her chest. When she looked down, she saw the handle of a knife blade sticking out of it. The Queen collapsed. Her eyes were open. Caroline coughed up blood and then looked at Obsidia and pulled her close and whispered, "Save my children."

Her eyes closed and her head slumped forward. Obsidia checked her pulse at her neck.

"Oh my God," Obsidia cried out, "Edward, the Queen is dead."

43
THE SECOND BATTLE OF BRITAIN

"Yes!," Mordred shouted as he banked his manticore away from the Tower.

The Queen had died by his hand. That meant that Dwifae held the reigning monarch of this land is his arms, a mewing, puking king. He would soon put an end to the child's agonized cries.

He scanned the skies looking for his other five winged mounts. There were four archers out there, in addition to Dwifae. He should have seen dragons dropping from the sky by now.

"There's one," Dipeka said. She raised her bow and pulled back the bowstring. She was astride Boudicca, who caught the manticore's scent on the wind at the same time that Dipeka spotted it. The rider was weaving around buildings, trying to find her and her friends.

"Stay with us," Angus said.

"Not when I can get off an easy shot," Dipeka answered on her comm link. She and her dragon dove down, anticipating where the rider and beast would emerge back out into the open.

The desert elf was experienced and he was lucky. He had seen the reflection of Dipeka and Boudicca on the glass window of a building he was flying next to. When her line of sight of him was blocked, he yanked back hard on the reins and made the beast pull a sharp turn and double back. Dipeka and Boudicca shot ahead of him. Now they would be his prey.

"Behind you," Angus yelled, "break right."

Dipeka shifted her weight right and Boudicca heeded her command. A flaming arrow shot under Boudicca's left wing. He was not aiming for her, Dipeka realized. He was trying to kill her dragon.

Angus reached over his left shoulder and pulled an axe free of its restraint. He aimed for the rider's head and sent it flying, but it went wide. The second axe also missed its target. The rider looked over his shoulder and laughed at Angus, who had pulled up high behind his target, keeping the manticore and rider between himself and his two spinning weapons. The rider turned back in time to see both blades upon him as they flew to return to Angus. Both the desert elf and his mount were cut cleanly in two.

A second manticore and rider were closing in on Angus from behind. Before Dipeka could raise her bow and take aim, Henry let his spinning meteor hammer fly. It wrapped around the elf's neck tightly. Victoria angled her wings so that she and Henry slowed suddenly, yanking the rider from his beast.

"Here, kitty, kitty, kitty!," Henry yelled as they dragged the rider through the air. The elf struggled and kicked to loosen the noose around his neck. The manticore was intrigued, and started to pursue them. The connection between the rider and beast had been broken. It now saw the struggling, wounded elf as food.

"Dipeka," Henry said, "are you in position?"

"I'm on its tail," she said.

The manticore was focused on tracking its former rider and ignored both Henry above and Dipeka and Boudicca behind. She got off five rapid arrows before the beast realized that it was someone else's prey. Its wings stopped beating and it fell lifeless into the river.

"You can let go now," Dipeka said.

"Roger," Henry answered. He opened his hand and let the meteor hammer free just as they were passing over the HMS Belfast, a retired warship anchored in the Thames across from the Tower. The cord vanished as the elf fell on the deck of the ship like a bomb.

Henry reached into the bag on his hip and felt his meteor hammer was back where it belonged.

44
FOR QUEEN AND COUNTRY

"She's dead," Obsidia said. She did not know what to do. She pulled the knife from Caroline's chest and dropped it at the sight of her sovereign's blood. "Call an ambulance," she said to Edward numbly.

The air was beginning to fill with the sound of sirens. An ambulance was not what his queen needed, Edward thought.

"Loki," he cried, "come here. I need you."

"Edward, what are you doing?"

"The dragons," he said. "The dragons can make this right."

"They can't help her," Obsidia said crying, "she's dead."

"Not if I can help it. Loki," he yelled, "I need you here now."

Like an unholy angel, Loki swooped into view and landed on the edge of Waterloo Tower. He looked down and saw Edward and Obsidia and the body at their feet, then scanned the skies. There were still five manticore and riders out there, five threats to his home.

"Loki," Edward said, "if I wish it, you have to grant it, right?"

Loki stopped searching the heavens and looked down at Edward.

"If I give you a wish, you must fulfill it, right?," Edward said.

Loki nodded cautiously, watching Edward carefully.

"This is the Queen, Loki. This is our Queen. Yours and mine and Obsidia's and everyone's. If I wish it, can you bring her back to life?"

Loki held his claws out in front of him, rolling them from side to side, trying to beg Edward off from asking the question.

"I know you don't want to tell me, but you must. If I wish it, can you bring her back?"

Loki nodded reluctantly. He pointed to Edward, then to his own chest, and then down to the Queen.

Obsidia instantly understood. The Queen could live once more, but only if Edward gave up his life for it.

"No," she shouted, "there has to be some other way."

Loki shook his head.

"Take me", Obsidia said. "I'm a woman. She's a woman. Take my life."

Loki shook his head again.

"A big wish comes with a terrible price," Edward said quietly. "I guess we learned that one, didn't we, my love?"

"You can't be serious, Edward. You can't go through with it."

"I may look like I'm just the funny little birdman of the Tower to most people. But I am the Yeoman Warder Ravenmaster of Her Majesty's Royal Palace and Fortress Tower of London, Member of the Sovereign's Body Guard of the Yeoman Guard Extraordinary and I took an oath long before you were born, my love, to give my life if necessary to protect the Crown. It is both my duty and my honor. This I do proudly for Queen and country."

"Edward," Obsidia cried, "what about our baby?"

He pulled her close and kissed her softly. "Obsidia, I waited what seemed like two lifetimes to find you. That was a miracle by itself. I became young again so I could be the man you deserved. That was a second miracle. Our baby, that's about the biggest miracle that could ever be. You made my life complete. Just tell me one last time that you love me."

"I love you, Edward. And I'm going to keep loving you for the rest of my life."

"Wherever I'm going, I'm glad I have your love to take with me." Edward looked up at Loki. "Let's do this. Loki, I wish that you would bring Queen Caroline back to life."

Loki bowed his head and clamped his eyes shut. A bright blue stream of light flowed from Edward's chest to Loki's outstretched claw. In a few seconds, it was done and Edward collapsed. The blue light lingered on Loki's hand for a moment and then the particle shower began to move, but it did not go directly to the Queen. It flew over to Obsidia and caressed her face as it went by.

Perhaps, Obsidia thought with a tearful smile, it was Edward's last goodbye.

The light entered the Queen and Obsidia saw the bloody wound on her chest begin to close. The pallid waxiness of Caroline's face faded and her cheeks became rosy once more. She coughed and struggled to rise.

"Ma'am," Obsidia said, bending to attend to the Queen, "you're hurt. Don't try to get up."

As Caroline stood, she saw the Ravenmaster slumped on the ground, leaning his head against the tower wall.

"My God, Edward," the Queen said, "what have you done?"

45
TILL BIRNAM WOOD DO COME TO DUNSINANE

Merlin wove through the trees in the forest of Birnam, trying to dodge the blasts that Morgana was sending his way. They had been fighting for almost five days in the umbilical cord that connected the human world with this one. It was only a few miles long and a half-mile wide and parts of it were burning out of control.

He had been so close to finishing, to reciting the last of the incantation that would have forever separated humanity from the monstrosity that Morgana had become. Without that, mankind would be defenseless against her magic and her hordes. At least the elven and the dwarves had a chance to defend themselves. They were no strangers to magic and could mount a defense. How could a human defend himself when a troubled whisper could persuade the matter he was made of to give up its twists and its bonds and unhook itself from the anchor of reality? There was no shelter from a lightning storm not powered by electricity, but a more brutal form of nature, greed and hatred.

Even if he did not complete the spell, the ends of the two dimensions would eventually heal themselves and cast the bubble in which they battled into the endless void of the netherspace. That would take at least a year at this rate, a year that he was certain that he could not endure. Morgana was younger than he was and all she had to do was outlast him even for a moment. If he died, she would find a way to open both sides of the bottleneck that Merlin had trapped them in. It would become a ramp for her invasion forces to march into the other world.

During their cat-and-mouse game, Merlin checked the end of the bubble that connected to the human world. Every minute, a season passed on Earth, each hour meant that two more decades had expired. Almost twenty-five centuries had passed in the five days they had been battling. The little river village he could see below had grown into a city. The watch fires had given way to electrical incandescence. Huts and hovels were swept away by floods, rebuilt, and consumed by fire. Men began to build with wood, then stone, then steel and glass.

With a moment to rest, he finally had time to collect his thoughts. He could not finish the incantation without lowering his defenses, futilely exposing himself and ensuring his own death. Trapped inside the bubble, he could not slip the bonds of time. Out there, he could. If he opened one end of the bottle, the other side would open. At that end, in the dimension that Merlin had created, time was progressing much slower than on Earth. Mordred would be alive, but he would still be a young man — a spoiled boy tyrant who would be ruling in his mother's absence — an inexperienced general.

And what of himself and Morgana? If he imploded the bottle, he would have to make sure that he was on the Earth side and she was on the other. The blast could kill him, Merlin thought. Then again, it might kill Morgana. That was something he could look forward to — or at the very least, it would leave her so weak that it would take her years to recover.

All he had to do, Merlin concluded, was immediately return to the bottle after he had been blown out and finish the incantation, like putting a punctuation mark at the end of a long sentence, sealing off both worlds from each other forever.

He had one advantage that Morgana lacked — he could slip back through time. He had only watched the city grow beneath him. He had not been a part of it. There was no way that he could trip up his own timeline.

That was it. That was his only hope.

"Morgana," Merlin said, projecting his voice from every corner of their tiny world. "I give you one last chance to surrender to me or face oblivion."

"By the gods," she responded bitterly, "you are still as foolish and arrogant as the day I met you. Surrender to me, and I will end your life quickly."

She had answered him, just as he had hoped. She had grown stronger than he, but she lacked the experience and control of a truly great wizard. She had neglected to shield herself and he could almost sense her exact location. She was as near to the other end as he was to this one. If he focused the undoing of the spell that created the bubble close to her, the energy would travel with equal force in both directions. She would be shot out her end, like a dart from a Thadan's blowpipe. The force would dissipate by the time it reached him, but it would still shatter this end. He would fall to the ground. If he survived the blast, he might be able to counter the effects of the Earth's pull on him and slow his descent.

"*Andwywn beth gwnaed*," he chanted, seeing the exact point where the detonation had to occur in his mind. "*Andwywn beth gwnaed. Andwywn beth gwnaed. Andwywn beth gwnaed*," he repeated over and over again, faster and faster.

The air at the point of Merlin's mental focus began to shimmer, causing the pinesap in the trees nearby to boil, splitting the bark. The trees burst into flame. He forced the darkness to stay inside a sphere of white energy. In a few seconds it grew to half-mile across.

Morgana stared down the length of the bottle and saw the energy sphere growing in size. She tried to counteract Merlin's incantation with one of her own.

"You don't want to die, do you, Morgana?," she heard Merlin say in her head. "An explosion such as neither world has ever seen is coming. Will it kill you? Probably not. Will it roast you alive? Maybe. Will it burn away your beauty? Definitely."

"Are you a madman?," Morgana cried out, abandoning her attempt to defeat Merlin's spell. "You'll kill yourself."

That was enough. She had given away her exact position to him. They had each tread over the very ground she was standing on several times over the last few days while they hunted and stalked one another. He just had to keep her distracted a few seconds longer.

"I'm old, Morgana," Merlin's voice in her head shouted. "I was old when mankind was new. I've lived long enough. Can you say the same about yourself?"

"*Andwynn beth gwnaed — Awron,*" Merlin screamed out loud. The command was given to the half of the energy shell closest to Morgana. He told it that it should no longer resist. It had to give into the dark energy inside, to become one with it, to speed the combined mass on its way, to consume Morgana.

A wall of light and heat and the stuff the universe was made of just after it was born came racing towards Morgana. She ran away from it in vain, but it overtook her and consumed her like a wall of avalanching snow sliding down a mountain peak. It broke through her side of the bottle, like a brick tossed through a stained glass window, and tossed her high into the sky. The plasma began to disperse as soon as it left its launch tube. It was still concentrated enough to consume a brigade of Orc warriors that had waited just outside the bottle for their mistress' return in victory.

Merlin had tried to keep the other half of the energy sphere intact, but finally lost hold of it with his mind. The residual energy that had not consumed Morgana now began to race back towards him. He encased himself in the same blanket of force that had held the dark energy in place while it built. He was swept up and pushed out and over the lip of the barrier.

He was back in his world. The sky was dark and he could see the stars that he had once left behind. He was falling.

Had it been days, years, or millennia? It did not matter. He was falling and he was so tired that he could not remember the words to make himself stop.

46
THE BONDS OF MATRIMONY

Merlin had to keep his vigil in the sky. His instincts were to help his students, but he could not. If he died coming out the bottleneck, then all of what had happened would never have been. Even if Morgana was dead, her son could still mount an invasion of this world.

There was a blinding flash and the center of the vortex exploded, spewing plasma and gas. Merlin saw himself in the middle of the firestorm, falling. Unrestrained, it would take fifteen seconds for his body to hit the surface of the Thames.

Apollo made a power dive, aiming for a spot in space where he could intercept the unconscious body of Merlin while transporting the live one. They pulled beside the wounded wizard, matching his speed as the ground rushed towards them. Merlin reached out and grabbed his unconscious self's robes. They were little more than ash and dissolved under his own touch. Merlin grabbed onto himself just as Apollo opened his wings to slow their plunge. The dragon struggled to shift their momentum to pull out of the dive without causing his wings to snap off at their base. They leveled off just a few feet from the surface of the water, then rose high into the air, wheeled and came about, landing on the Wharf just in front of the Traitors Gate.

The Merlin that had fallen out of the sky began to stir and opened his eyes.

The Merlin that had rescued himself had an odd feeling, of having experienced this very scene, but from the opposite point of view.

"I've written it all down," Merlin said, pulling the moleskin diary from his jacket.

An archer swung his manticore around the Tower Hotel and saw two Merlins by the water's edge. He ignited an arrow and let it fly, hoping that it would kill both of them. Instead, it hit the moleskin diary in Merlin's hand, sending it flying. The book caught fire and pages were torn from it and were borne off by the wind. The Merlin that had taught the students at the American School waved his hand and summoned the book back, extinguishing it as it flew. The rescued Merlin saw the mounted archer had reloaded his bow and was about to pull back the string.

The weaker Merlin said, "Allow me," to his stronger self. With a gesture, the elf rider and his mount disappeared, banished to the dark side of the moon.

Lightening began to crash all around them.

Merlin yelled to himself, trying to be heard over the roar of the wind and the crash of thunder. "This will happen on June 3rd, not June 23rd."

The fallen Merlin took the moleskin book and nodded, and began to unmoor himself in time. "June 23rd. Got it," he called out and then faded into the past.

Dwifae had been hiding in the shadows on a roof nearby, but the opening of the vortex had drawn him out. He still had the child and it had not stopped crying since he had caught it in mid-air back at the Palace.

Mordred spotted him as his vizier raced to get directly

under the vortex.

"Good news," Mordred cried as his mount closed on Dwifae's, "their Queen is dead. You hold the new King of the Britains."

"Look down, Sire," Dwifae said. "She lives."

Mordred's gaze went to the tower where he had left the Queen dead. Now she walked. It could not be.

"This thing's no use to us now," Dwifae said and cast Gregory free.

Caroline looked up and saw something small had been jettisoned by one of the riders circling above.

"Gregory!," she screamed.

Loki and Obsidia both looked up and saw the little prince was falling. He flailed his arms and kicked uselessly.

"Loki, get the baby," Obsidia ordered.

What Loki wanted was revenge. He wanted to fly up and tear into both of those riders and dine on their entrails. They had killed Edward and they must suffer a dragon's revenge.

"Do you hear me, Loki? The baby. Get the baby."

Loki leapt into the sky, putting himself under the falling child. He held his position in space high above the Tower for a moment and then began to drop straight down, at a rate slower than the child's. He extended his front claws and snatched the little prince, clutching him tight to his chest. Loki extended his wings fully and glided forward. He would turn and bank and give the child to Edward's mate. Then he would find those two and have his revenge.

Loki struggled to keep a hold of Gregory without hurting him. The child was trying to break free. Loki did not hear the manticore flying up behind him. The flying lion overtook the dragon. It opened its massive jaws and bit down hard on the long wing bone that connected to the dragon's flight shoulder, snapping it in two.

Loki held onto to Gregory tight and spun around,

grabbing the manticore's soft belly with its talons and held on. The creature let go of Loki's wing and howled in pain. It bucked, sending its rider into the Thames. The weight of the dragon was too much for the lion to carry and remain in flight. Loki was using the manticore as a living parachute.

Obsidia grabbed the Queen and pulled her down as Loki hit the top of Waterloo Tower with his back. On instinct, she shielded the Queen with her body. Ancient stone exploded, sending shards flying. Obsidia's head, neck and back were gashed and pounded by the chunks of flying limestone.

Their momentum carried Loki and the manticore forward and they dropped down onto the lawn next to the White Tower. As Loki's back hit the ground and he skidded forward, he brought his good wing around over his body.

The Queen raced down the roof hatch of Waterloo Tower and ran out towards the spot where the dragon had crashed. The manticore struggled to its feet and made a move towards Caroline and Obsidia. Loki grabbed it with the talons of his left clawed foot once more, getting a hold of its neck this time and squeezing. The beast tried to break free of the grip, shook violently, and fell dead.

As the two women approached the injured dragon, the inner part of the Tower of London filled with police vehicles. Men in riot gear holding pump action shotguns rushed forward, aiming their weapons at Loki. Prince Francis ran to his wife's side.

"Nobody move," the Queen commanded. "The dragon saved my son. He's injured and he's probably scared. Everyone stay calm."

Against the Queen's orders, Obsidia stepped forward.

"Loki," she said in a soothing tone. "Are you all right? Can I have the baby?"

Loki made a curious sound. "Shush," he said.

When he pulled back his good wing, Gregory was lying

on his broad chest, fast asleep.

All five of the students met up in the sky above London.

"Mordred still has Guinevere," Art said. "Has he made a break for it?"

"No," Dipeka said, "we haven't seen him."

"He hasn't gotten past us," Henry declared.

A huge green body went falling next to them. And then another. And dozens more.

Orcs were parachuting from the mouth of the vortex. The wind was carrying them over the middle of the river.

"Great," Amanda said, "can Orcs swim?"

"Stay up here and don't let Mordred through," Art said. "Angus, come with me."

As Art and Angus landed on the Wharf next to the Tower, they jumped off their dragons. Art motioned for Angus to remove his helmet.

Standing at the water's edge, Art said, "Call your girlfriend."

"Which one?"

"The one that lives underwater."

"Jardana?"

"Exactly," Art said.

Angus called out, "Jardana, Jardana, Jardana!"

The water in front of the Wharf began to bubble and the young nymph leapt high. Angus caught her in his arms as she solidified.

"You remembered me!," she squealed appreciatively.

"Jardana," Art said, "we need your help." He pointed out where the first of the massive green soldiers were landing in the water.

"Orcs. Ick," she said.

"Yeah, we need you to help us defeat them, can you do that?," Art said.

"Nope," Jardana said, rearranging her red hair using

her reflection in Angus' chest plate. "My mother says we are forbidden to interfere with humans. We can only protect our own. Angus, do you think I'm pretty?"

"Pretty? I think you are gorgeous. Beautiful."

"Do you like me?"

"Very, very much. I do."

She smiled, kissed him, and then did a backflip out of his arms and stood on top of the water.

"He said, 'I do'," Jardana called out. "I say, I do, too. I have husband!"

The surface of the Thames began to move rapidly back and forth, like water being sloshed about in a tub. Thousands of Naiads popped up out of the river.

"Husband!," they all began to cry out in celebration.

"Angus is now Naiad by marriage," Jardana declared. "Orcs are my husband's enemy. That makes them our enemy, too."

With that, the Orcs that were in the water were pulled under and held there. Art noticed that the Orcs were no longer floating down on parachutes, but falling from the sky, trailing collapsed fabric behind them and hitting the surface of the water hard. The Naiad quickly dragged those that were able to struggle to the surface under again.

Art looked up. Amanda was flying by each parachuting Orc she could approach and slicing the tops off their canopies with her sword. Henry was using his meteor hammer to rip other parachutes apart and Dipeka was puncturing the few that got past Amanda and Henry with her arrows.

When the Orcs realized that there was no hope that they would be able to reach the ground without dying, they stopped jumping.

"Let's saddle up, big guy," Art said.

Angus waited until his helmet was back in place and they were both airborne before he spoke.

"Man, you got me hitched. Was that your plan all along?"

"No," Art said truthfully. "I thought that you'd be able to persuade her. The marriage was her idea."

"Marriage?," Dipeka said on the comm link. "Who got married?"

Angus sighed. "I think I just did. It's a long story."

Mordred had retreated to a rooftop with Dwifae. There was no hope for their original plan. The Queen lived and the child was safe with its mother. The Orcs briefly offered an alternative hope, leaping into this world to form the vanguard of the invasion. Orcs may be stupid, but they were not suicidal. When they could see that entry into this world meant either death at the hands of the Naiad or death from a fall from two thousand feet, they retreated. By now, Mordred was sure that they had moved out of the bottleneck.

"Sire, we have to make a run for it. Dump the girl and you might make it."

Mordred pushed his manticore to fly faster and Dwifae followed close behind.

"I could dump the girl," the Prince said, "or I could try to distract them."

"Distract them how?"

Mordred looked into the mind of Dwifae's manticore and drove it mad. It now moved without reason and attacked without thought. He set the beast to attack the dragon riders.

The manticore clawed its way across the sky. Dwifae could barely hold on. Its fangs were bared, and an unthinking, blind rage was driving it. It lunged for Henry, but missed. It came around and started chasing Dipeka until Angus caught its eye.

Art saw Mordred flying almost straight up into the vortex. "He's making a run for it and he's still got the Princess.

"Merlin's going after him," Angus said, seeing their

professor in close pursuit.

"Go on," Amanda said, "I'll catch up and soon as I take care of this one."

The other four flew off, hoping to intercept Mordred before he entered the vortex.

Amanda and her dragon hovered in place, waiting for the manticore to attack again. When it did, she dropped down like a hummingbird and slashed with her sword, easily slicing off the lion's right wing. Amanda made for the vortex in a hurry without bothering to see what happened to the beast or Dwifae, its rider.

47
THE TEARS OF A QUEEN

Mordred was forcing his mount to expend every last bit of energy it had. He did not care. As soon as he crossed back into his world, he would land at his army's camp and this beast be damned. Once surrounded by his troops, a thousand Merlins could not reach him.

The students could not intercept Mordred and fell in behind Merlin.

"Go back," Merlin commanded them. "You'll kill yourselves."

"He has the Princess," Art said. "We can get her back."

"I don't care about the Princess," Merlin said.

"Well, I do!," Art yelled. "We trained for you. We fought for you. We won for you. You owe us this."

"The bridge between the two worlds is collapsing, Arthur," Merlin called out. "Turn back now while you can."

"Not without the Princess," Art said as he urged his dragon forward, closing the gap between himself and Mordred.

"I'm with you, boss," Angus said.

"Me, too," Dipeka said.

"Make that three," Henry added.

Amanda said, "It just wouldn't be a party unless we all went."

Mordred's mount cleared the far end of the bottleneck just as there was a blinding white flash.

For a few seconds, the vortex shone brighter than a hundred suns at midday. The Queen pressed Prince Gregory's face to her chest to shield him from the glare. Loki extended his unbroken wing over Obsidia. Within a few seconds a massive shockwave followed. Every window on the Tower Hotel's glass facade exploded, raining shards below. Old buildings all around them, but not the stone structures of the Tower of London itself, were flattened. The area around the Tower for a mile in every direction lost electricity as power lines exploded.

The Queen directed that Prince Gregory be taken to safety. Ignoring even her husband's wishes, she refused to move from the Tower until the body of Edward Flummox-Jones was borne away.

Royal Air Force General Lord Nigel Walker saluted the Queen smartly as he approached her. She barely acknowledged him while she stood and waited for the paramedics to bring Edward's body down from the Tower. She had made a promise and she was going to keep it.

"Ma'am," General Walker said, trying to choose his words carefully, "we've calculated the force of the explosion. I regret to inform you that there is no way that Princess Guinevere or any of the others could have survived it. I am very sorry for your loss, Ma'am."

She knew that would be the answer. She had sent word to her Air Force that she wanted to know the truth. Now she had it.

"Thank you, Lord Walker."

"Is there anything else I can do for you, Ma'am?,"

Walker asked.

She shook her head and the General withdrew. Just then, the gurney bearing Edward came through the stone archway at the bottom of Waterloo Tower. At that moment, she did something that queens are never supposed to do.

She cried.

48
THE LAND OF LIGHT AND JOY

The bells of London stood guard over the city for a thousand years. In ancient times, the start of wars and the cessation of violence were announced by the bells of every church steeple across the land. Before text messaging, before the Internet, before television, before radio, before newspapers, even before town criers who walked the ancient cobbled streets proclaiming, "All is well", there were the bells. The news of the death of a king or the birth of a prince was proclaimed by the sound of tons of bronze in motion. Obsidia heard the sound of the bells that morning. She did not have to send to know for whom the bells tolled.

They tolled for the Princess, kidnapped and killed by invaders. They pealed for the children who saved England, who saved the world, and who died trying to rescue Guinevere. They cried out for the men and women of Britain's police and military who tried in vain to thwart the attack. But for Obsidia, they rang for her husband and the dragons he had been raising in secret, testifying to his bravery and their sacrifice.

Instinctively, she touched her abdomen. It was too

soon to feel the life growing inside her stir, to feel it kick and flutter, but she knew it was there. He or she was Edward's child and one day she would tell little Edward Junior or Edwina of their father's bravery and the destiny that lay before them.

Obsidia had not wanted to go to hospital for herself. She wanted to ride with Edward's body just to stay by his side for as long as she could. The medics on scene saw how badly she was injured, torn and battered and bruised and bleeding, but she pushed them away.

She felt a hand touch her shoulder. "Mrs. Jones," the voice said, "Obsidia, there is nothing you can do for him now. I will see he is taken care of."

Obsidia turned in anger, ready to fight whoever tried to stand between her and Edward. The woman at her side was the Queen. Obsidia's anger evaporated. Caroline took both of Obsidia's hands in her own.

"I know what Edward did. I know the sacrifice he made. When he gave me his life, I also received some of his memories and feelings. The strong ones, anyway. I know that he loved you very much. I know that you only just told him of the child you carry. You're bleeding and you're hurt. He would want you to take care of yourself and your baby," she said.

Obsidia felt ashamed and embarrassed. "Ma'am, you shouldn't be worrying about me. I'm sorry we could not save the Princess. I'm sorry ..."

"Shhh," the Queen said. "You've got nothing to be sorry about. Your husband was the last Ravenmaster of the Tower of London. It was a silly legend, I suppose. But from this day forward, I decree that there shall always be at least three dragons at the Tower of London. And, if your child, and your grandchild, and your great-grandchild want the position, they shall follow in the footsteps of Edward Flummox-Jones, the First Dragonmaster of our

Realm."

The Queen leaned forward and kissed Obsidia on both cheeks.

"I promise I'll stay here until they bring Edward down," the Queen vowed. "I swear it."

Obsidia felt fine now, but the doctors were not prepared to let her be discharged yet. She would miss the memorial service at St. Paul's Cathedral, intended to honor the memories of all of those who had lost their lives in the terrible tragedy.

The Queen had declared just a single national day of mourning for her daughter and then, surprisingly, a day for each of the children who perished with the Princess. Tomorrow was Art Williams' day, followed by days to honor Amanda Keating, Angus Wilcox, Dipeka Jaswinder, and Henry Ying. A week from today, when the doctors estimated that Obsidia would be well enough to attend, was the day meant to honor Edward. For now, she would have to watch the service on the BBC from her hospital bed.

Obsidia heard a tap on the window of her hospital room, sounding like someone had tossed a pebble against it. That was impossible. She was in a room on the top floor of the London Bridge Hospital, just across the River Thames from the Tower of London. It was eight stories up. Perhaps a bird struck the window. She settled down to watch.

Then she heard another tap, this one was louder. Then another, even louder still. Finally, there was a crash as a rock the size of her head shattered the window and rolled across the floor of her room, stopping at the foot of her bed. She looked out through the torn blinds and saw the two female dragons, Aphrodite and Matilde, circling outside, level with her window. When Aphrodite saw Obsidia staring at her in disbelief, she motioned with her small arms, pointing upwards, and then banked away. Matilde swung into view and did the same. They orbited over the Thames for a moment, until Obsidia finally guessed what they were trying to communicate. She pointed straight up and gestured with her hand. Aphrodite nodded and the two dragons flew up and out of sight.

Obsidia had to think of what to do next for a moment. When she arrived at hospital, she was wearing her Beefeater's uniform, but the doctors and nurses in the emergency room cut her out of it when they started sewing up her many wounds. She did not have any clothes hanging in the closet, not even a bathrobe.

A nurse, wearing purple hospital scrubs, came into Obsidia's room to see what caused the noise.

"Your clothes," Obsidia said brusquely, "give them to me. Now!"

Over five thousand people had come to St. Paul's Cathedral that morning. At the front of the church, in large gold picture frames were blown-up photographs of the Princess, Angus, Dipeka, Amanda, Henry, and Art. There was a photograph of Edward there, as well, taken during his second middle age. His glasses were gone, his hair was dark and full, and his teeth beamed in a joyous smile. Beside them were pictures of the police officers and soldiers who also died.

A large number of the Princess' classmates from the Benendon School sat together in their uniforms in the middle of the cathedral. On the other side of the aisle were an equal contingent from the American School in London, most wearing suits and dresses purchased for the occasion. They all fidgeted uncomfortably waiting for the service to start.

The President of the United States had flown all night aboard Air Force One to attend with the First Lady. He was seated next to the President of the People's Republic of China. The Australian Prime Minister was behind them with his wife and sat in the same row as the Indian Prime Minister and her husband. The British Prime Minister and his Cabinet were there to mourn with all the others, as well. All the dignitaries were seated further back in the church than protocol would normally dictate.

The first few rows of chairs immediately in front of the altar were reserved for the families of those who had died just a few nights before. Mildred Williams held her husband's hand and kept dabbing her eyes with her handkerchief. Angus' parents, the Wilcoxes, sat to their right. Across the aisle, Indian High Commissioner Pramoda Jaswinder consoled his wife. The Keatings, Amanda's parents, were on their left. Just behind them was Beverly Ying, Director-General of the Hong Kong Economic and Trade Office.

When the Queen entered the church from behind the altar, her eyes fixed on the mothers of the children who, like her, had lost one of their own. By all rights, she should be sitting with them, especially since each of them had been made to endure their sacrifice to save her son and to try to save her daughter. Duty demanded that she take her place on the side of the altar. Such was the place for the Defender of the Faith. Prince Francis took her arm and guided her to her chair.

The Archbishop of Canterbury, backed by priests and altar boys, stepped forward. "I am the resurrection and the life," he began.

The assembled congregation stood and answered in unison, "Grant them an entrance into the land of light and joy."

"Please open your programs to hymn number 376," the Archbishop said, "'Joyful, Joyful, We Adore Thee.'"

The door to the hospital's roof was shoved open from behind. Obsidia ran onto the roof, the feel of gravel crunching beneath her bare feet. The nurse's purple scrubs were too large for her and hung loosely on her frame, but the woman's white rubber soled shoes were too small for her feet. She decided to go barefoot. She knew that hospital security must be just a few minutes behind her.

She looked around and then felt a rush of air blowing on her from above. Aphrodite and Matilde landed in front of her and bowed their heads in acknowledgement.

"What is it?," she demanded.

Matilde looked over to Aphrodite, who motioned with her massive head. Aphrodite stepped forward and threw open her tiny arms, opened her eyes wide, and smiled.

Ta-dah!, she seemed to be saying.

Obsidia shook her head. "I don't understand."

Aphrodite held out her right arm and kept her claw parallel to the ground. She made a slight chopping motion for emphasis, then varied the height slightly and repeated it.

"Are you trying to tell me something about the children?"

Aphrodite pointed at her with the finger of one of her claws and nodded.

"Can't you just tell me?," Obsidia asked, frustration rising in her voice.

Aphrodite looked over at Matilde, who sighed and nodded her head in agreement. Aphrodite stepped even closer to Obsidia and placed her open palm on the woman's forehead.

Instantly, Obsidia's vision went black. As her eyes cleared, she saw flashes of purple lightening all around her. The roar of the wind and the crash of thunder buffeted her ears. The wizard, riding on the back of Apollo, was far ahead, heading straight up into the mouth of the vortex. On his heels was Art, astride Margaret, and the other children were close behind. They entered the eye of the storm, the primal forces of creation swirling all around them. There was an explosion that ripped them from the fabric of the universe. Then nothing. No light. No dark. No pleasure. No pain. Obsidia ceased to be, except for her thoughts.

Then she felt light and joy, a cooling breeze brushing against her cheek. She smelled a fire burning and meat roasting. Most importantly, she heard the sound of young voices laughing. A flurry of messages drilled themselves into her consciousness, but ones without words, only sensations and emotions.

Her eyes snapped open and she stared up into the narrowed gaze of Aphrodite.

"I've got to tell someone. I've got to tell them all right now." She looked across the rooftop. Further up the river she saw the dome of St. Paul's glistening in the morning sun. "I need you to take me there, now."

Aphrodite shook her head and pointed at Obsidia's abdomen.

Obsidia patted the dragon's chin. "I'll be fine," she said reassuringly, "and so will the baby."

Aphrodite lowered her shoulder so that Obsidia could climb on her bare back. Obsidia settled herself in place, wedging her knees against the dragon's neck. Aphrodite took a step forward and spread her massive wings, catching the morning air, which lifted them just as the dragon's second step took them off the edge of the roof. Obsidia grabbed two spikes at the base of Aphrodite's neck and held on tightly.

They banked over the river and flew through the Tower Bridge, just above the roadbed. Obsidia looked over at the Tower of London and saw Loki standing atop the Traitors Gate, his injured wing was bandaged and held in place at his side, but his good wing was open full and he shook it and bellowed a salute as they flew by. London Bridge passed beneath them. The streets for three blocks around the cathedral had been blocked for the sake of security, but they could not close the sky, not to dragons anyway.

They touched down lightly in the small stone plaza in front of the church, causing a knot of police and military men to scatter. Obsidia slid off the dragon's back and pointed to one of the policemen.

"Don't upset the Queen's dragon," she ordered and ran towards the steps at the entrance of the cathedral.

One of the soldiers took half a step to try to block Obsidia, but then felt a deep bass rumble in his chest and looked over at the dragon staring at him through eyes that were molten red slits. The growl was coming from the bottom of the creature's throat and its open mouth betrayed an army of dagger-like teeth. The soldier decided to let Obsidia pass.

The assembled multitude inside the church was finishing the hymn, singing:

"Ever singing, march we onward,
Victors in the midst of strife,
Joyful music leads us Sunward
In the triumph song of life."

The great organ's last note echoed and reverberated through the building.

All of the congregants turned as one when they heard the massive bronze door behind them open with a bang. The aisle down the center of St. Paul's was more than a block long, but Obsidia crossed it at a barefoot run in just a few seconds.

"Your Majesty," she cried out, "I have news of the children."

The Queen rose and, when she saw it was Obsidia, moved towards her. Prince Francis tried to restrain her, but she pulled her arm free and moved down the steps to beneath the center of the dome.

"The children," Obsidia said, trying to catch her breath, "they're alive."

A gasp went up in the church. Mildred and the other mothers pushed their ways forward to surround Obsidia.

"They survived the explosion!," Obsidia said.

"Where are they?", Mildred demanded.

"I don't know, but I know they're together and they're all safe. For now."

Prince Francis stepped forward and grabbed Obsidia's arm. "And my Gwennie? Is she all right?"

Obsidia shook her head. "I don't know. But they're going to find her. If she's alive, they're going to bring her home."

Art felt the radiance of the sun on his face, but he wanted to sleep forever. The smell of roasting meat made his stomach growl. Five more minutes, he bargained with himself. He would get up in five more minutes and get some barbecue to eat. He heard girls' voices laughing. The thought slowly worked its way through his mind that he had not fallen asleep on the beach in front of his parents' place on Martha's Vineyard. That was last summer. This was now.

Art sat upright. He was still dressed in his armor, except that the black carbon shell now gleamed like it was made from stainless steel. Excalibur hung in its scabbard on his belt. Ajax and Margaret looked down at him, peering over the shoulders of Dipeka and Amanda, who were joined by two other girls their age. The newcomers had long pointed ears and large almond-shaped eyes and were dressed in tops and leggings made of filmy linen gauze. One of the new girls whispered something in Dipeka's ear and they all laughed some more.

Angus sat up slowly next to Art, trying to shake the sleep from his head.

They were in the middle of a forest glen. A small stream ran by, gurgling as it rushed over smooth stones. Small round white buildings surrounded the clearing at ground level.

As he looked up, Art saw more of them, decorated at their rooflines with a fine golden filigree edge and swirls of pastel coloring. They rested on the branches of the massive trees of the forest. There must have been thousands of them.

"I don't think we're in London anymore," Angus said as he looked around.

As Art stood, he was met with a thunderous wave of cheers and applause. There were ten thousand people in the open meadow that spread out below him, all refugees who had escaped the Pandorium.

"Arthur! Arthur! Arthur!," thousands of voices started to chant.

"He carries Excalibur," another cried.

The cry of "Excalibur" went up and there were greater cheers.

"King Arthur has returned," someone cried out.

Merlin pushed his way between the two dragons followed by Henry. His white beard was now long and he leaned on a long, gnarled wooden staff.

"Arthur," he said, "it's about time you woke up. If you're going to raise an army and lead it into battle against Morgana and Prince Mordred, we've got a lot of work to do."

THE END

TO BE CONTINUED IN
THE WITCHING HOUR,
PART II OF
THE MIDNIGHT REALM CHRONICLES

ABOUT THE AUTHOR

Stephen Cody is a writer who lives in the fetid, turgid heat
and humidity of Southern Florida with his wife, Rita, and
their four children. He is the author of
Lying in State and *Soulless*.

Made in United States
Orlando, FL
27 March 2022

16214711R00186